# BLUES IN
## THE NIGHT

# BLUES IN THE NIGHT

ROCHELLE KRICH

BALLANTINE BOOKS • NEW YORK

*To our newlyweds, Meira and Daniel*
*and*
*To our newest blessings—*
*Adena Esther*
*Jonathan Jarod*
*Julia Anne*

*Our hearts are full.*

## ACKNOWLEDGMENTS

To all those who so generously and graciously shared their time and knowledge: LAPD Detective Paul Bishop; Dr. Vivian Burt, Director of Women's Life Center at the UCLA Neuropsychiatric Institute; Paul Glasser, associate dean, Max Weinreich Center at the YIVO Institute; Jane Honikman, founding director of Postpartum Support International, Santa Barbara; Dr. Jonathan Hulkower, attending psychiatrist, Cedars Sinai Medical Center; Dvora Kravitz, marriage and family therapist; D. P. Lyle, M.D.; Deputy District Attorney Mary Hanlon Stone; Dr. Sara Teichman; and Dee Thompson, Executive Director, Twentynine Palms Chamber of Commerce.

To Leona Nevler, whom I've always admired, for her enthusiasm and support.

To my agent, Sandra Dijkstra, for her steadfast faith and wisdom.

To my wonderful editor, Joe Blades, who has rolled out the welcome mat and embraced Molly and *Blues in the Night* with exuberance.

To my son David, my Jewish encyclopedia; to my "aunt" Regina, for her help with Polish, and to Sonia, with Yiddish; to my cousins Ben and Stella, who tell the best Yiddish jokes, and to their daughter Gail, for sharing some of her experiences that found their way into Molly's life.

To the people who give my life meaning—my husband, Hershie, my children, grandchildren, and family.

All my thanks.

Rochelle Krich
www.rochellekrich.com

# A Note on Pronunciations

Yiddish has certain consonant sounds that have no English equivalents—in particular that guttural "ch" (achieved by clearing one's throat) that sounds like the "ch" in Bach or in the German "Ach."

Some Yiddish historians and linguists, including the Yiddish Scientific Institute (YIVO, or Yidisher Visenshaftikhe Institut), spell this sound with a "kh" (Khanukah, khalla). Others use "ch" (Chanukah, challa). I've chosen to use "ch."

To help the reader unfamiliar with Yiddish, I've also doubled some consonants ("chapp," "gitte").

"Zh" is pronounced like the "s" in *treasure.*
"Tsh" is pronounced like the "ch" in *lurch.*
"Dzh" is pronounced like the "g" in *passage.*

Here are the YIVO guidelines for vowel pronunciations, which I've followed in most cases, except for those where regional pronunciations vary ( *"kliegeh"* instead of *"klugeh,"* *"gitte"* instead of *"gutte"*):

*a* as in *father* or *bother* (*a dank*—thanks)
*ay* as in *try* (*shrayt*—yells)
*e* as in *bed*, pronounced even when it's the final letter in the word (*naye*—new)
*ey* as in *hay* (*beheyme*—animal)
*i* as in *hid*, or in *me* (*Yid*—Jew)
*o* as between *aw* in *pawn* and *u* in *lunch*, (*hot*—has)

*oy* as in *joy* (*loyfen*—to run)
*u* as in *rule* (*hunt*—dog)

With a little practice, you'll sound just like Molly's Bubbie G.

—Rochelle Krich ("ch" as in *birch,* but that's another story)

# CHAPTER ONE

IT WAS THE NIGHTGOWN THAT HOOKED ME:

*Sunday, July 13. 1:46 A.M. Near Lookout Mountain and Laurel Canyon. An unidentified woman in her mid- to late-twenties, wearing a nightgown, was the victim of a hit-and-run accident that left her unconscious and seriously injured. There were no witnesses.*

That's how my copy would read in next Tuesday's edition of the *Crime Sheet*. We're not talking Chandler or Hammett— just the facts, ma'am. There would be no speculation about the nightgown mentioned in the police report, or about the woman wearing it.

Had she been in distress? I wondered. Desperate, maybe, her hair flying behind her like a banner as she dashed across the serpentine road, oblivious of the oncoming car? Had she been running for help, or away from something or someone? Had she been looking behind her in that final moment before the car slammed into her, several tons of metal crushing muscle and delicate bone, or paralyzed by the headlights, feral eyes gleaming menace in the dark, moonless night?

My editor, who constantly carps about lack of space, would probably cut the nightgown. People don't care what she was wearing, Molly, he'd argue. For me, the nightgown was key. And in my opinion, it's details like this that give the *Crime Sheet* its quirky flavor.

I'm a freelance reporter and I collect data from the Los Angeles Police Department for a section in the local independent throwaways that people read to find out what crimes are taking place in their neighborhoods and figure out how nervous they should be. I also write books about true crime under the pseudonym Morgan Blake. I've always been inquisitive ("Excellent grades marred by interrupting class with too many questions"), and ever since I can remember, I've been drawn to crime stories, true and fictional. So with a journalism degree from UCLA, I set about channeling my curiosity into a career.

As to my love of crime fiction, I inherited that from my maternal grandmother, Bubbie G (the *G* is for Genendel, a name Bubbie has forbidden any of us to mention although I think it's cute). Bubbie, who immigrated to Los Angeles from Europe with my late grandfather in 1951, taught herself English and cut her teeth on Erle Stanley Gardner. Soon she was devouring four or five mysteries a week—cozies, hardboiled, Agatha Christie to Elmore Leonard—and whenever she babysat us kids, she'd read to us from Dr. Seuss and a few chapters from the latest mystery she'd picked up from the book sale table at the library. Of course, she skipped some of the choice words, something I didn't discover until I became addicted myself.

None of my siblings (there are seven kids in the Blume *mishpacha*; I'm number three) share Bubbie G's love of mystery, which gives Bubbie and me a special bond. The mystery gene skipped over my mom, Celia, who, aside from teaching high school English, has published one romance novel under the pen name of Charlotte D'Anjou, my father's favorite pear. (Bartlett came in second.)

I suppose it's funny that we both use pseudonyms, though our motives are different, and there's nothing funny about mine. My mom does it because it fits her romantic sensibilities, and I suspect she's not ready to test the reactions of her students and principal. I do it to protect myself from the criminals I write about, people for whom I have a healthy fear and from whom I'd like to keep my identity and address secret.

Because mystery fiction is different from true crime. There are experiences Bubbie won't talk about, ever. There are events I choose not to remember that worm their way into my consciousness despite my efforts to keep them out. It's those events and Bubbie's unspoken past, not curiosity, that compel me to try to find out the why of the horrible things people do to each other. And there are moments when the sadness of the fractured lives I'm investigating makes me wonder whether my mother doesn't have the right idea.

Lookout Mountain, the spot where the woman was hit, is about half a mile south of Mulholland, which is halfway between the city and the San Fernando Valley. I added the information to my HOLLYWOOD computer file and, with a stack of note-filled pages and several photocopies of police reports in front of me (some divisions will give me photocopies, others will allow me to take notes "under scrutiny"), I proceeded to enter the details of other misdemeanors and felonies in the Hollywood area:

*Sunday, July 13. 3:37 A.M. 8400 block of Fountain. A man broke into a woman's home and raped her.*

*Sunday, July 13. 8:08 A.M. 8500 block of Beverly Boulevard. A suspect, angry about his cellular phone service, threatened his service consultant, saying, "I'm going over there to shoot and kill you."*

*Monday, July 14. 9:58 P.M. 5700 block of San Vicente Boulevard. Sometime during the morning a thief removed money from a woman's artificial leg.*

You get the picture.

I had finished inputting half the police data and was returning to my office with a refilled coffee mug when the phone rang. The Caller ID on my desk phone told me it was my mother, who knows I generally don't take calls when I'm writing. It's so easy to destroy the gossamer filaments of creative thought, so hard to spin them.

I'm an excellent worrier, and my mind ran through several dire possibilities as I picked up the receiver. "Is everything okay, Mom?"

"Everything's fine," she said, panting. "I hate to interrupt you, Molly, but Edie wanted me to call right away."

For my sister Edie, everything has "right away" significance. "You're not interrupting, Mom. Why are you so out of breath?"

"Edie let us have a five-minute break from class," she said, referring to the weekly Israeli dance lessons my sister gives. "She wants to set you up with someone. He's very special. Brilliant, funny, sensitive, handsome."

One of Bubbie G's favorite jokes is about a *shadchan* (matchmaker) who raves to a young man's parents about a girl who has everything: beauty, intelligence, a sterling character, wealth.

What *doesn't* she have? ask the skeptical parents. A long pause before the *shadchan* replies: Teeth.

It's even better in Yiddish.

"What's the hitch?" I asked now, sandwiching the cordless phone receiver between my head and shoulder as I stirred artificial sweetener into my coffee.

"There's no hitch. He's thirty, just a year older than you are. Never married."

"What does he do?"

My mother hesitated. Teeth, I thought, and then I heard her say, "He's a rabbi."

I laughed out loud. "I don't date rabbis. I don't even *like* most of them." An exaggeration, but the idea was too ridiculous. "What was Edie thinking?"

"She says he's a real catch, Molly. She wants to set this up quickly, before someone else grabs him."

"Let them grab." Ever since my divorce two years ago, my sister Edie has made it her mission to find my true *bashert*—my destined love. It's probably easier to find a Kate Spade bag on a clearance table.

"One date can't hurt. Edie says you know him, by the way."

"Edie probably booked the Century Plaza for the wedding and ordered the flowers for the *chuppa*." The wedding canopy. "What's his name?" I took a long sip.

"Zachary Abrams. He's—"

I coughed violently, spraying mocha droplets over my laptop and the papers on my desk. "I went out with Zack Abrams my junior year in high school, Mom. Don't you remember? He French-kissed me." All of which Edie knew. No wonder she hadn't called me herself.

"That's more than I care to know," my mother, the romance writer, said dryly.

"Zack's a rabbi? You're sure?" I was back in his parents' gray Pontiac, steaming up the windows with stuff that would be rated G today, and the memory was quite pleasant, to tell you the truth.

"The rabbi at B'nai Yeshurun is retiring," my mom said, referring to a modern Orthodox synagogue about half a mile from my parents' home. "Zachary Abrams is his replacement. Edie's friend Harriet is a member. She thought of you and phoned Edie this morning."

"You know that's the *Hoffmans'* shul." The Hoffmans are my ex-in-laws. Since the divorce I've bumped into them several times—the Orthodox Jewish world in L.A. is small—and the encounters have been polite but strained.

"I can see that it might be awkward, Molly. But you shouldn't let that get in the way."

"Get in the way of what?" *Way* too small, I decided.

My mother sighed. "So should I tell Edie no?"

"Tell her yes," I said, surprising myself and my mother, whose "Really?" conveyed the relief of a hostage negotiator braced for failure. "Just for old times' sake."

I had no intention of hooking up with a rabbi, or with Zack, with whom I had unfinished business, but I was curious to see what twelve years had done to him. They had added the hint of a few lines around my brown eyes, an inch to my five feet four, and five or six pounds that, like the tide, ebb and flow but make no discernible change to my topography.

After mopping up the coffee from my keyboard and papers, I refastened my unruly blond hair with a banana clip and tackled the rest of the police reports. An hour later I was done, and after stretching my cramped neck and back muscles and flexing my fingers, I sat down again and accessed the piece I was writing, an update on the chromium six some of us Angelenos are apparently sipping with our lattes. Yes, just like *Erin Brockovich*—life imitating art based on life—but I guess our city council members hadn't seen the movie, because they were planning to study the effects of the chromium for five years before deciding what to do, if you can believe it.

I took out my notes and started writing, but the young hit-and-run victim kept calling to me, saying she had a story to tell. No, I don't hear voices, but sometimes I have a sense about things. I think I get that from Bubbie G, too.

I wondered if the woman had died.

# CHAPTER TWO

*Tuesday, July 15. 11:48 A.M. 8600 block of Pico Boulevard.*
*A suspect used a victim's prescription without permission to ob-*
*tain a painkiller that had been prescribed as a controlled sub-*
*stance. (West Los Angeles)*

MY BREAKFAST ROOM TABLE LIES BURIED UNDER PISA-
like towers of magazines, newspapers, and junk mail that I move
to the spare bedroom every Friday afternoon—religiously, I guess
you could say—to make room for the silver Sabbath candlesticks
my ex-husband's parents gave me when Ron and I became engaged. When I discovered that Ron was sleeping with his cousin
Susan's best friend, Tilly—while I was in his mother's kitchen
frying latkes for the family Chanukah party, Ron and the zaftig

blonde were apparently sizzling in the living room—I contemplated throwing the candlesticks out along with him.

But the candlesticks are beautiful, if a little ornate, and I figure I earned them. That and the engagement ring, which I traded for a new, ultra-thin, ultra-light laptop and laser jet printer and a pair of Manolo Blahnik shoes. And half of Ron's considerable earnings as a day trader during the fourteen months of our marriage.

Gives a whole new meaning to "mutual" funds.

I unearthed the past two days' editions of the L.A. *Times* and found two inches of print about the unidentified hit-and-run victim in Monday's California section (formerly called Metro, don't ask me why they changed it):

> Anyone having information regarding a hit-and-run early
> Sunday morning on Laurel Canyon and Lookout Moun-
> tain, please contact Detective Andy Connors at the Holly-
> wood Division. . . .

They hadn't named the woman, but that didn't mean the police hadn't identified her. I checked today's edition of the *Times* but found nothing else.

In collecting data for the *Crime Sheet*, I've come to know several detectives in the LAPD divisions I cover. Some are as much fun as root canal. They'll hover over me like Goodyear blimps while I'm jotting down notes about the crimes listed on the board, as if they're worried I'm going to steal it. Others enjoy shooting the breeze and will make life easier for me by photocopying sanitized police reports that I can read at home. Andy Connors is one of the latter, and I know him better than some.

I phoned Hollywood and scanned a Neiman's catalog while I waited for him to come on the line. So many shoes, so little closet space.

"Connors," he announced, pronouncing the name *Cahners*. Sixteen of his thirty-eight years had been in L.A., but they had barely dimmed his flat Boston accent.

"Andy, it's Molly Blume."

"The sexy, beautiful journalist, Molly Blume? Still breaking hearts?"

"Only two this morning. It's a slow day." I couldn't help smiling. "What about you?"

"Nah, I'm waiting for you."

We chitchatted for a minute, flirting comfortably the way we always do, both of us knowing that nothing would come of it for many reasons, including the fact that I'm Modern Orthodox Jewish and he's Irish Catholic. Then I asked him about the woman.

"Lenore Saunders," he said promptly.

So she had a name. "Is she . . . ?"

"Hanging in there. Internal bleeding, broken leg. She came out of surgery fine, and they upgraded her from critical to serious yesterday. It could've gone the other way. She's one lucky lady, considering—" He stopped.

"Considering what?"

"Considering she lost a lot of blood. But she's young, twenty-six, so that helps. What's your interest, Molly? Do you know something?" His voice held quickened interest, the panting of a dog sniffing a bone.

I had the feeling that wasn't what Connors had been about to say. "No. I just read about her in your police report."

"And you're thinking you may have a story, huh?" He sounded disappointed. "You're doing a piece on hit-and-runs?"

"Actually, I'm curious about the nightgown. Why would this woman be out on Laurel Canyon at two in the morning, wearing a nightgown? What kind was it?"

"Versace. You're doing fashion now? What happened to true

crime? Although judging by what they're charging for clothes nowadays, it's the same thing."

"Was it a regular gown?" I asked patiently. Andy likes his fun. "Sweatpants? A robe?"

"It was silk, or something that looked like silk. Thin straps. Cream-colored, with lace. Probably looked sexier without all the blood."

I winced and blinked away the mental image. "Was she barefoot?"

"She had on one of those backless sandals. We found the other one several hundred feet away."

Cinderella after the ball. "Who ID'd her?"

"The mom, Betty Rowan. Lenore was supposed to have dinner with a friend Sunday night. When she didn't show, the friend called Lenore's apartment, then the mom. The mom phoned hospitals till she found her."

Different last names, which meant Lenore was married, or had been. Probably the latter, since there didn't seem to be an anxious husband in the picture. I asked Connors, and he confirmed that she was divorced. I'd discarded Ron's surname along with my wedding band and wondered why Lenore, like so many other women, hadn't done the same.

"Where is she now?" I asked.

The hospital he named was a five-minute drive from my apartment, which is on Blackburn west of Fairfax. It would be easier to walk it, considering how hard it is to find street parking, and I hate paying those exorbitant parking lot fees.

"If you're thinking of taking her Godiva chocolates and flowers, save your money and time," Connors said, reading my thoughts. "She's not having visitors. No point, anyway. She's asleep most of the time and doesn't make much sense when she's awake. Could be the trauma, the doc says, could be the sedation and the aftereffects of the anesthesia."

"Has she said anything about what happened? Does she remember anything about the car that hit her?"

"The two times I talked to her she didn't remember a thing. No surprise, considering she had more meds in her than Eli Lilly when they brought her in."

That perked my interest. "She overdosed?"

"I didn't say that. She just had a lot of stuff."

"What kinds of meds?"

"Sorry."

"Come on, Andy. It isn't classified information. I can get it from at least ten hospital staffers." I could, too. I'm skilled at obtaining information, but Connors could save me time.

"Prozac, Atavan, Haldol," he said after a moment. "The mom played dumb at first but coughed up the names when the docs insisted they couldn't treat Lenore in the dark."

"Why the big secret? So the daughter's depressed. Half the country's on Prozac, the other half is thinking about it," I said, jotting down notes on the Neiman's brochure. "Did Mrs. Rowan say why Lenore was depressed?"

"She said there was no one reason. Apparently, Lenore's been depressed for years."

I found it hard to believe Betty Rowan didn't know the cause of her daughter's long-term depression. In my family, everyone knows everything about everyone. Well, just about. "What about the doctor who prescribed the meds?"

"Her shrink. He wouldn't discuss Lenore. Doctor-patient confidentiality, something even you can't get around."

I could picture Connors's smirk. "What's his name?"

"I can't tell you that."

"I can find out."

"Go ahead."

One of the reasons Connors and I get along well is that I know when to stop pushing. "So if Lenore was all doped up," I said, thinking aloud, "maybe she just wandered out of her house onto Laurel Canyon. Does she live near the scene of the accident?"

"She lives in West Hollywood, just west of Crescent Heights and south of Santa Monica."

I calculated the distance. About two miles, maybe more. "So she *could* have walked." And in L.A., walking around in a nightgown in the middle of a warm July night doesn't necessarily signal trouble or invite intervention. But why would she walk to Lookout Mountain?

"Even if she wandered into traffic," Connors said, "that doesn't excuse the bastard who hit her and drove off. The doc said another ten minutes, she would've bled to death."

The thought made me shudder. "Where exactly did it happen? At the intersection of Lookout and Laurel Canyon?"

"Just north of Lookout. Why?"

"I'm trying to get a picture. What about the guy who called it in?" According to the report, he'd used his cell phone to notify the police and waited till the paramedics arrived. "Anything new with him?"

"He won five bucks on a Quick Pick," Connors drawled. "Why the big interest, Molly? Running out of material?"

"I told you, I'm intrigued," I said, but Connors had struck a chord. Two months ago I'd mailed my editor and agent the 512 pages of my final draft on the Verone case: a father convicted of injecting his son with the AIDS virus because he didn't want to pay child support. You may have heard of it.

I'd spent a much-needed month—not nearly long enough— catching up with the minutiae of my life and relaxing, taking long walks on the beach, letting the salty air and gently lapping waves purge the gruesome images I'd been living with for almost a year. Then my agent called, and my editor (she loved the manuscript and would be sending me her notes soon), both wanting to know what was next.

I wanted to know, too. I'd been bouncing ideas around in my head like Ping-Pong balls, looking through boxes of yellowed newspaper clippings, searching for a crime that would engage my mind and heart for the next year or longer. So far I'd come up empty. Maybe I was trying too hard. Maybe I was hoping that occupying myself with the woman in the nightgown would free my mind and open the door to my muse, who seemed to be on vacation.

That was part of the *why*. The other part—the tug I'd felt the minute I'd read the police report—I couldn't explain to Connors, because I couldn't explain it to myself.

"C'mon, Andy. The guy didn't see it happen?"

"He hasn't changed his story."

"What if he was driving the car that hit her? Maybe he felt bad about leaving the scene and came back but was afraid to admit he was the one. Did you examine his vehicle?"

"Did you brush your teeth? What if you stick to what you do best, okay? Leave the detecting to me." His tone was light, but he sounded annoyed.

"It was just a thought. A few more questions?"

"I'm just a guy who can't say no. Just like you, Molly Blume. 'Yes, I said yes, I will, yes,'" he whispered intimately, then laughed.

I sighed. The first time we'd met, and several times since then, Connors had teased me about my name—just my luck, I'd thought, a detective familiar with *Ulysses* and Molly Bloom, Joyce's sexually frank and willing heroine who could fit right in with Carrie and the others on *Sex in the City*. In college I became adept at saying no, no, no to guys who thought they were wowing me with their literary breadth while their hands and lips made exploratory moves. In defending herself, my mother, who has an M.A. in English literature, claims she and my dad were prepared for a boy and had to choose a name quickly for the birth certificate. Actually, I like Molly, which is a variation of my paternal great-grandmother's Polish-Jewish name, Mala. In Hebrew, it's Malka. I like that, too.

"Does the mom know what Lenore was doing near Lookout Mountain and Laurel Canyon?" I asked.

"She says she has no idea."

I detected a note of skepticism in Connors's voice. "You don't believe her?"

"I didn't say that." He sounded amused.

"But you implied it."

"I didn't imply. You inferred. Next."

I scowled at him through the receiver. "What are you holding back, Andy?" I knew he was, and that he was savoring the knowledge.

"I've told you everything I can."

Not really an answer. "Lenore was depressed, right? She was medicated. What if she wandered into traffic deliberately? What if she tried to kill herself?"

"See you around, Molly."

# CHAPTER THREE

L<small>ESS THAN AN HOUR LATER ZACK ABRAMS PHONED.</small>

"Edie gave me your number and told me now would be a good time to call," he said. "I hope I'm not interrupting your work."

Have I mentioned that my sister works faster than DSL?

"Actually, your timing is perfect. I was taking a break." Over a decade had passed since I'd last seen him, and I swear my face was tingling just from the sound of his voice. Or maybe it was the caffeine rush from devouring three Hershey's Milk Chocolate with Almonds—my reward for finishing the first draft of the chromium-six piece. "Welcome back to L.A.," I said, remembering my manners and wondering if he felt as awkward as I did.

"It's good to be home. How are you, Molly?"

"Wonderful." I wouldn't have admitted otherwise, but it was pretty much true. I had a family I adored, a career I loved, and security, thanks to an ex-husband who was someone else's problem now. Not Ron's cousin's friend. Like the latkes, she had been a side dish. "Edie said you're a rabbi. I was kind of surprised."

He laughed. "You still cut to the chase, don't you?"

"As I recall, having a pulpit isn't exactly what they predicted in your yearbook. Most Likely to Break Girls' Hearts, right?" Ron's photo had been in the same book—Most Likely to Succeed in Business. He'd certainly sold me a bill of goods.

"I was hoping you wouldn't remember," Zack said with wry amusement. "I guess I'll never live that down."

"Probably not," I agreed. "I thought you were going to law school."

"So did my parents and Harvard."

"What happened?"

"If you're really interested, I'd be happy to tell you the details in person. Off the record, of course. You have to say that to reporters, don't you?"

"Off the record." This was going well. I relaxed and swiveled in my chair. "Do I get to ask questions?"

"As *I* recall, it wouldn't matter if I said no."

No argument there. I am nothing if not persistent. "You can always refuse to answer."

"Somehow I think you'll prevail. You're a terrific reporter, right? Kidding aside, Molly, it's wonderful that you followed your dream."

"I do all right." I was tempted to think he'd been pining for me all these years, following my career and byline, but I figured Edie or her friend Harriet had told him. "Where are you staying?"

"With my parents, until I find a place. I arrived a week ago and haven't had much chance to look. I'd love to see you, Molly. I know this is last minute, but how about dinner tomorrow? Unless you have other plans."

Bantering on the phone had been fun, but the thought of seeing him made my stomach muscles curl. I could say no. I *could* have plans: gardening in my landlord's yard after the heat of the July day passed, editing the chromium-six story one last time before I e-mailed it to the paper, seeking a perfection I'd never achieve. Maybe watching the rerun of *Law and Order*, which I'd missed on its first airing.

"Dinner sounds nice," I said.

"Great. I hear Rafi's has excellent food. I can do early, around five or six, but I have to be back for *ma'ariv*." Evening services. "Or we can do it after *ma'ariv*, after nine, if that's not too late."

"Late is better for me."

"For me, too—that way we won't have to rush. I'll make reservations for nine-fifteen, if that's okay, and pick you up at nine. Where do you live?"

"Nine-fifteen is fine. I'll meet you there."

On blind dates I prefer driving my own car. I hate that awkward ride when I'm trying to get a conversation going with a stranger who can't make eye contact because his eyes (I hope) are on the road. Plus, if the date's a disaster, I can always plead another engagement and escape. Zack wasn't a blind date, but I wanted to feel in control of the evening. I certainly hadn't been in control twelve years ago.

# CHAPTER FOUR

THE LAST TIME I WAS IN A HOSPITAL WAS SEVERAL MONTHS ago, to donate blood for the citywide drive run by Bikur Cholim (*ch* pronounced as in Bach), a Jewish organization that tends to the needs of the ill. The time before that was nine years earlier, when my Zeidie Irving, Bubbie G's husband, had a heart attack and died while we kids were outside his room waiting for the nurse to move him from his chair to his bed.

Lenore Saunders was on the fifth floor in the South Tower. I walked through the lobby, steeling myself against the hospital smells and sights. Nurses carrying color-coded vials of blood. A gurney with a frail, elderly man with skeletal fingers and skin so transparent I could see the subway map of capillaries on his skull. A guy ahead of me, probably a messenger, was holding an oversized white cardboard envelope with a diagram of two breasts. I watched the breasts swinging back and forth as he bounced down the hall, someone's fate in his indifferent hands.

On the fifth floor I found Lenore's room, directly across from the nurses' bay. I was about to enter when a voice stopped me.

"She's not having visitors," I was sternly informed by the heavy-bosomed, forty-something black nurse sitting at the large semicircular desk. "Doctor's orders." She returned her attention to the marching blips on one of the monitors in front of her and made a notation on a chart.

I walked over and read her name tag. Jeannette Plank. "We have some more questions," I said. Sometimes the *we* works; sometimes it doesn't.

Jeannette looked up. "You're with the police, then." Brown-black, almond-shaped eyes regarded me as they would a suspect spider, with reluctant deference and no fondness. "She was awake a few minutes ago when I checked on her, but Dr. Lomeli doesn't want her upset."

"Of course not. I promise I won't stay long." That earned an approving nod. "Lomeli's her psychiatrist?"

"Dr. Lomeli's head of internal medicine. Her psychiatrist is consulting on her meds." The nurse checked her log. "Dr. Lawrence Korwin. I told that to the other detective, but I guess you people don't talk to each other, huh? Did you want me to page Dr. Lomeli?"

I'd heard of Korwin. He was a big-name shrink. "Not right now, thanks." I wrote down both doctors' names. "How is Lenore doing?"

"Stable. Her vitals are much better today, but she's still disoriented. Could be the aftereffects of the anesthesia and the sedation. They're talking about moving her to a regular-care floor tomorrow if she continues to improve."

That was encouraging. "Is Mrs. Rowan with her daughter now, Jeannette?"

"You just missed her. I made her go to the cafeteria. I don't think she's had a morsel since she got here early this morning. I told her if she didn't take care, I'd have to get her a bed, too." The nurse clucked.

I tsked in return. "Has anyone else been by to see Lenore?"

"A man stopped by ten, fifteen minutes ago and brought her these." She tapped a tall, straw-beribboned glass vase of sunflowers on her desk console. "No one else today, at least not on my shift. I was about to put them in her room."

"I'll do that," I offered. "Did he give his name?"

The nurse shook her head. "He was nice-looking, tall, brown hair." She narrowed her eyes. "I'd put him in his late twenties," she said, though I hadn't asked.

"Thanks." We were on the same team now. "I'll go see if Lenore is up to talking."

Jeannette handed me the vase. "Ten minutes," she warned, pleasant but firm, collaborator turned nurse again.

Inside the room's doorway I stood for a moment, listening to the oxygen whooshing through tubes into the injured woman's delicate nose, watching her eyes flutter open and shut like butterfly wings, as if fighting sleep or welcoming it, I couldn't tell. Attached to her thin wrist was an IV tube. More tubes ran from the receptors on her chest to the monitor above her bed that recorded her vital signs. Her long dark hair, splayed against the pillow, intensified the pallor of a thin, bruised face that hinted at uncommon beauty.

An ugly mustard-yellow plastic carafe on the nightstand filled with limp white daisies was the only spot of color in the room. There was no other place to put flowers. With apologies to the daisies, I set the towering sunflowers, unabashedly gaudy in their cheeriness, next to the carafe and read the attached card.

*Feel better soon, Lenore. God bless.* Signed Darren Porter.

Not a family member or boyfriend, I decided. A coworker? Neighbor? Casual acquaintance?

Lenore's blue-veined eyelids were doing that fluttering thing again. I sat on the chair next to the bed, wondering who Darren was and why he'd brought her flowers.

Glancing toward the doorway, I saw Jeannette at her desk. She was looking at me and holding up seven fingers. As in seven minutes left. If I ever needed someone to watch over me, I wanted Jeannette.

I turned to Lenore and said her name a few times, softly at first, then louder. When there was no response, I slipped my hand through the railing and touched her hand. She stirred.

"Lenore?"

She opened her eyes, dark brown pools flecked with amber, and moved her head slowly until she found me.

I scooted to the edge of my chair. "I'm so sorry about what happened, Lenore. I'd like to talk to you about it, if you want."

"I want to talk to Robbie," she said, her voice a hoarse whisper. "Is he coming?"

"I don't know."

She sighed. "I don't think he's coming. He's very angry with me."

"Why is Robbie angry with you, Lenore?" Connors had warned me that Lenore was confused, and I was shamelessly ready to take advantage.

"You *know* why. Because of what happened. Everybody says it was my fault, but it wasn't. You're the only one who believes me." She groped for my hand and tightened her slim, cool fingers around mine. "You do, don't you?"

"Yes, I do." I wondered who she thought I was, and what I believed. "Do you remember trying to cross Laurel Canyon early Sunday morning, Lenore?"

She blinked a few times as if trying to focus. "They keep asking me that. Momma, and the detective. Robbie, too. Dr. K was angry. He said I don't have to remember. He said I don't have to talk about it if I don't want to."

Dr. K as in Korwin, the shrink. "Of course not."

"I don't even remember *being* on Laurel Canyon, but I guess I was." She looked at me, a question in her eyes.

"You were in your nightgown," I told her, eliciting a puzzled expression. "Was there an emergency that made you run out in your nightgown, Lenore?"

"I don't think so. I wish I *could* remember," she said, her wan smile embarrassed and mournful. "Sometimes it's almost there, you know? And then it's gone. Momma says it's all the pills they're giving me. Maybe I should stop taking them."

"Hopefully, they'll take you off the medication soon, when you're feeling better."

"I *want* to remember."

"Maybe something frightened you, and that's why you can't remember. Your mind does that to protect you. Or maybe someone upset you. Did you have an argument, Lenore? Is that why you ran out?"

There was a flicker of something in her eyes. Then she stiffened, and the eyes went blank, as if someone had flipped up shutters and blocked the view. "No, nothing like that." She released my fingers and placed both hands on top of the sheet.

I wondered what chord I'd struck and how to proceed. "Was it Robbie?" I asked, keeping my voice gentle. "You said he was angry. Or was it someone else who was angry?"

"Shh." She put a silencing finger to her lips. "Don't tell. *Promise.*"

"I promise." I waited a moment. "Did you have a fight with Robbie, Lenore? Is that what happened?"

She sighed. "Robbie isn't coming. He's very angry."

Back to square one. "Why is he angry, Lenore?"

"You *know* why. Because of Max."

"Who is Max, Lenore?"

She narrowed her eyes and studied me, as if she were seeing me for the first time. "You're not Nina." She sounded surprised and a little fearful. The hands grabbled at the sheet.

I didn't answer. Who were Nina and Max? Who was Robbie? A spouse? Boyfriend? Father? And what about Darren Porter?

"What's your name?" Lenore asked.

"Molly Blume."

"I don't know you." She said this as a fact, without suspicion or accusation.

"No," I agreed.

"Are you a friend of Nina's?"

I shook my head. "I don't know Nina."

"Why are you here?"

That was a good question. It's a mitzvah—a positive commandment—to visit the sick, but God and I both knew that curiosity more than concern had brought me here. "I'm a writer, a freelance reporter. I read about what happened to you, about the accident. I wanted to know if you remembered any details."

"Are you going to write about me?"

"I don't know," I said. "Would that be all right?"

She glanced at the door and shifted nervously on the bed. "They won't like it."

"Who won't like it, Lenore? Robbie?"

"I wrote everything down. Dr. Korwin says it helps, but it doesn't, not always." She eyed me, taking my measure. "You want to know what I wrote, don't you?" she challenged, a trick question for the nosy reporter.

"If you'd like to tell me," I said.

With a visible effort, she lifted her head an inch or two.

" 'The truth doesn't always set you free.' *That's* what I wrote."
Her head dropped back against the pillow like a leaden weight.

The anger hadn't been directed at me, then, but at hope that
had seduced and betrayed. "Why is that, Lenore?"

"Because it's my fault." The small movement, the spent
anger—both had exhausted her, and her eyes welled with tears.
"Everyone says so, so it must be true, and I'll never be free."

"Why was it your fault, Lenore?"

"I thought I was going to have a second chance, but I don't
deserve one." Her swollen lips trembled. "I'm so sorry!"

"Sorry for what, Lenore?" I sensed that she was retreating to
a part of her mind where I couldn't reach her.

"Ask Nina. Tell her I said."

"Excuse me, but the doctor said my daughter's not supposed
to have visitors."

The short, stick-thin woman entering the room was probably in her mid-forties, judging from the fine wrinkles around her
eyes and mouth and the slight sag of the skin at her jawline and
neck. Her hair was almost black, like her daughter's, but bottle-
harsh with red glints. She'd plucked her eyebrows into thin black
semicircles that gave her a surprised, oh-my-goodness look.

She walked to the other side of the bed. "Are you okay,
baby?" she asked, smoothing her daughter's forehead. "You'll have
to come back another time, Detective," she said, not looking at me.

"You're a detective." Lenore's soft sigh, like her eyes, was
filled with the hurt of betrayal.

"No, a writer," I said.

"A *reporter*, you mean!" the mother said with loathing, as
though pronouncing a four-letter word. She glared at me, twin
dots of red on her cheeks. "You told the nurse you were with
the police."

"No, I didn't. I'm not here to cause you or your daughter
pain, Mrs. Rowan. I read about what happened, and I—"

"Get out!" the woman hissed with the venom of a rattler. "We don't need prying eyes, and we don't need you printing more lies in your paper. My daughter was almost killed, isn't that enough? Have you no shame?"

It's the moral dilemma I face in my line of work: my need and right—and the needs and rights of my readers—to know versus the right to privacy of the people whose lives and stories I'm examining and writing about. I face it over and over, and it never gets easier, or clearer.

The nurse filled the doorway. "Is there a problem?"

"No problem," I said. "I'm just leaving."

"And you can take those flowers with you! You can't buy us with flowers!" Lenore's mother turned to the nurse. "She's not a detective," she told her in a tattling-schoolgirl tone. "She's a reporter."

Ignoring a tight-lipped scowl from Jeannette, I took out a business card and placed it on Lenore's nightstand, next to the daisies. Their droopy heads mirrored my mood.

"I hope you feel better, Lenore. You have my home and cell numbers. If you want to talk, day or night, just call." I squeezed her hand and was surprised when she squeezed back.

"My daughter has nothing to say to you!"

Lenore's gesture had told me otherwise. I felt three pairs of eyes watching me as I walked out of the room.

# CHAPTER FIVE

*Wednesday, July 16. 9:27 P.M. corner of Carlos Avenue and
Tamarind Street. A 31-year-old woman received a 150,000-
volt shock at the hands of an assailant, who approached her on
the street, said, "You . . . bitch, give me the money," and then
used a police-style taser on the victim's right arm. (Hollywood)*

RAFI'S IS ACROSS TOWN FROM WHERE I LIVE, ON PICO
Boulevard west of Robertson, in the heart of the west side Jewish community. It offers Middle Eastern cuisine and some traditional Jewish dishes, and sushi. I love sushi, and so do most of
my friends and family, including Bubbie G, but my dad won't try
it. It's the latest addition to kosher Jewish cuisine, right up there

with Chinese, although of course we don't have crab or other shellfish or anything else that isn't kosher.

The restaurant has only a few parking slots. I pulled my black Acura (preowned is the preferred euphemism) next to a white Suburban hogging one and a half spaces and wondered which car, if any, was Zack's. I was twelve minutes late thanks to my two older sisters, Edie (the housewife/dance instructor) and Mindy (the attorney), who had been coaching me via a conference call about what to wear. My mom wasn't involved. She's a freer spirit, and she realized long ago that advising me would propel me in the opposite direction.

Which it did. I had put on and quickly discarded my sisters' choice—a conservative navy suit and virginal white camisole I'd bought for a cousin's bar mitzvah—and replaced it with a black Lycra skirt hemmed well above the knees and a short-sleeved, scoop-necked clinging white silk sweater that stopped just short of offering a peek at my Wonderbra-enhanced assets. It was July, it was hot. Rabbi or not, this was me.

With a last look in the Acura's vanity mirror, I licked my Oh Baby M.A.C.–glossed lips and tousled my curls, wishing I hadn't put off redoing my highlights. Then I locked the car and walked to the restaurant. Inside, I scanned the packed, dimly lit room, looking for the Zack Abrams I'd known, trying to imagine him twelve years older with thinning hair and a paunch, possibly with a beard now that he was a rabbi (I'd forgotten to ask Edie).

I didn't see him. I *did* recognize a psychiatrist who had told me at the end of our first (and only) date that although we'd both exhibited high levels of anxiety, he thought the evening had gone well and was interested in seeing me again—probably to administer a Rorschach inkblot.

I've had worse dates. Like the depressed motivational speaker who didn't stop talking about his ex-wife. Or the orthodontist who showed up at my door with toothpaste on his lips and offered to check my teeth for gum recession. Or the investment broker who ordered angel hair pasta and curled one strand at a time around his fork with intense deliberation until I wanted to strangle him al dente. I could write a book. Ron, by the way, was a great first date and an excellent boyfriend. He just turned out to be a shitty husband.

And then I saw him. Zack, I mean. He'd been talking to an attractive young blond woman at a table across the room, and his back had been toward me. When he'd turned around, our eyes met.

My heart thumped. It really did. He turned back to the woman and must have said something funny, because she laughed intimately. Same old Zack, I thought with a mix of disappointment and annoyance as he made his way around some tables. And then he was standing in front of me, taller than I'd remembered but no less captivating, fit and clean-shaven and Rupert Everett debonair in a black sports jacket, blue shirt and tie, and a black suede yarmulke much larger than the teeny colorful cotton ones a succession of girlfriends had crocheted for him. I'd never finished the one I'd been working on. Nineteen rows of tiny, intricately patterned stitches, and we were suddenly over.

We stood there for a few seconds, not saying anything, just taking each other in, the way people do when they haven't seen each other in years. At least, that was part of it. For a few seconds I was back again in his parents' Pontiac, felt the heat of his lips on mine. My face was flushed, my palms clammy. I wondered what I'd do if he leaned over and kissed me, but of course he wouldn't, he was a rabbi now. Which was just as well.

"You look beautiful, Molly." His gray-blue eyes stared into mine. "You haven't changed at all."

"Neither have you." His thick, wavy jet black hair had a

sprinkling of premature silver at the temples and sideburns that I found sexy, like the tiny lines that formed around his eyes and mouth when he smiled, which he was doing now. His smile was magic.

I don't remember walking to our table. I do remember worrying that we wouldn't have anything to talk about, but we ordered dinner and drank white wine—he sipped, I quaffed—and I found myself relaxing as we played catch-up over the sushi and miso soup and well into the main course.

"Have you seen . . . ?" and "Are you still in touch with . . . ?" and "Did you know that . . . ?" and "Can you believe . . . ?"

We had done well. We were doctors, lawyers, electricians, contractors, stockbrokers, plumbers. We were homemakers and teachers and politicians and CEOs. We sold medical equipment, homes, insurance, clothing, cars, and telecommunication systems.

Most of us were married and raising families. A few, including Zack, were still single or, like me, divorced. Zack didn't mention Ron, but I assumed he knew about us. I wondered why he'd never married, whether he'd come close.

There were other names we didn't mention, because I didn't want to dampen the mood, and I suppose Zack didn't, either. Names that hung in the air like invisible specters. Jonathan Kaymer, who succumbed to lymphoma a year after high school. Batya Glazer, newly married and pregnant, her parents' only child, having a snack in a Jerusalem pizza shop when a suicide bomber detonated explosives, killing Batya and fourteen others. Mark Lodenberg, a stockbroker on the ninety-eighth floor of the south World Trade Center tower that terrorists had attacked.

And Aggie Lasher, my best friend, whose brutal murder five years ago continues to haunt me and pushes me to explore the caverns of the dark side of the mind, searching for answers that I have come to realize may not be there.

"I guess you're the only writer in the group," Zack said. "I read your work, you know. Your books and feature articles. I look for your byline all the time." He chewed a roasted potato.

No further comment, so I assumed he was being diplomatic. His opinion shouldn't have mattered, but of course it did. I've published numerous articles and one book and received my share of good reviews and some klunkers, along with varied comments from readers and friends ("You're not Shakespeare," one of my college classmates opined). I'm still vulnerable to criticism and wish I'd develop a turtle skin like Bubbie G, whose *"pfuff"* blows off hurtful comments like a dandelion's fur.

"You're very good, Molly," Zack said. "I mean, *really* good. Your language, your style. The way you capture the essence of the people you're writing about, the pathos."

"Don't forget my syntax," I said, uncomfortable with his praise now that he was giving it.

He cocked his head. "Why can't you take a compliment? Just say, 'Thank you'?"

"Thank you," I murmured, annoyed with the flush of pleasure working from my neck up to my face.

He studied me for a moment, chewing another potato. "So what are you working on now?"

I told him about the book I'd just finished, about the chromium-six piece, about the *Crime Sheet*, which made me think about Lenore. She'd been on my mind since I'd visited her yesterday, and I wondered how she was doing.

"What made you decide to write true crime?" he asked.

"I'm not sure." *Aggie Lasher*, but that wasn't something I wanted to go into. "Let's talk about you. When did you decide to become a rabbi?"

"Sometime in my second year in Hakotel." He saw my raised brow. "You're surprised I went there?"

"I'm surprised you lasted," I said, my tongue loosened by the wine. I smiled sheepishly. "Sorry." Hakotel, which means "wall," as in the Western or Wailing Wall, is an Orthodox, post–high school Jerusalem yeshiva for motivated, self-disciplined males interested in intensive, all-day Talmud study. Not exactly a match for the Zack who had flitted not only from girl to girl but from interest to interest. Often, though, when we were alone, I'd sensed a deeper, more serious side. . . .

"See, that's what I missed most about you, Molly. Your subtlety." He was smiling, too, apparently amused. "I think they saw me as a challenge."

I decided to let that pass. "How long were you there?"

"Three years. I loved every minute. The learning, the rabbis, the guys, the environment. The falafel," he added, probably fending off some smart-ass comment from me.

"The falafel's great," I agreed. "And the schwarma." Ribbons of succulent lamb sliced off the meat as it's roasted on a skewer over a grill. "I spent a year there, too." Studying in a girls' seminary, touring, like most of my classmates. "Funny that you and I didn't bump into each other." I wondered what direction my life would have taken if we had.

"So you know Yerushalayim," Zack said, using the Hebrew for Jerusalem. His voice was wistful, as though he were talking about a lover, not a city. "It's like no other place in the world, isn't it? I didn't want to leave."

"Why did you?"

"My parents were pushing. Time to come back, figure out what to do with my life."

After returning to the States, he'd received rabbinic ordination and had been assistant rabbi in a large synagogue near Philadelphia for two years when the B'nai Yeshurun position became available. He'd missed L.A., smog and all.

"Your parents must be thrilled to have you back," I said. "And they must be *kvelling*." There's no perfect English translation. Proud as hell comes pretty close.

"So they tell me." His smile was becomingly shy and self-conscious. "Although I get the feeling they're still disappointed that I turned down law school, and they worry about the politics of being a rabbi of a large shul. Three hundred fifty members, according to my dad, is three hundred fifty bosses. Not counting the spouses."

"Including the Hoffmans," I said. "Ron's parents? Ron and I were married, but we divorced two years ago." Something Zack no doubt knew, but I felt a sudden need to make sure, don't ask me why.

Zack nodded. "I was sorry to hear things didn't work out." He paused. "But I guess you and I wouldn't be sitting here if they had."

"I guess not." For a second I wondered what he'd heard, and from whom—Ron, maybe? his parents?—and I had to stop myself from continuing down this familiar path that led nowhere. "So are you nervous about all those congregants?"

"It's the challenge of the pulpit. I figure I'll win them over one at a time. That should take me about, oh, give or take six years." He flashed a wry smile, then speared a chunk of chicken cutlet. "Actually, this'll be my first *Shabbos* officiating, so wish me luck. Rabbi Newman was there over thirty years, and the congregation adored him. It's hard to compete with a legend."

I had vague memories and several wedding-album photos of the pleasant, slouch-backed, gray-haired man who had officiated under my *chuppa*. Ron and I met with him once before the wedding and then two years later, when I received my *get*, the Jewish divorce that granted me freedom.

"I'm sure you'll be fabulous, Zack. You have experience, and you have the perfect rabbi's voice." He did—deep and resonant and gravelly. "And if you have problems with the men, you can charm the ladies, just like you did in high school."

He laughed. "My reputation was highly exaggerated."

"You had a new girlfriend every three months," I reminded him. "I lasted only two, by the way." I could talk about it easily now, but at the time I'd been stung, had spent more nights than I care to remember crying myself to sleep.

"Then I owe you a month, don't I? I'd like to make amends."

His tone was light, but the way he was looking at me, as if I were the only person in the world, made my face feel warm. I'd been taken in by that look before, had practiced writing *Mrs. Molly Abrams* on the inside cover of my AP History folder on the strength of it.

"You just got back," I said. "You're going to meet tons of eligible women. Looks like you've already made one conquest." I nodded toward the blonde sitting at the table across the room.

He half turned to see where I was looking, then faced me. "Reggie's a member of the shul, a real estate broker. She's trying to find me a house. We're just friends, Molly."

"Hmmm."

"I'm not looking to play the field." He was serious now. "I want to settle down, raise a family."

"Sounds like a good idea. The shul board will approve." That came out more cynical than I'd intended.

He looked at me appraisingly. "You don't trust me?"

"You dumped me. One day we were an item, the next day it was over." The words had come unbidden into my mind and had rolled off my tongue. I was surprised by the anger that pricked at me and wondered if this was why I'd come, to tell him.

He nodded. "I was an immature punk, but that's no excuse. I've always felt bad about the way I acted. I'm really sorry, Molly."

"Forget about it. It's not like I think about it every day." He had a forlorn, lost-puppy look I'd never seen before. My anger evaporated like air escaping a balloon, and I felt silly for having nurtured it for so long. But that's what we do, isn't it?

"I wasn't ready for a relationship," Zack said. "With the other girls, I knew there'd never be anything serious. With you—" He picked up his goblet and twirled the stem. "I was hoping we could start where we left off."

There was something electric in the air. I think we both felt it.

I sighed. "You're a *rabbi*, Zack."

"You make it sound like a communicable disease."

"I've had some unpleasant experiences with rabbis, Zack." One, really, but I tend to generalize for effect. "It's left me wary."

"Don't tar us all with the same brush. I teach and try to be a spiritual guide to people who need my help. That doesn't mean I'm not a normal guy."

"It isn't just that."

He waited.

"I'm divorced, Zack. My skirts and sleeves are too short. My necklines are too low. I wear pants and use four-letter words, but not in front of my parents or grandmother."

He smiled. "At least you have *some* standards."

"I'm *serious*, Zack. I ask questions and make comments that ruffle people's feathers, even if the people happen to be rabbis. I like who I am and what I do."

"I like who you are, too, Molly. You're bright. You're funny." He paused. "You're real."

"Your board members don't want 'real.' They want 'suitable.' "

"Aren't we jumping the gun?" He gazed at me. "If you thought it was pointless, why'd you come tonight?"

"I was curious."

"Me, too. We're having a good time, right? So why don't we just enjoy the rest of the evening and see where it goes."

Twelve years had given him maturity and sensitivity, and I was drawn to him now more than before. But . . . I looked at my watch. "Actually, I have to go. I have a deadline for a piece I'm finishing, and I have to get up early tomorrow morning."

"Okay." His eyes and voice said he knew I was lying. "Maybe we can get together again sometime."

After paying for the meal, he walked me to my car and waited until I pulled out of the parking lot. I watched him in the rearview mirror and was halfway toward La Cienega when I realized he'd never told me why he'd decided to become a rabbi.

My answering machine was blinking. I wasn't in a rush to find out who'd called—probably Edie or Mindy, wanting a debriefing.

I switched on the ceiling fan, changed into my sleepwear—a yellow tank top and briefs—removed my contact lenses, and scrubbed my face free of makeup. Then, sipping a cup of apple-cinnamon tea, I played my one new message, the last of over a dozen on an overly full tape I'd neglected to erase.

"You said to call," a woman said in a low, clear voice. "I need to talk to someone. I'm af—"

And that was it. End of tape, end of message, but from the few words I knew it was Lenore.

# CHAPTER SIX

*Thursday, July 17. 6:48 A.M. Corner of Highland Avenue and Santa Monica Boulevard. A 37-year-old Asian man chased a 21-year-old African American man with a knife, saying, "I'm going to kill you. Die, bitch, die." (Hollywood)*

I AWOKE WITH THE HEAVY, JITTERY FEELING I GET WHEN it's about to rain or I'm hours away from a migraine. It was the date with Zack, I figured, and the restless night it had caused, and the explanation I'd have to give my sisters, and myself. I did thirty minutes on the treadmill, my feet pounding rhythmically along with my heart as I worked up a sweat and wondered why I'd walked away from something that could have been so good.

Of course, I *knew* why. I didn't need a psych degree to figure out that it was because he'd dumped me before, because Ron had done the same, even though I'd been the one to call it quits, and I'd be an idiot to risk that kind of hurt again.

But damn, I wanted to see him.

I went into the kitchen for a cup of coffee and saw the reminder note I'd stuck to the fridge with a magnet.

FAST DAY—DON'T FORGET.

It was Shiva Assar b'Tamuz, the seventeenth day of the Jewish month of Tamuz, the day on which the Romans first breached the walls of Jerusalem in the era of the Second Temple. It was also the beginning of the Three Weeks, and maybe that explained my jittery feeling.

I dread the Three Weeks. They take place in the heat of the summer, beginning with this fast, and culminate twenty-one days later on Tisha b'Av, the ninth day of Av, a longer and more stringent fast that commemorates our national mourning over the destruction of both Holy Temples.

During the Three Weeks we refrain from luxuries, like listening to music, buying or wearing new clothes, cutting our hair, celebrating marriages, bar and bat mitzvahs, or other happy events. Within the Three Weeks are the Nine Days of Av, and they are even more somber and stringent. We don't swim or do laundry and, except on Shabbat, we don't eat meat or drink wine.

I'm okay with the stringency. I can survive for three weeks without Bloomingdale's or a concert at the Hollywood Bowl or the latest Kevin Spacey flick. And it isn't the solemnity that bothers me, or the fasting. I can certainly use an intense dose of introspection now and then, and I'll admit it's hard for me to feel the enormity of the loss of the Holy Temples when I have no concrete connection with either one. So the protocols of mourning help.

It's the unease that I dread. It's the apprehension that sneaks in and holds us hostage while we wait to hear of some tragic event—and there is always one, usually more than one—that will arrest our hearts and make us say, "Oh, of *course*, it's the Three Weeks." So we are grief-stricken but not really surprised when we hear, during these Three Weeks or Nine Days, that a driver lost control of his bus and plunged over the mountainside, taking thirty-one young campers to their deaths; or that a toddler drowned in his family's pool; or that a mother had a fatal fall when hiking with her family. Or that a lovely, sensitive, pious young woman, Aggie Lasher, was murdered.

And we hold our breaths, not wanting to hear more, anxious for these Three Weeks to be over so that we can cast off their pall and allow ourselves to relax our guard once again, to feel joy.

You're probably thinking, "superstition," and I can't prove you wrong. But like most of my friends and family, during the Three Weeks I exercise caution. I don't use my cell phone when I'm driving, and I won't have any elective surgery done, and during the Nine Days I try not to go anywhere that requires air travel. I am careful not to wave a red flag in Satan's face. I don't want him to see me.

After showering and getting dressed, I phoned my mom to talk to her about Zack. I needed a gentle push, and I knew what she'd say: Not everyone is Ron. But I never did get to talk about Zack, because she told me about a forty-seven-year-old father of eight who had died of a strep infection that had traveled to his brain a day after a routine dental appointment.

*The Three Weeks . . .*

My father had heard the report at the morning service in shul. Not someone we knew, but the sadness was there all the same. There were meals to organize for the family while they were sitting shiva, my mom told me, funds to raise for the widow. Our community is prepared for tragedies like this, and I knew the family's needs would be met with compassion and efficiency. But this woman would never again feel her husband's touch; eight children would have to forge their way without a father's guiding hand.

I volunteered to help cook the Friday night Shabbat dinner, and I spent a little longer than usual on my morning prayers, which I sometimes skip altogether when I'm distracted or rushed or lazy. I prayed for the bereaved family and wished I could do more. I thought about how precious life is, and how we don't always get second chances. I thought about Zack, and then about Lenore, and wondered again what she'd meant by not deserving a second chance, about the message she'd left on my machine.

Jeannette Plank wasn't happiness to see me. The nurse glared at me, brown eyes narrowed into raisins, lips curled in derision, and brushed me off with a quick turn of her head that sent her cornrows flying.

"Ms. Saunders phoned me," I said. "She asked me to come."

Jeannette opened her eyes wide in mock surprise. "Is *that* right? Did your momma teach you to lie like this, or did you take special lessons?"

"I didn't lie to you last time, Jeannette, and I'm not lying now." I ignored the rolling of her eyes. "You assumed I was a detective. I never said I was."

"You never said you *weren't.*"

"No, I didn't," I said without apology. I should have come last night. Maybe the nurse on duty would have been less hostile. Then again, Lenore's mom had probably made me persona non grata with the entire staff.

"Well, you can't see her," Jeannette said, and pulled her lips into a grim, self-satisfied line.

I was becoming annoyed. "I think that's her decision to make. Please tell her I'm here. She said she needed to talk to me."

"Uh-huh."

"I can bring in my answering machine tape if you don't believe me." I can do sarcasm, too.

"Well, you're out of luck. She's not here anymore."

I frowned. "Has she been moved to another floor?"

"Lady, she's *gone*. D-E-A-D. You want to see her, you'll have
to talk your way past St. Peter."

# CHAPTER SEVEN

I STOOD THERE, UNCOMPREHENDING. "BUT SHE SOUNDED *fine* last night."

Jeannette placed her hands on her shapely hips. "Oh, so you're a doctor *and* a detective, is that right?"

I barely heard her. "She was *fine*," I repeated stubbornly, as if that would make it true. "She phoned and wanted to talk to me." If I had come last night . . . I thought again. "When did she die?"

Maybe it was the distress in my voice. Whatever the reason, Jeannette answered more civilly. "Sometime in the night, but I don't know exactly. She was on Seven South. That's where they moved her yesterday morning."

"They moved her?"

Jeannette nodded. "She was doing much better."

"Obviously not. Who made the decision?"

"Things happen." Ignoring my question, Jeannette punctuated this philosophical truth with a shrug. "If you want details, you'll have to talk to her doctors or family."

She seemed eager to end the conversation, and I wondered whether Mrs. Saunders was contemplating a lawsuit.

On the seventh floor I stopped at the first nurses' bay and was told by a youngish male nurse with crew-cut bleached-blond hair that neither Dr. Lomeli nor Dr. Korwin was available.

"I'd like to speak to someone about Lenore Saunders," I said. "I understand she died last night."

He exchanged a quick look with a female nurse. "Are you family?"

Something was going on. I felt a prickling of unease at the base of my spine. "A friend. Can you tell me what happened?"

"You'll have to talk to the police," he told me and pointed me to another bay at the end of the long corridor.

I walked down the corridor and from a distance saw Connors. He was talking to a tiny, white-faced Asian nurse who was twisting her hands. I caught his attention and the slight not-now shake of his head, and stayed with my troubled thoughts for ten long minutes until he loped over to me.

He's a tall, lanky man, around six feet two and string-bean thin, and stands with his shoulders kind of hunched and his head bent, as if the height is too much for him and he's thinking about folding himself in half. He has a long, thin face; a long, sharp nose; and intelligent hazel eyes that miss nothing. His light brown hair is receding, and he has a bald spot that even a yarmulke won't cover, but he's sexy as hell and looks better in his tight jeans than I ever will. He wears cowboy boots, too, and I figure he thinks he's McCloud, if you remember the Dennis Weaver series that never took off like *Columbo*.

Connors motioned for me to follow him about a hundred feet away from the bay.

"Losing your touch, Molly?" He gave me a slow grin. "What took you so long to get here?"

"What's going on, Andy? Why are you here?"

"I could ask you the same thing." There was something more than curiosity in his voice. Official, almost.

"Lenore left a message on my answering machine last night. She wanted to talk to me."

"Guess you should've come last night," he said, not unkindly.

I flushed.

"Hey, I was teasing. You couldn't have known."

"She sounded *fine*, Andy. And the nurse I spoke to on Tuesday said Lenore was doing better, enough so they moved her to a regular floor. What happened? Did she start bleeding again?"

"I suppose you could say that."

I scowled at him. "Don't play games."

An orderly came down the hall, wheeling a cart. Connors waited until the man had passed, then lowered his voice. "It looks like she killed herself. Not pretty."

In my research I've seen my share of grisly crime scene photos, but I'm never prepared. I steeled myself. "How?"

"Apparently, she lifted a pair of scissors from a surgical cart or nurse's pocket and played tic-tac-toe on her wrists."

"God!" I swallowed hard and tried unsuccessfully to block the mental picture of Lenore on the bed, her blood turning the white sheets crimson. "Who found her?"

"The nurse you saw me talking to, a little after four this morning. She was making rounds and found Lenore dead. Twenty-six years old." He shook his head. "What an effing waste."

I looked at the nurse, who was talking to another staff member, her eyes darting anxiously at Connors every few seconds like a car blinker. "Does Mrs. Rowan know?"

Connors nodded. "She got here around a quarter to six, ten minutes before I did. They had a hard time keeping her from going into the room. She said she had a bad feeling all night about her daughter."

"Meaning?"

"Lenore was real depressed last night. The mom came early this morning to make sure she was okay. Evidently, Lenore tried to kill herself before."

I frowned. "Then why wasn't she on a psych ward? What does Dr. Korwin say?"

Connors raised a brow. "You *do* have your ways, Molly Blume. How'd you get his name?"

I smiled in answer.

"He's playing it close to the chest," Connors said. "He admits he was worried and says he talked to Lomeli last night about maybe transferring her to psych."

"Covering his butt."

"Probably. She may have been more agitated than usual because they were weaning her off the antidepressants. But he insists they had no reason to think she was suicidal. He's shaken up. So is Lomeli."

"Probably worrying they'll be sued." I had a thought. "Do we know for a fact that Lenore was taking the meds?"

Connors frowned. "Why wouldn't she?"

"When I visited her on Tuesday, she told me she hated not being able to remember and blamed the pills. She said maybe she should stop taking them. I didn't think she was serious."

He looked at me, interested. "I don't think they were giving her much, but I'll check it out with the nurses. It'll be on her chart."

"She could've fooled them," I said, warming to my theory. "She could've pretended to swallow the pills, and flushed them down the toilet. Or saved them."

"You're reading way too many suspense novels," Connors said, but he sounded thoughtful. "What else did she tell you?"

"Lots of stuff, most of it confusing. She said the car accident was her fault. She thought I was someone named Nina."

Connors nodded. "I told you she was loopy. Korwin said the aftereffects of the anesthesia can last days for some patients. And they were sedating her with Haldol."

"She kept talking about Robbie, saying he was angry at her because of what happened to Max. She didn't explain who they were, and then the mom came in and ended the conversation. Aren't you curious?"

"I'm more interested in Lenore's state of mind. Did she seem depressed?"

I reviewed the visit in my mind. "She was weepy talking about the accident, but she didn't sound suicidal." Not that I'm an expert. "She was more disoriented than anything else, but that was two days ago."

"Because of the Haldol and the antidepressants. But if you're right, and she stopped taking them . . ." He rubbed his chin. "Interesting theory, Molly. If it pans out, I'll owe *you* one. So will Lomeli and Korwin and the hospital. Takes them all off the hook."

I didn't answer. I was too busy reviewing in my mind the message Lenore had left, something she'd said. . . .

"Knock, knock," Connors said. "Anybody home?"

I looked up at him. "She said she was afraid, Andy. On the tape, I mean. Well, she started to. My tape ran out." I returned his skeptical gaze with my own cool one. "She said, 'I'm af.' What else could that mean?"

"I'm a fool? I'm a failure? A flirt? Shit, it could be anything." He sounded impatient.

"What if she didn't kill herself?"

He sighed. "The mom said she's suicidal. Two days ago you

suggested that Lenore ran across Laurel Canyon trying to kill herself. So this time she found another way and did it right. What's the effing problem?"

Everything he said made sense, but for some reason I was resisting. "She kept saying this Robbie was very angry with her. She was nervous when I asked her if they had a fight."

"She told you a lot of stuff, none of which made sense. *Nina,*" he added with a smirk.

I ignored it. "She didn't sound depressed when she phoned. She didn't sound confused, either." I was reaching here. She'd said what? Ten words? I didn't volunteer that.

"Which only proves she was off her meds."

"What if she phoned me because she was afraid someone was going to kill her?" Even as I spoke, the words sounded ridiculous.

"More likely she was afraid she was going to kill herself." He placed his large hand on my shoulder. "Maybe she was hoping you'd come talk her out of it, and maybe you're feeling guilty 'cause you didn't show," he said with a gentleness I'd never heard. "But it's not your fault."

Connors is too smart. I felt my face becoming warm. "I didn't think it was urgent, but I should have come."

"It wouldn't have been a permanent fix. The mom told me why Lenore was so depressed. It's not something you could have helped her with, Molly. She killed herself."

"I guess you're right." Writing about crime tends to make me see its shadow everywhere. "What did the mother tell you?"

"You'd have to ask her. It's not my story to tell." He stood and unfolded himself. "Try not to obsess, okay?"

## CHAPTER EIGHT

LENORE'S MOTHER WAS WHERE CONNORS HAD SAID SHE'D be, in the visitors' lounge that bridges the north and south towers. She was standing in front of the large picture windows that look out on the courtyard below, next to a short, brown-haired, bearded man in a well-cut navy suit that worked hard to camouflage his portliness. He was talking to her in quiet, soothing tones, and she was bobbing her head like one of those cute toy dogs people used to keep on their dashboards. From what I could tell, like those dogs, she didn't seem to be taking much in.

I heard snippets of what he said—"Call me," "help you," "need anything." Her dull "Thank you, doctor" in reply. A moment later he squeezed her shoulder, and then he was duck-walking past me toward the south tower. Probably the shrink, I decided. Lomeli would be wearing a white hospital coat.

She watched him go, eyes red-rimmed, face mascara-streaked, those penciled eyebrows clownlike now. Her entire body exuded weariness and despair. I had just decided to leave her alone with her grief when she looked up and saw me. Her face tightened as I walked over, so I knew she'd recognized me.

"My baby's gone," she said tonelessly. "Dead."

"I heard. I'm so sorry, Mrs. Rowan." I've talked to mothers who have lost their children, but never when the loss is so raw. "Is there anything I can do to help? Maybe make some phone calls for you?"

She shook her head. "There's not many people to call. She's an only child, and her daddy's been gone twenty-five years."

I wondered about Lenore's ex-husband but didn't ask. "Can I get you some coffee? Something to eat?"

"What is it that you want?" she demanded, her eyes cold brown marbles. "A lead story?"

I hesitated, not wanting to intensify her pain, then decided she had a right to know. "Your daughter left a message for me last night. She needed to talk to me."

The mother snorted. "Do I look like a fool?"

"I can play the tape for you," I offered for the second time today, minus the sarcasm. "It ran out before she finished talking so I can't be sure, but I think she started to say she was afraid."

Betty Rowan chewed on her lip and thought that over for a minute. I didn't rush her.

"She was depressed bad yesterday," the mother finally said. "Maybe she was afraid she was going to do something . . . like what she did." Tears filled her tired, reddened eyes.

That's what Connors had said. It certainly made sense.

"Did you see her?" Mrs. Rowan asked.

I shook my head.

"They wouldn't let me see her. I'm her momma, and they wouldn't let me see her, and then they took her away."

"Sometimes it's for the best," I said, mouthing one of those platitudes that had made me clench my teeth when my great-aunt Estelle died at seventy-eight, six months after she suffered a stroke that left her partially paralyzed with limited speech.

"How did she do it?" Betty Rowan asked. "Last time she took a razor blade to her wrists. But I guess she couldn't do that here, in the hospital."

"I don't know," I lied.

Betty nodded. "Her psychiatrist swore she wasn't at risk. That was him talking to me a minute ago. Did you meet him?"

"No."

"He's sweating bullets, worrying am I going to sue. So is Lomeli." Her smile was bitter. "I have half a mind to, but suing's not going to bring my baby back." Her mouth worked as she fought back tears.

"I'm so sorry," I said again, inadequacy and guilt sitting like heavy bricks on my shoulders. "She wanted to talk to me last night. I wish I'd come to the hospital."

"Well," the mother said. If I was asking for absolution, I'd come to the wrong place. "You talked to her the other day. What did she say?"

Two days ago Betty Rowan had ordered me out of her daughter's room, but most family members of the deceased, I've found, are eager to feed on crumbs of conversation, and so I would have to do.

"She didn't say much that made sense, probably because of the sedation," I told her. "She thought I was Nina—?" I ended with a question mark in my voice.

"Weldon," the mother finished automatically, as I'd hoped she would. "Mousy thing. I don't know what Lenore saw in her."

"I guess they were close."

"*Too* close." She was frowning, and I wondered if she was jealous of their relationship. "I suppose I'll have to call her. I have her number somewhere in my purse."

"Do you want me to call her for you?" I'll admit I'm not sure how much of my offer was prompted by curiosity, how much by my sincere desire to help.

The woman stiffened, almost imperceptibly. "No, that's all right. She'll take the news worse, coming from a stranger. She was here yesterday, and Lenore was doin' so much better." Betty ran a hand through her hair. "What else did Lenore tell you?"

"She said Robbie was very angry with her, that he wasn't going to visit her. Because of Max. She said that twice. I assume Robbie is her ex-husband." A guess, but Betty didn't deny it.

The woman tightened her lips. "Did she say why he was angry?"

"No. She said that the accident was her fault, that she'd hoped for a second chance, but didn't deserve it."

"She was too hard on herself." Betty shook her head. "I told her over and over, but she didn't believe me. I seen this coming. Dr. Korwin says no, but a mother knows." She pressed her hand against her heart.

"You think she tried to kill herself the other night?"

"I guess so. I guess she did, poor baby." The mother sighed. "She wanted out of her pain."

"Why was she so depressed?"

A spark of anger kindled in her eyes, but she smothered it. "It doesn't matter now."

"Mrs. Rowan, something's been puzzling me. Why would Lenore be in a nightgown trying to cross Laurel Canyon in the middle of the night?"

She shook her head. "I have no idea."

"Doesn't that bother you?"

"There's a lot that bothers me, and not much I can do about it," she said, the anger sparking again. "Did you ask Lenore?"

"She didn't remember being there."

Betty nodded. "It was the medication. She didn't know what she was doing."

"But why would she go to Laurel Canyon? Does she know anyone who lives around there?"

"It doesn't make a difference, does it? Why she went there, what happened, whose fault it was. She's at peace now, in God's hands." She glanced down the hall toward the south tower. "I'm going to talk to the detective, find out when I can see my baby."

Without another word she walked away. I stood there for a moment, thinking about our conversation. It occurred to me that Betty Rowan had talked to me not because she was seeking comfort from Lenore's final words, but because she was nervous about what her daughter had revealed.

# CHAPTER NINE

NORTH OF SUNSET, CRESCENT HEIGHTS BOULEVARD changes its name and densely populated residential/commercial character and morphs into Laurel Canyon, a tree-and-mountain-bordered two-lane road that quickly merges into one as it snakes its way up to Mulholland, then widens again on its descent into the San Fernando Valley.

On your right as you're driving up, you'll see a few apartment buildings and homes ranging from modest to grand, as well as convenience stores and an espresso bar and, for a short stretch, a side road that allows you to escape part of the rush-hour traffic I found myself in now—too many cars packed into the coils of a sluggish intestine. Also on your right, just north of Hollywood Boulevard, is the dark yellow marquee with black Grecian-style letters that marks the entrance to an area called Mount Olympus, where the streets are named for Greek and Roman gods.

On your left is mountain wall. In some spots the wall is a bare, unadorned reddish-brown; in others it's dressed for company, wearing a petticoat of oleander, eucalyptus, fir, the occasional palm, and other trees that stretch to the sky. There are houses, too, some street-level and rather shabby, some wedged into the mountain, most of them higher up and grander, their foundations supported by sturdy wooden beams that seem to be doing the job. Signs placed at intervals along the canyon road warn against smoking and flooding, and while I'd love to live in one of those aeries, breathing in the scent of wildflowers, taking in the spectacular views of city and valley, I worry about the heat and dry air that, every now and then, bakes the trees and brush into tinder for the fires that lick at those sturdy beams and snap them as if they were Pick-Up Sticks, leaving the parched earth and the houses sitting on them defenseless against the rush of swollen rains.

Every so often I *am* tempted. The area is beautiful and enticing, and the houses I saw last year and the year before and the year before that are still standing. Like I said, though, I'm an expert worrier.

Lookout Mountain is one of the few streets on Laurel Canyon with a traffic light. Nearing the signal, I wondered exactly where Lenore had been standing when the car had struck her, and darted nervous looks around me, as if the road still bore bloody evidence of Sunday morning's events. There were a few stores on my right, but I doubted that they'd been open at that time.

The light turned green. According to Connors, Lenore had been found north of Lookout, so I continued a few hundred feet, passing the famed wide stone steps and bridge of the three-and-a-half-acre former Houdini estate, all that remains of the original mansion that fire destroyed in 1959.

At Willow Glen I turned right. I'd never been here before, and I felt hemmed in by the densely packed, two-story homes and unnerved by the cars coming toward me on the narrow, serpentine one-lane road that climbed higher and higher. I guess if you live here you get used to it, but I felt as though I'd done 180 curls on an Ab Roller. The good news, I told myself, was that there were plenty of potential witnesses. Connors or another cop had no doubt questioned the residents days ago, but experience has taught me that a great deal depends on the questions asked, and the questioner—people are often leery of becoming involved in a police investigation. And maybe Connors hadn't talked to everyone. Maybe I'd be lucky.

Luck had eluded me so far. After returning from the hospital, I'd spent the rest of my morning and most of the afternoon accomplishing little. I blamed it on the mild headache from fasting, a headache that lingered for a while after I dry-swallowed two Advil tablets, but I knew it was Lenore, and that I'd failed her.

There were several pages of Weldons in the Pacific Bell directories (I have the whole set, covering the city and Valley), half a dozen with the initial *N*, but not one Nina. I began with the six, heard six answering machine messages—two delivered by male adults, three by females, and one by a squeaky-voiced, singsongy child whose parents obviously thought he was the cutest thing since Macaulay Culkin.

I had fared no better trying to track down Darren Porter: There were numerous Porters, many of them with the initial *D*, but none of them were home except for a Doreen, to whom I apologized for calling the wrong number. People, of course, aren't always home when you want them to be, which was why I'd braved the traffic and come here now, close to dinnertime.

I fared no better now. None of the residents had seen Lenore in her nightgown. None had witnessed or heard the accident, even those within yoo-hoo-ing distance of Laurel Canyon. Back in my car, feeling embarrassingly winded by the climb and determined to exercise more, I continued along Willow Glen and took one hairpin turn after another until I arrived at Apollo and what seemed like the crest of Mount Olympus. In any case, it was crest enough for me.

The street was graceful and wide, lined with Italian cypress trees standing proud as sentinels in front of predominantly white houses that reflected the muted brilliance of the setting afternoon sun. After inhaling a lungful of what I hoped was smog-free air, I crunched along the walk to the topmost house, a brand-new white stucco two-story with a white-tiled roof, mullioned windows, and multiple balconies. No landscaping yet, and no car in the driveway. No sign of occupancy, for that matter, but I rang the bell and waited a few minutes before giving up.

The occupants of the next few houses were home, but they hadn't seen or heard Lenore or anything related to the hit-and-run. I was disappointed but undaunted, charmed by the vista and the ever-present cypress trees and the winding streets that suddenly changed identities (Jupiter becomes Oceanus, Apollo becomes Electra), much like the mercurial and capricious gods for whom they'd been named and whose escapades had kept me company during the summer months of my adolescence.

Several stops later on Hermes was a house I could easily covet: clean lines, weathered redwood planks, a peaked shingled roof, huge windows uncluttered with drapes or shutters. Two cars—a black Jeep Wrangler and a red Mercedes—sat in the driveway, and a tall, dark-haired, ponytailed woman in tight jeans and a crisp white cotton sleeveless blouse opened the door after I introduced myself, the cell phone at her ear a jarring note to the rustic splendor.

Her name was Jillian, and she was trying hard not to show her impatience. "A police detective was here a few days ago," she told me. "I was out of town that night."

"What about your husband?"

"Fiancé. He didn't see or hear the accident."

"I'm wondering if he saw the woman wandering around this area," I said, wishing I had a photo of Lenore. "She was wearing a nightgown."

Jillian shook her head. "He would have told me."

"Maybe I could ask your fiancé."

"Ask me what?" A man appeared in the doorway behind Jillian, then moved to her side and slipped his arm around her thin waist. He was a few inches taller than the woman and good-looking, with well-cut dark blond hair framing a broad face and friendly hazel eyes. They both looked to be in their mid-thirties.

"She's a reporter," Jillian told him, handing him the card I'd given her. "She's looking into that hit-and-run the police asked us about."

The fiancé tightened his lips and nodded. "Horrible thing. I hope they get the creep." He glanced at my card, then up at me. "Molly Blume, huh? I'll bet you get kidded about that. So you're writing a story about her?"

"Something like that. I was wondering if you saw the woman wandering around. She was wearing a nightgown."

"Wish I could help you out, but I went to sleep a little after midnight. Fell asleep during Leno—not his fault, mine." He smiled, chagrined. "Sorry."

So, I learned, were most of the residents, aside from those on vacation—sorry and asleep the night in question. Where were insomniacs when you needed them?

I had gone up and down Apollo and Hercules and had back-tracked up Venus, then come down again on Achilles, which leads into Vulcan. The street names and their fickleness were losing their charm, and I was losing my sense of direction and optimism. I was sick of Italian cypress trees. I dreaded the climb back up to my car. My headache was back, my clothes were sticking to me. I was tired and thirsty and hungry. I needed a bathroom. I thought of Cyrano—"I press on, I press on"—and did the same, wondering whether I'd find my white plume.

I trudged onward and found myself back on Hercules, then detoured onto Zeus, a short, isolated thunderbolt of a street that comes out of nowhere apparently only to intersect Hercules. I braked my Nikes to a stop in front of a silver Toyota. A girl wearing below-the-navel, low-cut white short shorts and a yellow crop top was sitting on the side of the hood, her caramel-tanned legs and arms scissored around the lean, cut-off jeans-clad torso of the porcupine-black-haired boy whose lips were locked on hers.

"Excuse me?" I called.

They pulled apart and stared at me, unembarrassed. I stared back. She had curly strawberry blond hair, a constellation of freckles splashed across the bridge of her short nose, and a ring in the navel of a midriff as flat as a sheet of wood. He had a row of studs in his left eyebrow and nostril, more on his upper lip. I wondered how it felt to kiss all that metal and remembered that braces had never stopped anyone, including me.

"A woman was injured in a hit-and-run around two o'clock Sunday morning," I said, beginning my script.

"Are you a cop?" Studs asked.

"Freelance reporter," I told him.

"Cool," he said, looking unimpressed. I didn't take it personally.

"A detective was here, but my parents were out of town that night," the girl offered. "I was babysitting my sister, but I didn't hear anything."

"Were you here that night, too?" I asked Studs.

"He wasn't," the girl said, too quickly.

I looked at her, then at him. "Is that right?"

"Yeah." He concentrated on digging a hole in the ground with the toe of his athletic shoe.

"You're lying," I said, as if I were commenting on the weather, which was pretty damn hot.

"I don't have to talk to you," he said. "You're just a writer." Back to his toe.

How quickly they turn. "No, but Detective Connors—he's handling this case—is going to ask you the same thing after I talk to him, and he'll know you're lying. Why, I can't figure, unless you were driving the car that hit her."

His head jerked up. "No *way!*"

I waited.

He looked at her, eyes flashing panic like a neon sign. She sighed. Birds chirped.

"I was here with Abby, okay?" he said, sullen. "I came around ten, after her sister was asleep. I left around three. But we didn't see or hear anything. You can believe it or not, I don't give a shit."

"My parents'll kill me if they find out," Abby said.

"I won't rat you out to your parents," I promised. "I'm trying to find out if anyone saw a woman around here that night. She was wearing a cream-colored nightgown."

They exchanged startled looks. My white plume, I thought with a prickling of excitement.

"Is she the same woman that got hit by the car?" he asked.

I nodded.

"So is she, like, dead?" Studs asked.

Like, "Yes."

"Jeez." He blew out a deep breath.

The girl licked her lips.

"Where did you see her?" I asked him.

"Who said I saw her?" Narrowing his eyes, trying to tough it out.

I examined my nails.

"Suppose we *did* see her," he said a moment later. "Do we have to, like, talk to the cops?"

"Probably."

"Shit," Studs muttered.

I wondered if the metal on his face was stunting his vocabulary.

"Then my parents will know." The girl was grazing on her upper lip with her teeth as if it were a snow cone.

"So where did you see her?" I repeated.

"She came running out of a house," Studs said, his tone resigned.

"Which one?" I started to look around me, but he shook his head.

"Not here. Up there." He pointed in the direction I'd come from. "On Hermes," he said, rhyming the name with *germs*. "The wood one with the big windows?"

My dream house, occupied by Jillian and fiancé. Interesting, I thought. Then I frowned. "You can't see that house from here."

"We weren't in my house," Abby said, her face a becoming shade of pink that hid her freckles. "We went to this new house way up on Apollo. Once my sister's asleep, she never wakes up," she added before I could call her on it.

"What were you doing there?" I asked, although I had a pretty good idea.

"Fooling around." The pink in her face had deepened. "The owners haven't moved in yet. It's locked, but there's a way to get in from the back."

The single-minded determination of thieves and horny adolescents. "You could've fooled around in your own house, with your parents away and your sister asleep."

"We were getting high," she admitted. "I was nervous that

my sister would smell the stuff and tell my parents. Anyway, it's way cool being in an empty house."

I could see that. "So what happened when the woman came out of the house?"

"The guy came out, too," Studs said. "He grabbed her arm and she yelled at him to get his effing hands off her. She was screaming at him, cussing him out. Eff you, eff you. She said she was going to kill herself, that he'd be sorry."

"What did the man say?"

" 'Make sure you do it right this time.' Something like that."

Nice guy, I thought. I turned to Abby. "Does that sound right?"

She nodded.

"Then what happened?" I asked.

"Then she ran off, I guess all the way down to Laurel Canyon," Studs said. "We didn't see her again."

"Did he follow her?"

"Not right away. A few minutes later we heard a car, so it must've been his."

"Which car?"

"No idea."

"What time was this?"

He shrugged. "I dunno." Neither did Abby.

"Where were the two of you when this was happening?"

"In the backyard. You could hear every word."

"We were looking at the stars," Abby said. "It was totally awesome."

"It was cool," Studs agreed.

Not for Lenore, I thought, who would never again see the stars. "Then how did you see him grab her?"

"We heard yelling in the house, so we went there to see what was going down. They didn't notice us. It was dark, and they were kind of busy." He allowed himself a smirk.

"Did the woman call him by his name?"

"She called him a *couple* of names. Asshole, son of a bitch. Bastard." The kid was off the hook now, grinning and enjoying himself.

"I think she called him Ronnie," Abby volunteered.

Ronnie, or Robbie? "Did you hear him when he came back?"

"Nope. We didn't stick around that long. We went back to Abby's."

"What about the woman? Do you know when she arrived?"

Both of them shook their heads.

I gave them business cards, asked them to call me if they remembered anything else, and headed back up the hill. When I looked back a moment later, they were back on the hood of the car, revving up their motors.

The gods would be proud.

# CHAPTER TEN

THE FIANCÉ OPENED THE DOOR. "SOMETHING ELSE I CAN do for you?" he asked, smiling, one hand on the doorpost, the other in the pocket of his jeans. Welcome to my neighborhood.

"Leno wasn't on that night," I told him.

The smile slipped. The hand came down. "What?"

"You said you fell asleep watching Leno, but Leno isn't on Saturday night." Chugging up the hill had jogged my memory and produced this nugget.

He quickly regained his composure. "I didn't mean Leno *specifically*," he chided good-naturedly and chuckled. "I meant whatever was on TV. Are you reporting to Nielsen?"

I smiled to show I appreciated his wit. "It's Robbie Saunders, correct?" A reasonable assumption, given the argument Studs had heard, and what Lenore had said about Robbie being very angry.

His frown confirmed it. "I'm not interested in being interviewed for your story," he said, all traces of bonhomie gone from his voice, his body stiff as a plaster cast. "So if you'll excuse me?" He took a step back and started to shut the door.

"We know Lenore was here that night."

That stopped him. I'd debated going to Connors, and the *we* was my insurance in confronting a man who I thought had something serious to hide and might take extreme measures to keep it hidden. I'll admit I was nervous.

He pulled the door shut behind him and eyed me coolly. "Am I supposed to know what the hell you're talking about?"

"Your ex-wife?"

"I know my ex-wife's name," he said, giving me a steely look that could have razed a building. "I haven't seen her in weeks."

"She's the woman who was injured by a hit-and-run driver on Laurel Canyon near Lookout Mountain. I'm surprised you didn't know."

His face was a kaleidoscope of emotions that finally rearranged itself into dark somberness. "Lenore's mother told me," he said with what sounded like genuine concern. "I have no idea what Lenore was doing there. I was—*am*—terribly upset. Lenore and I have our problems, but I've never wished her harm."

"Lenore thinks you're angry with her. She said that's why you haven't visited her in the hospital."

"I'm not angry with her. Things are—" He glanced behind him at the door, then faced me, his hands raised in helpless surrender before they dropped to his sides. "I'm in touch with her mother. She tells me Lenore is doing well."

Either he didn't know Lenore was dead, or he was pretending. I decided telling him would only infuriate Connors, who would want to gauge Saunders's reaction when he learned the news. I also wondered why Betty Rowan had been evasive when I'd asked her what Lenore was doing near Laurel Canyon.

"I'm puzzled because when I talked to you earlier about the hit-and-run victim, you didn't tell me it was your ex-wife," I said. "Neither did your fiancée."

"Because it's none of your business," he snapped, his voice rising along with the color in his face. "It's not my job to feed the appetites of your voyeuristic readers. Is that it? Are you done prying into my life?"

"Does your fiancée know?"

"Yes, she knows." He was glaring now. "Leave her out of this."

"Mr. Saunders, don't you find it an odd coincidence that Lenore was down the hill from your home when she was struck?"

He sucked in air, and I could see he was fighting for control. "I find it *very* odd. The police think she may have been disoriented."

I nodded. "Because she was on antidepressants and sedatives."

"I see you've done your homework." He was assessing me, trying to figure out how much I knew.

"Why was she depressed?"

Something twitched in his face. "You'd have to ask Lenore."

"But even if she was disoriented, Mr. Saunders, why would your ex-wife be wandering around in a nightgown near your home?"

"I have no idea." He shrugged. "Maybe she had a nightmare. Maybe she was sleepwalking. She's done that before."

"Witnesses saw her run out of your house early Sunday morning."

Saunders snorted. "You don't give up, do you?"

I pulled a notepad from my purse and opened it to a page on

which I'd scribbled my grocery list. "You followed and grabbed her arm," I pretended to read. "She screamed at you, called you names. She told you she was going to kill herself." I looked up.

"I was sleeping," he said in a bored voice, a patient man indulging lunacy. "Who are these witnesses?"

I referred to the notepad. "You told her, 'Make sure you do it right this time.' "

He shook his head. "Not a nice thing to say."

The guy was cool, as Studs would say. "She ran down the hill. You followed minutes later in your car." I put the notepad away.

"And then?" he prompted, the intensity in his eyes giving him away.

A welcome breeze feathered my face. "And then I think your car hit her."

He shook his head sadly, my lunacy confirmed.

"Maybe it was an accident," I said. "Maybe you went looking for her, because you were sorry about the argument, sorry about what you said. Worried about what she'd do to herself. It was a dark night, no moon out. Maybe you didn't see her."

"Maybe you've been in the sun too much."

"If it was an accident," I said, "they'll take that into account. But you should go to the police before they come to you."

"I've already talked to the police. They're satisfied. Check my car." He pointed to the Jeep. "Go ahead. You won't find a scratch on it."

"Body shops do good work." I'd already given the Jeep and Mercedes a quick once-over, but unlike my brother Joey, I'm not an expert.

Saunders sighed and massaged the back of his neck. "Okay. Game's over."

"It's not a game, Mr. Saunders."

"It never happened. You're desperate for a story. Who do you write for, *The Enquirer*?"

"Witnesses saw you with her and heard you arguing. Why don't you tell me what happened? The police are investigating, they'll talk to the same people I talked to."

"This block is deserted, as you've probably discovered," he said. "The people who live in the next three houses down have been on vacation since the beginning of July. Who are your witnesses, owls?"

"They were in the new house on Apollo."

"No one lives there yet." Half turning, he opened the door and stepped onto the stone floor of the entry hall, his smile smug. Checkmate.

"That doesn't mean it was empty that night."

"Lenore wasn't here," he said calmly, not missing a beat. He cocked his head. "How do you know your witnesses aren't making all this up?"

"I don't. That's why I'm here, verifying the facts."

"Verify this," he said, and slammed the door in my face.

I was surprised he hadn't done it sooner.

# CHAPTER ELEVEN

*Friday, July 18. 8:08 A.M. 2500 block of Silverwood Terrace. A woman became angry at her husband and threw a frozen chicken at him. The suspect is described as a 52-year-old woman standing 5 feet 6 inches tall and weighing 170 pounds. (Northeast)*

I'M AN EARLY RISER, BUT I HAD OVERSLEPT AND WAS IN my usual morning-after-the-fast state, sluggish and bloated, like a turkey on the day before Thanksgiving. I always eat too fast and too much. (Last night it had been a bowl of my mom's to-die-for potato-celery soup, basil and tomato pasta, and Greek salad, followed by a pint of Häagen-Dazs Cookies and Cream from my freezer.) What bothers me is that I don't seem to learn.

After showering and dressing, I swallowed two Advil tablets

with my coffee and toasted English muffin, crunched a Tums for dessert, and after reviewing and e-mailing my *Crime Sheet* column to my editor, I set about preparing the Friday night Shabbat dinner I'd promised to make for the Birkensteins, the bereaved family my mother had told me about. I'm no Emeril, but I enjoy cooking and entertaining, and I had put my kosher cookbooks to good use when Ron and I were married. Living alone, it's hardly worth the effort, so I welcomed the opportunity and couldn't help wondering who, if anyone, was preparing meals for Betty Rowan.

With the phone receiver wedged between my head and shoulder, something that was beginning to give me a chronic pain, I phoned Connors and plucked chicken hairs while I told him what I'd learned. If my readers could see me now. . . .

"Proud of yourself, are you?" he asked when I'd finished.

"Are you going to talk to Saunders?" The chicken balded and rinsed, I washed two celery stalks, set them on the cutting board, and began slicing.

"For your information, we already did."

"But that was *before* I told you what those kids saw."

"Actually, Saunders came to the station early this morning to clear things up. He told us what happened. We're satisfied he's not the hit-and-run driver."

I stopped slicing. "You're kidding, right? They had a heated argument, Andy. He said he hoped she did a better job of trying to kill herself, then drove down the hill after her."

"He told me all that. He realizes he should have told us she was there that night when we first talked to him, but he panicked. He didn't want to get involved, have his name in the paper."

I put down the knife and took the receiver in my hand. "But he *is* involved!"

"He didn't see it happen. He looked for her because he was worried, but he didn't see her. He drove about half a mile, then gave up and went home."

I rolled my eyes though Connors couldn't see me. "You actually *buy* that?"

"It was dark, Molly. No moonlight. He thinks she hid when she saw him coming and waited until his car passed her. She's proud like that, he said."

"Are you going to check out his car?"

"You keep asking that. What's with you and cars lately? Are you opening up a dealership?"

Today his humor grated. "Well, *are* you?"

"We did—both cars, in fact. He's not the guy, Molly. I know you're disappointed."

"There are body shops—"

"The paint is old," he interrupted me, impatient. "There's nothing to indicate that either vehicle was involved in an accident."

I thought for a moment. "According to the police report, Lenore was hit at one forty-six. I assume that's when it was called in, right?"

"Right. And before you ask, Saunders doesn't know exactly what time she left, or when he drove down the hill."

"Very convenient."

"Was he supposed to check his watch? Oops, time to drive down the hill and slam the ex-wife." Connors sighed. "Give it up, Molly."

But I couldn't. There's a maxim in Judaic law that I learned in my high school Bible class: *modeh b'miktzat, modeh b'kol*. If someone admits he lied about part of a charge, chances are he lied about the charge in its entirety. Or as Bubbie G would say, "Half a truth is a whole lie." I didn't think Connors or a D.A. would appreciate Talmudic reasoning or a proverb.

"I just can't believe he didn't see her," I said instead. "What if she was trying to run away from him, Andy? Maybe that's why she didn't see the car coming. Doesn't that make him responsible?"

Connors didn't answer right away. "It's a possibility I've considered," he allowed grudgingly. "Another is that he saw her on the way back, after she was hit, and did nothing about it. But we don't have a Good Samaritan law, Molly. As to the first possibility, I can't prove it, and unless I can, I'm going to leave it alone. Which is what you should do."

"Why?"

He expelled a deep breath. "Do you know who Robert Saunders is?"

I frowned. "Should I?"

"His family is old money. Saunders is a land developer and he's running for city council. He has a lot of supporters, including the mayor."

I'm not much into city politics, so I wasn't surprised that his name hadn't been familiar. "You didn't mention this before."

"I didn't know until yesterday, when Lenore's mom clued me in."

"If Saunders is running for city council, no wonder he doesn't want all this to come out."

"We don't know that there's anything to come out."

"You know there is."

"He's well-connected, Molly."

"So?" I didn't like what I was hearing.

"So it's not a good idea to sling accusations against someone like him unless you have solid proof. Which I don't have."

Anger stirred inside me. "*Please* don't tell me you're backing off because he has money and friends in high places. If you do, I'll vomit."

"Have you forgotten about presumption of innocence? Just 'cause he's a politician doesn't mean he's a liar."

"Can *you* spell Gary Condit?" I asked in a *Mister Rogers' Neighborhood* voice.

Connors hung up. I turned on the radio to KF101, the oldies station. With my mind on Saunders and "My Boyfriend's Back" in the background, I finished slicing the celery, chunked an onion and four pared potatoes, one red and one green pepper, some mushrooms, and spread everything on the bottom of a foil-lined baking pan. I sprinkled garlic powder and paprika on the chicken, which I placed on top of the veggies, then smothered everything with half a jar of sweet-and-sour duck sauce. It's my sister-in-law Gitty's recipe—easy and foolproof—and goes great with rice, which I planned to steam just before I delivered the meal.

I covered the chicken with tinfoil and set the pan into the oven. I phoned Connors again.

"What now?" he grumbled when he came on the line.

"I just remembered something else Lenore told me."

Connors sighed. "Why am I not surprised?"

"When I asked her if she remembered trying to cross Laurel Canyon, she said everyone was asking her the same thing. You, her mother, Robbie. Why would Robbie care unless he was worried about himself? And when did he ask her, if he didn't visit her?"

"Okay. Interesting." Connors's tone was grudging. "Is that it?"

"When I asked Lenore about her fight with Robbie, she said she promised not to tell."

"This just came to you, did it? Or are you undergoing hypnosis?"

"Did Saunders say why Lenore was in his house, Andy?"

"Yeah, he did."

"But you're not going to tell me."

"They say women are intuitive. I guess they're right."

"Come on, Andy. Give."

"The man's entitled to his privacy, Molly. I know that's hard for you to accept."

"Her car wasn't there. So how did she get there unless Saunders picked her up?"

"She told him she took a cab."

"In her nightgown?"

"Can you drop the effing nightgown, Molly?"

I could sense that he was this close to hanging up again. "The fiancée wasn't there Saturday night, and Lenore shows up in a nightgown. What does that tell you, Andy?"

"That Saunders is a popular guy?"

"Did you tell him she killed herself?"

Connors sighed. "Yeah, I did. For what it's worth, he seemed genuinely upset."

Especially if he drove her to it, I thought.

# CHAPTER TWELVE

HALF AN HOUR LATER THE DUCK SAUCE WAS PERFUMING my apartment and I located Nina Weldon. I'd spoken to seventeen Weldons the night before, none of them Ninas, and had left my name and phone number for three women whose answering machine messages hadn't revealed their names. Now one of them had called back.

"What's this about?" she asked, more curious than anything else.

I couldn't tell her age from her voice, which was tentative and soft. "I'm calling about Lenore Saunders. Her mother said she was going to call you?"

"God, it's horrible, isn't it?" she said. "First the hit-and-run—I just *knew* something was wrong when she didn't show up

Sunday night. And now this. I can't believe she's dead. I just can't." She started crying, quiet, whimpering sounds like the bleats of a lamb.

"I'm so sorry. Lenore told me the two of you were close."

"We were *best friends*. I don't know what I'm going to do now that she's gone." She sniffled.

"How long did you know her?"

"A little over a year. What's your name again?"

"Molly Blume."

"Did you just meet her? Because she's never mentioned your name."

Something new in her voice puzzled me. Not suspicion . . . "I visited Lenore in the hospital. Actually, she said I should talk to you. I'm a freelance reporter."

"Oh, is this about Dr. Korwin's project?"

She sounded relieved, and I realized what I'd heard before: jealousy. "What project is that?"

"Dr. Korwin has a clinic for women who are depressed. He's doing a major study on it. That's how Lenore and I met. We were in group together."

"Do you think I could meet with you, Nina? I'd like to talk to you about Lenore, and what happened."

She hesitated. "I don't know much. Lenore was hardly able to talk when I visited her in the hospital. Are you planning to write a story about her?"

"Possibly. I'm interested in your impressions. Is today good for you?" I pressed before her hesitation could take root. "I can make it any time until five." After that, I'd be cutting it too close for Shabbat, which starts before sundown.

"No, I'm sorry. I'm leaving for work—I'm a medical receptionist—and I won't be home until six."

"How about Sunday? We can meet anywhere you like."

"I have no intention of betraying Leonore's confidence."

"Of course not. Whatever you feel comfortable telling me."

"I still don't understand what you want to know." Her tone was almost plaintive.

"To be honest, I'm not sure. But when I talked with Lenore, she said, 'Ask Nina.' So I guess that's what I'm doing," I said, hoping my light tone would relax her.

"Ask me what?"

"She said what happened was her fault, that she didn't deserve a second chance. That's when she told me to talk to you. It sounded important to her," I added. "The next night, just hours before Lenore died, I guess, she left a message on my machine."

Nina sucked in her breath. "What did she say?"

"Why don't I tell you when we meet."

"Okay," she said, still reluctant. "Sunday, at ten?"

"Fine. Where?"

"My apartment." She gave me her address on Havenhurst between Romaine and Santa Monica.

"That's near Lenore's apartment, isn't it?"

"It's the building next door. I just moved there four months ago. We were *best friends*," she said again, mournful, angry, bewildered, the way I'd felt when Aggie had died.

On the way to the Birkensteins' I stopped at a kosher bakery on Fairfax Avenue. When I was a child the three blocks of Fairfax from Beverly Boulevard to Clinton were the heart of a Jewish community that was small and centralized. Today the community is much larger and has mushroomed—east to Hancock Park; west to Beverly Hills, Pico-Robertson, Beverlywood, and Santa Monica; south to the newly gentrified Olympic area; north, across the Hollywood Hills, to the San Fernando Valley and beyond. A venerable dowager showing her age, Fairfax has stiff competition from young, robust upstarts like La Brea and Pico and Ventura Boulevards.

Several years ago the city council gave Fairfax a face-lift. The sidewalks were repaved and prettied, creating access ramps for the wheelchairs and walkers of the elderly, many of whom reside in nearby retirement facilities. Cheerful green awnings replaced tattered, faded ones, spring hats with veils softening the wrinkles of old faces. Trees were planted. But unlike the Farmers Market and its specialty shops, only a few blocks south, Fairfax will never be quaint, and to the chagrin of the disdainful giant CBS eye two blocks east that pretends not to see her, she will never be a lady.

Fairfax is an uneven chorus line of banks and bakeries, of social welfare agencies and nail salons and thrift shops and stores that sell produce, fresh fish, pizza, menorahs, nuts, fake Persian rugs, Israeli CDs, smoked cod, shoes, deli, and the mah jongg cards I buy every April for the weekly game my sisters and I play.

The population of shoppers is still primarily Jewish—first- and second-generation Ashkenazis of western European heritage, Israelis, Moroccans, Russian immigrants—except for curious tourists and an occasional black or Hispanic or Asian student from the high school whose campus borders on the east side of the street between Rosewood and Melrose but is so removed from the neighborhood that it could be miles away. Walk up the block that boasts Canter's, a celebrity late-night hangout in its heyday that's making a comeback, and you'll find one or more of the homeless—malodorous, scruffy, sitting on the sidewalk and leaning against a store window—their lot worse but not so different from that of better-dressed, down-on-their-luck mendicants who ask, usually in Yiddish, for *a bissele tsedakeh far Shabbos* (a little charity for the Sabbath), all of them looking for crumbs like the pigeons on the corner.

The smells from the bakery, a heavenly vapor of cinnamon and yeast and chocolate and warm apple, beckoned to me, a genie promising riches. Inside, I took a number, waited patiently behind old Mr. Froman while he counted the coins he'd fished out of his pocket, and chatted with Elsa, the sixty-eight-year-old salesperson who had given me free sprinkle cookies when I was a child and helped me choose my wedding cake. I bought challah and pastries for the Birkensteins—crumb-topped, pocket cheese Danish and an assortment of cookies—and two Danish for myself, along with half a log of the best seven-layer cake I've ever tasted.

I thanked Elsa, and we exchanged the traditional *"Shabbat shalom"* (a peaceful Sabbath) greeting. Picking up my bags and pink string-tied boxes, I turned around and came face-to-face with Robert Saunders.

He raised a brow and smiled. "Well, *this* is a surprise."

"Isn't it."

Not a scintillating rejoinder from someone who earns a living with words, but I was unnerved at seeing him, suspicious of this heartiness that rang false in view of the fact that yesterday he'd slammed the door in my face. I wondered how long he'd been standing there and whether he'd followed me.

"A friend of mine told me Fairfax has the best bakeries," he said, "so I thought I'd check it out. What do you recommend?"

"Try the strudel, or the cinnamon buns." If he'd followed me, he knew where I lived, which didn't make me happy. I wished I'd used my pseudonym.

"Look, Miss Blume . . . can I call you Molly?" Without waiting for my response, he continued. "I'm glad we ran into each other. I didn't handle things well yesterday, and I'd like to explain, to tell you my story."

"I'd love to hear it." The change of heart, if genuine, explained his demeanor but was still puzzling. Maybe it was Connors's doing.

Saunders checked his watch. "It's twelve-fifteen. I have a client at one-thirty. Can we grab a cup of coffee nearby?"

I was curious to hear the story that had satisfied Connors, but the chicken and rice wouldn't last long in the trunk of my car. "I can't do it now. What about after your appointment?"

"Would three work for you?"

"Three is fine. There's a Coffee Bean and Tea Leaf on Beverly near Robertson."

"I know it." He nodded. "I'll see you there."

With my bakery goods and a bottle of red Joven wine from the Israeli-owned grocery a few stores down, I returned to my car and drove to the Birkensteins' on Curson north of Oakwood, a block that, like most of the streets in this neighborhood, is filled with duplexes and four-unit apartment houses rented by old-timers and, more and more, by young, hip singles.

Though I write about murder, I'm uncomfortable around death and mourning. Pushing open the Birkensteins' door (the front doors of a house in which family are sitting shiva are left unlocked during the day), I entered the apartment and found the kitchen, where I deposited the chicken and rice, the bakery goods and wine. The children were at the table, eating lunch and attended to by a woman who must have been a family friend.

Entering the living room, I counted the heads of ten or twelve visitors and sat on a sofa at a safe distance from the widow, who was perched uncomfortably on an armless chair with truncated legs, on loan from the local Jewish burial society, like the chairs my mom and dad had used when mourning their parents, and the Lashers, Aggie. Mrs. Birkenstein, her hair covered by a kerchief, eyes dazed, was stroking the head of the blond three-year-old boy at her feet whose arms were climbing her leg like vines.

She seemed lost in thought, and we joined in her silence—according to Jewish custom, it's the mourner who sets the tone and initiates conversation. I felt awkward at first, compelled to fill the void with words, but after a while I settled into the quiet of the room, my thoughts drifting from the bereaved family to Lenore and her ex-husband and her best friend, and back to the widow, who had broken her silence.

"You didn't know him well," she said to one of the men sitting in the front row of chairs.

"Unfortunately, no. But even from the few times we talked, he impressed me as being a very kind man."

Zack's voice. I was startled and wondered what he was doing here.

"And I've heard from so many people in the shul how wonderful he was," Zack said.

She smiled shyly. "He was a wonderful husband, and a wonderful father."

So the Birkensteins were Zack's congregants. My mother hadn't mentioned which shul Mr. Birkenstein had belonged to. My father probably hadn't told her. Even if he had, there was no way she or anyone else could have orchestrated my being here at the same time as Zack.

"We were planning to go on vacation next month," Mrs. Birkenstein said, her voice filled with regret and some surprise. "We had so many plans."

Shakespeare says there's Providence in the fall of a sparrow. Bubbie G says much the same thing, that what happens in our lives is *bashert*—predestined—though we don't understand God's designs, and we do have the ability to exercise free will (which explains Ron and some other mistakes I've made). I tend to agree, because it's comforting to think that God, who is busy running the world, isn't too busy to watch over me and nudge me in the right direction. I wondered whether He was nudging me now, and if so, why here, in this house of covered mirrors and hushed conversation, in this room where a new widow, her garment freshly rent, had not begun to absorb the reality of her loss. Maybe that was the point, I decided. Maybe God was reminding me that happiness is fleeting.

Or maybe this was, after all, just a coincidence.

Mrs. Birkenstein talked about her husband, her voice quiet but animated, tears glistening in her eyes. After a while, when she had lapsed again into silence, I rose and approached her.

I stole a look at Zack. He was sitting on a chair to my right. The surprise in his gray-blue eyes turned into something else that made me pleasantly flustered. I bent down and offered my condolences to the widow and left the room.

# CHAPTER THIRTEEN

LENORE HAD LIVED IN AN APARTMENT BUILDING TYPICAL of Los Angeles construction in the late Fifties and Sixties—two stories of banana-colored stucco and faded-orange Spanish-tile roof, small wrought-iron enclosed balconies, a center court with a swimming pool, underground parking.

The managers, Tom and Marie O'Day, invited me into a living room darkened to movie theater standards by double drapes— a necessity, Marie explained, because of the intensity of the afternoon western sun. They wore white Bermuda shorts and white sports-logo-emblazoned T-shirts that set off their darkly tanned, raisined skin, and had almost identical salt-and-pepper short, curly hair and friendly hazel eyes prematurely lined, probably by exposure to the same sun from which they were careful to protect their furniture. A large television screen showed a women's tennis match in progress, and the coffee table had been laid out with bowls of popcorn and pretzels and cans of soda and beer.

"We were shocked when her mother told us Lenore died," Marie said, her voice rising to compete with the droning of a former tennis champion turned commentator and the air-conditioning unit that sporadically emitted a bronchial cough. "Just shocked. Weren't we, Tom?" She turned to her husband, who was sitting next to her on an avocado green velvet sofa in pristine condition.

"Shocked," he agreed. "She was a nice gal. Pretty." He fixed his eyes on the television screen.

"Tom and I were planning on visiting her at the hospital when we heard about the accident, but we never got around to it. And now she's dead." Marie sighed. "We thought it was from her injuries, but a detective stopped by and asked us all those questions. Was she depressed, things like that. He didn't say, but I guess she killed herself." Marie looked at me for confirmation.

"Did she *seem* depressed?"

"Not as far as I could tell. She was a nice woman. Quiet, kept to herself. But not aloof," she added quickly.

Tom scooped a palmful of popcorn from the bowl.

"Do you know what kind of work she did?" I asked.

"She didn't work," Tom said. "Didn't need to. She had investment income."

Probably part of her divorce settlement, I thought.

"She had plans, though," Marie said. "She was taking acting and singing lessons. She had a beautiful voice. And I think she wanted to be an author. I'd see her sitting at the pool, writing. It's just so sad what happened, isn't it, Tom?"

"Rotten shame."

"How long was she living here?" I asked, sipping the iced tea Marie had insisted on serving me.

"Seven months," Marie said.

"Did you ever meet her ex-husband?"

"Son of a bitch," Tom muttered.

I turned to him. "Why do you say that, Mr. O'Day?"

He looked at me and blinked. "What?"

"Mr. Saunders was a son of a bitch?"

"Was he?" He shrugged. "I wouldn't know. Never met him." He returned his attention to the screen. "That ball was on the line, you imbecile!" he shouted.

"Tom takes his tennis seriously," Marie said, gazing with affectionate humor at her husband.

It's the way my dad and mom look at each other after thirty-six years of marriage. It's what gives me hope but sets the bar high. "So I see." I smiled. "Did you ever meet Mr. Saunders?" I asked her.

"No. I knew she'd been married, but I didn't like to pry. She always got this sad look in her eyes when the subject came up."

"No boyfriend?"

"Not that I know of." Marie leaned closer to me. "Between you and me, I think she was hoping they'd get back together."

Interesting. "Did she tell you that?"

"Not in so many words. It was just a feeling. She had their wedding picture out, and a few other photos of the two of them. I saw them once when I was in her apartment. Why would she keep those pictures out after they were divorced?"

Why, indeed. "Did Lenore tell you that her ex-husband is engaged?"

"Is *that* right?" Marie looked disappointed. "Well, maybe I was wrong, then. I know she wanted to get married, to have children. She *loved* children. She'd bring candies and little toys for our grandkids when they'd come to visit. But she seemed shy around them."

"Move up to the net!" Tom urged.

"When was the last time you saw Lenore?" I asked.

"The detective asked us that," Marie said. "Saturday afternoon, when she was getting her mail."

"Did she seem upset?"

Marie considered. "Come to think of it, she wasn't herself. She usually asks how we're doing, things like that. This time she was in a hurry, distracted."

"So you didn't see her when she left the apartment late Saturday night?"

Marie sighed. "No, I'm afraid not. Her car was here, though, in her parking spot. The detective asked that, too."

I was pleased to know that Connors had followed up, but not surprised. He *is* thorough. "Did Lenore have a lot of visitors?"

Tom snorted and chomped on popcorn.

"There was this woman who came by all the time," Marie said. "Nina something. I don't know her last name, but she moved into the next building. She came by Wednesday afternoon to pick up some things Lenore wanted. Of course, I checked with Lenore before I let her into the apartment. You can't be too careful nowadays, can you?"

"No, you can't," I agreed.

"That's about it as far as visitors, aside from her mother, and I only met her once, not counting twice this week. She was here more in the last few days then in all the time Lenore lived here. Well, I'm sure she visited other times, I just didn't see her. And maybe Lenore had other visitors. Her apartment's toward the back of the building, and it's not like I'm watching it all the time."

"Interfering," Tom announced.

"Oh, go on now." Marie shoved him playfully.

"Do you think you could show me Lenore's apartment?" I asked. "Of course, I wouldn't touch anything, and you'd be right there the whole time." I had few clues about Lenore, and seeing how she lived might give me a sense of her personality.

Marie widened her eyes and looked as if I'd asked her to strip naked. "Oh, I couldn't do *that*! It wouldn't be right. I even had to stop Lenore's mother from going in yesterday afternoon, because the detective told us not to touch anything until he had a look, although I don't know why. It's not as though she was murdered."

"I think it's routine." I felt a flicker of interest and wondered whether, despite his denials to me, Connors suspected foul play, or whether he was just being careful. "Do you know a Darren Porter, by the way?" I repeated the description Jeannette Plank had given me.

Marie shook her head.

"Double fault," Tom muttered, disgusted.

I couldn't have said it better.

# CHAPTER FOURTEEN

"LENORE *WAS* AT MY HOUSE THAT NIGHT," ROBERT SAUN-
ders said with the air of someone determined to be gracious.
"But I didn't see her after she left."

We were at The Coffee Bean and Tea Leaf. With the tem-
perature in the high eighties and not much of a breeze, my
white cotton blouse was sticking to me like Saran Wrap. I would
have preferred the air-conditioned, coffee-scented indoors, but
Saunders had practically insisted on sitting at one of the small
round outdoor tables. He probably figured that whatever he told
me would be dissipated into the air or drowned out by the
throaty rumble of cars forming a steady caravan along Beverly
Boulevard and the clatter and groan of the buses belching fumes.

It's not Paris, but on cooler days I enjoy sitting outside,

feeling *très* cosmopolitan sipping a cappuccino as I watch the foot traffic and ponder life or my work or a sale at Nordstrom's. Down the block are several banks and medical offices and Jerry's Famous Deli, where I ate nonkosher sandwiches in my rebellious years, and the former site of a mystery bookstore I frequented that relocated to Westwood a couple of years ago. Up the block is Robertson, which has evolved from Decorators' Row to a boulevard that has added to its furniture showrooms high-end dress salons and movie theaters and features The Ivy, a posh restaurant you've probably heard of. You have to be careful at Robertson and Beverly, though, because it's one of those intersections equipped with a camera that will take a photo of your license plate if the light changes red before you get to the other side. The DMV will send you the photo in the mail, along with a $270 citation. I know, because I got one a few weeks ago and am still debating whether I should go the Comedy Traffic School route or do it online.

"What was Lenore doing at your house?" I asked, taking a bite of the mozzarella-and-tomato French bread sandwich Saunders had insisted on paying for, along with a blueberry scone. Many of the products at the Coffee Bean in L.A., in case you're wondering, are kosher, but not conspicuously so.

"What are you planning to do with what I tell you?" Saunders countered, holding a losing hand but unwilling to throw in his cards.

"I don't know."

"At least you're honest." With a smile so strained it looked painful, he leaned toward me over the small table, his hands cupping a cardboard container of steaming coffee. "I'm in a tough spot, Molly," he said, his voice and the use of my first name suggesting an intimacy of longtime friends. "Jillian's not thrilled that I didn't tell her about Lenore's visit, and—"

"Why didn't you?" I interrupted.

"Because I knew she'd be upset—not with me, with the situation. It's not as though I invited Lenore to come over. And whether you believe me or not, Lenore's death is extremely painful for me, not to mention for Lenore's mother. Lenore was all she had. I don't see what's to be gained by publicizing all of this, except creating *more* pain. It's a private matter."

"And you're running for public office."

A frown flitted across his handsome face. "I suppose you think that makes me fair game for media scrutiny. I'd agree, if this were about me—my character, my background, my track record. But it's not. It's about Lenore."

"Why are you telling me all this?" I asked. "Why are we here?"

Saunders took a sip of coffee. "Detective Connors told me you're not about to let this go, and the information is there for you to dig up. He also said you're ethical. I'm hoping once I explain everything, you'll agree to keep this to yourself."

"I can't make promises. And if I can find the information, so can others."

"There was a small mention in the *Times* two months ago. But if you start asking questions . . ." His voiced trailed off. "How about this: I talk to you now. If you agree it's not of public interest, it stays between us, unless someone else starts investigating. In which case I give you an exclusive."

"*If* I agree," I said. "I'll have to corroborate whatever you tell me."

"It's not all that complicated. Can I ask you something, Molly? What's your interest in Lenore?"

"I read about her accident in a police report, and I was intrigued."

Saunders sighed. "There's nothing intriguing about what happened. Pathetic, maybe, and tragic, now that Lenore's taken her life, but hardly intriguing."

"She was wearing a nightgown when she was struck by a car about two miles from her home, at almost two in the morning. I find that intriguing."

"I didn't invite her to spend the night, if that's what you're implying." He was prickly with defensiveness.

"I'm not implying anything. You lied to the police, and to me."

"I didn't owe you a statement," he said with a trace of yesterday's irritation. "And I didn't *lie* to the police. They asked me if I'd witnessed the accident or knew anything about it. I hadn't. And I had no idea the victim was Lenore until her mother told me what happened."

"But you didn't mention that Lenore was at your home just before she was hit."

"I didn't think the two events were connected."

"And I don't write fiction, Mr. Saunders." I took another bite of my sandwich.

He opened his mouth to say something, then closed it. "Okay," he said a moment later, his tone grudging. "I suspected. But Lenore's visiting me had nothing to do with what happened to her, and I didn't want Jillian to be upset. I *did* tell Detective Connors everything this morning. I know I should have done that right away."

His sheepishness was convincing and charming. I decided he'd make a great politician. "So why was Lenore at your house?" I asked again.

"She needed help. She showed up after midnight, in her nightgown. She was agitated, disoriented. She said she was afraid she might hurt herself if she was alone and asked to spend the night."

I frowned. "Why at your place? Why not her mom's?"

"I don't know."

I gave him a look that said, try harder.

"She's always depended on me," Saunders said, clearly reluctant. "Even after the divorce."

"Whose idea was the divorce?"

An expression I couldn't figure out crossed his face. Pain, anger. "Mine."

"It's odd that she'd come to your house, now that you're engaged. Unless she knew that your fiancée wouldn't be there?"

"I don't see how. She just wasn't thinking clearly. Anyway, I told her she couldn't stay and offered to drive her to her mother's house, or to a friend. She was irrationally angry—probably because of the drugs. That's when she stormed out."

"How did she get to your house?"

"She told me she took a cab. She was a little woozy from the meds when she showed up. I guess she was afraid to drive."

"In her nightgown," I said.

"She probably didn't realize what she was wearing."

I supposed that was possible. "So she stormed out, yelled at you, threatened to kill herself, and you said, 'Go ahead, do it right this time.' "

"That wasn't my finest moment." His face was flushed. "Lenore was always threatening to kill herself. She was manipulative, needy. I didn't take her threat seriously, but I was worried about her. So I got into my car a few minutes later to give her a ride home, but I couldn't find her."

"How many minutes later?"

"I don't know. Five, maybe? I didn't check my watch. At first I thought she was lost, because the streets here curve, and they can be confusing, especially at night."

"Lenore was struck on Laurel Canyon just north of Lookout," I said. "How is it that you didn't see her when you exited on Willow Glen?"

"Because I didn't *take* Willow Glen," Saunders said, allowing himself a small satisfied smile. "I drove up and down the streets looking for her, then took Mount Olympus to Laurel Canyon. I figured Lenore would go that route because it would take her closer to home, and it was safer."

"And when you didn't find her, you didn't think that maybe she took Willow Glen?"

Saunders shook his head. "Why would she head farther north?"

"Because, as you said, it was dark, and she was confused by the streets, and her pills. Obviously, that's where she *did* end up."

"Obviously." Saunders nodded. "But at the time, it didn't occur to me that she'd take Willow Glen. At first, when I couldn't find her, I figured she'd managed to get to Laurel Canyon before I did, so I drove south. When I didn't see her, I assumed she'd heard my car when she was heading down Apollo and hid until I passed. Lenore was very stubborn, Molly. And she was furious with me."

I understood stubborn and angry. I'd stormed out of the house once after a fight with Ron and refused to get into his car when he'd followed me. "How far did you drive down Laurel Canyon looking for her?"

"Past Hollywood Boulevard. When I didn't see her, I figured she was hiding, like I said, or she'd flagged a cab. So I turned around and took Mount Olympus home."

"And all this happened *before* the car hit her," I said, not bothering to hide my skepticism.

"I have no idea when she was hit. Willow Glen and Mount Olympus at Laurel Canyon are over a mile apart." Saunders stared into his coffee container. "I keep going over it in my mind. What if I'd caught up with her and persuaded her to let me take her home? What if I'd taken her threat more seriously and let her stay the night?" He looked up at me. "Even if I had, she probably would have killed herself, if not yesterday then some other time."

*"Why?"*

That pained, angry look crossed his face again. He shifted restlessly on his seat and gazed up the street, as if searching for an escape. I thought that, like Connors and Betty Rowan, he would avoid answering, but he cleared his throat and I tensed in anticipation.

"I haven't talked about this for some time." He spoke so softly that I had to lean closer to hear him above the noise of the traffic, but I couldn't miss the quiet despair in his voice. "Last March, almost a year and a half ago, Lenore killed our two-month-old son."

I don't know what I'd expected, certainly not this. My heart felt heavy with sadness, and a sort of regret at what I'd pried loose. "I'm so sorry," I said, the words lame to my ears. Even if I hadn't been shocked, I don't think I would have known what other words to offer.

"She was suffering from postpartum psychosis," he said, still not looking at me. "You hear about it more these days, and I guess the signs were there, but I didn't see them at the time. Afterward, of course, it was so clear." His voice was bitter with anguish and self-recrimination. "Max was colicky and fussy. Lenore was nervous and weepy. She wasn't eating, she couldn't sleep. She was tired and listless, and little things would set her off. She'd stay in bed except for getting up to check on Max, which was all the time. She kept asking me if I thought he was okay, did he seem normal."

I remembered my sister Edie's wildly fluctuating moods after her second child was born. Laughing one minute, sobbing the next. But that had lasted only a few days.

"I figured most mothers go through that, you know?" Saunders said, turning to face me, and I found myself nodding in sympathy. "Having a baby is an adjustment, and it takes longer for some women to get into a routine that works. I thought

Lenore was tired because of the sleepless nights. And she didn't have a support system. We'd moved to Santa Barbara just before the baby was born. In retrospect, the timing was a mistake. Her mother and mine were in L.A., and I was setting up an office in Santa Barbara, but I had to be in L.A. quite a lot. I know now I should have been home more, but I thought I was doing what I could. I hired a full-time housekeeper. I offered to hire the nurse we'd had the first few weeks after Max was born. We all thought it was a good idea—me, my mother, Lenore's mother. Lenore refused. She accused me of doubting her ability to mother her own child. She insisted she was feeling better every day, stronger, more confident."

Saunders stopped, and I made no move to prompt him.

"I realized later there were things she didn't tell me. She didn't want me to worry. She wanted to prove she could do it. But she wasn't herself. She was a different person, not the woman I'd married. Then one Thursday . . ."

His jaw worked hard, and tears formed in his eyes. "Max was two months old. I came home from work late, around ten o'clock. Lenore was in the glider in the darkened nursery, rocking the baby. She was cradling him in her arms, singing to him, and she didn't seem to be aware that I'd entered. I stood there for a minute or so watching her. I didn't want to disturb her. They looked so sweet, my wife and my son." The tears were streaming down his face now. He wiped them with his broad fingers.

"I called her name softly, not wanting to wake the baby if he was sleeping. When she didn't look up, I walked over to her. Her eyes were closed, and so were Max's, and I thought they'd both fallen asleep. When I bent down to take the baby and put him in his crib, she opened her eyes.

" 'Max is sleeping,' she said. 'He was crying and crying, and I was so worried, but he's going to be okay now. He's sleeping.'

"I offered to put him in his crib, but she held him closer to her breast. 'If you wake him, he'll cry,' she said. I reached a hand to stroke his cheek. It felt cold, but I still didn't realize anything was wrong, because the only light was coming from the hallway, and I couldn't see his color, which was a bluish gray.

" 'If you fall asleep you might drop him,' I told her. Again I bent down to lift him. Again Lenore resisted, but I pried Max from her arms. And that was when I noticed that there was something wrong with the angle of his head.' "

Saunders removed a tissue from his jacket pocket and blew his nose. "According to the autopsy findings, Lenore shook Max so violently that she broke his neck. She said that he'd been crying continuously for several days, that nothing she'd done had soothed him, that she'd sensed that his cry wasn't the same, that he wasn't the same, but when she'd asked me, I hadn't seen or heard anything unusual. She said she realized this time why he sounded different. A voice told her there was something inside him—" Saunders stopped and sighed deeply before continuing. "There was something terrible inside him, and it was going to get stronger and stronger, and she had to shake it out of his body or it would kill her and the baby."

As Saunders talked, images of Lenore violently shaking her crying baby forced themselves on me. I felt ill and couldn't imagine how he lived with the pain.

"Did you believe her?" I recalled what Lenore had told me. That no one believed her about what had happened to Max. No one except Nina.

"I *wanted* to," he said with sad earnestness. "Lenore's doctor said hers was a textbook case. He explained that she'd had a postpartum psychotic episode, and everything he said made sense. The symptoms were all there. And Lenore was obviously severely depressed. The day of Max's funeral she tried to kill herself in jail. She broke a makeup mirror and used a piece to slash her wrists, and she overdosed on medications she'd somehow hoarded. She tried again a few weeks later. I felt terribly sorry for her, and I blamed myself for not having seen the signs, for not having protected Max."

I didn't know a pleasant way of bringing up my next question. "You felt sorry for her, but you divorced her."

He flinched as though I'd struck him, then nodded. "Maybe another man would have been stronger. I couldn't get past the fact that she'd killed our son. I hired the best criminal defense attorney we could find. I was there for her during the trial, and after. I just couldn't stay in a marriage that had died."

There are violent deaths to a marriage, I thought, and there are petty, sordid ones. "What happened during the trial?"

"The jury found her guilty of manslaughter, and the judge decided against jail time. She was in a psychiatric hospital for six months, and as far as I know, she's been continuing therapy with Dr. Korwin, and on medication." Saunders sighed. "But I guess the guilt was too much for her."

I understood now why Lenore had felt she hadn't deserved a second chance. Connors, of course, had known all along. That's why he was so sure she'd killed herself.

"Lenore wouldn't want all of this to come out again," Saunders said, his tone urgent. "Her mother certainly doesn't. One of the reasons I returned to L.A. was to get away from the notoriety. The media coverage was worse than the trial." He was scowling at me, as if I were personally responsible.

"I'm surprised there hasn't been more coverage here now that you're running for office," I said.

"Me, too." He grimaced. "I'm waiting for the shoe to drop. So far it hasn't." He looked at me pointedly.

I pitied the man. If what he told me was true—and why would he lie?—he'd suffered a horrible tragedy, and I had no interest in forcing him or anyone in his family or Lenore's to relive it. I understood now why Betty Rowan had been evasive when

I'd asked her if she knew what Lenore was doing on Laurel Canyon.

But what about the events of last Sunday morning? According to Andy Connors, neither of Saunders's vehicles had struck Lenore. Still, I was skeptical about Saunders's story. I wondered whether he'd pursued Lenore—to protect her, as he claimed, or to harass—and forced her into the street; whether he'd seen her lying there, injured, and had decided not to come to the aid of the ex-wife responsible for the death of his son.

# CHAPTER FIFTEEN

THE VACUUM WAS GROANING WHEN I LET MYSELF INTO my parents' house. After calling "Hello?" and receiving no answer, I went upstairs to my old bedroom and unpacked. I don't usually spend Friday night with my parents. They live on Gardner south of Beverly, over a mile from my apartment, and since I don't drive on the Sabbath, I have to sleep over. Sometimes I prefer the solitude of my apartment, the uninterrupted introspection; sometimes, as my sister Edie claims, I'm determined to prove my postdivorce self-reliance. The truth is that, as comfortable as my parents try to make me feel, since the divorce it's been odd returning to the bedroom I left when I got married. Like Hardy's Tess, I am maiden no more, trying to find my place.

I stepped into the hallway, where my brother Joey was

pounding on the bathroom door, yelling at my sister Liora to get out and ignoring Noah, who was demanding to know the whereabouts of a tie Joey had borrowed without asking. I find it comforting that, even though half my siblings are married and out of the house, nothing has essentially changed.

Friday afternoon before Shabbat candle lighting in my parents' home was always frenzied. Hair dryers droning, music blaring, pots clanging, doors slamming, feet pounding up and down the stairs, an occasional expletive, the ensuing rebuke. My mother assigning last-minute chores that we bounced among us like a volleyball. My dad charging into the house, dangerously late as usual. We kids jockeying to be first in the shower and last to set the table or candles, or make sure the refrigerator lightbulb was unscrewed and the oven and clock timer set. On Friday afternoons we were an orchestra warming up, strings and percussions and winds warring in a crescendo of discordant solos until the conductor raised his hands and cacophony was magically transformed into one pure note that soared and swept you with it.

Of course, I vowed Friday afternoons in my own home would be different, calmer. Of course, they weren't. I suppose there's a Jewish equivalent of Murphy's law: No matter how early or late Shabbat begins, you're always racing to be ready. And maybe that's the point. The activity bordering on the manic helps me appreciate the serene silence and peace ushered in by the lighting of the candles.

There was a time when I didn't appreciate Shabbat at all, when I wore the rules and readiness like a straitjacket I longed to throw off, and did, for a while. But that was years ago, when I was hurt and angry and bewildered, looking to blame everyone, especially my parents and God.

My mother was crouching in front of the open oven door, basting something that smelled wonderfully of lemon and garlic and tarragon. I called her name, and she stood up, her face flushed from the oven's heat, a few dark brown tendrils moist against her forehead.

In a short denim skirt and a white T-shirt, sandals on her tanned legs, she looked closer to forty than her fifty-five years. She has slipped graciously into middle age and her skin is relatively unwrinkled, although she grumbles that menopause has thickened her body into a size ten, and she frowns, between tints, at the gray that has invaded the shoulder-length, chestnut brown hair she tucks under a hat or a wig whenever she goes out or when we have company.

She beamed at me, her dark brown eyes crinkling in pleasure. "Molly. I didn't hear you come in."

With the baster in one hand, she drew me close with her other hand, transformed by an oven mitt into a bear's paw, and kissed my cheek. I'm twenty-nine years old, but when my mother kisses me, I'm a little girl again, safe in the comfort of her arms.

"Anything I can do to help?" I asked.

"Everything's under control, which is a miracle, but thanks. I'm just going to fill the urn." She dropped the mitt on the counter and checked her watch. "*Shabbos* is at seven forty-five. I have ten minutes to shower and put on makeup, assuming your father's done."

"Go ahead. I'll fill it." We don't cook on Shabbat, so we boil water beforehand for tea or instant coffee. My family uses an electric hot pot, plugged in until Shabbat is over. You can also use a kettle and leave it on a *blech*, a heavy sheet of metal, placed over a stovetop and a burner set to a medium flame.

She studied me. "Are you okay? You seem preoccupied."

"I'm fine. Just thinking about stuff. A woman I read about in a police report," I added when I saw my mother's concerned look. Since leaving Saunders, I hadn't been able to clear my mind of Lenore and Max, both violently dead.

She nodded. "How was your date? I didn't even ask."

"It was okay."

"Just okay?" she said, careful not to sound disappointed.

"I like him," I admitted. "I liked him twelve years ago, too. I don't know if I can trust him."

"We'll talk while Daddy and the boys are in shul." She smiled and patted my arm.

A few minutes later the hot pot was burbling. I went to the backyard, cluttered again with outdoor toys and a wading pool for the grandchildren, and snipped an assortment of roses—whites, citrus-scented yellows, and my favorites, Double Delight, with their heady, intoxicating perfume. The roses reminded me of the sunflowers Darren Porter had brought Lenore. I'd forgotten all about him and made a mental note to check him out on Sunday, maybe before my talk with Nina.

I'd already checked out Saunders's story. After our meeting, I'd gone home and accessed the online Santa Barbara newspaper archives and printed out numerous articles about Max's death and Lenore's trial.

The jury, though sympathetic, had found her guilty of manslaughter. The judge had suspended sentencing and granted probation on the condition that Lenore would enter a psychiatric hospital for a six- to nine-month stay and serve one year in a residential treatment program that would provide progress reports every three months.

Saunders hadn't exaggerated the media attention and ensuing notoriety. At the funeral, hecklers had forced their way past security guards, carrying signs that were seen throughout the trial and after: KILL BABY KILLERS! JUSTICE FOR INFANTS! NEVER MORE, LENORE! After the verdict and sentencing, a fracas broke out between Lenore's defenders, who felt she should never have been tried, and her bitter attackers, who suggested that the judge had been swayed by Saunders's wealth and status. A few even hinted that he'd been bought. No wonder Saunders hadn't stayed in Santa Barbara.

There were background articles about Lenore, too. She was born in Twentynine Palms, about forty miles east of Palm Springs, an only child raised by a divorced mother. After two years of community college she moved to Los Angeles and met Saunders two years later while working as a receptionist in one of his companies. A year after that they were married. Their son, Max, was born the following year.

Everything I read corroborated what Saunders had told me. Still, I wanted to talk to Andy Connors, but he hadn't returned my calls. He was probably avoiding me. I would try him again on Monday, but I was impatient to compare what Saunders had told us separately, and I wanted to verify something that had been niggling at me for the past hour.

How long had Connors known about Lenore's past? Talking with Saunders at the restaurant, I'd assumed that Connors had known all about it from the start—that Betty Rowan had told him. But driving home I remembered Connors telling me that the mother hadn't known why Lenore was depressed.

Either Betty had been less than candid with Connors, or Connors had lied to me. "Because it's none of your damn business, Molly," I could hear him drawling, and I could accept that, even if I didn't like it. But if he hadn't known about Lenore's past at that point, what had he been withholding from me? Maybe—*probably*—nothing important, but it bothered me.

Back inside the house, I arranged the roses in a round glass vase that I set in the middle of the dining room table, now covered with a white lace cloth. I counted seven place settings. My parents often invite company for Shabbat, but tonight it was just family.

Still thinking about Saunders, I phoned my apartment from my mother's kitchen and listened to my answering machine's

outgoing message (I hate my taped voice), followed by one beep.
I hoped it was Connors, but it was Marie O'Day.

I blanked for a moment, then remembered: She was the
manager of the apartment house where Lenore had lived.

"I would have called you sooner, but I misplaced the card
you gave me," Marie said a minute later when she answered the
phone.

"Was there something you remembered about Lenore, Mrs.
O'Day?" I'd excised a tiny cube of steaming hot kugel sitting on
the counter. Now I plopped it into my mouth, savoring the
potato and onion pudding, and cut another cube.

"Well, no. I'm sorry. But the detective was here not long after you left, to check her apartment. The most terrible thing!
Someone broke Lenore's front-door lock and vandalized the
whole place! I thought you'd want to know."

My stomach muscles tightened. "When?"

"Tom says it must have been sometime Thursday night or
early Friday. Whoever did it made a real mess."

Murder, not suicide. I didn't care what Connors said—I was
as sure as if I'd witnessed the act. My mind was reeling, and I
wished I hadn't called before Shabbat, which is supposed to be a
day of repose and tranquillity.

"Miss Blume? Are you there?"

"I'm sorry. Would it be okay if I came by Sunday morning?"

Marie hesitated. "I guess so. The police should be done by
then, and there's not much to protect." She sighed. "Poor Lenore.
I'm glad she didn't see this. She was very particular about her
things."

So, apparently, was someone else.

# CHAPTER SIXTEEN

Bᴜʙʙɪᴇ ɢ ᴡᴀs ɪɴ ᴛʜᴇ ɢᴜᴇsᴛ ʀᴏᴏᴍ, ʀᴏᴄᴋɪɴɢ ɪɴ ʜᴇʀ chair while reciting *tehilim*, psalms, which she does with the aid of a special magnifying lens and memory, now that macular degeneration has stolen most of her central vision and some of the spirit that helped her survive the internment camps during the war and life's dark surprises. She looked up at the sound of the door opening, smiled with a nod at my greeting, and motioned to me to wait.

Bubbie is a study in contrasts. She is feisty and independent, insisting on living in her own apartment despite her failing vision, yet she is tender and sentimental. She will haggle with a store owner over a nickel, but is generous to charities and delights in giving her grandchildren gifts for no particular reason. She loves off-color jokes, but you'll rarely see her without a prayer book or psalm book in her hand. My father, who became closer to Bubbie after both his parents died when I was so young that my few memories of them need prompting by faded photos and repeated anecdotes, says Bubbie's piety and constant prayers have protected our family time and time again. Years ago I asked my father why Bubbie's prayers hadn't saved Zeidie Irving, whom I had loved fiercely. Why hadn't God heard her prayer?

"God always listens," my father said. "Sometimes He says no."

At the time I hadn't been able to share my father's faith, and though I have come to accept what I don't understand, I still find myself struggling.

A minute or so later Bubbie shut her psalms book and touched her lips to the brown leather cover. I leaned over and kissed her lined cheek, inhaling the scent of baby powder.

"You look nice, Molly," she said. "A new blouse?"

"Ann Taylor." I'm always surprised by how much Bubbie can see with only her peripheral vision. "I like your dress, Bubbie."

She harrumphed. "This *shmatte*," she said, using the Yiddish for *rag*, but I could see the pleasure in her once bright blue eyes.

Bubbie G takes great care with her appearance. She points with pride to the fashionably dressed girl she was in the photos she managed to save before the war—tall and slim with long, wavy dark hair and a cupid-bow's mouth—and reminisces fondly about the young men who pleaded with the *shadchan* in Sosnow-ice, the Polish town where she was born and grew up, to peti-tion her parents on their behalf. Old age has shortened and thinned Bubbie's frame, turning shapely calves into a bird's twiggy legs. It has hollowed her cheeks and the craters that house her eyes and has silvered her short, thick hair, but it hasn't dimmed her style. *"Kleider machen Leute,"* she always says, using the German she learned when she lived in Munich after the war. Clothing makes the person.

My sisters have followed in her sartorial footsteps, but I suspect that Bubbie's patience has been tried by my mother, who lacks the shopping gene and doesn't always remember to put on makeup. And though I know Bubbie's unhappy about the brevity of my sleeves and hems and the pants I wear, she has never said a disapproving word.

Which doesn't mean she hesitates to speak her mind. *"Chapp nisht,"* she advised when I was dating Ron (the "ch" as in "Bach" is a guttural sound best achieved by clearing the throat). *"Du kenst ge'finen bessereh schoyreh."* Don't grab. You can find better merchandise. Well, I had *"chapped."*

"You like my lipstick?" she asked now. "Estée Lauder. Your mother got it free and was going to throw it out, it's not her color. But I said, give it to me. Why waste?"

"It looks great on you, Bubbie." She'd applied the cotton-candy pink unevenly on her thin lips, refusing to ask for help because that would allow her failing eyesight a victory.

Pushing herself off her rocking chair, Bubbie found her cane and, ignoring my offered arm, marched, with me at her heels, down the hall to the dining room sideboard where my mother, a lace mantilla on her head, was about to light the candles in the nine-arm silver candelabra my siblings and I bought for my parents' twenty-fifth wedding anniversary. She had lit two candles as a bride, another when each of us was born.

My father hurried into the room, one hand adjusting the brim of his black hat over his mostly gray hair, the other checking his watch.

He smiled when he saw me. "Hi, sweetheart." Then he turned his head toward the hall and bellowed, "Noah, Joey, I'm leaving!" and without catching his breath, "Liora, Mommy's lighting, turn off the hair dryer!"

He gave me a bear hug and planted a kiss on my forehead,

another on Bubbie's cheek. His lips lingered on my mother's. "Good *Shabbos*."

"Wait for the boys, Steven," my mother said, fixing his tie, the top of her head resting just below his square chin.

"Shul won't wait. Tell them to catch up." And he was gone.

My mother lit her nine candles, and I lit my two, neither bride nor maiden, reciting the blessing and the accompanying prayers of gratitude and requests. Out of the corner of my eye, I watched as Bubbie G, anger pinching her pink-stained lips, held a thin, lit candle in a silver tube that served as a match and, admitting temporary defeat, allowed my mother to guide her hand to the *Shabbos* candles she couldn't see.

That night, for the first time in months, I dreamed about Aggie. She was wearing the long-sleeved navy cotton sweater and ankle-length khaki skirt I'd last seen her in when she stopped at my apartment that Wednesday evening five years ago in July, at the beginning of the Three Weeks, on the way to a community-wide recitation of psalms for a young mother just diagnosed with cancer. Come with me, she urged, but I was too lazy to change out of my shorts, and I didn't think my prayers would help. So I stayed in my apartment, and Aggie drove to the gathering, and somewhere between the side street where she parked her Corolla and the hall where hundreds of women were beseeching God, Aggie disappeared. They found her body a day later in a Dumpster behind a restaurant several miles away. For a long time after that, I couldn't pray at all. Because if Aggie wasn't protected, what chance did I have?

"Come with me," she called now.

I reached for her slender hand, but she vanished up a steep, darkened street. I raced after her, my chest soon pounding with exertion, my breath labored, as I turned one corner after another on winding streets that seemed so familiar to me. For a second I caught a glimpse of her, angel-like in a long, silky white lace nightgown, and then she disappeared, and though I ran and ran, calling her name over and over, I never saw her again.

# CHAPTER SEVENTEEN

*Saturday, July 19. 9:25 A.M. 1700 block of North Western Avenue. An assailant came from behind and struck the victim on the back of her neck. "Stay the . . . away from my boyfriend!" the assailant screamed and cut the victim on the left forearm with a razor. (Hollywood)*

B'NAI YESHURUN WAS FILLED TO HIGH HOLIDAY CAPACITY when I arrived half an hour after services began—a sold-out performance for the handsome young rabbi. Taking a seat at the back of the women's section, I opened a siddur to the Shabbat morning prayers and debated the wisdom of having come here, a decision instigated by curiosity and the serendipity of my seeing

Zack at the Birkenstein home, and abetted by my mother and grandmother.

"If Rachel didn't go to the well, she would never have met Jacob," Bubbie G had advised when I went to her room to kiss her good night.

So here I was, a stranger ill at ease in the synagogue I'd attended for the year and a half of my marriage, usually at the side of my former mother-in-law, Valerie, and surrounded by her friends. I scanned the rows of straw hats, hoping not to see the chin-length frosted blond hair under the trademark UFO-size brim. She was in her customary spot—second seat, second row. Ron was probably here, too.

A familiar-looking woman several rows in front of me was smiling broadly at me. I smiled back, anxiously searching my memory, and was relieved when the answer came to me: Edie's friend Harriet, the scout who had reported to my sister about Zack.

Harriet winked at me. Facing forward, she leaned toward the woman next to her, the brims of their hats butting. The woman twisted her neck in a great imitation of Linda Blair in *The Exorcist* and gave me a quick appraisal before turning back and whispering into the ear of the woman to her right. A conga line of more turned heads and appraising looks, more knowing smiles. By the time the information reached the end of the pew, they'd have me married to Zack and the mother of his three children.

"*Mazel tov,*" I muttered under my breath, not sotto voce enough, judging from the curious stare of the fifty-something woman sitting next to me.

I blushed.

She returned her attention to her siddur.

I did the same, silently reciting the familiar Hebrew words but not concentrating. Harriet and her friends' telephone game, silly as it was, had heightened my anticipation of seeing Zack, an anticipation dampened by the prospect of an encounter with my ex-mother-in-law, who is always a lady, and with Ron, who is unpredictable.

And I couldn't stop thinking about Lenore and Aggie, and the fact that the two had become entwined in my dream. The nightmare had unnerved me, but of course, it made sense. I'd begun Friday saddened by Lenore's life and the futility of her death, and had gone to sleep troubled by the certainty that she'd been murdered, that I'd let her down just as I'd let Aggie down. The question was, who had killed Lenore, and why?

Saunders's name kept popping into my mind, but that was hardly surprising. He had reason to hate Lenore, and I was convinced he hadn't been completely honest with me. That didn't mean he'd killed her. I knew next to nothing about Lenore, about the people who loved her and those who wished her ill.

And why *would* Saunders tell me all? If Lenore had run across Laurel Canyon to avoid him, he certainly wouldn't admit responsibility. Even if he'd only witnessed her being struck, or had seen her later, lying on the road, the fact that he'd scurried home instead of going to her rescue wouldn't sit well with the public.

I had tried last night to place myself in his shoes. In the darkened theater of my bedroom, I'd summoned up the Greek chorus of the farce that was my marriage: Fury, Humiliation, Anguish, Sorrow. I had hated Ron then, had told him so. I had come close to wishing him ill. But if he were struck by a hit-and-run driver . . . ?

I no longer have enough vested in Ron to hate him, but even if I did, I'd like to think that I would rush to his side, as I would to help any human being. And I could never imagine killing him.

Then again, Ron had killed our marriage, not our child.

I've read about postpartum depression—not the short-term "baby blues" Edie and Mindy had, but the kind that lasts for weeks or months or longer. I know it's not uncommon. I looked around the synagogue, at the young and not so young mothers and their toddlers, some sitting obediently, some giggling or racing up and down the aisles before a "Shush!" tethered them, at least temporarily. Our community encourages large families, and six or seven children isn't considered unusual. I wondered how many of these women who seemed so relaxed with motherhood had struggled with the kind of severe depression that had brought catastrophe to Lenore and her infant son and other families that we read about in the news, like Andrea Yates, who drowned her five children in the bathtub. And what about the fathers of these dead children, and the grandparents?

The congregation stood, and I realized with a start that ten minutes and several prayers had passed me by. I hurried to catch up, struggling to give meaning to my words. Soon the morning service was completed, and we followed in our Bibles as a young man toward the front of the shul stood at the *bimah*, the elevated table on which the Torah scroll is placed, and read this week's portion, Pinchas.

Another reading from Prophets, and Rabbi Newman approached the lectern. He had aged since I'd last seen him, almost two years ago—his back was more rounded, his hair almost as white as his fringed *tallis*. He was smiling, and his eyes shone with affection as he looked around the room, a shepherd counting his flock.

"It's time to say goodbye. . . ." He spoke about his history with the shul, about the wonderful memories he would always have, about his plans to devote his time to Torah study and the enjoyment of his grandchildren.

"This week's *parsha*, Pinchas, ends, fittingly, with transition," he continued. "Moses handing over his leadership of the children of Israel to Joshua. Just as Moses had complete faith in Joshua, I have complete faith in Rabbi Zachary Abrams. We are fortunate that Rabbi Abrams has returned to Los Angeles, even more fortunate that he has chosen to lead our congregation, and I know that you'll show him the kindness, warmth, and respect that you've always shown me and my family."

Rabbi Newman stepped down. I know it's silly, but on some level I don't think I really believed that Zack was a rabbi until he was standing in front of that lectern, handsome in a well-cut navy suit, looking composed and self-assured and, well, rabbinic. A colony of butterflies fluttered in my stomach, just as they had at Noah and Joey's bar mitzvahs. I wanted so badly for him to do well, don't ask me why.

He had us at "Good *Shabbos*." He held us captive with his easy smile, with the warmth and earnestness and authority in his gravelly voice as he talked about Pinchas, the zealot who brought peace to the nation and an end to the plague that had ravaged it, about the daughters of Tzelafchad who argued successfully that they were entitled to inherit their father's portion of the promised land, about the census-taking that ends the Torah portion.

"Everyone was counted during that census," Zack said. "Every one of you here counts—every man, every woman, every child—as individuals, and as members of this congregation and this community." He paused and smiled again. "And I'm counting on each of you. *Shabbat shalom*."

Harriet turned around and threw me a triumphant smile. "Isn't he wonderful?" she mouthed.


After the service, in the large rectangular hall off the synagogue where the weekly Shabbat refreshments are served, Zack recited the kiddush over the wine and collected congratulations from the women, who beamed at him adoringly, and *"Yasher ko'achs"* (loosely, "Well done") from the men, who slapped him on the back and pumped his hand so vigorously that he'd probably need orthopedic surgery.

When the crowd showed no sign of thinning, I made my way toward him, squeezing around clusters of people talking and holding plates of pastries and potato and noodle kugels. Halfway there I almost bumped into Ron.

"Hey, babe, I *thought* I saw you," he said. "What brings you here, me or the *chulent?*" he asked, referring to a traditional Sabbath lunch stew—meat, potatoes, several kinds of beans, and barley, cooked Friday afternoon and left overnight in the oven or Crock-Pot.

"Oh, it's *you*, Ron. Definitely."

He leaned close. "You miss me, don't you?" he whispered, treating me to a pungent whiff of herring and liquor.

"Every minute of every day." I moved back. "Ron, what can you tell me about Robert Saunders?" My ex-husband is the Joan Rivers of the business world.

"The guy running for city council? He's a *macher*." A big wheel. "Family money, plus his own. He lost heavily in the market last year—didn't we all?" Ron grimaced. "He'll recoup. He has some major investors backing him in that new housing development in the Santa Monica Mountains and some other projects. There's a zoning problem, but he'll probably resolve it. He always does. Why? Are you writing about him?"

"No. His name came up in conversation."

Ron winked. "Whatever. Just spell my name right in the acknowledgments. Did you see my folks? They'll want to say hello. Wait right here."

Like an idiot, I waited. Why he thought his parents were interested in greeting their ex-daughter-in-law, I don't know, but it's typical of Ron to pretend that everything's all right and pull everyone into his fantasy. That's what makes him such a great day trader, and what attracted me to him in the first place, along with his energy and ambition and zest for life.

I watched him work the room, slapping backs, laughing, high-five-ing all the way. I wish I could say a life of duplicity had left its mark, but he's a Jewish Dorian Gray—wholesome, boyish good looks with a shock of angelic blond hair masking the blackness rotting inside. Okay, maybe blackness is an exaggeration, but it really burns me that he continues to fool everyone, including probably himself. He's on the synagogue board, he's involved in community organizations that have honored him for the large sums he donated before the dot-coms in which he traded lost their dots. People love him and regard him as a poster boy for Modern Orthodoxy. I had loved him, too.

Of course, they don't know about the adultery. Only my family and Ron's know, and his parents still think I jumped to conclusions about their only child, their golden boy, though I can't fathom how anyone can call the flowers and jewelry I never received and the hotel rooms I never stayed in (all charged to his business credit card) conclusions. I started snooping after Edie reluctantly reported seeing Ron with his cousin's friend Tilly at a Dodgers game, where he scored more than the Dodgers. (His parents: Edie was mistaken.) I followed him into a Westwood movie house and caught Ron and Tilly snuggling, with his hand up her skirt. (His parents: Ron was comforting her over bad news. And how could I be sure what he was doing when the theater was dark?)

As for Ron, he admitted to me (and later denied to his parents and mine) that he'd fooled around. He hadn't *technically* committed adultery (thank you, Bill Clinton), though he had no explanation for the condoms I found in his laptop case next to a DVD that would have curled Rabbi Newman's hair. I told him he was a hypocrite to stay on the board of a synagogue. He insisted he had an illness, like kleptomania. He'd done *teshuvah* (repentance). He wanted me to stay. He would get help. He was full of regret. I told him he was full of crap.

Sometimes I regret not revealing why we'd divorced. I'd done it for a number of reasons: Because it was the right thing to do. Because in exposing Ron I'd be spreading *"lashon harah,"* gossip, which is a sin. Because nobility spared me the pitying looks and comments for the woman scorned. Because it gave me leverage in obtaining my get, my Jewish divorce.

Knowing Ron, even if I *had* told, he would have found a way to twist his way out of the truth and lay the fault at my feet.

"Ron is a healthy young man with normal needs," Valerie had told my mother.

To which Bubbie G had responded, in Polish: *"Niech cie szlak trafi."* May a thunderclap strike him. I say that phrase whenever he pisses me off.

A moment later my ex-mother-in-law was in front of me, flanked by Ron and her husband, Louis. She's a well-dressed, attractive woman—about my height, five-five, and a few pounds lighter—with green contact lenses, ash blond highlighted hair, and interesting facial planes shadowed now by that oversized brim. Louis is neither handsome nor plain, a man you'd never pick out of a crowd. He's around five-eight, and he and Valerie often wonder aloud how they sired a tall Adonis like Ron.

"Good *Shabbos*, Molly," Valerie said. I think she would have preferred coming face-to-face with her gynecologist.

"Good *Shabbos*."

" *'Shabbos,"* from Louis, who was gazing at something over my head, avoiding eye contact.

Only Ron was having a good time, which was just like him, he's so oblivious. I felt sorry for my ex-in-laws. I got along well with them when Ron and I were married, and have no quarrel with them now. They have a right to take their son's side, and heaven knows he can be convincing. I've come to accept that bad sons happen to good people.

"So what brings you here?" Valerie asked.

"I'm spending *Shabbos* with my parents and thought I'd try out this shul."

"Please give them my best. Did you hear the new rabbi's speech? Wonderful, wasn't it?"

"A little too long," Louis said. "Ron knows him. Same high school class. Ron convinced the board to hire him."

I almost groaned aloud.

"What are friends for?" Ron smiled. "Molly dated him in high school. He was a jock, and now he's a rabbi. Go figure."

"People change, dear," Valerie said.

"That's what I keep telling Molly, but she doesn't believe me." Exaggerating a sigh, he placed his hand on my back and lowered it so that he was cupping my butt.

*Niech cie szlak trafi.*

Louis coughed. Valerie smiled tightly, looking as happy as if she were having a Brazilian bikini wax.

"Nice seeing you," I said, moving out of Ron's reach. "I'll tell my parents you said hello." Every few months, in between girlfriends, Ron calls and suggests that we give it another try, probably to practice his moves. He was obviously having a dry spell now.

I stepped around another cluster of people, prepared to approach Zack, but he wasn't where I'd seen him. I spotted him near the long refreshment table in the center of the rectangular room and found him engrossed in conversation with the blond real estate broker I'd seen in the restaurant. From the way she was looking at him, she wasn't discussing interest rates.

"Her name is Reggie," Ron said, coming up alongside me.

"She's hot, isn't she?" He ran his hand down his jacket, simulating striking a match, and blew on his raised fingers. "Zack knows how to pick 'em. But the lady has competition."

I saw what he meant. Standing near Zack were five or six hatless (ergo, unmarried) young women I hadn't noticed, all waiting their turns at the well.

Even Rachel would have hoisted her buckets on her shoulders and gone home.

# CHAPTER EIGHTEEN

NEAR THE END OF LUNCH I ASKED MY BROTHER NOAH about Lenore. Next month he'll be a third-year law student at UCLA, he's top of his class and driven, and I thought he'd be pleased that I was asking him instead of Mindy, whose success is an inspiration and an albatross. I would have preferred questioning him out of the presence of my other siblings—we Blumes are an outspoken group—but Noah was walking to his girlfriend's after lunch, and from there to afternoon and evening services at the shul, and wouldn't be back until after Shabbat. Carpe Noah, I decided.

"Say a woman has a fight with her ex-husband and walks out on him," I began after I got his attention. "The husband gets in his car and follows her, she runs into the street, and she's struck by a hit-and-run driver."

"*Chas v'shalom,*" Liora said. God forbid.

"Was she killed as a result?" Noah asked.

"No."

"What kind of car?" asked Joey.

I smiled patiently. "I don't know. It doesn't matter."

"What did they fight about?" asked Liora.

The questions illustrate the difference between my youngest sister and brother, who share physical characteristics and nothing else. They are average height—he's five-nine, two inches shorter than Noah; she's five-four—and have wavy brown hair and hazel eyes. Joey, twenty-two, has a B.A. in computer science and a passion for cars that began when he got his first Hot Wheels at the age of two. Liora, nineteen, finished a year at a Jerusalem girls' seminary and is majoring in biology at Santa Monica City College. Since her return in May, she's gone on countless blind dates, hoping to meet her *bashert.* I suspect she's hoping I'll meet mine, too, so that neither of us will feel awkward at her wedding.

"That doesn't matter either," I told her. "Here's my question, Noah. Is the ex-husband criminally liable for her getting hit?"

"So it *could* matter," Leah said.

"Let your brother answer," my father said without looking up from the slice of rye he was slathering with mustard. He's owned a construction company for over thirty years and has learned to tune out noise.

"We just learned this last semester." Noah ran a hand through his light brown hair, the same color as mine before I added highlights. "Was it a busy street?"

"Laurel Canyon, a little before two in the morning."

"Not much traffic then," Noah said, "but the street curves a lot. Did he force her into the street?"

He was enjoying this, and I was glad I'd asked him. "I don't *think* so. But I do think she was running to avoid him."

"Does she have a history of erratic behavior?"

"She tried to kill herself. More than once," I added.

"That's good." He nodded.

"That a woman tried to kill herself is good?" Bubbie G had been half dozing at the table, her chin on her chest.

Noah flushed. "Of course not, Bubbie. What I mean is, it goes toward building a case against the ex-husband." He faced me again. "If he knows she has a history of suicide attempts, and it's a busy street, a prosecutor could go for second-degree murder."

"No kidding." I nodded, impressed. "On what grounds?"

"Conscious disregard of human life. But you'd have to prove that he followed her, and that she ran into the street to avoid him. Did he report the accident to the police?"

I shook my head. "He claims he didn't see it."

Bubbie harrumphed.

"I'm with you, Bubbie." I cut a slice of seven-layer cake and slipped it onto my plate.

"Well, if you can prove he was there," Noah said, "the fact that he didn't report what happened will go against him. And if you can't get a D.A. to indict, the family would have a much easier time with a civil case. There's a lower burden of proof."

Either way, Saunders would be in deep water, his political career as dead as Lenore. I wondered how far he would go to avoid being tried for manslaughter. I also wondered if Betty Rowan knew about Lenore's late-night argument with her former son-in-law.

"Why did this woman try to kill herself?" my mother asked.

"It's so sad," I said. "Tragic, really. She was suffering from postpartum psychosis and killed their son." I summarized what Saunders had told me.

There were no interruptions from Liora or Joey, no questions. They looked somber like everyone else at the table, especially Bubbie G.

"I'm sorry," I said. "This isn't the best conversation for the *Shabbos* table."

"Are you going to write about this?" my mother asked.

"I don't know." I'd promised Saunders I'd wait, but if Lenore had been murdered . . .

"Why do you write about such morbid stuff?" Liora shuddered.

I pulled off a layer of the cake, cold from the refrigerator, the way I like it.

"In the camps, there was a woman with a baby," Bubbie said.

We all turned to look at her, surprised. Bubbie rarely talks about her experiences in the war.

"Not in my barracks," Bubbie continued. "But my friend Salka was there, and she told me about this woman who was so lucky, she carried so small the Nazis didn't know she was pregnant. She had the baby—Salka and a few others helped her. A boy. She didn't have enough to eat, so she didn't have enough milk, and the baby cried and cried and cried, and some of the women, they were afraid the guards would hear the baby and they would all be punished. Killed, even. They called the baby 'it,' Salka told me. Because of *it*, we are going to die, they said. What are you going to do about *it*?"

Bubbie stirred a spoon in her glass of tea. "The mother was afraid to go to sleep. One time she woke up, and a woman had her hands on the baby, but the mother pushed her away. Every day she would hold the baby at her breast, always at her breast, just so he wouldn't cry. But then he was crying all the time, because there was no milk, maybe a few drops. And she knew one day she would wake up and the baby would no longer be there." Bubbie paused.

"So what did she do?" Liora prompted when Bubbie made no move to continue.

Bubbie sighed. "What *could* she do? She pressed him to her

breast and sang to him, pressed him closer and closer, held him tight and kissed him until the crying stopped for good."

Liora's face blanched. "She *killed* her own child?"

"She loved him to death," Bubbie said softly. "This is what Salka told me." She turned to me. "But this is very different, Molly, from the woman you are telling us about."

"Very different," I agreed, chilled to the bone. "What happened to her? Did she survive?"

"Depends what you mean. The war, yes. But for years she heard the baby crying. Morning and night. The doctors gave her pills, but they didn't help. Now, I don't know." Bubbie shrugged. "And your woman?"

I hesitated. Why talk of murder when, after all, it wasn't a fact? "She killed herself."

Bubbie nodded. "Sometimes, this is the only way to stop hearing the crying."


After the stars came out, we listened to my father's rich baritone as he recited the havdalah blessings that separate Shabbat from the rest of the week. I held the braided candle high ("as tall as you want your *bashert* to be," Zeidie Irving had always teased), my thoughts stealing to Zack and quickly bouncing away, what was the point?

I packed my things and helped my mother wash the Shabbat dishes and pots that Joey hadn't been able to fit into the dishwasher. He had gone out with friends, and Noah with his sweetheart. Liora had disappeared into her bedroom and emerged forty-five minutes later wearing an ankle-length gray silk skirt and a pale pink silk sweater set. Her below-the-shoulder hair brushed into a sable luster, cheeks pinked, eyes bright with nervous excitement, she was waiting impatiently for her blind date, recommended by a friend's sister, the last in a series of young men committed to full-time yeshiva study for one to three years or more before pursuing careers in business, law, accounting, computers, or teaching. My family had already vetted his, and his family, ours, and both sets of parents had agreed to supplement the salary Liora would earn for those first years of marriage.

(Bubbie G's joke about a father grilling a suitor:

"You'll have expenses," the father says. "An apartment, clothing, food, a car."

"*Hashem* (God) will provide," the suitor replies.

"Tuition for children is high," the father points out.

"*Hashem* will provide."

"You'll want a house one day, other things."

"*Hashem* will provide."

After the suitor leaves, the wife asks, *"Nu?"*

"A very fine young man," the father says. "And very respectful. He called me God three times.")

Almost all of Liora's friends and classmates are dating young men with similar aspirations and backgrounds, and while I have reservations about these whirlwind courtships between couples barely out of their teens (twelve dates and you were engaged; three months later, wed), the majority of these unions are happy, and I, who had dated Ron for a year and married him at twenty-five, am in no position to judge.

I do worry, though, that Liora is unprepared for the burden of being the sole breadwinner, especially if she becomes pregnant, which is probable since she won't use birth control, and I hope reality won't trample on her romantic idealism. My parents, who have been ambushed into this world of arranged marriages, still seem somewhat shell-shocked, but trust that Liora will be happy.

Bubbie G is more pragmatic: *"Di libeh iz zis, mit broyt iz ze besser."* Love is sweet, but it's better with bread.

I wonder sometimes what course my life would have taken if

I had been content years ago to wear ankle-length skirts and sweater sets and had embraced a spouse and life like the ones Liora and her friends were pursuing. But I am not my sister, and though I would have preferred to save my family and myself the pain of my divorce, I don't really have regrets about the road not taken.

The bell chimed. While my father went to the door, I peered through the slats of the wood blinds on the breakfast room window at the black-hatted young man rocking on his heels on our front porch. A handsome face, expressive eyes, hands stuffed into the jacket of his black suit.

Was this the one?

My manuscript had finally arrived with a letter from my editor, who reiterated how much she liked the book. It's a heady feeling, receiving praise from a person whose opinion you value on the work you've labored so long to produce, never quite sure whether it's wonderful or awful or mediocre. I basked in the moment, then read her general comments and fanned the manuscript pages, looking for her notations. I'd been eagerly awaiting the edited pages for almost six weeks, and ordinarily would have immediately sat down to begin addressing her suggestions, but I was too distracted.

I listened to my phone messages while sorting through the other mail. Nothing from Connors, which was disappointing but not surprising. He probably didn't want to hear my "I told you so." Two messages from my sister Edie, who had heard after Shabbat from her friend Harriet that I'd been in shul, and what did that mean?

And a message from Betty Rowan, saying she'd like to discuss something that might interest me.

# CHAPTER NINETEEN

*Sunday, July 20. 9:02 A.M. 3400 block of Fay Avenue. A woman left her house with the kitchen window open. While she was gone, burglars stole five jewelry box drawers, 80 pieces of costume jewelry, a $50 wristwatch, a glass jar containing about $50 in coins, a Disneyland tip tray, a $90 rope chain, a $50 bracelet, three anklets, a pair of 14-karat gold earrings, a* Wheel of Fortune *electronic game, a $10 jewelry box, a $300 jewelry box, a $120 portable CD player and one CD. (Culver City)*

LENORE'S APARTMENT WAS A MARTHA STEWART NIGHTMARE.

The living room/dining room carpet, barely visible, was littered with books, magazines, videocassettes, and CDs, and clumps of white polyester stuffing that trailed from the gaping wounds of taupe chenille sofa cushions. Open kitchen cabinets had surrendered their possessions, many of which lay shattered on the Formica counter or on the linoleum, immobilized in a gooey puddle pouring out of a felled bottle of Murphy's Oil Soap.

Back in the living room, I surveyed the books on the floor. Paperback romances, thrillers, two hardcovers that I'd recently seen on the *New York Times* bestseller list. There was a large, black glossy book on acting techniques and several texts on postpartum depression. *Overcoming Postpartum Depression and Anxiety, Evaluation and Treatment of Postpartum Emotional Disorders, Rock-a-bye Baby: When Baby Blues Won't Go Away* (by Lenore's shrink, Lawrence Korwin), *Sleepless Days: One Woman's Journey Through Postpartum Depression, Behind the Smile: My Journey Out of Postpartum Depression* (Marie Osmond's book). The titles alone were enough to depress me.

Buried under the books were Lenore and Robbie's wedding album, along with the wedding photo and other candid shots of the stunning couple that Mrs. O'Day had spotted, their cracked glass frames giving the lie to their smiling faces.

All the drawers in Lenore's dresser had been turned upside down. The stripped mattress was on the floor, along with colorful heaps of skirts, dresses, sweaters, shoes, purses, belts, and half a dozen silk pajamas in jewel tones. An emptied jewelry box lay on top of the box spring, the white fingerprint powder stark against the mahogany.

In a lavender hatbox in front of the closet I found assorted memorabilia. High school souvenirs, including programs for several drama productions in which Lenore had played the lead; ticket stubs to movies; a Twentynine Palms Public Library card; a dried orchid corsage pinned to a tiny card that said *To the most beautiful girl in Twentynine Palms* and was signed *Love, Jeff.* A Santa

Barbara hospital nursery card listing the date and time of birth
for Baby Boy Saunders, along with his weight, height, and the
name of the attending physician.

There were numerous photos of an adolescent Lenore with a
smiling brown-haired girl, presumably a close friend; more wedding photos; several poses of Robbie and Lenore, big with child;
of the new mother with her infant son, his tiny face peering out
from a yellow receiving blanket. There were several poses, too,
of the family, one with Lenore holding the baby, others in which
she was gazing at the beaming father cuddling his son. I studied
Lenore. It seemed to me there was something strained about her
smile, something uncomfortable in the way she was holding the
baby. Or maybe I was reading something that wasn't there.

There were other, older photos, their glossy coats smudged
with fingerprints, their edges worn, of an infant girl with a cap
of dark hair, presumably Lenore. In some of the photos she was
with a much younger and happier Betty Rowan and a handsome
man, probably the ex-husband. In others, she was alone with her
father. In most of the poses he looked extremely serious and
somewhat aloof, as though he'd already decided to leave his wife
and daughter.

I went into the bathroom. The toilet tank lid had been removed, vials had spilled their pills, and in what I assumed was
just spite, whoever had done this had plastered toothpaste and
ointments and smeared lipsticks and foundation over the marble-
ized counter and mirror. The contents of a Lucite trash can had
been strewn on the white-tile floor. I poked at a mound of tissues with the toe of my sandal and unearthed a familiar flat plastic wand with an absorbent tip. I tore off a swatch of toilet paper
and picked it up.

"Find anything?"

I jumped and turned toward the doorway. "Jeez, you scared

me." Connors was slouched against the post, arms folded. I wondered how long he'd been standing there. "She was pregnant, wasn't she?"

He straightened up. "The manager told me you were here Friday, and here you are again. The department should put you on the payroll."

"The department can't afford me. So *was* she?"

He hesitated. "Yes."

Lenore's second chance. It all made sense now. "How long have you known?"

"They did a beta qual in the ER when they brought her in."

I nodded. This was what Connors had been holding back. "But you weren't going to tell me."

He smiled. "Inasmuch as it's none of your damn business, no."

I dropped the wand onto the tissues. "This changes everything, doesn't it? Why would Lenore kill herself if she was pregnant?"

"Saunders said he was going to tell you all. Did he?"

I hate it when people answer a question with a question. "Yes, Friday afternoon. It's a terrible story."

"And it explains why Lenore killed herself. She panicked when she found out she was pregnant. She was terrified she'd kill the baby, just like she did last time."

I thought about the books in the other room. "She was in therapy, Andy. She was on medication, taking control of her problem."

"You're talking logic. Who says Lenore was thinking logically? And she told you she wanted off the meds, remember?"

He had a point. "Why did you ask the O'Days not to let anyone in her apartment?" I countered. "Because she was pregnant, right? It made you wonder."

"Routine procedure. Until the M.E. determines cause of death, we have to treat it as a possible homicide."

"You're lying."

He smacked his hand against his chest. "I'm hurt, Molly. Really hurt."

I waved my hand around the room. "Is this routine, too? Someone killed her, Andy. You know it."

"We don't *know* it. It's certainly a possibility."

"You honestly believe this is just a *coincidence*?"

"It *could* be a coincidence. But I doubt it."

"So . . ."

"Just because someone trashed her apartment after she died doesn't mean she was killed. Suppose Lenore had something in her apartment that could compromise someone. Maybe he or she panicked when Lenore died and decided to retrieve it."

"Maybe it's just easier to call it a suicide, Andy. Then you don't have to figure out who did it. Case closed."

"Are you done?" he asked, his voice filled with quiet anger.

"Sorry." Sometimes I go too far. "She *called* me, Andy. She said she was afraid."

"How did the killer slash Lenore's wrists without getting caught, Miss Marple? Wouldn't she have resisted, yelled for help? Someone would have heard her."

"Maybe he smothered her with a pillow."

"We would've seen that right away. If she was asphyxiated, the skin on her head and neck and upper body would've been a deep purple. And there would've been some hemorrhaging on the pink lining around the eyeball. Red dots. The M.E. didn't see any of that. And there's no sign she struggled. No tissue or blood under her nails."

"What if the killer upped the Haldol and waited until she was out?"

"Then why slash her wrists?"

"Because the other times she slashed her wrists. So this would fit her pattern. Why are you fighting this?"

"Why are you so determined to prove she was killed, Molly? Because you need to be right?"

"If I'm right, it means I failed her!"

We stood there for a moment glaring at each other, breathing hard, not speaking.

Connors sighed. "For what it's worth, I think it's possible Lenore was killed. So, yeah, that's why I asked Mrs. O'Day not to let anyone in Lenore's apartment. And if it makes you feel better, I considered her phone call to you. So they're going to do an autopsy."

That surprised me. "Don't they always?"

"Usually, if there are past documented suicide attempts, it's pretty much an open-and-shut case for the coroner. They might do a psychological autopsy, have the shrink review the circumstances, then rule it a suicide. I'm hoping we'll have the results by Tuesday. I don't want any of this getting out, Molly, or word of the break-in."

"Mrs. Rowan knows, right? And Mrs. O'Day, the manager, told *me* about it, and she probably told others. So I hardly think it's a state secret."

"Fine. But I don't want you telling anyone Lenore was pregnant. If I read about it, I'll know it came from you."

"Why not from her mother?"

"I haven't told Mrs. Rowan. Lenore's doctors didn't say anything to her either—it's privileged information. I'm serious, Molly." He scowled at me to press the point.

I nodded. I've never abused Connors's trust, which is why he's willing to share information with me. And I don't take his willingness for granted. "Did Saunders know?"

"He says no. He seemed shocked when I told him. Which doesn't mean squat."

"Maybe Lenore went to his place Saturday night to tell him she was pregnant with his child."

Connors smiled. "Believe it or not, Molly, the possibility occurred to me."

I smiled back. "Just helping out."

"If necessary, we'll do DNA testing to determine paternity. But we're a long way from that."

"The fiancée may have known. She wouldn't be thrilled."

"Again, stating the obvious. Let me do my job, okay, Molly?"

I glanced around the room again. "Did they take anything?"

He raised a brow. "Are you saying you don't know their names yet?"

I suppose I had that coming. "Come on, Andy."

"Aside from the contents of the jewelry box, you mean. According to Mrs. Rowan, Lenore had some serious jewelry, including a diamond choker and a tennis bracelet, all compliments of her ex. That's gone, plus a coin collection from her father. They left a full-length mink coat, also from the ex."

"Maybe they're members of PETA," I said.

"Yeah. And it's less risky to take stuff you can slip in your pocket." He looked around the room. "Whether or not Lenore was killed, I think the robbery and vandalism were just stage dressing. Whoever did this was looking for something. I have no clue what, or whether he found it."

"The journal," I said.

Connors frowned. "What?"

"Lenore told me she was keeping a daily journal. Dr. Korwin told her to. And Mrs. O'Day said she always saw Lenore writing. Maybe Lenore wrote down stuff somebody didn't want known."

# CHAPTER TWENTY

"I DON'T KNOW ANYTHING ABOUT THE HIT-AND-RUN,"
Nina Weldon said. "Lenore was sleepy when I first visited her in
the hospital, probably from the medication. And I didn't want to
upset her with questions."

We were in Nina's breakfast nook, which she'd painted a
cheery yellow, seated across from each other at a knotty pine tres-
tle table she told me Lenore had helped her pick out. She'd set
the table for company—royal blue linen place mats; china plates,
teacups, and saucers with a blue-and-yellow floral-wreath design;
a crystal bowl filled with fruit; a cobalt platter with cinnamon
buns that smelled heavenly but probably weren't kosher. It was
rather formal for an interview with a reporter, and I had the feeling she didn't entertain much and welcomed the opportunity.

Betty Rowan had called Nina Weldon mousy—an unkind description, but true. She was remarkably colorless in this room of bright yellows and blues, as though she'd used up her allotment of pigments on her surroundings and accessories. She was the *before* woman in magazines and romantic comedies who had fine features but needed a dresser and hairstylist and a Bobbi Brown makeover to transform her into a butterfly. Right now she was a moth: drab, shoulder-length brown hair; faint, unshaped brows; quiet brown eyes, invisible lashes; pale lips that disappeared into skin the color of oatmeal. She was somewhere in her thirties, I guessed, around five feet six or seven, neither slim nor heavy, her shape camouflaged by a beige tentlike dress.

Her hands were surprisingly beautiful, long and slender, but she'd bitten her unringed fingernails all the way to the nail bed and they looked raw. The hands flitted from place to place—her chin, the table, her mug, her lap. Again, I thought of a moth. I wondered if she was nervous because of me, or whether this was her natural disposition.

"I spoke with her ex-husband on Friday," I said. "He told me Lenore was at his house Saturday night, just before it happened. Did she tell you she was going there?"

"I didn't see Lenore on Saturday." She gazed at me with interest. "Did he say why she was there?"

"He said she wanted to spend the night because she was afraid she might harm herself." I was watching Nina carefully, but saw no reaction. "He told me about their son. I don't know how anyone gets over something like that."

"You don't, really." She ran a finger over the rim of her coffee cup. "Lenore *was* depressed lately. Something was bothering her, but she didn't want to talk about it."

"Do you know if she was taking her medication?"

"I have no idea."

"Maybe she wrote in her journal about whatever was bothering her. She told me she was keeping one, at Dr. Korwin's suggestion."

"Dr. Korwin has *all* his patients keep journals." She pushed a strand of hair behind her ear. "To be honest, I don't feel comfortable discussing Lenore."

"Especially with a reporter." I smiled. "I don't blame you. But Lenore *wanted* me to talk to you. She said so in the hospital. 'Ask Nina.' I think she has a right to have her story told, don't you?"

Nina cocked her head. "Are you going to write about her?"

"Yes." With Lenore dead, probably murdered, I *needed* to do it, although I suppose I'd been headed in this direction from the moment I read about her in the police report. "So far, everything I know is from the media coverage of the trial and whatever her ex-husband told me. The newspaper accounts aren't flattering, and her ex-husband . . ." I left the sentence unfinished. "As Lenore's best friend, you could shed another view. You probably knew her better than almost anyone else."

Yes, I was being manipulative. No, I didn't feel great about it, but I hoped it would make her open up. I took a sip of coffee and watched her eyes, which gave no clue as to what she was thinking. Her fingers played a sonata on her napkin.

"What do you want to know?" she finally asked.

I relaxed against my chair. "What she was like. Her hobbies, her likes and dislikes. What kind of perfume she wore. What her life was like before and after her son's death."

"Her favorite color was blue," Nina said quietly. "She wore mostly Calvin Klein perfume, sometimes Angel. She didn't like sports, but she loved games and puzzles and amusement parks and cotton candy. She was always interested in what you were doing. She made you feel special." Her lips quivered, and she stilled them with her hand. "Did you see her smile?"

I shook my head.

"She had a beautiful smile, and a great laugh that started way down in her stomach, and she loved to sing. She didn't smile or laugh or sing when she came to the clinic, and that's where we met, so I don't know what she was like before Max died, but I do know she never stopped blaming herself for what happened." It was a long sentence, and she paused to take a breath. "She told me that the best two things that ever happened to her were Robbie and Max, and then she lost both of them."

"She must have been devastated when he divorced her."

"There were problems," Nina said. "Even before Max died. Lenore didn't think she measured up to the people in Robbie's world, including his family and his business associates. She was a working girl from a small town. His family practically built L.A. She wasn't as sophisticated as his crowd. She was nine years younger than Robbie, too."

"I read that her mom raised her alone."

"Her dad skipped when she was a baby, and her mom barely made ends meet. I think that was why Lenore fell so hard for Robbie—because he could give her security. The fact that he was older was a plus."

"A replacement for her father?"

Nina nodded. "That's what Dr. Korwin told her. But Robbie was in L.A. on business a lot, and that was hard on Lenore." She paused. "But to answer your question, yes, she was devastated about the divorce. She was shocked when he told her. Thank God she was in therapy at the clinic. I don't know how she would have handled it on her own."

I thought about the photos I'd seen in Lenore's hatbox. Lenore's father had divorced her mother. Saunders had divorced Lenore. She must have felt that history was repeating itself.

"She was lucky to find a friend like you there," I said. "Actually, I find it odd that she went to her ex-husband for support when you and she were very close. Especially with the fiancée there."

"We were *best friends!*" Her lips quivered. "We told each other *everything!*" She sounded hurt, almost angry. A moment later she blushed, probably embarrassed by her show of passion.

I thought about the pregnancy. *Maybe not everything.* "I'm sorry. I know it's hard to lose someone you love." I didn't want to think about Aggie, but there she was.

"Actually, Lenore knew Jillian was going out of town," Nina said. "I think her mother mentioned it."

Not what Saunders had said. I felt a prickling of excitement. "Her mother and Robbie are on good terms?"

Nina nodded. "When he and Lenore married, he bought a house in L.A. for her to live in so she could leave Twentynine Palms and be closer to Lenore. She lives there rent-free, and Lenore said he still helps her financially."

Maybe that explained Betty Rowan's reluctance to involve Saunders in the hit-and-run. "That must have been uncomfortable for Lenore, having her mother chummy with her ex-husband."

"She *hated* it." Nina grimaced. "It was awkward for her, and it made her feel more isolated from everyone."

"Lenore told me everyone blamed her for Max's death. What about her mother?"

"*Her* mother, *his* mother. Practically everyone in Santa Barbara. They all *said* they understood about Lenore's postpartum illness, but she knew they blamed her. Dr. Korwin told Lenore she couldn't change what they think. He was trying to help her move on with her life."

"I think I saw him when I was in the hospital the day Lenore died. He was talking to her mother."

"Dr. Korwin is *wonderful.*" Nina's eyes sparkled, rescuing her face from ordinariness. "He doesn't just treat postpartum illness. When I came to him I was in a terrible depression. It was—" She stopped. "It was a dark time for me. I couldn't hold down a job. Most days I stayed in bed. I had no hope. But Dr. Korwin gave me hope. He did that for so many other women who are depressed for all sorts of reasons. Lenore, too. She told me over and over how grateful she was to Dr. Korwin, how he'd changed her life. She adored him."

"Patients often become attached to their therapists." I smiled.

Nina stiffened. "Dr. Korwin would *never* allow that to happen. There was nothing inappropriate in their relationship."

The mouse had turned into a lion. "Of course not. I didn't mean to suggest that there was. I'm glad he was able to help her."

Nina relaxed her shoulders, apparently mollified. "He tried, but she didn't always follow his advice. He didn't approve of her seeing Robbie."

"Was Lenore still in love with Robbie?"

"She thought so. Dr. Korwin told her she was holding on to Robbie because she was trying to re-create her life before Max died. It's one of the things she was working on, letting go."

"She must have been upset when Robbie became engaged. Has he known Jillian long? What's her last name, by the way?"

"Horton. Their families have been close for years." Nina hesitated. "Actually, they were engaged when Lenore met Robbie. That's one of the reasons Lenore wanted to move away when they married. Robbie's mother disapproved of her and blamed her for the broken engagement. As if Robbie didn't have anything to do with it." She sniffled.

I shook my head. "It's always the woman's fault, isn't it?" I wondered whether Jillian had known about Lenore's pregnancy, and if so, how she'd felt having her marriage plans threatened a second time by the same person. And what about Saunders's mother? "So when did they reconnect? Jillian and Robbie, I mean."

"Robbie moved back to L.A. a year ago, after the trial. A few months later he filed for divorce. Lenore thinks he was seeing Jillian way before then. She didn't come out and say it, but I think she suspected something was going on even before the baby was born. I think that's the real reason she wanted to move to Santa Barbara, to put some distance between them. A little over a month ago, when the divorce was final, Jillian moved into his house in Mount Olympus. Lenore was very upset."

I couldn't imagine being pregnant and worrying that my husband was lusting after someone else. Thank God I'd found out about Ron before it was too late.

Nina moved another strand of hair behind her ear. "You said she left a message on your answering machine. What did she say?"

"That she needed to talk to me. She started to say something else, but my answering machine ran out of tape."

Nina's hands fluttered against her chest. "What do you think it was?"

"It sounded like 'I'm afraid.' Do you have any idea what she meant?"

"The only thing I can think of is that she was afraid she'd harm herself. Because she did, didn't she?" she said softly, her eyes flooded with tears.

I reached over and patted her hand, wishing I could be of more comfort. "How did Lenore seem when you visited her?"

"The first two times she was confused. I wasn't even sure she knew I was there." Nina wiped her eyes with her napkin. "On Wednesday morning I talked to her on the phone, and she seemed much better. She asked me to bring her makeup and other stuff from her apartment. I took that as a good sign."

I had to agree. "When were you there on Wednesday?"

"The first time, on my lunch break. I went to her apartment first to get her things. She was stronger, more alert. She was asking about people in the clinic, taking an interest in things. When I came back at seven-thirty, she was depressed again. Something must have happened to upset her, but she didn't want to talk about it."

"Did Lenore ever tell you she was afraid of anyone, Nina?"

The question seemed to startle her. She frowned. "Why do you ask?"

I'd promised Connors not to say anything about the suspicion of foul play, but that was all. "Someone burglarized her apartment."

Nina's hand flew to her mouth. Her eyes widened. "I don't— *When?*"

"Sometime Thursday night or Friday morning."

"Oh, my God! What a horrible coincidence!" She shuddered, and I watched her expression go from shock to bewilderment to suspicion. She stared at me. "Unless it's *not* a coincidence. But that doesn't make sense either. Why would someone break into Lenore's apartment because she killed herself?"

"The police think it *could* be coincidence," I said, making amends to Connors. "Or maybe someone was looking for something he didn't want found."

"Like what?"

I decided not to mention the journal.

Nina was frowning, preoccupied. I was out of questions, at least for now. I thanked her, and she nodded and walked me to the door, still lost in thought.

I asked if I could call again.

"I suppose so," she said without enthusiasm.

"By the way, what kind of nightgowns did Lenore like?"

She blinked a few times, as though trying to focus. "What?"

I repeated the question.

"Lenore didn't wear nightgowns. She liked pajamas." The idea must have amused Nina, because she smiled for the first time. "Are you going to put that in your book, too?"

# CHAPTER TWENTY-ONE

GARDENING RELAXES ME. I LOVE RUNNING MY FINGERS through clumps of earth, inhaling the rich scent of loam and fertilizer. I even enjoy pulling weeds and sometimes wish life could be as black and white, and that I could yank out of my life the problems or people who annoy me.

Gardening also lets me think, which explains why I was out here now in my landlord's tiny yard while the sun was baking my SPF 30–coated legs and forearms and plastering my white T-shirt to my back. I'd protected my head and face with a wide-brimmed straw hat my mother had bought me.

When I write about true crime, I generally know who dunit. My goal is to explore the why, to make sense of what often seems senseless, to trace the origins of a brutal act so that you and I can feel reassured that something like that won't happen to us.

I've interviewed a criminal who killed for twenty dollars, and a seventy-three-year-old man who shot his neighbor because a tree was littering his yard. My first true-crime book, *Out of the Ashes,* was about a neo-Nazi who torched a church, killing twenty-three congregants, including five children, maiming and disfiguring many others, and leaving scars that were invisible but would probably never heal. My second, as I mentioned, is about a father who injected his son with the AIDS virus so he wouldn't have to continue paying child support.

I was writing about Lenore, but I had no idea who killed her. My talk with Nina had been illuminating and provocative, giving me details about the dead woman and the people in her life, but not enough to help me understand why someone would kill her. *Because she'd killed Max?* I doubted that Saunders would exact revenge a year and a half after the fact. *Because she was harassing him and his fiancée?* A restraining order would have done the trick, and I wasn't even sure Lenore *was* harassing them. *Because he was partly to blame for her hit-and-run or had left her to die in the middle of Laurel Canyon?*

Saunders had phoned while I was at Nina's, wanting to know what I'd decided to do. He was flying to Phoenix for a business appointment and would contact me when he returned tonight, or early tomorrow morning. Betty Rowan had phoned again. She sounded eager to talk to me "as soon as possible, in person." We were playing phone tag, and I'd left another message on her answering machine and my cell number in case she called when I was out. I'd spent another hour trying to locate Darren Porter with no luck. I'd forgotten to ask Nina whether she knew him.

"Nice garden," a voice said behind me.

I was hunched in front of my petunias. Swiveling my knees,

I craned my neck up at Zack. My hat fell to the ground. "Didn't your mother teach you to knock?"

I reached behind me for my hat, but he was faster. He picked it up and set it on my head.

"Your landlord told me you were back here. He's watering the front lawn and saw me ringing your bell. He took pity on me." Zack didn't look rabbinic now in his khaki Dockers, white Polo shirt, and brown loafers.

I picked up my garden basket and stood, brushing dirt from my red shorts. "You should feel honored. He's very particular about my gentlemen callers."

My landlord is a scrawny, bowlegged, seventy-seven-year-old three-time widower who hitches his pants practically up to his eyebrows and loves sitting on his small porch people watching. He's looking for number four ("Companionship, sure, but I wouldn't say no to something better"), and like Edie and Mindy, he's concerned about my marital status, though so far he hasn't approved of any of my dates. I'm convinced he scans my mail.

"I heard you were in shul yesterday," Zack said, squinting into the bright light. "Why didn't you say hello?"

"I figured the well would be dry."

He looked puzzled. "What?"

"You were busy. I didn't want to intrude." I snipped dead leaves off a rosebush.

"You wouldn't have intruded. I'm glad you came. So what'd you think of my *d'var torah*?" His sermon.

"Pretty good," I said, refusing to swell his head. "Connecting the census and counting on everyone was a nice touch."

"I'm glad you liked it. It seemed to go over well."

"Not with everyone. Ron's father thought it was too long."

"So did my dad. My mom thought it was perfect. Moms are great." Zack smiled and wiped his forehead. "It's hot out here. Can we talk inside?"

"About what? Are you here to recruit new members or get free editorial advice?"

He tented his brow. "Did I offend you the other night, Molly? Or is this about what happened twelve years ago?"

"I'm not offended. I'm just not interested in taking a number."

"You make me sound like a bakery."

"Were you out last night?" I asked, raising my arm and pointing the gardening shears at him.

"Yes. Can you put those down? I haven't had a tetanus shot in a while."

"With Reggie the Realtor? Or were you with one of the other nubile young congregants who adore you and want to bear your children?"

"Actually, I was at the Birkensteins'. I thought Mrs. Birkenstein might want to talk." Not a hint of a smirk, though he was entitled.

"Oh." I lowered my hand, feeling like one of the garden slugs I'd dispatched a few minutes ago.

"Can we start over, please?"

My face was burning. "Fine."

"In the house? Because I may faint from the heat, and I don't think the board will approve if they find their new rabbi passed out in your flower bed."

I sat him in the living room, cooled by an air-conditioning unit, while I undressed and splashed cold water on my face, put on makeup, and slipped into a yellow print skirt, a white cap-sleeved blouse, and a pair of sandals. When I returned he was standing in front of my bookcase, which is crammed with Judaic texts and true-crime books—the sacred and the profane—and photos of my family, some still waiting to be framed.

"This is a great one." Zack pointed to a shot of the Blume clan.

"That was taken two years ago, at my brother Judah's wedding. I love it that photographers are doing black-and-white now, don't you?"

He nodded. "You're lucky you have a large family. My parents always wanted more kids, but it never happened. Are you close?"

"Yes. But we have our moments. You don't want to be around us then." I smiled. "Did you have lunch?"

"No, but I don't want you to bother."

"It's the least I can do after almost eviscerating you. How about tuna sandwiches and lemonade? That's all I have on the menu."

"Tuna and lemonade sounds perfect."

He followed me into my kitchen, which is not much larger than an airplane's galley but allows me to reach everything without moving. I rinsed three lemons and set them on the tile counter, then hunted in a cabinet for the lemon juicer and a pitcher.

"Let me help," he said, moving so close that I could smell the musk of his aftershave.

I sliced a lemon and handed him half, our hands grazing, and watched him out of the corner of my eye while I took out a container of tuna salad from the fridge, along with seven-grain bread, lettuce, and my last tomato. I know this sounds silly, but there was something adorable and at the same time incredibly sexy about the way he approached his task—forehead creased in concentration, lips pressed together, his right hand vigorously twisting the lemon as if he were determined to wring every last drop.

He must have sensed that I was looking at him, because he turned to me. "What?"

"I hope you like onion and celery in your tuna," I said with mock sternness to cover my flustered state.

"Love it." He picked up another lemon half.

I spread tuna on the bread and topped it with tomato slices and lettuce. "She's interested in you, you know. Potato chips or corn chips?" I may not have a well-stocked fridge, but I have a serious stash of junk food, which is why my nieces and nephews, who are nosh deprived at their respective homes, love coming to Aunt Molly's.

"Potato. Reggie the Realtor?" Zack nodded. "I really thought she was calling so often because she wants to find me a house."

"Hmmm."

He flashed me a smile. "I guess I'm naive. It's a little awkward since she's a member of the shul, and I don't want to hurt her feelings. She's very nice."

"You may have to marry her."

He nodded. "Or buy a really big house that I can't afford."

I slipped the sandwiches onto plates and sprinkled potato chips on the side. Martha Stewart had better watch out. "So what are you going to tell her?"

"That I'm seeing someone." He turned toward me and reached out his hand.

For a second I thought he wanted mine. Then I remembered the lemons. I gave him another half. "Are you?"

"You tell me."

You know in *Sabrina*, when Humphrey Bogart is staring at Audrey Hepburn after he tells her he's sorry he screwed up and he can't live without her, and she's staring back, and the camera zooms in, and the background music swells, and she's all tingly 'cause she knows he's going to kiss her? That's how I felt.

"So basically," I said, my heart racing as we stood inches apart in the tiny, hot kitchen, "what you're telling me is that you're using me?"

"That would be right. Assuming you're willing to be used. It's for a good cause," he added.

"Then how can I say no?"

146

There was enough chemistry between us to activate a nuclear reactor.

"There's just one thing," he said. "I lied."

I braced myself. "What about?"

"I'm not a tuna and onions guy, but I'm willing to give it a try."

# CHAPTER TWENTY-TWO

OVER SANDWICHES AND LEMONADE, HE TOLD ME HIS story. He'd been fooling around that first year at Hakotel, going through the motions of studying the Talmud during the day to justify to his parents why they'd sent him to Israel and skipping night sessions to hang out with American friends, male and female, in the hot spots along Ben Yehuda, a street in central Jerusalem teeming with activity well into the morning hours.

"Nowadays, with the fear of terrorist attacks, the schools have tightened the rules," Zack said. "But when I was there, you could stay out pretty much all night and no one would know. And there's no drinking age in Israel."

I nodded. The girls' seminaries have always been stricter, even more so now, but I'd slipped out more than once to meet friends for pizza or drinks, or guys. Liora, pure soul that she is, hadn't even been tempted.

"Then two things happened," Zack said.

He had been so drunk one night that he'd passed out and didn't remember returning to the dorm. He'd slept through the entire day and feigned illness to the rabbi who counseled and supervised the young men, but he'd sensed that he hadn't fooled him. So a week later, ready to party again, he couldn't refuse when the rabbi asked him to tutor a student who was having difficulties. At first, Zack had been annoyed with the rabbi and with this student who was killing his fun, but as hour followed hour, he found enjoyment in helping the young man and in the material that had become suddenly more interesting in the teaching.

And in the morning he learned that the bus he would have taken to Ben Yehuda had been attacked by snipers who killed seven passengers, including one of his friends.

"I felt as though someone had slammed me into a wall," Zack said. "If Rabbi Frank hadn't asked me to do this favor, if I'd taken that bus. . . . It was clear to me that God had saved my life, and He wouldn't appreciate my wasting it."

"But why the rabbinate?" I asked. "Why not law school, the way you'd planned?"

"I was never passionate about law. It just seemed more appealing than anything else. When did you know you wanted to be a writer?"

"In utero."

"That late, huh?" He smiled. "I wish I'd been that focused. Anyway, I started tutoring younger kids and helping them with their personal problems. I loved doing it, and I loved my studies, and I was torn between teaching or counseling when Rabbi Frank suggested I could do both as a pulpit rabbi. All of a sudden I knew this was what I wanted." He took a sip of lemonade.

"I also found out that it was Rabbi Frank who took me back to the dorm when I passed out. The nightclub manager had phoned him."

It was odd, I thought. An act of violence had brought Zack closer to God, and had driven me away. I wanted to tell him about Aggie, but something stopped me.

Zack was still hungry. I sat at the dining room table and watched while he fixed himself another sandwich and helped himself to more chips. There's something about a man making himself comfortable in your kitchen that suggests a certain intimacy. I liked the feeling but was afraid to trust it.

"So what brought you to my shul yesterday?" he asked when he returned to the table.

"I'm not sure." I told him how I'd felt seeing him at the Birkensteins', that maybe God was nudging me. "Plus my grandmother forced me. Who told you I was there? Harriet?"

"Ron. He says you still have a thing for him."

I did, mostly pity. "Ron and I are very much over. Is that why you came, to find out if it's true?"

"Actually, your grandmother forced me." He smiled. "I came because I thought we had unfinished business, Molly. I phoned you earlier in the day, by the way, but I guess you were out."

"I was interviewing someone. Why didn't you leave a message?"

"I don't like voice mail in general, and I wasn't sure you'd return my call. Later your line was busy, so I figured I'd take my chances and stop by. So is this for an article or your next true-crime book?"

"It's for a book about a true crime, but I don't know the truth yet, or how it'll end up." I told him about Lenore—about my hospital visit, about her death and what I suspected, about my talks with Connors and Saunders and Nina.

Zack had been shaking his head every once in a while.

"You think I shouldn't be getting involved?" I asked, prepared to bristle. I suppose Connors was on my mind.

"Not at all. I admire your passion, and I find all this fascinating." He took a bite of the sandwich. "You may be right about the journal, Molly. In which case Saunders is a likely suspect."

"But why would he steal her journal? What could Lenore have written that he'd want to suppress?"

"That she was pregnant with his child."

I shook my head. "Even if the police thought Lenore killed herself, Saunders had to figure they'd know from the ER doctors that she was pregnant. Which they did."

"But not necessarily with his child. We don't know that either."

"Nina told me Lenore was still in love with him, Zack," I reminded him. "The apartment building manager suspected the same thing."

"Which doesn't mean Lenore wasn't intimate with anyone else."

"Why would she sleep with someone else if she was in love with Saunders?" I said with some impatience.

Zack shrugged. "Loneliness? Anger? Maybe she wanted to make him jealous."

"Maybe." I pleated my napkin. "Well, if Saunders isn't the father, who is?"

"I didn't say he's *not* the father. I said the police wouldn't *know* that unless she wrote it in the journal."

I pressed my palms against my temples. "Is this Talmudic discourse? 'Cause you're giving me a headache."

"Just establishing the facts," he said seriously. "You have to examine all the possibilities. Who else would have worried about Lenore's journal?"

He was really involved. I was amused and pleased and unprepared, because Ron had shown little interest in my work. "Whatever floats your boat, babe," he'd say, as though I were crocheting doilies. I think he was surprised when a publisher bought my first book, and not unhappy that my advance was modest—I wasn't showing him up.

"The fiancée may have stolen it, to protect Saunders," I said. "That would explain the vandalism. She must have resented Lenore a great deal. And there's Lenore's mother."

"The mother?" Zack looked skeptical.

"She left two messages saying she wants to talk to me. I can't think why, unless Saunders asked her to get me to back off. Maybe she stole the journal to protect him. The building manager says she only saw Mrs. Rowan visit Lenore once, aside from a few times last week, and according to Nina, Mrs. Rowan and Saunders are still tight. That's odd, don't you think? And she hasn't been very forthcoming."

"In what way?"

"She implied she didn't know why Lenore was on Laurel Canyon Saturday night. As if she didn't know that Saunders lives there." I tried one of Bubbie G's harrumphs, but didn't do it as well.

"You can't blame her for not wanting to tell all to a reporter, Molly. No offense." He smiled.

"Offense taken," I said, but he had a point.

"I can see the mother stealing the journal," Zack said, "but not killing the daughter. Which means we're dealing with *two* people. Quite a coincidence."

I took a few chips from his plate. "Suppose the mother believes it was suicide but thinks the police will investigate as though it were a homicide. *I* thought so, until Detective Connors told me differently this morning. So she steals the journal for Saunders, or because she doesn't want it to be a Book-of-the-Month-Club pick."

"Okay." Zack nodded. "But if the mother stole it, why would she vandalize the apartment?"

I rolled my eyes. "To make it look like a burglary."

He frowned. "Why bother? How would the police know the journal is missing if they didn't even know it *existed*?"

That was a good question, and I'd already considered it. "People knew about the journal. Nina, Dr. Korwin—he has all his patients keep journals. *I* knew about it, and Lenore probably told some other people. What if one of them mentioned the journal to the police, and the police discovered that it was missing?"

Zack didn't answer right away. "Does the mother have a key to her daughter's apartment?"

"She must, because the manager told me she stopped Mrs. Rowan from going into Lenore's apartment on Thursday afternoon. Detective's orders." I frowned.

"What?"

"I had a thought, but now it's gone." I shrugged to make light of it, but I hate when that happens. "Oh, well. It'll come back to me."

"We've overlooked three possibilities. One, Lenore may have written things in the journal that were connected to her ex-husband's political campaign or his business or to someone else entirely."

"*You've* overlooked it. I haven't." I stacked our plates. "What's the second possibility?"

"That this has nothing to do with the journal. Maybe Lenore had something else that someone wanted to retrieve."

I nodded. "And the third?"

"What Detective Connors suggested. That Lenore really *did*

kill herself, and the burglar was anxious to retrieve something incriminating before someone else, either the police or a family member, found it."

It was certainly plausible, and I couldn't rule it out. "But then why would Lenore tell me she was afraid?"

"Because she was thinking of killing herself and hoped you'd talk her out of it. Or because she was afraid of having another child."

"But why me? I hardly knew her, Zack. Why didn't she phone someone close to her—her mother or best friend? Her shrink, for that matter."

"You visited her in the hospital. You showed concern. Maybe she connected with you."

"I don't know." I took the plates to the kitchen. "As to your first two possibilities, I plan to check into Saunders and some other things."

Zack followed me. "Be careful, Molly. If you're dealing with someone who could be a killer . . ."

"You just said there might not *be* a killer."

"And if there is?"

"I'm careful."

"I'm sure you are, but—"

I stopped him with a look. "I'm a big girl, Zack. I can take care of myself."

"So I'm not allowed to worry?"

"Worry all you want, but keep it to yourself." To be honest, I liked knowing that he was concerned. I washed a dish and handed it to him.

He picked up a towel from the counter. "I'm giving a class tonight, but how about dinner tomorrow? You can fill me in on your progress."

"Monday night is mah jongg with my sisters." I could have

canceled with Edie and Mindy's blessing, but I didn't want him to think I was too eager. "What about Tuesday?"

"I have a bar mitzvah boy coming at nine, right after *ma'ariv*. How about an early dinner? Five-thirty?"

"Fine."

"Great. I'll pick you up at five-fifteen," he said, and this time I didn't say no. "By the way, the shul board is throwing a party the Tuesday night after Tisha b'Av. Meet the new rabbi. Can I have them send you an invitation?"

"I've already met the rabbi."

"I'd really like you to come, Molly."

"That's almost three weeks away." In three weeks we could be over.

"So?"

"You don't need me there. You'll be busy meeting people."

"Exactly why I *will* need you. To protect me from Reggie the Realtor and all those nubile young women you mentioned." He smiled.

I told him to send the invitation and promised I'd think about it.

# Chapter Twenty-three

I SPENT THE AFTERNOON WORKING ON MY MANUSCRIPT edits, reviewing my notes on my talk with Nina, and learning through news articles on the Web that Robert Saunders had been poking his developmental fingers into much of L.A. and other Southern California counties for almost ten years, and that not everyone was happy about it.

I hate what's happening to my city. I don't yearn for the days when Wilshire Boulevard from downtown L.A. to the Pacific Ocean was all farmland. That was long before I was born, and I do love shopping and catching a movie at Century City and Santa Monica and other malls. But now the malls, with their multilevel department stores, movie complexes, restaurants, boutique shops, and kiosks, are encroaching like locusts on residential neighborhoods, including my own, and creating traffic snarls from early morning until late at night that would make Gandhi weep.

Twenty-plus years ago developers replaced the pony-ride park my grandparents used to take us to on Sundays with the Beverly Center, an ugly monstrosity that squats like an elephant, occupying an area bordered by La Cienega and San Vicente, and Beverly and Third. On the other side of La Cienega they built the Beverly Connection, whose labyrinthian parking lot must have been designed by someone on LSD. Across Beverly to the north they erected the Sofitel Hotel, from whose upper-floor windows you'd have a great view of the Hollywood Hills if it weren't for the Pacific Design Center, two large shiny buildings (one is Lego blue, the other green, and I hear the next one will be yellow) about as picturesque as Play-Doh.

About three years ago they razed Chasen's, an L.A. landmark where movie stars used to celebrate post Oscars, and built Bristol Farms, a high-end produce market. More recently they completed a huge mall called The Grove that houses a Nordstrom's, a Banana Republic, and other stores and restaurants and clubs that surround and overwhelm what remains of the original Farmers Market. There were city council meetings where homeowners protested, but the bulldozers had their way, and while I admit the mall is gorgeous (I heard it was designed by the architect of the Las Vegas Bellagio) and I enjoy relaxing near the pond and fountains, it now takes me five times as long to drive from Fairfax to La Brea.

Ron had been right about Saunders's interest in the Santa Monica Mountains. He'd submitted plans for a large housing subdivision with a nearby complex of hotels, restaurants, movie theaters, department stores, specialty shops—practically a city. He was also developing property in Malibu and Westwood, and now that I think about it, it may have been his name that I saw a few months ago on placards of protest planted on Westwood lawns. One newspaper piece about the Malibu project (the headline was GOBBLE, GOBBLE) reported a shouting match between a homeowner and Saunders's representative at a council meeting.

In every case, Saunders had faced opposition. In every case, ultimately, he had won. I wondered whether his success was a result of his persuasive powers or his connection with good friends in high places.

This time I took Mount Olympus, a more direct route to Hermes. The street was wider and easier on my stomach and offered a breathtaking view of the city when I reached the top.

"Robbie isn't here," Jillian told me, something I already knew. She'd opened the door to show only a sliver of her face, which didn't look all that welcoming.

"I was hoping to clarify a few things he told me on Friday. I assume he told you that he and I talked?"

"Robbie and I have no secrets." A little smugness, a little disdain.

"Then maybe you can help me." I smiled to show we were all friends now. "I'd hate to think my trip up here was a waste. Not that the view isn't worth it."

"It would be better if you talked to Robbie," she said, a shade more pleasant. "He'll be back tomorrow."

"No problem. It's just that I spoke to one of Lenore's friends today. She said some things about you and Robbie and Lenore, and I thought it was only fair to hear your side."

Jillian's eyes narrowed. "My side about what? Exactly what did she say?"

"Could we talk inside? It's rather warm out here."

After a brief hesitation, she opened the door. I stepped into the cool stone-tiled entry and followed her down three steps into an enormous living room with dark hardwood floors and a vaulted, two-story wood ceiling.

We sat at opposite ends of a chintz sofa, the only furniture in the room aside from a stone-based glass coffee table covered with campaign brochures bearing Saunders's handsome smiling face. She was wearing jeans again and another crisp white cotton blouse, this one with three-quarter sleeves. Her dark hair hung down her back. I noted a few gray strands at her forehead, some lines around her brown eyes.

"Your home is magnificent," I said. It was the first truth I'd uttered since I'd arrived.

"Thanks. We're in the process of redecorating, as you can see. This couch and table are temporary, of course." She glanced at the offending pieces, then back at me. "It's hell finding the right decorator."

"I know what you mean," I murmured, my lapse into honesty over. My decorators had been a Pottery Barn catalog and a sales-man at Plummers, a furniture store on Venice Boulevard in Culver City that used to have the added attraction of being near an En-tenmann's shop, no longer open, where you could get day-old doughnuts for half price. "How long have you been living here?"

"A little over a month. Robbie owns a lot in Beverly Hills, near both of our parents, and we plan on building there—after the wedding, of course. We'll probably come here weekends, just for the view."

"It's quite a view." I glanced at the floor-to-ceiling windows and felt renewed envy. "Do you have a wedding date?"

"December tenth at the Biltmore downtown."

The Biltmore is a beautiful hotel with a ballroom that has a gilded ceiling and old-world charm, and new-world prices. I picked up a brochure. "Between planning the wedding and cam-paigning for the city council election, the two of you must be very busy."

"It's a little crazy, but it's exciting. Robbie has a great deal to offer. He'll make a wonderful councilman, and after that, who knows?" Jillian smiled.

"He's a land developer, right? I understand he's planning a new subdivision in the Santa Monica Mountains."

"I don't know much about that. You'd have to ask Robbie." A note of caution had entered her voice.

"Did I read that there was a problem with the zoning?"

She shrugged. "There are always problems, but Robbie manages to solve them. He's very good at what he does."

"I'm sure." I glanced around again. "How long has he owned this home?"

"Down to business, right?" Jillian looked amused. "What you're really asking is, did he and Lenore live here? The answer is yes. And no, that's not why I want to move. It's been over two years since Robbie and Lenore lived here, so her presence is long gone. Although she seems to be haunting us from the grave, doesn't she? Don't quote me on that," she warned, suddenly nervous.

"I won't." I smiled. "I take it you didn't like her."

Jillian laughed. "What makes you think that?" She tucked one leg beneath her and assumed a serious expression. "Look, Miss Blume—"

"Molly." You'd be amazed how much people open up once you're on a first-name basis.

She nodded. "Lenore's dead, Molly, and it's a tragedy that she killed herself, but I won't pretend to be sorry that she's out of our lives."

"I admire your honesty."

"I'm not sure Robbie will. I think you'd better come back tomorrow."

"Her best friend says if you hadn't come back into the picture, Robbie wouldn't have divorced her."

"That's crap. Robbie was thinking divorce even before Max died. Lenore wasn't coping with mommyhood, but she refused to let Robbie hire a nurse. Changing diapers and dealing with a crying baby wasn't his thing. I encouraged him to stick with her through the trial and afterward. Maureen did, too. His mother," Jillian said when I looked blank.

Public opinion, I suspected, but I asked her why.

"Because it was the right thing to do. There are rules, and you play by them. She was his wife, he had a responsibility."

She was playing with the huge square-cut diamond on her ring finger that matched the diamond studs in her ears. I wondered if this was the original engagement ring, or a new one. Maybe Robbie had a direct account with DeBeers.

"I understand that you and Robbie were seeing each other before the divorce was final. Even before the baby was born."

She shrugged. "Robbie and I were friends long before Lenore ever *met* Robbie."

"You were friends who happened to be engaged before. And you moved into this house right after the divorce."

"The marriage was over! *Dead.*" She glared at me, nostrils flared, face flushed. "Lenore didn't want to accept it. She was making ridiculous demands. Robbie was outrageously generous, but every time they'd be close to a settlement, she'd up the ante."

I'd obviously touched on a sore point. "But eventually she agreed."

"Her mother finally made her see reason. Thank God." She took a calming breath. "I thought you promised Robbie you were going to keep this quiet." She sounded nervous again and probably regretted her outburst.

"*If* I can corroborate what he told me. So far, I'm hearing conflicting stories, Jillian."

"I really shouldn't talk about this."

Maybe it was anger at Lenore or frustration with Robbie.

Whatever it was, I sensed she wanted to tell her story. Most people do, which makes my job easier. "To be honest, Jillian, everybody I've talked to so far thinks Robbie treated Lenore badly. I'm interested in the truth, and I'd like to be fair, but—"

"You want the truth?" Jillian unfolded her leg. "Lenore manipulated Robbie into marrying her."

"How did they meet?"

"She worked for him. She began as a secretary, and within a year she managed to become his personal assistant. I have to give her credit. She's bright and she did a good job, and she was *so* interested in his business." She drew out the word, adding a breathless, vampy quality. "Have you met her?"

"Once, in the hospital."

"She probably wasn't at her best." Jillian's smile was nasty. "She's very pretty and incredibly charming, and she's got this sweet, innocent, you're-my-hero act down pat." She wrinkled her nose, as if sniffing dog doo. "Robbie ate it up."

"That's how she manipulated him?"

"That's how she started. Then she seduced him so she'd get pregnant."

This wasn't the Lenore Nina had described, and I wondered how much Jillian's bitterness had colored her view. "It could have been an accident."

"With Lenore there are no accidents. She probably used an ovulation chart to make sure the time of the month was right. She *knew* Robbie would marry her, and she'd be set for life. Like mother, like daughter." Jillian saw the surprised look on my face. "You didn't know? Lenore was conceived out of wedlock, just like Max. Her daddy married Betty, then skipped when he knew he'd been taken for a ride."

"Lenore told Robbie this?"

Jillian snorted. "She didn't even tell him her parents were divorced. She told him her father died when she was an infant.

Maureen had the family checked out. She told Robbie, but he was determined to marry her."

"He could have told Lenore to get an abortion."

"That wasn't the point." She shook her head impatiently: I wasn't getting it. "He was infatuated with her. He thought he *loved* her." She made it sound like a dirty word. "There was no talking him out of it. Believe me, we tried."

I was annoyed by her patronizing attitude. "You and Maureen?"

"Someone had to talk sense to him. Robbie's father wasn't around to do it. Maximillian died eight years ago of a heart attack. Max was named for him," she added.

"Maybe Robbie really *did* love her."

"He hardly *knew* her. Their backgrounds were totally different, their interests, their social circles." She waved the hand with the rock. "She didn't fit into his world."

"But you do."

"Yes, I do. And I'm honest enough to say so. Our families have been close for years. We even went to the same schools. Robbie realized he'd made a huge mistake. Lenore was uncomfortable around his family and friends, so he rarely saw them, and when that wasn't good enough for her, they moved to Santa Barbara, and she was lonely. Robbie is used to entertaining clients. It's an important part of his business. Lenore *hated* entertaining."

"I can see how that would destroy a marriage," I said, risking a little sarcasm.

"You think I'm a snob." Jillian shrugged. "You can teach someone how to dress and choose wines and set a table, but you can't teach her how to be witty or sophisticated or how to fit in. Life isn't like the movies. I think Lenore watched *Pretty Woman* too many times."

I decided I didn't like Jillian. "I guess she did."

"There's a reason the wealthy marry each other, Molly. It's not elitism. It's compatibility and practicality."

"I can see what you mean. And that's why you and Robbie are getting married?"

"That, and because we love each other deeply."

And because Robbie is successful and wealthy and probably owns more homes than a Monopoly set. "You've waited a long time to be happy together. You must have been upset when Lenore threatened that happiness a second time."

"Lenore wasn't a threat. She was an annoyance. Robbie had no interest in her."

"But she was interested in him. That's why she came here Saturday night, right?"

Jillian sighed. "She told Robbie she was afraid she might harm herself, but she's cried wolf before. Robbie feels terribly guilty that he sent her away, but how could he have known she *meant* it this time?"

I furrowed my brow and hoped I looked genuinely puzzled. "This is where we have a discrepancy, Jillian. Lenore told her friend she came here that night with every hope of reuniting with Robbie. Why would she say that?"

I could see her entire body tensing, as though I'd yanked an elastic tape at the top of her head.

"I have no idea."

"She also said— Well, maybe I *should* come back, when Robbie's home," I said with a hint of awkwardness. "I don't want to cause a problem between the two of you."

"Robbie and I tell each other *everything*." Her voice was as cool and smooth as sorbet. "What else did Lenore allegedly say?"

"That she and Robbie were intimate."

Jillian's hands formed fists. "That's a lie."

I shrugged to show my helplessness. I was just the messenger.

She was silent a moment, and I watched her face, wondering what she was thinking.

"The police told Robbie Lenore was pregnant," she said. "But you already know, don't you?" She looked at me shrewdly. "That's what Lenore told her friend. That's what you were alluding to. You wanted to see if I knew. Well, for your information, Robbie told me. We have no secrets."

She'd used a variation of the phrase three times so far, twice in the last minute, almost like a mantra. Maybe saying it helped her believe it. "So Saturday night Lenore told Robbie she was pregnant with his child. That's why she thought they'd be getting back together."

"It's ridiculous. She probably slept with someone else and used him as a sperm donor so she could trap Robbie. Robbie hasn't had anything to do with Lenore since the divorce, aside from some business dealings. He made the mistake of putting her name on some property when they were married. Maureen warned him, but he wasn't thinking clearly."

"I don't mean to be insulting, Jillian, but my ex told me he was at business meetings when he was really fooling around with someone."

"You don't understand. It was *painful* for Robbie to be around Lenore. Every time he saw her, he thought about Max. He'd come back terribly depressed, and I had to let him work it out, because he couldn't talk about Max, not even to me or Maureen. So the last thing in the world Robbie would do is get involved with Lenore again."

I had to admit that was a good point. Still . . .

"And why would he risk being trapped again?" Jillian added. "We love each other. We're looking forward to a wonderful life together. He's almost sure to win the election. Why would he jeopardize all that?"

There was a brooding quality to her voice, and I wondered whether she was trying to convince me or herself. "You're probably right. But if he wasn't intimate with Lenore, why would she expect him to believe the baby was his?"

Jillian snickered. "Lenore's so doped up most of the time, she probably doesn't know what's true and what isn't. Robbie told me he said as much to her. That's when she started cursing him and threatening to kill herself." She leaned back against the sofa. "Well, you know the rest."

I did know the rest, and that's why I was bothered. "She was wearing a nightgown when they found her, Jillian. And she doesn't own nightgowns. You might want to ask Robbie about that."

The doorbell rang. Jillian excused herself and walked to the entry hall. A moment later I heard a woman's voice.

". . . stop by and return the invitation proof, dear. I think the font is a little busy, don't you? And the text— Oh, hello."

The woman who had entered the room smiled at me automatically, then turned to Jillian, who was two steps behind her.

"I didn't know you had company, dear."

"This is Molly Blume," Jillian told her. She sounded nervous. "She's a writer. Molly, this is my future mother-in-law, Maureen Saunders."

Mom and son resembled each other. She had the same hazel eyes and broad face, and her hair, cut in a chin-length bob, was a honey blond. She was wearing a white linen suit that looked expensive, Fendi shoes that definitely were, and a purse with the signature Chanel logo that I'm sure wasn't a knockoff. The silk scarf draped on her shoulder was no doubt signature, too.

"A pleasure to meet you. Molly is such a charming name. You don't hear it often these days."

"Thank you. It's a pleasure meeting you, too." I almost curtsied.

"I don't believe I'm familiar with your work."

"I'm a freelance reporter, and I gather data for the *Crime Sheet*. I also write books about true crime. *Out of the Ashes* is my latest." Never miss an opportunity to promote.

"It sounds rather grisly." Maureen shuddered. "Not something my book group would be interested in, I'm afraid." She smiled.

I'd have to live with the disappointment.

"I assume you're here to interview Jillian about Robert's campaign? I'd be happy to answer any questions you may have. We're biased, of course, but we think Robert has so much to offer." Her smile was warmer now, genuine.

"Actually, I'm writing about Lenore." A look of unbridled hate crossed her face. A second later it was gone, and I wondered if I'd imagined it. "I know it's a painful topic, Mrs. Saunders, but I hope you'd be willing to talk to me about her."

"I don't think so." She spoke politely but with great distaste, as though I'd suggested that she go mud wrestling in her white suit. "To be honest, Miss Blume, I don't think you *do* know how painful a topic it is. I lost a grandson, my late husband's namesake. My son lost a son."

"I'm sorry," I said quietly, meaning it. "It's not my intention to cause you pain."

"Then what is?" She turned to her future daughter-in-law. "Jillian, I'll wait in the dining room while you show Miss Blume out." To me she said, "Lenore was a tortured young woman. I can only hope that she's found some peace."

I wondered if that was true.

# CHAPTER TWENTY-FOUR

THE FIFTH-FLOOR EVENING CHARGE NURSE, MIRNA ZHIR-
kovsky, was a tall woman with a bouffant blond hairdo, a thick,
trunklike torso, sturdy legs, and muscular arms that could easily
flip patients like pancakes.

"How can I help you?" she asked in a thick Russian accent,
her *h*'s invested with a guttural "ch" sound.

"I wanted to ask you a few questions about Lenore Saunders," I said. "She was a patient here last week."

Something flickered across her broad face. "I cannot discuss
Ms. Saunders."

The hospital's legal department had probably issued a direc-
tive. "I understand." I flashed my most sincere smile. "I'm not
here to ask about her condition. When I spoke with Jeannette

last week, she told me a young man brought Ms. Saunders flowers. Apparently, Lenore didn't receive any other visitors on Jeannette's shift, but I'm wondering if anyone visited Lenore on *your* shift."

The nurse narrowed eyelids heavily shadowed in blue. "Why you want to know?"

"I'm writing a human interest piece about Lenore, just trying to reconstruct the last few days of her life."

She kept her eyes on me while she thought that over. "Her mother comes every day," she finally said. "Dr. Korwin, too. A very nice man. And a friend comes twice."

"Do you remember the friend's name?"

The nurse frowned. "Maybe if you tell me, I remember. A plain woman."

"Was it Nina?"

She nodded. "Yes, Nina." She pronounced it Nyeena. "She is crying when she comes, with a face like this." Mirna assumed an elongated, hangdog expression. "I say to her, listen, you are visiting your friend, she will think things are very bad if you are so sad."

Sound advice. "Were there any male visitors?"

"Besides husband, you mean?" She shook her head. "No one."

"When was he here?" I asked in a casual tone.

"I see him only one time, Monday night. He does not stay long. Dr. Korwin, he comes and tells husband he must go, patient needs sleep. Then the husband talks to the mother. I'm thinking he is coming the next night, but no. Maybe he comes during day."

"Lenore must have been happy to see him."

She shrugged. "Happy, I don't know. She is crying, begging him not to go. I think she is afraid she is going to die, because he tells her, don't talk like this, is not going to happen. I don't mean she's afraid she is going to kill herself," the nurse added quickly, her eyes wary. "I mean from accident."

On the elevator to the seventh floor, I reviewed my conversations with Saunders. Had he said that he hadn't visited Lenore, or had I assumed it? Lenore had been inconsistent, telling me that Robbie, among others, had questioned her about the accident, then bewailing the fact that he wasn't going to visit her.

*"Robbie isn't coming,"* she'd said. *"He's very angry."* Which didn't mean he hadn't been there before. Maybe he'd regretted sending her away, telling her to "do it right this time."

I thought about what the Russian nurse had overheard. "Don't talk like this. It's not going to happen." Had Saunders been reassuring Lenore, or warning her that her hopes of their reuniting was a fantasy?

On the seventh floor I located Sally Huang, the nurse who had been in charge of Lenore the night she died. She was as petite as Mirna Zhirkovsky was large, with short black hair and eyes and thin lips that she bit nervously while I introduced myself and told her why I was here.

She shook her head in a rapid, birdlike fashion. "I'm sorry, I can't talk to anyone about Ms. Saunders."

I gave her my I-only-want-to-know-who-visited-Lenore spiel. It didn't work.

"Do you know who was Lenore's last visitor that night?" I persisted. "I'm hoping to get an interview with him or her for my article."

"I'm sorry. I really can't talk to you."

You have to know when to fold 'em, as Kenny Rogers says.

Downstairs in the lobby the gray-haired volunteer at reception peered at me through bifocals attached to a chain and told me she had no idea who had visited Lenore Saunders on

Wednesday night. From her unguarded expression, I decided she hadn't been warned not to discuss Lenore, which made sense since the hospital was worried about suicide, not murder.

"Don't you have sign-in sheets for visitors?" I asked.

"Yes, we do," she said cheerily. "But we only keep them for the day. And to tell you the truth, not everyone signs in. Have you checked with the nurse who was on duty? She'd probably be able to help you."

I had learned very little at the hospital, hardly enough to warrant the parking fee. At home I checked my messages: Mindy, confirming mah jongg tomorrow night at her house. Zack, telling me what a great time he'd had even though I'd made him wipe the dishes and how much he was looking forward to Tuesday night. Betty Rowan had phoned.

"It's about the call Lenore made to you before she died," Betty said. "And something you need to know." She sounded anxious, not like she had the other two times.

So did Jillian, in her message. "What I told you today is off the record, Molly. About Lenore being pregnant, and everything connected with it? Robbie's very private, and he'll be upset if he finds out I told you. So will Maureen. Please call me so that I know you received this message."

If you've ever been interviewed, you know it's not uncommon to have second thoughts about what you've revealed. You get caught up in the telling, you forget who you're talking to, what you've said. It's happened to me when I've given print and radio interviews, and I'm a reporter. It explains why people read quotes attributed to themselves and go, "No way did I say that!"

But aside from one comment, Jillian hadn't asked me to keep her comments off the record. So I had every right to use the material, and I didn't feel guilty, especially since Lenore's pregnancy would be public knowledge soon.

Which didn't mean I relished talking to her. I debated

putting off the call, then picked up the phone. I've been on the other side, waiting anxiously to hear from my agent or my editor, and I've never liked it.

Jillian repeated what she'd said in her message. I explained my position, told her my intention was not to cause her any embarrassment or trouble, but I couldn't promise what I would and wouldn't use. She hung up without saying goodbye.

I phoned Betty Rowan, but her line was busy. I wondered what it was she needed to tell me. Something about Lenore and Robbie? About Jillian?

Robbie and his women. . . .

According to Jillian, Lenore had been desperate to hold on to Robbie. Maybe Jillian had been desperate, too, enough to believe whatever he told her.

Connors had said Lenore had been on Haldol, which is an antipsychotic, presumably part of her treatment. I didn't know if she was delusional. Maybe so. But I found it hard to believe she'd imagined an intimate encounter with Robbie. More likely, they'd met to discuss business, and business had turned to something else. Maybe Robbie had been drinking, maybe he'd been lonely. Maybe they'd talked about Max and their loss. . . .

I didn't think he'd leveled with Jillian, and I think Jillian knew it, too. Now Lenore was dead and the truth had died with her, unless she'd written it down in her journal, which was missing.

I remembered what Zack had pointed out: just because Lenore had slept with Robbie didn't mean she hadn't slept with anyone else. Someone else could be the father. Lenore might have written that down in her journal, too.

I tried Betty again. The line was still busy. I warmed up leftovers my mom had packaged for me, turned on the TV, and listened as a big-haired female anchor announced an update on the police investigation into the apparent suicide of a woman in a hospital as a possible homicide.

"Sources have confirmed that the dead woman, Lenore Saunders, formerly married to local developer Robert Saunders, was pregnant," the anchor said. "Lenore Saunders was found guilty over a year ago of killing their two-month-old son in a trial that rocked Santa Barbara. The former Mrs. Saunders was being treated by local psychiatrist Lawrence Korwin, whose new book . . ."

Seconds later coverage switched to a grim-faced Korwin, who repeated "No comment" to a persistent female reporter. The psychiatrist sounded annoyed and nervous, probably because he was worrying about a prospective lawsuit.

Robert Saunders and his family wouldn't be happy either. Neither would Connors. I phoned Hollywood station and left him a message, assuring him that I hadn't leaked anything to the media or anyone else. Then I worked on my manuscript until my eyes were bleary and the words stopped making sense.

I was in bed when Zack phoned. We talked well into the night, past two o'clock, and I remember saying, aren't you worried that you won't be able to get up early for shul, but I was the one who fell asleep with the receiver at my ear. I'm pretty sure I was smiling.

# CHAPTER TWENTY-FIVE

*Monday, July 21. 1:38 P.M. 6600 block of Yucca Street. A man was thrown from a fourth-floor apartment balcony by a suspect who approached the victim, asked if he was OK, then offered to provide the victim with protection. When the victim declined, the suspect demanded money, then threw the victim from the balcony. (Hollywood)*

THE KORWIN CLINIC WAS HOUSED IN A TWO-STORY, BEIGE-pink stucco building in Reseda in the San Fernando Valley. The offices, examining rooms, and common areas (game room, dining area, exercise room, visitors' room) were on the first floor; the bedrooms for residential patients, on the second. In its prior life the structure had been an assisted-living facility.

I learned all this from Eileen, the pleasant, matronly brown-haired receptionist, while I waited in a small anteroom to see Lawrence Korwin, with whom I'd scheduled an appointment before leaving my apartment this morning to do my rounds at the various police stations, gathering data for the *Crime Sheet*. I had visited Northwest, Culver City, and Wilshire. I still had West Hollywood and Hollywood to cover (the *Crime Sheet* hopes to expand coverage to include the Valley soon), but I wanted to do the latter when Connors was there. I'd phoned the station several times, but he was out in the field.

There were handsome, full-color brochures on a wood coffee table in the reception area. I picked one up and learned that the clinic was staffed by a team of psychiatrists, psychologists, and other experts with vast experience in the field of women's mental health, including but not limited to mood disorders and premenstrual, natal, postpartum, and perimenopausal depression.

"We've been open only two years, and we're really doing well," Eileen informed me proudly. "Many of the women are outpatient, but we're getting so many new residential patients that we'll have to start turning people away. Six months ago I didn't know if we were going to make it."

"Have you been with the clinic long?"

"From the start. This is a dream come true for Dr. Korwin. He was nervous about doing something on such a large scale, even with backing. But the book's prepublicity helped, and now that it's out, we're getting calls from women all over the country. It just came out last week. Have you read it?"

Lenore had the book, so Korwin had probably given her an advance copy. "Not yet. But I plan to."

I'd looked up Korwin online on the Google search engine and had read about the thirty-eight-year-old psychiatrist's background and accomplishments. Pages and pages of dissertations, and several reviews of his new book. I hadn't heard of it until I'd seen the copy in Lenore's apartment, but plenty of others had: He'd made the L.A. *Times* and *New York Times* nonfiction best-seller lists, and his Amazon ranking as of this morning was forty-three. That was in Stephen King and Grisham territory. My best Amazon ranking for *Out of the Ashes* was 987, and that was only for an hour. The next hour the book plummeted to 5,081, where it hovered for a day before settling into the twenty thousands. This morning it had been at 76,892, which isn't bad, considering the book has been out for a year. (Have I mentioned that I'm compulsive?)

"It's absolutely wonderful." Eileen handed me the glossy hardcover sitting on her desk. "Dr. Korwin publishes medical monographs all the time, but he wanted to reach women who didn't have easy access to a mental health practitioner or didn't realize they needed help."

I looked at the cover. *Rock-a-bye Baby: When Baby Blues Won't Go Away.* Below the title was a drawing of an empty cradle rocked by the hand of a shadowy figure of a mother. Underneath that was Korwin's name. Below that, *What every woman needs to know.* The back cover was crowded with testimonials from medical practitioners to Korwin, whose friendly, bearded face smiled at me from the back inside flap, above an impressive alphabet of degrees.

"He's doing *Good Morning America* and *The Today Show,* " Eileen said. "He's been asked to chair a symposium in the Netherlands next year. It's been amazing and overwhelming. You're lucky he had a cancellation, or he wouldn't have been able to see you until next week."

I wondered if he still had time for his patients. "Is Dr. Korwin married?"

"To his work." Eileen smiled. "He's the most caring person I've ever met and takes great interest in every patient. They all adore him."

What Nina had said. "Does he see every patient personally?"

"Absolutely." She seemed offended by my question. "Dr. Korwin does the initial evaluation, and consults with the doctors on staff to create a therapy program. And he follows up regularly. You said you're a reporter. Is this for a newspaper or magazine article?"

"I'm not sure yet." I glanced at my watch.

"He's running a little late." She picked up the phone receiver and pressed a button. "Dr. Kor— I'm sorry. I just wanted to remind you that Miss Blume is here." She put down the receiver, her face flushed. "He'll see you now. We've had a stressful few days because of a crisis, and he hasn't been himself."

"You mean Lenore Saunders's death. I saw on the news last night that she was Dr. Korwin's patient."

Eileen sighed. "What a horrible tragedy. I don't think I've ever seen Dr. Korwin so shaken. Her mother phoned on Friday, and I didn't know what to say. And of course, patients have been calling nonstop, needing reassurance."

Korwin met me at the door and escorted me to one of the black leather chairs in front of an oversized mahogany desk cluttered with books and papers. My kind of guy. He was wearing suspenders over a light blue shirt that strained across his gut. His handshake was firm, and his eyes were a warm brown.

"Sorry I kept you waiting," he said when he was seated. "It's been a little hectic the past few days."

If he was tense, he was covering up well. "Congratulations on your book. Your receptionist filled me in. *Good Morning America. The Today Show.*" I smiled. "You'll be a household name right up there with Tom Cruise."

"Eileen's my biggest fan." Korwin's grin was ingenuous. "It's a real kick at first, and my parents are thrilled. Now they can tell all the neighbors that their weird kid made it big. But you wanna know the truth? I hate flying, and I hate hotel rooms, and I hate the whole media circus. I'd rather be here at the clinic. This is where it comes alive for me." He waved his hand.

I like to think that I'm a good judge of people, and I have to say he sounded sincere. "So why do it?"

"It sells books, so it makes my publisher happy, and they'll publish my next book. Listen, I'm grateful the shows *want* me. Despite what you said, Tom Cruise I'm not." He pointed to his paunch. "Without the media exposure, I'd reach a handful of women. My goal is to reach thousands, tens of thousands. The more, the better."

"Women suffering from postpartum depression." I took out my notepad.

"Women who are pregnant or contemplating becoming pregnant or have just given birth. Ten to twenty percent of new moms suffer from postpartum depression, maybe more. One to two in a thousand suffers from postpartum psychosis—again, maybe more. I want to help them and protect them from themselves, and protect their babies. And if elected . . ." He smiled again. "Sorry for the speech. I get carried away."

"Good speech." I smiled back. "So what's the difference between depression and psychosis?"

"You know about baby blues, right? Happens to most moms right after birth and lasts a couple of days. Postpartum depression is more intense and doesn't go away after a week or two."

"Describe 'intense.' "

"A woman with postpartum depression feels uncontrollably miserable and has some, but not necessarily all, of the following symptoms. She's crying daily, has trouble sleeping, and not just 'cause the baby's keeping her up all night. She loses interest in doing anything, can't concentrate or make decisions. She feels listless, worthless, guilty, inadequate as a mother. She worries excessively over her child's health. She loses her appetite, and feels an overall sense of helplessness. She thinks about death and suicide."

A catalog of gloom and despair. Was that what Lenore and other mothers like her felt all day, every day? I scribbled madly to keep up, engulfed with a wave of sadness. "What about psychosis?" I asked, wondering how anything could be worse than what Korwin had just described.

"It's far more severe and usually strikes in the first two weeks to one month after delivery, although it *can* start later. In extreme cases, it can lead mothers to harm themselves or their babies. By the way, we're the only Western country that puts postpartum psychotic mothers in jail. Other Western countries, like England and Italy, recognize that new moms are particularly vulnerable to mental illness that could, in some cases, lead to infanticide."

I shuddered. It was a horrible word. "What are the symptoms?"

"Obvious mood swings, extreme insomnia. Excessive concern about the infant. Hallucinations—seeing or hearing things that aren't there, like hearing voices when no one's around. Or delusions—having thoughts that aren't based on reality. A mother may be convinced that someone is trying to harm her, or that her baby is the devil."

What had Lenore seen in her baby's eyes? What had she heard in his cry that had caused her to shake him to death? I tried to picture a mother gazing at the face of a newborn and seeing the devil, but it was beyond me. It was a place I didn't want to go.

"The risk of psychosis after childbirth is twenty times higher than the risk before pregnancy," Korwin added. "Did you know that?"

I shook my head.

He grunted. "I'm not surprised. We doctors know all about gestational diabetes, preeclampsia, and preterm delivery, but even though postpartum depression is more common, it hasn't received equal attention in contemporary medical literature, training, and clinical practice."

"Until Andrea Yates."

"That's postpartum *psychosis*, not depression," Korwin corrected, his voice stern.

"Sorry." I'd obviously pushed a button.

"It's upsetting when the media carelessly label Yates and other women like her who killed their children 'depressed.' Postpartum depression and psychosis are two completely different entities. PPD doesn't lead to psychosis. It's not like a flu that can become pneumonia."

"Okay."

"It's not just a question of semantics, Miss Blume. Say you're a mother with PPD and you heard a news broadcast about Andrea Yates or someone like her, and the reporter said she'd killed her child because she'd been suffering from PPD. Can you imagine how stigmatized you'd feel, how terrified that you might end up killing your own child? And what if that stigma prevented you from seeking help?" He stopped, his point made, but he was still frowning.

"I can see what you mean. So postpartum depression is a relatively new diagnosis?" I asked, seeking safer ground.

"Actually, in 460 B.C. Hippocrates talked about puerperal fever and theorized that suppressed lochial discharge traveled to the brain, where it produced agitation, delirium, and attacks of mania."

"Lovely theory." I had no idea what lochial meant, but it didn't sound pleasant. And "discharge" has never been one of my favorite words.

"You like that?" Korwin smiled. "Here's another. An eleventh-century gynecologist thought that if the uterus was too moist, the brain would fill with water, and the excess moisture would spill into the eyes, causing the woman to involuntarily cry. I know," he said, seeing the expression on my face. He leaned forward, his hands clasped. "My point is that postpartum depression has been around a long time. Left undiagnosed and untreated, it can have devastating consequences. In New York State, by the way, the law says new moms have to be advised that one in ten women will have a depressive episode, and that one or two in a thousand will suffer postpartum psychosis. I'd like to see that happen nationally."

I could see why Nina and Lenore admired him. He was passionate about his field, caring, charismatic. "Won't that make moms with baby blues more nervous?"

"Better nervous than unaware. And remember, baby blues go away after a few days. The goal is to have women who need help *get* that help."

"Why wouldn't a woman who's feeling all those symptoms want to get help?"

"Good question." He nodded his approval. "Maybe she can't distinguish between feeling miserable and feeling exhausted and overwhelmed. Maybe she's embarrassed to admit she's depressed. She's getting congratulatory phone calls and visits, the baby's being showered with gifts. She's supposed to be thrilled. Or maybe she thinks she's a failure if she admits she needs help. So she tells herself things will get better if she hangs in there."

Korwin was echoing what Lenore had told Robbie. "So what *is* the cause of postpartum depression?"

He leaned back against his chair. "There are several factors. First, there's the patient's medical history. Did she suffer from depression before becoming pregnant? Depression in women, by the way, is twice as common as in men. Is there a history of depression in the family? If we're dealing with psychosis, is there a previous history of postpartum psychosis, or of a bipolar mood disorder or schizophrenia? Second, what about the home situation? Was she unhappy to learn she was pregnant? Was her partner unhappy to learn she was pregnant? Is she having marital problems? Did she recently have a stressful incident in her life? By the way, adolescent moms have a much higher rate of postpartum depression."

According to Jillian, Robbie had wanted a divorce even before the baby was born. And Nina had said that the marriage had problems, that Lenore was unhappy because Robbie was away so much, that she'd suspected him of cheating on her. Had Lenore worried that Robbie would leave her and go back to Jillian, just as her father had left her mother?

"And then there's the biochemical component," Korwin said. "Estrogen has been shown to inhibit depression. Immediately after childbirth, there's a dramatic drop in progesterone and estrogen, which causes changes in the chemicals in the brain. We think that in some women, those changes can trigger postpartum depression or psychosis."

"So what's the treatment?"

"Depends on the diagnosis. For baby blues, I recommend encouragement followed by a few hours at Elizabeth Arden once the baby sleeps through the night." Korwin smiled. "For postpartum depression, psychotherapy is highly effective, combined with antidepressants. For psychosis, you're talking psychotherapy, antidepressants, and antipsychotic drugs, and the patient has to be hospitalized—for her safety and the child's. In both cases, if the mom is nursing or pregnant, we're limited as to what drugs we can safely use without harming the infant or fetus."

Which explained why Korwin had wanted to wean Lenore off her medications. "Do you treat psychotic patients here?"

Korwin nodded. "We have twenty-five rooms and a staff of psychiatrists and nurses. We also offer on-site electroconvulsive therapy for depression and psychosis. It has no effect on a fetus, if the mom is pregnant, or on breast milk."

I grimaced. "It sounds barbaric."

Korwin smiled. "Most people have your reaction. ECT has a bad rep, but I've seen it do wonders. There are side effects—temporary memory loss, headaches, confusion. But they go away."

"I'll skip, thanks." I flipped a page to the questions that had really brought me here. "Dr. Korwin, what's the prognosis for a woman who's had postpartum depression or psychosis if she has another child?"

Korwin shook his head. "Without help, not good. There's a much higher incidence of repeated depression—twenty-five to thirty-three percent, maybe higher. With psychosis, recurrence can be as high as a hundred percent. But there's been experimentation with different prophylactic treatments. In fact, we're in the middle of a clinical trial here right now, using an estrogen patch with progesterone, antidepressants, and psychotherapy on a controlled group and a placebo on the other. The results are encouraging. Can you imagine what that would mean to millions of women if we're successful?" Korwin's eyes shone with excitement.

"It would be wonderful," I agreed. "I have another question, Dr. Korwin. Hypothetically—"

He cut me off with an exaggerated groan. "I *hate* hypotheticals."

I smiled. "Hypothetically, if a woman was treated for postpartum depression or psychosis and became pregnant again, would it be likely that she'd try to kill herself because she feared being depressed and possibly harming her child?" That's what Connors had suggested, and I wanted an expert opinion.

Korwin scratched his beard. "I'd have to know more about her history and how she presents and her diagnosis. What her symptoms were, the severity of her condition. Whether she's tried to kill herself before."

"She has, twice. The first attempt was after she killed her infant son."

Korwin's face registered surprise, which quickly turned to anger. He sat up straighter, his teddy bear softness gone. "You're not asking a hypothetical, are you?" He studied me as though I were a bacterium on a microscope slide. *Journalistus nosyus.* "And you're not here to interview me about my book or about postpartum depression. You're here about Lenore Saunders." He shot me a baleful look.

"I *am* interested in the subject, and yes, I'm writing about Lenore. I apologize for not being up-front, but I didn't think you'd agree to see me if I told you. I wanted to understand more about postpartum depression and psychosis so that I could understand her. Since she was your patient, I thought I'd come to you."

"You could have done research in a library or on the Internet. You didn't need to come here. If you'll excuse a nonmedical term, Miss Blume, that's a crock." He picked up a pen and tapped it on the desk. "So what rag are you writing for? Or is this for a TV movie of the week?"

He was entitled to sarcasm. "Actually, I write books about true crime. I was troubled by the circumstances of Lenore's hit-and-run, so I talked with her when she was in the hospital. The next night she left a message on my machine." The pen tapping had stopped, so I assumed I'd sparked Korwin's interest. "She said she needed to talk to me, that she was afraid. I waited until the morning to see her. By then she was dead. To be honest, I feel guilty."

"I'm not a priest, and if you need a therapist, I can recommend a few good ones."

I didn't answer.

He took a breath, and when he spoke again, his tone was less hostile. "Lenore's death is a shocking, senseless tragedy," he said quietly. "We're all trying to come to terms with it. It's not easy for any of us."

"You were an expert defense witness during her trial, and her therapist for over a year. You must have been close."

"I'm close with *all* my patients," he said curtly. "What's your point?"

Touchy, touchy. "That you probably know what she was thinking better than anyone else."

"I'm a psychiatrist, not a mind reader. Aren't the police saying it's homicide?"

The thought occurred to me that if Lenore had been killed, Korwin would be off the hook—legally, professionally, morally. "They're considering the possibility, but they're not ruling out suicide."

Korwin's phone rang. He picked up the receiver and uttered a sharp "Yes?" A pause. "Tell her I'll call her back in a few minutes." Another pause. "I *understand* that she's upset." He hung up the phone and pinched the bridge of his nose. "It's been like that all day. Where were we?"

"We were talking about Lenore's death. My question is, when she found out she was pregnant, would she have panicked and become suicidal?"

Korwin tsked. "Come on, Miss Blume. You know I can't discuss Lenore. Doctor–patient confidentiality."

"Even if she's dead?"

"She still has a right to privacy. Suppose you were my patient, and you knew that after you died, I could reveal things you'd told me in confidence. Wouldn't you think twice before confiding in me? Wouldn't that inhibit the therapy?"

"Probably," I admitted, disappointed. "But isn't it important to know whether Lenore was suicidal? If she wasn't, it's more likely she was killed."

"I don't need you to tell me my job, Miss Blume. I've already talked to the police and told them what I could about Lenore, based on the law." In a less officious voice, he added, "Believe me, I want to help, but I won't compromise my ethics."

"Even to identify a killer? If Lenore told you she was afraid of someone specific—"

"She never did," he said brusquely. "She never said anything about it." He was frowning, his eyes focused somewhere beyond me, and he sounded troubled.

"Maybe it has to do with her pregnancy," I said. "Did Lenore tell you who the father was?"

Korwin snapped his attention back to me. "Which part of confidentiality don't you understand?" he asked, annoyed again. He picked up a folder. "I have about ten calls to return and patients to see. If that's all?"

"Can we get back to my hypothetical?"

He sighed deeply, and for a moment I thought he was going to refuse. Then he put down the folder and swiveled in his chair.

"Hypothetically, if a pregnant woman has a history of ongoing depression and feelings of worthlessness and suicide attempts following postpartum psychosis that caused her to kill her child, and depending on whether she was taking medication for her depression and the efficacy of the medication, would she kill herself—is that your question?"

I leaned forward. "Yes."

"No comment."

He looked pleased with himself, and I had to admit he'd played me well. "Because you don't have an opinion," I asked, "or because your attorney advised you not to answer?"

Korwin smiled. "It was nice to meet you, Miss Blume. Sorry

I couldn't be of more help, but I have to play by the rules. No hard feelings?"

"No hard feelings." I slipped my notepad into my purse and stood. "Thanks for your time, and for all the information. I really *do* find the subject fascinating."

"Buy the book," he said and smiled again.

# CHAPTER TWENTY-SIX

CONNORS WAS AT HIS DESK IN THE ALMOST EMPTY DETECtives' room when I arrived at the Hollywood station at fourthirty after gathering *Crime Sheet* data from West Hollywood. Most detectives begin the day around seven-thirty and leave at two-thirty, so I was pleased to find him there.

He was doing paperwork and grunted in response to my hello.

"Aren't you happy to see me?" I asked.

"Overjoyed. You complete me," he said, his tone dour.

"I don't know who leaked the news about the possible homicide or the pregnancy. It wasn't me, Andy. Do you believe me?"

"Yeah, sure. Now you can sleep at night." He sounded tired.

I pulled over a chair and sat down. "I've left messages all weekend and several today. Where have you been?"

"See, this is why I'm not married, Molly. Nag, nag, nag. For your information, Lenore Saunders is not the only case we're working. What's up?"

"You first. Did you get the autopsy results?"

"They're doing the autopsy today, and we should have a full report, including some lab results, tomorrow. I told Mrs. Rowan yesterday that she could schedule the funeral for Wednesday. I think the Saunders family is taking care of the arrangements." He named a chapel in Universal City, near Forest Lawn.

"Talk about putting on a face for the public."

Connors shrugged. "FYI, there were only two sets of fingerprints on the scissors, Molly. Lenore's, superimposed on the nurse's."

"There's a box of latex gloves in every room, in case you didn't know." I'd noticed that when I visited Lenore. "The killer could've helped himself to a pair, done the deed, and then put the scissors in Lenore's hand."

"The gloves would've smudged the nurse's prints."

I thought about that. "What if he brought another pair of scissors to do the deed, and put the nurse's pair in Lenore's hand?"

Connors furrowed his brow. "It's possible," he allowed. "Let's wait to hear what the M.E. says. Preliminary report is still suicide."

I stifled a wave of impatience. "And the trashed apartment?"

"What I said before. She had stuff on someone. That someone wanted it back. Maybe it's the journal, maybe something else.

"What's the time of death?"

"The M.E. says sometime between eleven P.M. and five A.M., but we can narrow it down. Lenore was fine when the nurse made her three o'clock rounds. We're getting a record of any phone calls Lenore made that night."

"Did the nurse say Lenore was agitated that night?"

"She had a bad evening, so they gave her a shot of Haldol and, later, some pills. It was tricky, because of the pregnancy. They wanted to wean her off the meds, but Korwin was afraid that without them she'd be at risk."

"So someone posing as a nurse or doctor could have given her more Haldol. What about a list of all the people who visited her room?"

"Not many visitors on the floor that time of night, according to the nurses, aside from staff. Which is another vote for suicide."

"I imagine it's not hard to get a hospital uniform and walk around unnoticed. Even *without* a uniform." Attitude, I've learned, is everything. "And if Lenore's room was away from the nurses' station. . . . Was the station ever unattended that night?"

"Her room was at the end of the hall." Connors hesitated. "Actually, there was an emergency in her bay a little after three. A patient tried getting out of his bed and fell. And yes, the killer could have created the diversion. But that could just as easily have been a coincidence." He sat back and laced his hands behind his head. "Okay, your turn."

I gave him edited summaries of my talks with Nina, Jillian, and Korwin. Some things I wanted to think about first.

"You've been a busy bee," he said. "So what's your take, Miss Marple?"

I do believe he was impressed. "*A*, Lenore knew Jillian wouldn't be there that night. *B*, Jillian suspects that Robbie slept with Lenore, whom she pretty much hates, although he denied it. Jillian definitely has motive. So does Robbie's mom. *C*, Lenore didn't wear nightgowns. Which means she must have borrowed a gown from Jillian." I allowed myself a modest smile, then frowned.

"Let me call Ted Koppel. What else?"

"Sshh." For the second time something was tickling at my mind like a feather, and I needed to concentrate.

"You're telling me to be quiet?" Connors asked.

I put up my hand and he stopped talking. A few seconds later I figured out what had been bothering me. "Where's Lenore's key?"

Connors scowled. "What?"

"She left her apartment and presumably took a cab to Saunders. She needed her key and money for the cab, so maybe she had a small wallet or purse. And if she was going for romance, she'd take a lipstick, a brush, some other stuff. But she was found without any identification. So my guess is, she left her stuff at Saunders's house when she stormed out."

Connors didn't answer. I took that as a good sign.

"So who has the key now?" he asked after a few seconds in which I watched his face as he processed the question. I could picture the wheels grinding.

"Either Saunders or Betty Rowan."

"Explain."

"According to Nina, Betty and her ex-son-in-law are chummy. He bought her a house and he's helping her financially—probably because she convinced Lenore to agree to the divorce."

Connors looked skeptical. "Says who?"

"Jillian. So Betty owes him. Maybe Saunders asked her to put the purse back in the apartment. Or," I said, thinking aloud, "maybe he kept the key and used it to get into the apartment to search for the journal himself."

"And trashed it to make it look like it was a burglary."

I smiled. "I knew you had potential. By the way, Lenore's name was on some property Saunders bought when they were married. Also, Lenore was Robbie's personal assistant. She may have been privy to information he wouldn't want known."

"Like?"

"I don't know." I thought about the zoning problems Ron had mentioned. "When did you talk to Korwin?"

"We talked to him several times."

"And?"

Connors shook his head. "Sorry, Molly."

"Talk about his work, and he's Mr. Congeniality. As soon as I brought up Lenore, he was nervous."

"Why wouldn't he be? She was his patient. She's dead. You're a reporter asking questions he doesn't want to answer."

It was more than that. "He knows who the baby's father is, doesn't he?"

"If you're hinting, try to be more subtle."

"Was it Saunders? Just tell me that."

He laughed. "You're worse than the KGB. Korwin says he doesn't know. That's all I'm going to tell you."

Maybe Betty Rowan knew.

Isaac, my landlord, was rocking on the porch glider. Perspiration dotted his wrinkled forehead and had plastered the sparse gray-white strands of hair to his scalp.

"How's it going?" he asked as I walked up the three steps.

"Not bad."

We chatted a minute. He told me about the week's specials at the 99 Cents store and at the chain supermarkets. In return I gave him a few previews of the *Crime Sheet*. He loves bragging to his poker buddies that he's in the know.

"How's the boyfriend?" he asked.

"Which one?"

"The cute one who was here yesterday."

"Even cuter." I smiled. "Gotta go, Isaac. See you later." I took a step toward my door.

"I have your *New Yorker* and some other magazines," he said. "I wasn't here when the mail came. Ernie left them in front of your door, and I didn't want the gardener to get them wet when he hosed down the porch."

He hoisted himself off the glider and disappeared upstairs into his apartment. A minute later he returned and handed me an armful of magazines that looked as though a dog had danced on them.

Inside my apartment I flipped through them as I walked to the kitchen. Among them was a heavy large brown manila envelope with a return address I didn't recognize. The flap was open.

I walked back outside with the envelope. "This was open."

"I saw that." Isaac shook his head. "You oughtta tell Ernie."

I suspect that Isaac looks at my mail, but he's never opened anything before, so I didn't see why he'd start now. Back in the apartment, I kicked off my pumps and removed the contents of the envelope—a manuscript, accompanied by a cover letter, from a cousin's friend who wanted to know if I'd read his work and recommend an agent.

I put the manuscript and letter at the side of my desk. I'm happy to help new writers, but I'm always anxious about what to say if I don't like their work. And who am I to judge? I hated *The Bridges of Madison County*.

I had two voice messages—one from an irate Robert Saunders, whose call I had no intention of returning, another from Nina. Nothing from Betty Rowan. I was in the kitchen, enjoying a glass of milk with a Pepperidge Farm Sausalito cookie while looking through the rest of my mail, when the phone rang.

"I was just about to leave a second message," Nina said. "I can't believe what they said on the news, that Lenore was killed. It's so awful." Her voice quavered, and she sounded as though she was about to cry.

"They're not sure what happened, Nina."

"But if it's true . . . They said she was pregnant. She must have just found out, or she would have told me. I guess Robbie's the father, because she wasn't seeing anyone else. I guess she was trying to hold on to him."

"Did she tell you that they'd been together?"

"No. She probably thought I'd disapprove. But I wish she had, because I could have been there for her. She must have felt so alone. That's probably why she phoned me that night."

I put down my glass. "Lenore phoned you? When?"

"Late that night, or early morning. She left a message, but my machine is in the den, and I turn off the ringer in my bedroom at night so the phone won't wake me. So I didn't hear it, and I didn't see the message until morning."

I wondered why Nina hadn't mentioned this before. "What did she say?"

"That she wanted me to call Robbie and tell him to come. That she had to see him. I keep thinking that if I hadn't turned off my ringer, if I'd talked to her . . . It's so awful, isn't it? Every time I think about it, I feel like crying. I didn't go in to work, I'm so depressed."

"Maybe you should see Dr. Korwin, Nina."

"I couldn't get an appointment. The receptionist said she'd try to squeeze me in tomorrow."

I felt a twinge of guilt at having taken her spot. "Was there something you wanted to tell me, Nina?" She didn't answer. "You left a message for me."

"I'm sorry. I'm so . . . It's about Lenore's journal. The one she told you about?"

I felt a flicker of excitement. "What about it?"

"She kept a record in it of Robbie's business dealings. That was when she saw he was going through with the divorce."

"She told you this?"

"I was at her apartment one night when he called. She was

depressed and angry. She went into her bedroom to talk, but I could hear her yelling at him, saying she didn't trust him, that he kept lying to her and she knew it was Jillian's fault, but she didn't care. She was tired of his promises, she'd written it all down in her journal, everything, she could ruin him. . . ." Her voice trailed off. "Do you think I should tell the police?"

"Absolutely." I waited while she got paper and pen, and gave her Connors's name and phone number. "Do you know what she wrote?"

"I asked her, after she hung up. Names and dates, the amount of money involved. I don't know details. They wouldn't have meant anything to me, anyway. I think he must have threatened her, because she looked scared. *I* was scared. She told me she wasn't going to do it. She was just so *angry*. She wanted to worry him."

Robbie hadn't known that, I thought. Neither had the people whose names Lenore had recorded.

"That Wednesday when Lenore was in the hospital, when she was feeling better?" Nina said. "She asked me to bring her the journal."

I forced myself to sound casual. "Did you?"

"I couldn't find it, but I was in a rush to get to the hospital. I was planning to go back to look again, but then . . . then she was dead." Nina paused. "I think that's why she was so upset that night. Maybe she thought Robbie took it. That could be why she left you that message, telling you she was afraid. I don't *think* he took it, because how would he get into her apartment? And if he did, who broke in later and vandalized it?"

# CHAPTER TWENTY-SEVEN

"SALLY CAN'T MAKE IT TONIGHT," MINDY TOLD ME AS I followed her into her breakfast room. "Her husband had a last-minute business meeting, and she couldn't get a sitter."

Edie and my sister-in-law, Gitty, were seated at the table, stacking a double tier of tiles (called a "wall") against their racks. I exchanged hellos, inquired about Gitty's eight-month-old, and asked Mindy, nine months pregnant with her third child, how she was feeling.

"Put a fork in me, I'm done," Mindy said.

"Let's go," Edie said, leaning over to set up my wall. "Talk later."

Edie is thirty-four, the oldest sibling, and takes seriously the authority vested in her by her seniority. We have the same coloring—

brown eyes, blond, highlighted hair (she wears hers straight and chin length)—but she's inches shorter (five-one), and what she lacks in height, she makes up for in energy. We are polar opposites. I'm a last-minute kind of woman and tend to clutter, which I shamelessly blame on deadlines, imminent or forthcoming. Edie, who gives Israeli dance instruction three times a week and is president of her three children's school PTA, is ruthlessly efficient and organized. Magazines are alphabetized and discarded, read or unread, after a month (neatly excised articles are immediately filed). Unlike my fridge, where foods often turn interesting colors, hers harbors no produce with wilted leaves or dimpled skins, and her freezer has enough prepared food to feed the family through seven years of biblical famine. She's the only person I know who has never lost a sock, and her home is so spotless that her cardiac surgeon husband, Victor, could probably perform a triple bypass on her kitchen floor, whose five-year-old grout is bleached every week to its original whiteness.

Mindy, who has my mom's dark hair and grace under pressure, is thirty-one and has two daughters with Norman, a nursing home administrator. She's a tax attorney, not as organized as Edie, but unflappable and wise in ways that have nothing to do with her having graduated summa cum laude. I'm close to all my sisters, but Mindy's the one on whose shoulder I cried when my marriage was falling apart. I didn't want to worry my mom, and I sensed that Edie was impatient for me to sweep Ron out of my life. Like her china, shattered by the Northridge earthquake and quickly replaced, he was beyond repair.

Gitty is twenty-three. She's been married two years to my brother Judah, who owns a Judaica store, so she's relatively new to the family, and I'm sure she's received pointers from Victor and Norman. She's sweet but not cloying, a nutritionist who doesn't criticize the crap we eat at our weekly games.

Bubbie G calls Edie *a bren* (a dynamo) and Mindy, five-eight, *a hoicheh* (tall) and *a kliegeh* (clever). Liora is *a neshomeleh*, a sweet-heart. Judah is *a lamden*, an erudite person, Noah is *a brillyant*, a diamond, and Joey, *a mazik*, a rascal, a name that has stuck though he hasn't done anything rascally in years. I'm *a kochleffl*, a busybody, as if you didn't know, but am also *a lebedikeh*, a lively one. Ron is *a choleryeh* (accent on the second syllable), which is the Yiddish for "cholera." Aside from Ron, Bubbie hasn't given epithets to her grandchildren's spouses, so I suppose he should feel special.

I took my seat and built my wall. We play the American version of mah jongg, not the Chinese. It has elements of rummy-Q and gin but is more complicated and challenging. You play with fourteen tiles, which are dealt from the walls. Tiles come in three suits (red Craks, green Bams, and blue Dots), numbered one through nine. There are also eight Jokers, eight Flower tiles, sixteen Winds (four East, four North, four South, and four West), and twelve Dragons (red, green, and blue ones called Soaps).

You play the game by picking and discarding tiles, and passing a tile when a player calls it. Your goal is to assemble sets of tiles (singles or in groups of two, three, four, or five) into one of the hands created annually by the national league in New York, at which point you proclaim, "Mah jongg!" and collect winnings from the other players. Quarters to fifty cents from each player if you're playing face-card value, but the game is about fun, not money. It sounds impossibly difficult on paper, I know, and it takes a while to become familiar with the tiles and the sets and the rules. There are instruction booklets, and I could give you details, but it's like having sex. The only way to learn is to do it.

I love mah jongg. The feel of the cool, ivory tiles; the click they make when you're building them into a wall or arranging them on your rack. I love the idea that I'm doing something exotic, the smell and taste of the popcorn, the laughter and the gentle gossip and the release from the week's stress. I learned the game when I was eleven from my mom, who's been playing for over thirty years with the same core group of women. My sisters and I started our own game five years ago and Edie's friend Sally joined us a little later. Since her return from Israel, Liora has been playing sporadically, when dates and homework allow, but Gitty has become addicted like the rest of us. I rarely skip a game, only when I'm on a deadline.

I finished building my wall, and the game began. Gitty dealt tiles from her wall. There's an initial exchange of tiles, and we were all quiet, selecting possible hands. Then Gitty discarded a tile and named it, and the game took on its rhythm, each player picking a tile, discarding a tile, naming it. Five Crak, three Dot, Flower. . . . There were snippets of conversation—bulletins, really—about community news, movies we'd seen, family stuff. Talking is okay as long as it doesn't slow the game or disturb concentration.

"How was Liora's date?" Edie asked fifteen minutes later. We'd finished the first game, which she'd won, and were starting the second, exchanging tiles. "Does anybody know?"

"She'll go out again," Gitty said, "but she doesn't feel any chemistry." Gitty's only four years older than Liora, and the two have much in common.

"At least she's giving him a second chance." Edie discarded a tile. "Molly won't do that much for Zachary Abrams."

"We're going out tomorrow night."

"You didn't tell me." Edie looked up from her tiles.

"So how is he?" Mindy smiled.

"He's nice." I felt myself blushing.

"I thought you weren't going out with him again," Edie said.

"I changed my mind. When's your next appointment, Mindy?" See how smoothly I segue?

"Thursday. I'm hoping I won't be late this time, although

I'm not rushing to go to the hospital. A woman was killed there last week."

"Imagine not being safe in a hospital." Gitty shuddered.

"They're not sure it's murder," Edie said. "It may be suicide. She was pregnant."

"Why would she kill herself?" Gitty asked.

"According to the *Times* article, she had postpartum psychosis after her last child." Edie passed me three tiles. "She killed him. He was two months old."

"Oh, my God!" Gitty exclaimed. "How awful!"

"I guess she got what she deserved," Edie said.

"How can you say that?" Mindy demanded. "She was ill. She didn't know what she was doing."

Edie snorted. "Most women have postpartum depression. I did. You did. You get over it."

"We had the baby blues, not depression, certainly not psychosis. We were lucky, Edie. I have a friend who had postpartum depression. It took her a year to get over it, and that was with therapy and medication."

"Who?" Edie asked.

"What's the difference?" Mindy said, annoyed. Like Liora, she's careful about not gossiping. "She was miserable. She never slept, and she had these fears that she was going to put the baby in the microwave, which made her feel horribly guilty. That's when she knew she needed help."

I winced at the image.

"Exactly," Edie said. "You get help. You don't kill your child. That's just another excuse the lawyers are using."

"She was depressed, not psychotic. And what if you don't know you *need* help?" Mindy demanded. "It's easy for you to say—you've never been there."

"Well, you certainly don't get pregnant again if you can't

handle being a mother." Edie, as you may have guessed, would easily pull the lever on Andrea Yates.

"Actually, I talked to Lenore Saunders's ex-husband," I said. "He says Lenore *was* ill, that she really didn't mean to kill their child."

That stopped the game. I told them the whole story, from the time I'd read about Lenore in the police report through my afternoon talk with Connors.

"So what do the police think?" Gitty asked.

"They think she committed suicide, but I'm not sure. I also don't know what to make of Lenore. Her best friend thinks she walks on water. Jillian says she's a scheming, manipulative witch."

"Well, of *course* Jillian hates her." Edie made a face. "She was about to be dumped a second time. She sounds like a snob."

"She reminds me of Karen Beymer," Mindy said. "She was in charge of seating for the school banquet this year and offered to put me at a great table. I said, please put me with Sally and Helene, and she said, *well,* if you want to sit with your *pauper* friends." She wrinkled her nose.

We all groaned, then resumed play.

"What about the ex-mother-in-law?" Edie asked, discarding a tile. "Six Crak. She might not have wanted Lenore back in the family."

I remembered the look of intense hatred I'd seen on Maureen Saunders's face. "She's on my shortlist. I want to talk to Lenore's mom about her, and about Lenore, but we've been playing phone tag the past few days." I'd dialed her number several times before coming to Mindy's, but her line had been busy. She was probably making funeral arrangements. "I want to stop by her house on my way home."

"Five Dot." Mindy tossed a tile onto the table. "That late?"

"I want the five Dot." Edie placed the tile on the ledge of

her rack and added two five Dots from her hand, then discarded a tile. "Eight Crak."

"Actually, I was thinking of leaving a quarter to ten," I said, discarding a Flower. "She lives five minutes from here." Nina had given me the address, on Stearns between Olympic and Pico.

"And ruin the game?" Edie frowned.

"Sorry." We usually play until eleven. "I thought Sally would be here. I'm really anxious to talk to Lenore's mom about Saunders."

"Is he the Saunders who wants to build a large complex in the Santa Monica Mountains?" Mindy asked.

I nodded. "Why?"

"One of my clients invested with him, but was thinking of pulling out. He heard that Saunders is having trouble with the EPA."

"The environmental guys? I thought it was the zoning commission."

"Can we talk later, please?" Edie said.

"Maybe it's both," Mindy said. "Saunders told him not to worry. Apparently, he has a magic touch."

"Or he knows what palms to grease." I thought about what Nina had said. "Would your client be willing to talk to me?"

"I'll ask him."

Gitty picked a tile. "Mah jongg."

"I was one away," Edie groused.

The lights in Betty Rowan's house were on, a blue Honda Civic was in the driveway, but she didn't answer the door.

Her line had been busy when I'd phoned before leaving Mindy's. I tried her number again now on my cell phone. Still busy. A little late to be making funeral calls.

Twenty-four hours had passed since she'd phoned, anxious to talk to me. Maybe I'd read anxiety into her voice. Maybe her phone was out of order, or off the hook. Maybe she'd changed her mind about talking to me, or someone had changed it for her.

It was ten after ten. I walked to the house of the neighbor on the right and rang the bell. A minute later the privacy window opened, and a man asked me what I wanted.

"I'm sorry to disturb you," I said. "I've been trying to reach Mrs. Rowan since last night, and her line's been busy. I'm wondering if you've seen her today."

"Let me ask my wife."

I waited another minute for the wife, who told me through the privacy window that she hadn't seen Betty since yesterday afternoon.

"She lost her daughter," the woman said. "I expect she's feeling poorly. Maybe she doesn't want to talk to anyone."

A feeling of unease was creeping up my spine. "Do you by any chance have a key to her house?"

"I don't. You can try the neighbor on the other side, Zena Lopost. She and Betty are friendly. I hope she's okay," the woman added before shutting the little window.

I hoped so, too. The unease was spreading like an oil slick.

Zena Lopost had a key. "We thought it'd be a good idea, swapping keys, in case one of us got locked out or something. Why, is something wrong?"

From her voice I guessed she was somewhere around Betty Rowan's age. "I don't know." I repeated what I'd told the other neighbor. "Mrs. Rowan left several messages saying she needed to talk to me about her daughter, Lenore. So I'm worried."

Zena opened her door. She was older than her voice, probably in her mid-fifties. She was wearing a short zip-up, yellow cotton robe with white daisies and Dr. Scholl sandals. Her faded graying brown hair was in a braid that hung down her back, and her plain face was scrubbed free of makeup, if in fact she'd worn any. She told me she'd been in bed when I'd rung the bell.

"She was jittery yesterday," Zena said. "More than Friday. I was watching the TV with her when they said on the news that maybe Lenore was killed. She looked white as a sheet and started shaking. I don't know what's worse, knowing that your child killed herself, or that someone did it to her."

I had no answer for that.

"You're thinking that . . ." Zena didn't finish the sentence. "Let me get the key."

She was a tall, sturdy woman, and I was glad to have her at my side. We tramped over to Betty Rowan's house, two figures silhouetted by the moonlight. We hadn't exchanged a word since she'd stepped out of her house, and I imagine we looked the same, eyes staring grimly straight ahead, lips clamped together, hearts beating a little too fast.

Zena Lopost inserted the key, her hand steadier than mine would have been. She turned the knob, and the door groaned open as we stepped into a small living room, the way it does in a horror movie. Maybe it would've been funny under other circumstances, but it wasn't funny now.

The house was frigid with air-conditioning. Zena called Betty's name, then called her again, louder and shriller, I thought, the sounds echoing in the high-ceilinged room. We looked at each other then, communicating our unspoken fear, nodding. She followed me down a narrow hall through an empty bedroom into an adjoining bath, where Betty Rowan lay in the tub, the blood from one slashed wrist pinking the water while the other dangled over the side of the tub, fingers pointing to the spattered dark magenta drops and pink-handled razor on the black-and-white-tiled floor.

# CHAPTER TWENTY-EIGHT

*Tuesday, July 22. 1:01 A.M. 4200 block of Fountain Avenue.
An assailant told the victim, "You better go with us on a drive-
by. You don't have to do anything but you have to be in the car
with us. If you don't I'll kill you or your mother." (Hollywood)*

I DON'T THINK I'VE EVER BEEN AS TIRED AS WHEN I GOT
home from the station. I'd phoned Connors, even though Betty
Rowan's house was in Wilshire Division's jurisdiction. Zena and
I sat like statues on the living room sofa while we waited for him
to show up, which was five minutes after two uniformed police
and about ten minutes after the paramedics, although from the
smell in the room and the quick look I stole at Betty's grayed
face before I gagged and backed away, almost knocking Zena

down, I could tell she'd been dead some time. The coroner's van arrived half an hour later.

"Like mother, like daughter," Zena had said.

Connors didn't say anything sassy when he saw me. In fact, he didn't say much at all, which isn't like him. Maybe he was too tired, or maybe the look on my face made him think better of it. I introduced him to Zena, who explained how she had a key to Betty's house. He had me tell him why I'd come here tonight, something I'd already told the two cops from Wilshire and repeated to the Wilshire detective when he showed up a while later. Connors had phoned them.

"When was the last time you spoke to Mrs. Rowan?" the detective asked me. His name was Dobbins and he was in his thirties, with crew-cut brown hair and brown eyes, not as tall as Connors but wider.

"Thursday morning, at the hospital," I said. "We exchanged voice messages after that. She phoned me sometime on Saturday. I returned her call Sunday morning, but she wasn't in. She phoned me again Sunday afternoon or early evening. When I tried reaching her, her line was busy. I phoned again that night, then several times today."

"What made you think something was wrong?"

"Sunday morning Mrs. Rowan said she wanted to talk to me as soon as possible, in person. Sunday afternoon her message said it had to do with the call her daughter Lenore made to me before she died, and something I should know. But she never called again, and her line was constantly busy Sunday night, and several times when I tried her today." I didn't mention that during the marathon phone call with Zack I'd ignored several call-waiting beeps.

"But you didn't worry until tonight?"

I felt a flush crawling up my face like a spider's legs. "I

thought she was busy making funeral plans, or telling people what had happened."

"You tried to reach her," Connors said. "You couldn't have known."

I looked at him with gratitude. He knew what I was thinking—that history had repeated itself, that once again some-one had reached out to me and I hadn't been there.

Dobbins took Connors into the dining room, where they talked for a few minutes. When they returned, Dobbins questioned Zena. Had Betty said anything about wanting to kill herself?

"To tell the truth," Zena said, "I don't think they were all that close, especially since the baby died. The daughter visited only a few times after she moved back from Santa Barbara, and Betty didn't talk much about her. She took it hard—what happened to her grandson, and all." The woman sighed. "I saw the daughter about a month before she had the baby. She looked fine, but I guess she was depressed, even then. It just shows how you can't tell about people."

"So would you say that Mrs. Rowan wasn't depressed about her daughter's death?" Dobbins asked.

"When your child dies, it hurts." Zena stared at him with disapproval. "She wasn't carrying on, but that's not her style. She was quiet. I took her to supper Thursday night, and she didn't even seem to know I was there. She had a lot on her mind. She was worse when she heard them saying maybe Lenore was killed." Zena repeated what she'd told me.

"Did Mrs. Rowan mention having an argument with any-one?" Dobbins asked.

Zena shook her head. "Like I said, she was a quiet woman. Kept to herself."

"Had anyone threatened her?"

"Not that I know." She frowned. "Are you saying someone killed her?"

"We have to investigate all possibilities," Dobbins said. He disappeared down the hall and into the bathroom, where someone from the coroner's office was examining Betty Rowan's body.

Connors walked me to my car. "You're awfully quiet," he said. "You okay? Considering."

"Just thinking."

The lamplight cast half his face in shadow. "Don't beat yourself up about this, Molly. I meant what I said. You couldn't have known."

"I keep telling myself that. It's not helping."

"She phoned the station, Molly. Sunday evening. She asked to talk to me, said it was important."

I stared at him. "Did she say why?"

Connors shook his head. "I got her message and phoned her. She told me she'd just heard that maybe Lenore had been murdered, and she was afraid. I asked her why. She wouldn't say. I asked her was there someone specific she was afraid of. She said no. She asked could I send some cops to protect her. I said I was sorry, but we didn't have the manpower for that. I said maybe she should sleep at a friend's for a few nights, and she said maybe she would. I called her back an hour later, and her machine was on, so I figured that's what she did. When I called again in the morning, her line was busy, so I thought she was okay."

I didn't say anything for a while, and Connors didn't either.

"Did Nina Weldon call you?" I asked. "I gave her your number."

"Lenore's best friend?" Connors nodded. "She told me Lenore's journal was missing on Wednesday. So?"

I hesitated. "I think Betty Rowan had the journal. I think someone knew it and killed her for it and made it look like suicide." I looked at him, defiant.

"Me, too. Surprised you, didn't I?" He had a hint of a smile under eyes that were bloodshot. He needed a shave.

"Did you find evidence that someone looked through her things?"

"Not yet, but that just means whoever did it was careful. Keep that to yourself, okay?" he said with a mild attempt at his usual scowl. I guess he was too tired, too sad. "What else is on your mind?"

"Betty and Lenore, the fact that they weren't close. Mrs. O'Day said so. So did Zena. Nina said Lenore was upset because Betty and Saunders were thick."

He leaned against my car door. "Lenore killed Betty's grandson, Molly. Whether she was mentally ill or not, it's hard to forgive something like that."

"Exactly my point. They were practically estranged. But Betty Rowan was at the hospital almost all day."

"What that Lopost woman said. When it came down to it, she was still a mother. I can buy that."

"I'm not so sure. When I talked to her after Lenore died, I had the feeling she was mostly worried about what Lenore might have told me when she was sedated."

"Like what?"

"Stuff about Saunders, about Max. The whole mess." I waved my hand. "I think Saunders asked Betty to keep an eye on Lenore. Which explains why he gave her the key."

Connors shook his head. "You've lost me."

"Lenore's key?" I said patiently. "The one she must have left at Saunders's house? He gave it to Betty."

"Maybe Lenore gave Betty a key."

"Not if they were barely speaking. And if she had a key, why would Lenore ask Nina to pick up stuff from her apartment? Nina had to ask the O'Days to let her in. Why not ask her mother?"

Connors sighed. "And we know Betty had a key because . . . ?"

"Mrs. O'Day told me Betty was about to go into Lenore's apartment on Thursday."

"The day *after* the journal was missing, according to this Nina," Connors pointed out.

"She was there Wednesday, too. I called Mrs. O'Day."

"Well, why go back Thursday if she already had the damn journal?"

I was so tired. "Maybe Betty wanted to make sure Lenore hadn't written anything else incriminating."

"Possible." Connors didn't sound convinced.

"Or with Lenore dead, maybe Saunders asked her to make it look as though someone had burglarized the apartment."

He shook his head. "You saw the place. I can't buy the mom doing it."

I couldn't either. I was stumped.

"If Saunders had the key, why didn't he just go to Lenore's apartment himself?" Connors asked.

"And risk being seen? The O'Days saw Betty and didn't think twice about it. And Saunders *trusted* Betty. She'd been loyal to him, not Lenore. Betty was living in one of his houses rent free, and he was helping her out financially. That's what Nina told me."

"Suppose you're right," Connors said. "Saunders gave her the key, asked her to get the journal and maybe some other papers. Why would he kill her for it? That doesn't fit."

"It does if she read it and decided to keep it for insurance. With Lenore dead, maybe Saunders wouldn't be so generous."

Connors raised a brow. "So she was going to blackmail him?"

"Or someone else. Lenore wrote stuff in the journal about other people. Names and dates and the dollars involved."

"So who trashed the apartment?"

"You're the detective. Figure it out." I yawned and covered my mouth. "I'm going home."

He moved away from the car. "I'll follow you and check out your place."

I inhaled sharply. "You think I'm in danger?"

"Your name and phone number are on a pad on her night-stand, Molly, next to her phone. We spotted it, so the killer proba-bly did, too. Suppose he worries that Betty Rowan told you what's in the journal."

Fear formed a lump in my chest. "But we never connected."

"He doesn't know that."

Connors made me wait in his unmarked vehicle while he searched my apartment. He made me promise to double-lock my door, which I always do, and keep my windows locked, something I rarely do on nights like this when the outside tem-perature is cool but the room hasn't shaken off the day's heat. He also gave me his cell and home numbers.

"Call any time, even if it's something small," he said, which made me even more nervous.

After he left and the doors and windows were locked, I looked around the apartment. Nothing seemed disturbed, but could I be sure?

# CHAPTER TWENTY-NINE

THE ROAD TO TWENTYNINE PALMS IS PAVED WITH MILES of freeway. I left the house at nine, hoping to avoid rush-hour traffic, and took the 10 east. Once past downtown L.A., where the overpasses and underpasses of several freeways contort like an octopus's arms gone mad, I was making eighty to ninety, checking frequently for Chippies who might want to impede my progress.

It's a little less than a four-hour drive to Twentynine Palms, which is northeast of Palm Springs in the Mojave Desert's Morongo Basin. At least that's what the Mapquest directions showed, but I knew I'd make better time. I passed the Cal State L.A. campus, its initials carved into the steep green lawn; Covina and West Covina, Pomona. When you're driving eighty-plus miles an hour, this stretch of highway is a blur of car dealerships, shopping malls, office buildings, and movie theaters. Not a post-card picture of America the beautiful, though I was pleased to see they'd taken down the billboard advertising a recently closed Swedish massage parlor, fronting for a brothel, that had bordered a Pomona public elementary school. But my thoughts weren't on the scenery, and I was barely aware of the music from the radio.

They say if you want to find out who killed someone, you have to begin with the someone. Last night I'd suggested to Connors that Betty Rowan had been killed because she'd been planning to blackmail one or more people. In the light of day I'd pondered the presumption of my statement. The truth was, after seven days of talking to numerous people, I knew little about Lenore, about whom I'd heard conflicting opinions, and less about her mother, who I'd hoped could enlighten me. And now Betty was dead, too.

"Like mother, like daughter." Zena Lopost had said it when she'd seen Betty's body. Jillian had said the same thing, making a mean-spirited aspersion I couldn't accept at face value. Still, the phrase echoed in my mind and I wondered if it was true.

I was also trying to work out why, if Betty Rowan had the journal in her possession on Wednesday, she'd wanted to get into her daughter's apartment on Thursday. And why she'd phoned me again and again. Every time I thought I had it figured out, it fell apart in my head like a meringue. But thinking about it did make the drive seem shorter. When I looked at the clock again I was surprised to see that almost two hours had passed and I was nearing Palm Springs.

I'd been aware some time ago that the terrain had changed. Aside from the Cabazon shopping outlet that beckoned tempt-ingly on my left, there was mostly flat desert decorated with tall billboards every hundred feet or so advertising gambling on

Indian reservations, spas, and hotels. In the background were wide-hipped, reddish-brown mountains, and hundreds of small windmills exuberantly twirling with the grace and precision of Bob Fosse dancers. I had to grip the steering wheel as the wind buffeted the Acura, which is no lightweight, spraying the car with dust and gravel that was probably giving the exterior serious acne.

I turned off the 10 onto the 62. The scenery was stark here, miles and miles of sand dunes broken up mainly by highway signs that reassured me I was heading toward Twentynine Palms. I hummed along to some oldies ("Dream Lover," "Pretty Woman," "House of the Rising Sun"), and forty-five minutes later I parked in the lot of the high school Lenore had attended, a collection of eight or nine one-story, green-trimmed white buildings with palm trees on lawns of sand.

I stepped out of the car and was slapped by the desert air— 118 degrees, according to the Acura's gauge (two degrees higher than the *Times*'s prediction). People who live here and in other desert climates like Phoenix or Tucson will tell you the heat is dry and more tolerable, but hot is hot. I was wearing a scoop-necked, cap-sleeved white cotton blouse and a short tan skirt, but I felt as though I'd stepped into an oven. I hurried inside the first building, which housed the administration. I don't think Hansel or Gretel moved faster.

I'd phoned the school before leaving this morning and confirmed that a skeleton custodial staff was still around in the summer, along with the principal, Dr. Virginia Yawley, with whom I'd made an appointment, and her secretary. I was ten minutes early, but Virginia was available.

She was dressed in an elbow-length navy print blouse and navy skirt, and reminded me of a bird with her thin arms and legs and sharp, pointed nose and beaklike chin. Her short hair was gray, her skin heavily lined either from age—I put her in her sixties—or the brutal sun.

"You made good time," she remarked when I was seated in front of her desk. Her voice was birdlike, too. Thin and chirpy. "You wanted to talk to me about Lenore Rowan?"

I gave her my basic c.v. and told her I was writing about Lenore. "I need background information, and since she attended this school, I thought I'd start here."

Virginia sighed. "We heard that Lenore died under tragic circumstances. Her mother stays in touch with a few people here. I understand that the police are investigating Lenore's death as a possible homicide?"

"They're not certain. It may be a suicide." I hesitated. "I'm sorry to tell you Mrs. Rowan died last night. The police are investigating her death, too."

"Well," the principal said after a long moment. She sighed again. "Do they think the deaths are related?"

"I don't know."

She peered at me. "So you're here investigating, correct? That's why you're interested in Lenore's background information." Her tone was stern.

"Yes." I felt as though I were back in high school myself, about to be suspended. Which had happened a few times.

"They called me when she killed her son. The media, I mean." Her sharp look indicated that she included me with "them." "What was she like? Was she violent in school? Was she depressed? Did I sense she'd be involved in a tragedy like this?"

I waited, my open notepad idle on my lap.

"This is a small school, just under nine hundred students. I'd like to think I knew Lenore well. If you want me to say I thought she'd amount to trouble, I'm afraid you'll be disappointed. She was an extremely bright, ambitious, charming, talented young woman. I liked her very much and I'm saddened by her death," she said quietly.

"Was she popular?"

Virginia took a moment before she answered. "I wouldn't call her *popular*. She was beautiful—quite striking, actually. Some of the girls were jealous, but that's inevitable, don't you think? She was close with one or two," she added.

"What about boyfriends?"

"The boys chased after her. She dated quite a few, usually those several grades ahead of her, but my guess is she found most of them immature. And she was focused on what she wanted."

"What was that?"

"To leave Twentynine Palms. A lot of the kids leave, but most of them come back. Lenore didn't." Virginia gazed out the window at the open vista, probably trying to figure out what Lenore had found missing. "I came this way thirty years ago to visit Joshua Tree National Park and I stayed, because of my asthma, and because I wanted a simpler, less crowded life. It took me a while to adjust to the fact that there's no grass, just sand and brush and creosote. I thought the houses were all ugly." She shook her head. "But now I love it here. The stark beauty of nature all around you, the sense of community, the clean air, warm though it is." She smiled at me mischievously. "There's nothing like sunrise here, or the night sky. It's spectacular, stars so brilliant and so close you can practically touch them. I've sat on my deck and watched that sky thousands of times, and every time it catches my breath. It would be worth your while to stay overnight just to see it. Have you been to the park?"

I shook my head. It's on my list, which is pretty long.

"You should make the time and go. It's in our backyard, but we don't take it for granted. The boulders, the mountains, the cacti and wildflowers, the Joshua trees. They're short, stubby things with their arms reaching up to the sky. That's how the

Mormons named them, you know. Because the Israelites were victorious when Joshua's arms were raised." She glanced out the window again. "There's something spiritual about desert life, seeing God's grandeur. It's like witnessing the Creation. Most of us who live here feel that way. But I guess it's not for everyone."

I followed her gaze. Blue skies, endless open spaces ringed by mountains. I suppose that for some people, like Lenore, all that open space can box you in.

"Of course, we're tiny compared to L.A.," Virginia said. "Around twenty-six thousand, including the annexed housing of the marine base. And except for summer, we're swarming with tourists and Hollywood folk who come here to film pictures and commercials. But we're growing. Most of the marine families stay here after they're out of the service. We have a two-year college, fully accredited. That's where Lenore went. And we do have *some* culture. An artists' colony, galleries, a theater, restaurants, espresso bars. Even a drive-in movie." She smiled again, having her fun. "Maybe on your way home you can drive around and look at the murals painted on the buildings. They depict the history of Twentynine Palms and the people who settled it."

"How did the city get its name?" I asked, curious and wanting to please.

"A Colonel Henry Washington surveyed the area in 1855 and counted twenty-nine palm trees. A good thing he didn't see two hundred twenty-nine or some such." The principal chuckled. "But you didn't come for a history lesson. You're here about Lenore." She was all seriousness now. "She was happy enough growing up here, but she craved city life. Or I should say, her mother did."

"Mrs. Rowan pushed Lenore to leave?"

Virginia hesitated. "I don't know if you're familiar with Lenore's family history." She sounded wary.

"I know that her father left when she was an infant. I think that's why she married someone nine years older."

She nodded. "Betty was in my first graduating class. Her father was stationed at the marine base here. The mother worked in town in a doctor's office. Betty hated living here. She was counting the days till she could get out and all she talked about was moving to L.A. She'd skip school to watch the Hollywood people. I think she was hoping to be discovered. She was pretty enough, though not as striking as Lenore. After high school she took a job in one of the ritzy Palm Springs hotels as a desk clerk. That's where she met her husband. He was from Denver and vacationed in Palm Springs with his family every winter. Six months later she was married, and they moved to L.A."

"I understand that she was pregnant when they married," I said.

The principal gave me another one of those ruler-rapping looks. "For someone looking for background, you seem to know the important parts," she said dryly. "Supposedly Lenore was premature. There was gossip, but I can't say. In any case, the marriage didn't last long, as you know. I heard her husband didn't take to marriage or babies, and his family pressured him to divorce Betty. Lenore never said, but I think Betty made her feel it was her fault her father left. I'm always amazed by the burdens parents will place on their children." Virginia sighed.

"Why did Betty come back here if she hated it?"

"The husband went back to Denver and wouldn't send money. There was some talk he didn't believe Lenore was his, but I don't know that was so. Betty couldn't make it on her own, not with a baby to feed, so she moved back in with her parents for a few months, and then she was off again somewhere with some other man."

"And Lenore stayed with the grandparents?"

"They had Betty late in life, so they were older. They didn't want the responsibility." The principal's pursed lips showed what she thought. "Lenore was put in foster care. Betty came home a few months later and took Lenore back. She rented an apartment. Less than half a year later she left again, and Lenore was placed with another family. That went on for about five or six years. Betty would come back and take Lenore, then she'd get restless and disappear. Eventually she stayed, but she was always itching to get out. She finally did, for good, when Lenore married. She told her friends all about the house Lenore's husband bought her."

I tried to imagine what Lenore had felt like, being shunted from foster home to foster home, having her mother in her life one minute, gone the next. "Was Lenore depressed when you knew her?"

Virginia puckered her already wrinkled forehead. "I wouldn't say *depressed*. Pensive, maybe, like she had the world on her shoulders, although sometimes she was just a bundle of energy. It's amazing, with all that she went through, that she ended up normal, and she was determined not to let her past hold her down. But she wasn't carefree like the other girls." She hesitated. "There was talk that something had happened at one of the foster homes. Something with the father."

I felt a wave of revulsion. "Lenore was molested?"

She nodded. "And Betty was strict with her when she was in high school, maybe because she didn't want Lenore making the same mistake she'd made. I guess it didn't help, though. Lenore ended up chasing the wrong dreams and drinking from a cup full of sorrow, just like her mother. Now they're both dead."

# CHAPTER THIRTY

"I HAVEN'T TALKED TO LENORE IN YEARS," CATHY JOHN-son told me. "I was shocked to hear she killed herself. And now her mother's gone, too. It's all too much to take in."

Virginia Yawley had phoned Cathy, Lenore's best friend in high school, and the woman had agreed to talk with me. I'd driven to her white house, one of a cluster of white houses on large lots landscaped with sand and scrub and cacti. Between this cluster and the next was empty land. Blue skies above, the mountains around you. People in Twentynine Palms, Virginia had told me, liked their space, and their nature untouched. A city or-dinance regulated what kind of lights could be used, and what wattage, and how that light should be directed to protect the brilliance of the night sky, and no one minded.

People who live in the desert also buy mostly white cars, I'd noticed, and I understood why each time I got into my black Acura. The first time, leaving the high school, I'd made the mistake of sitting down before allowing the air-conditioning to cool off the interior, and the leather seat had practically broiled the undersides of my bare thighs.

We were sitting in Cathy's kitchen, the air cooler than outside but not cold. They used an evaporative cooler, not air-conditioning, she explained as she handed me a glass of refrigerated water. It worked like a swamp cooler, running air over water.

She was the girl in Lenore's photos, now a housewife and the mother of two—a three-year-old girl in nursery, and a newborn asleep in his crib. She had bags under her blue eyes, her brown hair needed a trim, and she'd apparently forgotten about the burp cloth that lay like an epaulet on her shoulder over a yellow blouse ballooned by her breasts.

"I have more milk than a cow," she told me happily.

Her husband was an engineer and worked on the marine base. Her father, a retired marine, did data processing for a firm in town. Her mother was a dental receptionist. After a year of community college Cathy had moved to San Diego, but returned six months later and couldn't imagine living anywhere else.

"I should've written to Lenore when her baby died," she said. "I didn't know what to say. We were best friends in high school, but once she got engaged, we drifted apart. I tried to keep up, but she stopped returning my calls. To tell you the truth, I was a little hurt."

"What was she like?"

"High energy, didn't need much sleep. Disgustingly bright. She'd get all A's without even studying. It wasn't fair." Cathy smiled. "She was real talented, too. She liked writing poetry. And she usually got the leads in the play productions. Some kids bitched that the drama teacher favored her, but I was happy for

Lenore. Her life was tough, what with having no dad and being in foster homes when she was a kid, and her mom never having money for extras. I think acting was a way for her to forget all that."

I recalled the books on acting I'd seen in Lenore's apartment. Maybe she'd been trying to escape the pain of her reality again—Max's death and everything that had followed.

"And she worked hard at it," Cathy said. "I remember one time she played Helen Keller in *The Miracle Worker*. She read books and books about her and watched the movie a hundred times. She wanted to get it just right. When you watched her perform, you would've sworn she was blind. Another time she played Elizabeth Proctor in *The Crucible*. She read up on the Puritans—what they ate, how they dressed, how they talked. That was her favorite play. She probably would've gone into acting if she hadn't married."

"Mrs. Yawley said some of the girls were jealous of Lenore."

Cathy nodded. "Well, she was beautiful and brilliant and all the guys were mooning over her. Your first instinct was to hate her, and if you didn't know her, you'd think she was aloof. I did, at first."

I took a sip of water. "Was she depressed, Cathy?"

She grimaced. "Who wouldn't be with a mother like that?"

"They didn't get along?"

"It was more one-sided. Mrs. Rowan was rough on her, and she'd always be throwing it in Lenore's face that she had to support her on her own. 'If your daddy hadn't left, I coulda this, I coulda that.' 'I don't know why I came back to get you, you're nothing but trouble.' Stuff like that. I'd hear her yelling in the background when Lenore and I were on the phone. One time Lenore stayed out past curfew, and her mom came to find her. She called her a slut in front of everyone. 'If I'd known what trouble you were going to be, I would've given you up for adoption, and your daddy'd still be around.' Probably wasn't the first time she said that."

Basically, what Virginia Yawley had suspected. "Lenore told you this?"

"We all heard it. There was a group of us at Denny's—four couples, including Lenore and Pete Riggs. It wasn't even late. Lenore's mom dragged her home, and Lenore didn't come to school the next day, she was so mortified. And of course, that ended it with Pete."

I had come home late one time after a date—a date with Zack, as a matter of fact. My parents had been waiting up for me, and the worried look on their faces had been enough to stop me from being late again without calling. "Her mother didn't trust her?"

Cathy turned her head toward the kitchen doorway. "He's up," she said, rising from her chair. "I thought I heard something. It gets so's you hear the tiniest cry, and your breasts start filling up. Isn't that amazing?"

She left the room and returned a few minutes later cradling a baby wearing a blue bottom-snapping T-shirt with a Donald Duck print. A moment later she was seated, the baby sucking noisily at her breast, his dark fuzz-covered head all but hidden inside her blouse. She made it look so easy, so natural. I couldn't help thinking about Lenore.

"I don't know if it was a trust thing," Cathy said. "I think Mrs. Rowan was afraid Lenore would waste herself on someone who wasn't *worthy*." She stroked her baby's head.

"Like Pete?"

"Like any of the guys Lenore dated. And there were plenty. She was with a new guy every time you blinked. They were nice enough but . . ." She looked at me and shrugged.

"They weren't rich?"

Cathy nodded. "Or not rich *enough*. I guess it's because Mrs.

Rowan had a hard life. After a while, that's what Lenore was looking for, too. Money, and a way to get out of Twentynine Palms. In college Lenore went on dates with guys she had no intention of marrying. They were wild about her, bought her expensive presents, more than they could afford. But it was never enough. She had higher goals."

The baby made a large, snorting sound.

Cathy removed him from her breast. "He drinks too fast and takes in too much air. Silly goose," she cooed. She held him up in a sitting position facing me, his lips ringed with white like in one of those "Got Milk?" ads, his eyes sealed in a contented half sleep, his tiny chest rising and falling. She patted his rounded back until he rewarded her with a large burp.

"Do you think Lenore loved her husband?" I asked after Cathy had returned the baby to her breast.

"Totally. She was obsessed with him. He was what she'd been looking for her whole life." Cathy hesitated. "But the money was definitely a part of it. I hate saying that, because she was my friend." She looked uncomfortable. "She visited once soon after she started working for him. She was staying with her mom for Easter. She kept talking about how wonderful and smart he was, and how he had this home and the other, and how much money his family had, how her mom was so thrilled."

"So Mrs. Rowan had met him?"

"No. She didn't have to. Mrs. Rowan wouldn't have minded if Lenore had married a three-armed convict as long as he had money. Lenore told me her mom was always thinking of ways to get rich. It's sad, isn't it?"

"Very sad," I agreed, thinking about the journal and blackmail. I wondered again why Betty Rowan had phoned me repeatedly, why on the last call she'd sounded anxious.

"The next time she came was after they were engaged," Cathy said. "She told me about the fancy engagement party they'd had at some country club, and where Robbie was taking her for their honeymoon, and the jewelry he'd bought her. She was like a kid who'd never been in a candy store."

I thought about Jillian's claim that Lenore had manipulated Robbie. "Did she mention during the first visit that he was engaged?"

Cathy looked startled. "No. Was he?"

I nodded. "Did she tell you she was pregnant?"

"Yeah. She kind of laughed about it, said something like, 'Well, I guess I'm not so different from my mom after all.' The funny thing is, I didn't think Lenore wanted kids. She wasn't comfortable around them, never wanted to earn extra money babysitting. I guess she changed her mind, or she got stuck."

Mrs. O'Day had said that Lenore always asked about her grandchildren. Maybe losing a child had changed her. "So you don't think she would have tried to trap Robbie by getting pregnant?"

Jillian's other claim, and I'd asked fully expecting Cathy to refute it, but she didn't answer right away.

"Lenore was very determined, very focused," Cathy finally said, uncomfortable again. "If that was the only way she could get him. . . . She'd waited a long time for him to come into her life, and from the way she talked, I think she would've done anything to hold on to him."

I'd enjoyed painting Jillian completely in the black and wasn't happy having to acknowledge that she might have been right about Lenore.

"I called her once after she had the baby," Cathy said. "I got the number from Mrs. Rowan. Lenore sounded like she was going to cry. She told me she didn't feel like getting up in the morning, and how did I do it? I'm sorry now I didn't call again."

"Do you think Lenore would kill herself?"

"She tried twice before, didn't she? That's what the newspapers said." Cathy sighed. "But now they're saying maybe she was murdered. I've never known anyone before who was murdered. Well, there was this woman in Twentynine Palms who was killed by a marine. Some lady wrote about it in a book that made us all sound like a bunch of hoodlums and lowlifes."

Virginia Yawley had mentioned the book. "I hope you're not going to paint the wrong picture of our town," she'd said, and I'd assured her that wasn't my intention.

"My mom used to play this song all the time," Cathy said. " 'The Lady from 29 Palms.' Did you ever hear it?"

I shook my head.

"It's real popular here, as you can imagine. It's on the town's Web site." She smiled. "I don't know who wrote it, but a few people recorded it. My mom has the one with the Andrews Sisters. Anyway, it's about this lady from Twentynine Palms who's real seductive and has twenty-nine Cadillacs and twenty-nine fur coats and diamond rings from twenty-nine guys whose hearts she's broken and who can't get to first base with her. Well, you get the picture." She smiled again. "But the point is, even though this lady gets gifts from all these guys and doesn't give anything in return, she doesn't sound happy." She bent down and nuzzled her baby's head with her lips.

"Whenever I hear that song, I think of Lenore."

# Chapter Thirty-one

"Your mail was open again," Isaac said. "I told Ernie, and he said it was probably kids. And your boyfriend was here."

"Oh, shit!" Shit, shit, shit.

"It's no biggie, Molly," Isaac soothed. "Just one envelope. I'll try to be on the lookout tomorrow when Ernie comes. Go put your packages away, and I'll get your mail."

I looked at my watch. 6:05. Zack had said he'd pick me up at five-fifteen. My packages—three large bags filled with finds from the Anne Klein, Banana Republic, and BCBG Cabazon outlet stores—were only part of the reason I was late. After leaving Cathy Johnson's house, I'd detoured through town to take in some of the murals Virginia Yawley had recommended. The ones I saw were huge—larger than I'd imagined and impressive—but I was too pensive to do them justice. Back on the 10 a while later, the Cabazon shops, on my right this time, so accessible, had promised mindless comfort and possible bargains.

And I'd forgotten all about the date.

Dropping the bags on my living room floor, I unbuttoned my blouse as I ran into the bedroom and searched my desk for the slip of paper on which I'd written down Zack's cell phone number. By the time I found it, I was in my underwear and he was at my front door.

"I'm *so* sorry I'm late," I told him through the privacy window.

"I heard about Mrs. Rowan this morning, and you weren't answering your phone all day, and you weren't home when I showed up. I didn't know what to think."

I do believe honesty is generally the best policy, but there are exceptions. I could explain that so much had happened since Sunday, that my head had been filled all day with thoughts of Lenore and Betty Rowan. All true, but egos are delicate things, and I didn't want to risk having him think I didn't care about him, because I really did.

So I blamed it on traffic.

"I was in Twentynine Palms, interviewing people," I explained. "I didn't have your phone number with me." That much was true.

"As long as you're okay," he said, which made me feel worse. "Are you going to let me in?"

"I'm in my underwear."

"I guess that's a no."

"Give me fifteen minutes."

I was ready in thirteen—shower, makeup, hair, a spritz of Jean Paul Gautier at my throat and behind my ears and knees. And clothes, of course. A baby blue short-sleeved silk sweater with a square neckline, a short black silk skirt, and black high-heeled one-strap sandals that give me sexy calves and blisters and a better workout than my treadmill at a twelve-degree incline. I figure it's a draw.

"Definitely worth the wait," he said when I opened the door. Then his eyes went from me to the packages I'd dropped on the floor, the ones that said CABAZON.

On the drive to the restaurant, he asked about my interviews, but I could tell he was making conversation and not really listening. I gave him credit for trying. With our reservation long gone, we had to stand twenty-five minutes in a waiting area the size of a telephone booth crammed with other hopefuls, one of whom stepped on the unprotected toes of my right foot and brought tears to my eyes.

By the time we were seated, it was ten after seven. Another twenty-five minutes elapsed before the apologetic waiter brought the tuna Nicoise salads we'd ordered hoping we'd be served quickly because Zack had to be in shul by 8:05. Which left us ten minutes to eat, before a couple came over to our table and greeted Zack. I recognized their faces—they'd been at my wedding—but didn't remember their names. My right foot was throbbing with pain.

"Great sermon, Rabbi," the husband said. While he and Zack chatted, his wife looked at me quizzically, trying to place me. A second later she did.

"It's Milly, right?" she said. "Nice to see you."

"Molly. Nice to see you, too."

She tapped her husband's arm. "They want to eat, George. You can talk with Rabbi Abrams in shul." She smiled at me knowingly and led him away.

"I'm really, really sorry," I said to Zack.

"It's okay."

"No, it's not. I ruined our evening."

"Forget about it. We have five minutes. Let's eat." He speared a potato.

"I lost track of the time."

"Well, I hope at least you bought some great stuff."

"So you *are* angry."

He put down his fork. "If you didn't have my cell number, you could have phoned the shul, Molly. I was worried."

"I didn't *ask* you to worry," I said, knowing I was in the wrong. "You weren't upset until you saw the packages."

"You wouldn't have been late if you hadn't stopped off."

"I forgot about the date," I said.

He cocked his head. "Is that supposed to make me feel better?"

"I should have told you right away. I had a lot on my mind. I found Betty Rowan dead last night. I was busy talking to people all day. It's not because tonight wasn't important to me."

"Okay."

"I just forgot. Haven't you ever forgotten anything important?"

"I can't remember."

I narrowed my eyes. "Are you being sarcastic?"

"No. I just can't remember. A dental appointment."

"What?"

"I forgot a dental appointment once."

"Are you implying that subconsciously I *wanted* to forget?"

"I'm saying I forgot to show up at the dentist's. Can we drop this?"

One time I'd found a barely noticeable dot of ink on a blouse. Instead of leaving it alone, I'd tried to get it out and ended up spreading it and ruining the blouse. I was doing the same thing now, but couldn't seem to stop.

"Are you hurt?" I asked.

"I don't know."

"Sometimes forgetting is just that, Zack. It doesn't mean anything."

The waiter approached wielding a totem pole–size pepper mill like a club. "Fresh pepper?"

"We'd like these boxed, please," Zack said. "And the check." He turned to me. "If that's okay?"

"It's fine."

Romance is like a soufflé—delicate, light, magical. I'd poked a hole in it, and once collapsed, no amount of air would revive it.

With a bag of frozen peas on my elevated right foot, I sat at my kitchen table and finished the Nicoise, then hobbled to the laundry room and put in a load of clothes that had kept my hamper from closing. While the machine did its thing, I wrote up my notes from my talks with Virginia Yawley and Cathy Johnson and brooded about the mess I'd made of what could have been a wonderful evening.

Mindy phoned. She'd talked to her client, and he was willing to talk to me.

"When?" I asked.

"He's leaving first thing in the morning for New York, so it would have to be tonight. If it's okay with you, I'll tell him it's a go, and he'll phone you now."

"Now" was good. I felt a flutter of excitement. "What's his name?"

"He'd rather not have you know. You have Caller ID that shows the caller's name, right? You'll have to deactivate."

"Come on, Mindy. How will I be able to verify something if I don't have a name?"

"He doesn't want to be involved. Take it or leave it, Molly."

I took it.

"By the way, what did you learn from Lenore's mother?" she asked.

"I didn't learn anything." I told her about finding Betty Rowan, saw in my mind the lifeless body floating in the pink-watered tub.

"Maybe you shouldn't get any more involved," she said, as I'd known she would.

"I'm careful. Don't tell the family, okay?" I didn't need half a dozen phone calls.

After hanging up, I pressed star eighty-seven on my phone keypad. Five minutes later he called.

"You want to know about Saunders," he said without pre-amble. He had a scratchy voice, probably a smoker. "He was flush with investors for the Santa Monica project. When the market went bad, investors dropped out. I was going to, but Saunders showed me he'd put in more of his own capital, and so did another major investor, Donald Horton."

Horton sounded familiar. And then I remembered: It was Jillian's last name. So the families had been more than socially involved. . . .

"Then I heard the EPA was going to be a problem. Saunders told me not to worry, that he had a contact in the EPA, and they were in the bag."

"I heard there was a zoning problem."

"There was some talk about that, too, but Saunders said he'd worked it all out."

"Did he tell you who his EPA contact was?"

"He wouldn't say, but I'm pretty sure it's Brad Messer. I think Messer helped him out before."

I wrote down the name. "Why are you sure?"

"One time I was waiting in reception. His secretary went to the rest room, so I was there alone. Saunders was yelling at someone on the phone. First he called him Brad. Then, when he got pissed, it was Messer."

"Maybe he was angry because Messer was giving him a hard time about the environmental concerns."

"Saunders was yelling at him, called him a greedy son of a bitch. He said he'd agreed to a hundred grand and not a penny more, that it was twenty-five grand more than last time, and the time before that. That if not for him—meaning Saunders—Messer would still be driving a Volvo instead of a Town Car."


At ten o'clock I was standing on the steps leading to the shul's glass door entrance, which was locked. I'd parked in the small lot behind the building near Zack's black Honda and a Camry I assumed belonged to the bar mitzvah boy's parent. I was waiting for parent and son to leave so I could enter. In my hand was a box from Maison Gourmet with two large slices of their sinfully delicious chocolate cheesecake, which Zack had mentioned was his favorite. If the course of true love never did run smooth, I was determined to pave the bumps.

About five minutes later I saw a mother and a glum teenager approaching the entrance. When they exited, I grabbed the edge of the door with my free hand, smiled at the startled mother and wished her a good night, and stepped inside.

The rabbi's study, I remembered, was to the right. I walked down the hall and raised my free hand to the slightly open door—cheesecake in my hand, a song in my heart—prepared to knock before entering, when I heard Zack's voice.

". . . are you, Lisa? It's Zack Abrams. Definitely a long time." He laughed. "I know. Most people are. What?" Another laugh. "Well, how about tomorrow night? Nine o'clock is good for me, too."

I limped down the hall and back to my car.

Isaac had left my mail at my front door, and I flipped through the envelopes and magazines while I ate both slices of the cheese-cake, which was pretty damn good. There was a hand-addressed invitation from B'nai Yeshurun for an evening with the new rabbi.

As if.

One of the envelopes, as Isaac had warned, was open. A large manila one with the same return address as yesterday's but thinner contents. Inside was a revised chapter from the author.

I wondered whether it was kids, as Ernie the mail carrier had suggested, or whether someone was snooping in my mail. To see if Betty Rowan had sent me the journal?

Bubbie G says that for some people the world stands on three things—*gelt, gelt, und gelt.* Money, money, and money. After talking to Virginia Yawley and Cathy Johnson, I was convinced that, sadly, Betty was one of those people, and that she was capable of blackmail. During the two hours it had taken me to drive back from the Cabazon outlets, I'd also arrived at a hunch as to why she'd phoned me.

Here's what I knew: On her first call, Saturday night, Betty had been eager to discuss something that would interest me. Ditto Sunday morning. Sunday evening she was anxious, and more specific (she'd mentioned Lenore's phone call to me and "something I should know"). And that was *after* the news broke that police were conducting an investigation into Lenore's death—news that, according to Zena, had shaken Betty up so much that she'd phoned Connors and told him she was afraid. I also knew that Betty had access and opportunity to enter Lenore's apartment.

Here's what I assumed: Betty had gotten hold of Lenore's journal sometime before Lenore died, probably at Saunders's behest. She read the journal, and when Lenore died, apparently a suicide, Betty decided to cash in on the journal's contents. She phoned people about whom Lenore had written incriminating information, and hinted or stated that she'd like to be paid for her silence. My assumption was based on the fact that she was dead, and that she had chased money most of her life.

Here's the hunch, and I'll admit it was just that: Betty strengthened her hand by mentioning that she could get big bucks for Lenore's story. A book deal, a movie. In fact, a published writer was already interested in Lenore, and Betty was considering working with her unless she received a better offer.

That writer was me, of course. Even if Betty hadn't named me, I was out there asking too many questions, interviewing everyone who had known Lenore. And when Betty had no takers, she decided to offer the journal to me—not for free, of course. You might argue that she phoned me those first two times because she suspected that Lenore had been killed. I'd considered that, but number one, she would've called the police, not me, and number two, she hadn't sounded worried.

Until the police decided Lenore might have been killed. Betty must have panicked, because she realized that one of the people she'd tried to blackmail was a very bad guy. That would explain why in her last message to me she'd been anxious, and why she'd referred to Lenore's call. *I'm afraid.* And why she'd phoned Connors.

That's as far as my hunch went. I still hadn't figured out why she'd called me that last time. Maybe she'd wanted to warn me that she'd mentioned my name, although I didn't see her as the caring type, and she certainly hadn't been fond of me. And why hadn't she just phoned the police?

And I still didn't know whom she'd tried to blackmail and whom she suspected of killing Lenore.

Someone who had killed Betty and tried to make it look like suicide. Someone who didn't know how much I knew, or what I had.

I told myself that Betty Rowan hadn't known where I lived. I'm not listed in the White Pages. But I can tell you that it isn't all that hard to learn a person's address, and how was it that Saunders had shown up at the bakery just when I was there? If he'd found me, so could anyone.

Connors had checked my apartment last night. I did it again now, searching room by room for evidence that someone had been here, had touched my things.

I had double-locked the front door but checked it again, and all the windows. I rummaged through my purse for Connors's card, debating whether to call him about the opened envelopes, but decided to wait until morning.

It was a long night.

# CHAPTER THIRTY-TWO

*Wednesday, July 23. 10:07 A.M. 100 block of South Flores Street. A man approached a house and knocked on a window several times. When a woman answered, the man told her, "It's good to have a lot of money because of bail." (Wilshire)*

THERE WERE MORE FLOWERS THAN PEOPLE AT THE FU-neral. Sunlight streamed through the chapel's rainbow-colored stained-glass windows onto the rich mahogany of Lenore's lily-bedecked casket. Tall bouquets of lilies and white roses stood on easels on either side of the casket and near the organist, who played mournful chords as people filed into the pews.

I sat at the back, a row behind Connors. I had checked with

him that morning, expecting that the funeral would be post-poned because of Betty Rowan's death, but the Saunders family had decided to proceed. I suppose they wanted to get the whole thing over with and pretend Lenore had never existed.

Robbie was in the front row, flanked by Maureen and Jillian, who had cast a nervous look at me when she walked into the chapel. She was talking to the middle-aged couple sitting next to her. Probably her parents. I wondered to what length Donald Horton would go to protect his major investment with his future son-in-law. A handful of people were seated in the pews behind the Saunders family. Probably some of Robbie's friends, maybe his closest political associates. Some of them had looked familiar as they'd entered the chapel.

Dr. Korwin was there, and Nina. She'd passed by me without seeing me, her eyes glazed and puffy, the black of her shape-less dress accentuating her deathlike pallor. She was probably the only true mourner here. Korwin must have been worried about her, because every once in a while he glanced at her with a fur-rowed brow. I'm sure there were friends from Betty's side, and Lenore's friends and other patients and staff from the clinic.

At one point Robbie turned around and our eyes met. A moment later Horton (at least I assumed that's who it was) turned around, too. Fingered, I thought, but the coldness in his eyes wasn't funny.

The service was short—only one eulogy, delivered by a somber, rail-thin pastor who did his best with the usual plati-tudes ("so young," "so tragic"), considering that the funeral was being paid for by the ex-husband and the deceased had killed his son. We all filed out of the chapel, and I waited in the narrow foyer for Connors, who was off in a corner talking with someone.

"Miss Blume."

I turned around and faced Maureen Saunders. "I'm sure this

is a difficult day for your family," I said, unable to think of anything more neutral. "Sad" would be untrue. "Great," though tempting, would be tacky.

"This isn't the time or place, so I'll make it short," Maureen said in a voice so low I had to lean closer to hear her. Her face was strained by a stiff smile she probably wore for the benefit of anyone watching. It made her look constipated. "If you continue to harass our family, we're prepared to take legal action. And I'd be careful about what you say in print. Suffice to say, we intend to be vigilant."

Maureen probably thought she'd have me shaking in my Escada pumps, but I've heard this before. I'm always careful about what I say in print, especially when I write about real people. My publisher expects no less, and although we're both insured, I don't relish a lawsuit. But my concern and care are to be accurate and truthful, not diplomatic. Otherwise, I'd be a political speechwriter.

Maureen joined Saunders, who was talking with a salt-and-pepper-haired man. He glanced at me, said something to Saunders, and left.

I watched mother and son exit the foyer through the double glass doors and walk down the concrete pathway toward the burial site. I wondered where little Max Saunders had been laid to rest.

Connors came up to me. "You don't look like you're having a good time. Who were you talking to?"

"Robbie Saunders's mom. She brought up the *L* word." As in libel.

"She's threatening you?"

"Only for four generations. You think he's here?" I asked in an undertone.

Connors looked around and leaned close. "Zorro?" he asked in a theatrical whisper.

"Are you done?"

"Oh, you mean the killer." Connors smiled. "If he is, he's not wearing a label."

"Did you get the autopsy report?"

"This morning. She was five to six weeks pregnant. They found toxic doses of Haldol in her blood, urine, and stomach contents. That explains why she didn't bleed as much from the wounds to her wrists. The meds slowed her blood pressure."

"You said she bled to death."

"It's unclear whether it was the meds or the cuts, or a combination."

"Which means what?"

"One, she sedated herself, then slashed her wrists. The M.E. says that's a typical suicide scenario. Two, the wrist slashing was a dramatic touch. It's her m.o., right? Three, the killer, if there is one, did the slashing to simulate her other attempts. I pick one or two."

I frowned. "Wouldn't the fact that she had toxic levels of Haldol indicate that someone killed her?"

"Not necessarily. Like I said, she was getting Haldol through injection and pills, so there were traces in her mouth and esophagus. And she may have swallowed pills she'd hoarded. Your original thought, remember?"

I remembered. It seemed like six years ago, not six days. "What about the angle of the wrist slashes?"

"Consistent with self-inflicted wounds or homicide, so that's no help. At least with Betty Rowan, we know. Her autopsy's scheduled for this afternoon, but it's definitely a homicide. She was strangled, and there's evidence that she was killed in her den and dragged to the bathtub after she was dead. FYI, we found a Kinko's receipt in her purse dated last Wednesday for photocopies. From the amount charged, I'd say she copied quite a few pages."

"Lenore's journal." Maybe she'd mailed selected pages to potential buyers. Saunders, I was certain, was one. Messer, a possible second. And who else? "I take it you didn't find it?"

Connors shook his head. "Assuming she had it, it's gone. There's no sign that anything was taken."

"How did the killer get in?"

"Side door. There are scratches on the lock, but a credit card would've done the job. The Lopost woman said Betty had been complaining that the deadbolt was jammed, but she hadn't gotten around to having it fixed."

I told Connors about yesterday's trip and what I'd learned. I also told him about my conversation with Scratchy Throat, naming Brad Messer but leaving out the connection with Mindy.

"Brad Messer, huh. How'd you hear that?"

"I can't tell you my source. I'd like to figure out a way to talk to him."

"Well, you just missed your chance." Connors turned and pointed toward the glass doors. "He was talking to Saunders two minutes ago. I met him once. He seemed nice enough."

It was broad daylight, but I felt a quiver of unease. "I wonder what he was doing here."

"Paying his respects, like everybody else. So what else do you have?"

I didn't mention my hunch, even though what he'd just told me strengthened it. I often write scenarios that seem to soar off the page but plummet to the earth like lead the next morning, and unlike Icarus, I wasn't willing to risk having the heat of Connors's sarcasm melt my wings.

"Basically, Betty Rowan liked money," I said, "and so did Lenore, the Lady from 29 Palms." I'd heard the song last night while visiting the town's Web site, and the Andrews Sisters' jaunty swing rendition kept playing in my head, making Lenore's life seem that much more pathetic.

He nodded. "Jimmy Durante, Freddy Martin, the Andrews Sisters, Vic Damone, P. Pastor, and a couple of others. I like the Sisters' recording best. Allie Wrubel wrote it in 'forty-seven. He lived in Twentynine Palms and used to play his hits on weekends in places like the Persian Room, which is now the Back Alley Bar. 'Zip-A-Dee-Doo-Dah,' 'The Lady in Red,' 'Venus Rising.' He died there, too."

Connors surprises me once in a while.

He went outside, leaving me alone in the foyer. I walked over to the guest book and flipped through the lined pages. Mostly names of people I didn't know, along with their addresses. I did recognize a few—Donald and Susan Horton, who I assumed were Jillian's parents. Lawrence Korwin, Nina Weldon. A few politicians, the ones whose faces had seemed familiar.

And Darren Porter.

# CHAPTER THIRTY-THREE

IF SANTA BARBARA HAD AN ORTHODOX COMMUNITY, I'D move there in a heartbeat, or at least buy a vacation home. It's about an hour and a half by car from L.A. on the 101 North, a pleasant drive that turns beautiful once you're in Ventura County, where the scenery is lush and serene. I've been to Santa Barbara several times with my family and have enjoyed the hiking paths, the gardens, and (my favorite) long walks on the beach. (Ron and I won fifteen hundred dollars at a Chinese auction, which we applied toward a belated three-night honeymoon at the just-opened Bacara Resort and Spa. What can I tell you? It's nice to be rich.)

The superior courthouse is on Anacapa, only eleven blocks from the ocean. I could smell the salt in the air and was tempted to detour, but it was five to two, and I had a two o'clock appointment with Donna Bergen, the prosecutor who had tried Lenore's case. I would have been here earlier, but after the funeral I'd stopped off at Darren Porter's Hollywood apartment and left a note in his mailbox, asking him to phone me. I entered the three-story building from the Santa Barbara Street side, and after passing through a metal detector, I was directed to the prosecutor's ground-floor office.

Donna Bergen was in her late thirties, tall and thin with a mop of curly black hair and brown eyes magnified by the thick lenses of her tortoiseshell frames. Her sleeves were rolled to her elbows, and her beige blouse was half out of the navy skirt whose matching jacket hung on her chair. She had a diet Coke six-pack on her desk with four cans gone from their plastic holders, which probably explained why she was so wired. She took a can and offered me the last one, which I declined because I'm trying to watch my caffeine. I think she was relieved.

"True crime, huh? I've been waiting for someone to pick up on this case," she told me. "If I had any talent, I would've written a book about it myself. Or better yet, a screenplay."

"What's so special about this case?"

"Come on, can't you see it?" She formed a camera box with her hands. "A poor but beautiful young woman marries rich. Her older husband is cheating on her. She kills her baby and walks free. I'm thinking Gwyneth or Nicole, Richard Gere or Pierce Brosnan. Maybe Catherine Zeta-Jones, but she'd probably want to bring her husband along, and damn, but I hate his sneer. So what's your angle?"

I wondered if Betty Rowan had gone that far in her speculations—if, in fact, I was right. I told Donna Bergen about the hit-and-run and my suspicion that Saunders had contributed to the accident or witnessed it. "Now I'm trying to figure out if

Lenore killed herself or was murdered. And if she was murdered, did Saunders do it. I assume you know she's dead?"

"Yeah, well, cry me a river." The prosecutor snapped off the tab from her can, then lifted the can in a salute. "Here's to justice, late though it is."

"The jury and judge apparently believed that Lenore killed her baby because she had postpartum psychosis."

Donna snorted. "And I have a million dollars."

From reading about several infanticide trials after my visit with Korwin, I knew that prosecutors are often skeptical about a postpartum defense. But Donna Bergen sounded bitter. "You don't think she was depressed?"

"Sure I do. Her husband was hitting the sheets with someone else while she was overwhelmed with being a new mom to a cranky baby. Who wouldn't be depressed? But that doesn't mean you get to walk after killing your two-month-old."

"You think Lenore really knew what she was doing?"

"I thought she had a bad day and too many diapers to change, and the baby wouldn't stop crying, so she lost her cool and shook him to make him stop and ended up breaking his neck. No intent to kill, but it's still reckless and conscious disregard of human life. So I was going for murder two."

"And the fact that Saunders was cheating on her played into it?"

"No proof." The prosecutor shook her head. "Saunders was careful. But even if I *had* proof, I don't know that I would have used it."

That surprised me. "Why not?"

"It's a double-edged sword." Bergen bent her head back and took a swig of her Coke. "Say I showed that he was screwing around with his former fiancée. If I argue that Lenore knew about it and was enraged and killed the kid to punish Saunders, then it's premeditated and I should be going for murder one. Which I would lose."

"Why?"

"*A*, I didn't believe that was the case. *B*, even if I *did* buy it, how would I convince a jury that Lenore knew about the affair, that she was enraged, and that she took out her rage on her own baby? Why not kill the husband or the lover? *C*, the jury *loved* her. The jury *usually* feels sorry for the mom. Your average person doesn't want to believe a mother would intentionally kill her own kid, even though it's happened. Plus Lenore was extremely convincing, and she looked like a grieving Madonna—not the singer." The prosecutor smiled. "Lenore was smart, too, smarter than Andrea Yates." She took another, longer swig.

I could see the soda chugging down her throat. "What do you mean?"

"Yates phoned the cops and her husband and told them what she'd done. That's why some people found it hard to believe her story. I believe it, by the way. Lenore didn't phone anyone. Saunders testified that he found her rocking the baby, and she told him she'd heard something wrong in the baby's cry a few days ago, and this time she heard a voice coming from the baby, telling her to kill the baby, so she knew the baby was possessed by a spirit and she had to shake it out of him, or he'd die."

Donna Bergen's recitation was dismissive, bored. In my mind I could hear Saunders, sitting across from me at The Coffee Bean and Tea Leaf, the grief in his voice real. "You didn't believe him?"

She shrugged. "I couldn't prove he was lying, but that's what my gut said. Maybe it's what she told him, and he believed it 'cause he had to if he wanted to keep her from going to prison."

"Why would he lie to protect her?"

"Guilt, because he wasn't there half the time to help her? Because he wasn't there to protect the kid? Because his affair drove her to it? I believe he honestly felt sorry for her, and the jury believed it, too. I think that's why he testified, to make Lenore look sympathetic—as her husband, he didn't have to. And he was there every day, visiting her. Stayed as long as they let him. His mother, on the other hand. If looks could kill . . ."

The prosecutor drained the can, crushed it, and lobbed it into a trash can several feet from her desk, where it made a clunking sound. She seemed pleased. "Which brings me back to my dilemma. Say I bring up the affair, and the fact that Lenore knew about it. If the jury thinks the knowledge *depressed* Lenore, I'm feeding right into the hands of the defense counsel, Victor Chapman, who happens to be one of the shrewdest guys I've ever been up against."

I recalled what Korwin had told me about the illness. "Because if she was depressed about the affair, that could lay a foundation for the postpartum depression?"

"Bingo." She beamed her approval. "Same problem with Lenore being pregnant when Saunders married her. If I argued that she didn't really *want* the baby, I'd be laying the ground for depression, and I knew Chapman and the defense shrink, Lawrence Korwin, were ready to step all over me." She grimaced, as if reliving the pain. "We had our expert, but he was no match for Korwin. And Chapman made mincemeat out of him. 'Is it possible . . . ? Is it possible . . . ?' " Bergen asked, mimicking a whine. "Saunders hired the best."

"What *was* your psychiatrist's evaluation?"

"That Lenore was fabricating. Everybody knows about postpartum psychosis. There are books on the subject, plenty of articles online. Oprah did a show on it. How hard is it to fake the symptoms? Hallucinations, paranoia, delusions. You don't have to be Meryl Streep. And Lenore gave an Oscar-winning performance."

I won't say the idea hadn't crossed my mind. *She read books and books about her and watched the movie a hundred times. She wanted to get it just right. When you watched her perform, you would have sworn she was really blind.* And Saunders had said Lenore had been a textbook case. I flashed to the books that had littered the carpet of Lenore's apartment, told myself Lenore had probably bought them after Max had died, because if not, Donna Bergen would have known about them and used them against her.

"Our guy also stated that women with postpartum psychosis usually show symptoms within the first month after the baby is born," Donna Bergen said. "And they usually, though not always, have some history of schizophrenia, manic depression, or bipolar disorder. Korwin blew him out of the water. He argued that depressed people don't always know they're depressed, so why would they go for treatment? He said she'd displayed symptoms of bipolar disorder. A need to be seductive, fear of abandonment, impulsiveness, a decreased need for sleep. Then he brought in Lenore's sad childhood—the dad skipping, the foster homes, the constant abandonment, the tough times. The jury was ready to elect him president."

I pictured the psychiatrist on the witness stand—charismatic, articulate, sincere. He was an authority on the subject and had believed Lenore, so why shouldn't I? "You think Korwin lied?"

"I've cross-examined experts who, for the right price, would argue that blue was pink and sound convincing. I'm not saying Korwin's one of them. He's tops in his field, has impeccable credentials. I think he saw what he wanted to see, and worked backward. If she had postpartum psychosis, she had to be manic or bipolar, right? So he found stuff in her past to support that belief. Doesn't mean it's true. It's like writing a term paper. You start with the hypothesis and do research. You use what fits, you leave out what doesn't."

I could see what she meant. "And the jury believed him?"

"Absolutely. Without him, we would've stood a chance. The

jury, by the way, was a dream come true for Lenore. Chapman knows how to pick 'em. Mostly males, who are suckers for a story like this. People without kids, people willing to believe that someone suffering from a chemical imbalance could hear voices that would tell her to kill her child. We had a few on our side, too. A parent of two small children. A woman who'd suffered from mental illness and didn't believe it could cause someone to kill. Obviously we didn't have enough." The prosecutor sighed. "I caught Lenore in a couple of lies, but she squirmed out of them, kept saying she didn't remember everything clearly. And the jury bought it. Korwin caught the lies, too. I saw him outside the courtroom during a recess right after she testified. He was one unhappy camper."

"Did he say anything to you?"

"What's he gonna say? 'Put me back on the stand, Ms. Bergen, I want to retract my testimony'?"

"What kind of lies?"

"It's in the transcript. You can read it if you want. You want to hear irony? Santa Barbara's the headquarters of Postpartum Support International and PEP. Postpartum Education for Parents. You'd think she would've gotten help if she'd wanted it. She claims she didn't know about it, didn't know she was depressed."

"Maybe she didn't."

"You sound like Chapman." The prosecutor made a sour face.

"So if she lied, why did the jury believe her?"

"I'll tell you why." She leaned toward me, her weight on her elbows. "They saw a new mom who had just moved to a new city, living away from her mother, married to a wealthy businessman who left her alone for days at a time so that he could make more money while she was alone with their colicky kid and cried all day and sank deeper into depression. Chapman made Saunders into the heavy. It was a brilliant job. If Saunders had been on trial, they would have locked him up and thrown away the key."

"But they still found Lenore guilty."

She shrugged. "They had no choice. There was a dead child, and Lenore killed him. California doesn't have a diminished-capacity defense, and the defense didn't go for an insanity plea, which they probably would've won. Hell, when she took the stand, *I* almost believed her."

"Why *didn't* they go for insanity?" That had puzzled me.

"They did at first. Chapman entered the plea. This was right after they arrested her, and she was just starting the meds. Then Lenore changed her mind. She insisted to Chapman that she wasn't insane, that the jury would see how much she loved Max, that they would believe that she would never have done anything to harm him. I thought Chapman was going to have a coronary." The prosecutor seemed pleased by the memory. "Chapman was hoping for manslaughter. I was hoping for second-degree murder, but the jury went with manslaughter. The judge granted probation, and she was in a hospital for six months. Her baby didn't even live *half* that long." Bergen's scowl was ferocious.

The bitterness was back in her voice, and I wondered if it was directed at the judge. "Some people thought the judge was bought."

"Bullshit. The judge believed Lenore's story, just like everyone else."

"Except you. So maybe it's true," I ventured.

"Except me. Look, I've seen cases where the mother really did kill a child because she was mentally ill. Those are tragic for everyone concerned, and I'm the first one to say, get her in treatment. But I've seen enough of these so-called postpartum defenses, and unlike male D.A.'s and judges whose brain cells seem to shrivel up when they see a crying mom, I can see the bullshit when it's there. And these malingerers make it look bad for every woman who really *does* have psychosis." The prosecutor gave me a sharp, appraising look. "*You* have questions, too, or you wouldn't be here."

"I'm trying to understand who Lenore was, what her relationship was with Saunders," I said, but of course, it was only half the truth. What *did* I know about the hit-and-run victim with whom I'd spoken only minutes, the woman who was either wonderful or manipulative, goddess or demon? Or was she somewhere in between?

"Maybe you're angry because you don't like to lose," I added, uncomfortable having the ball in my court.

She laughed. "Hell, *no,* I don't like to lose. Does anyone? But that's not why I'm pissed. I'm pissed because Lenore Saunders got away with murder. And I don't mean murder two."

Now I was confused. "So you *do* think she murdered her child to get back at her husband?"

She snapped off the tab on the remaining can and perched herself on the front of her desk. "There was this moment at the sentencing. Korwin was explaining that the therapy and medication were working, that Lenore was doing so well. He didn't sound as convincing to me, and I think Lenore was worried. She was watching him intently, and I was watching her." The prosecutor took a sip of the soda, drawing out the moment.

I inched forward on my chair, curious to hear what she was about to say, dreading it at the same time because I wasn't ready to give up the Lenore I'd been carrying around in my mind from the first time I met her.

"Then the judge pronounced the sentence," Donna Bergen said. "Probation, et cetera. And Lenore put her head halfway down for maybe a second or two, and her eyes kind of slid to the side." She simulated the movements. "That's when I saw it." She paused. "The smile."

# CHAPTER THIRTY-FOUR

THAT WAS IT? I WAITED, CERTAIN THAT SHE HAD SOME-thing more, but she sat there on her desk, watching for my reaction.

"Of *course* she was smiling," I said, annoyed. "She was happy. Why wouldn't she be?" Bergen had set me up for a *Sixth Sense* shocker and had given me *Ishtar*.

She wagged her finger at me. "This wasn't an 'I'm so happy I'm not going to jail' smile. That I expected. This was 'Gotcha.' 'Gotcha, you smart-ass prosecutor. Gotcha, ye suckers of the jury. Gotcha, judge. *Gotcha*, shrinks. I mean Korwin, too, not just our guy." She aimed an imaginary gun at imaginary targets around the room. "Gotcha. Gotcha. Gotcha. Gotcha. Gotcha. A second later the waterworks were there. The *good* Lenore was back."

The woman had a problem, I decided. Maybe it was all that caffeine. "Don't you think you're reading a great deal into a smile?"

"You had to see it," she insisted. "After the sentencing, Saunders came over and hugged her. I thought he looked relieved but kind of uncomfortable, but she was drinking him in like she'd been in the desert and this was the first water she'd seen in days. Then she put her arms around his neck and laid her head against his chest like she was his little girl. There were reporters and TV people, but they didn't exist for her. He was the only person in the world. And I realized then that he'd been the only person in the world who had ever mattered. Not the baby. She didn't give a shit about the baby."

I could have said a lot of things. That of course, Lenore was relieved to be free, that there was nothing unnatural about concentrating on her husband, from whom she'd been separated, or ignoring the media that had ripped into her so badly. I just sat there, visualizing what Donna Bergen had described, sorting out other things I'd learned about Lenore, wondering if she could be right.

"She played us all the way." A vein pulsed in the prosecutor's cheek. "After I left the courthouse, I got to thinking. Why *did* she change her plea? Why didn't she plead not guilty because of insanity? She was hearing voices, right? She thought her kid had an alien force inside him."

I thought for a moment. "The result would have been the same, wouldn't it? Whether she was acquitted on an insanity plea or placed on probation by the judge, she would have ended up in a hospital."

"With an insanity plea, she was looking at a year in a locked facility, minimum. Probably longer. She gets well too soon, the docs would be suspicious. And before being released, she'd have to go before a medical review panel. A much tougher process, I can tell you. With probation it was six to nine months with Korwin, and she's out. Plus, with the insanity plea, she would've been interviewed by more shrinks. And *that* was something she didn't want to do."

"But she took a serious risk," I pointed out. "She could have ended up spending years in prison."

"She knew she had a winning team. She had Chapman. She had Korwin. She'd convinced them, and she would convince the jury. She gambled and she won."

"She tried to kill herself twice," I said. "Doesn't that say anything?"

"They were gesture suicides, according to our shrink. Korwin, of course, didn't agree. Lenore didn't take enough Haldol to kill herself, and the wrist wounds weren't deep. I think she did it to convince Saunders how distraught she was. And it played well with the jury."

"Did you tell anyone about this?"

Donna Bergen laughed. "That I didn't like her smile? That she was madly in love with her husband? They'd tell me *I* needed to see a shrink. No point, anyway. With double jeopardy, I couldn't get at her. I *did* tell Korwin. I congratulated him on getting taken in by her and suggested he get her spayed. He got all hot under the collar, threatened to sue me." The prosecutor spun the empty can on her desk. "She did it because she thought the kid was in the way. The mother knew, too. I could see it in her face."

"Mrs. Saunders?"

"Mrs. Rowan. She visited Lenore one time in jail for maybe ten minutes. On the opening day of the trial she had this look on her face like she'd peeked under a rock and found something nasty. She didn't show again until the sentencing. Didn't testify for her daughter. Chapman told me she wasn't feeling well, but I think he ordered her to stay away unless she could pretend she believed Lenore and could put on a better face for the jury. I guess she couldn't. I guess a mother's love goes just so far."

From what I'd learned in Twentynine Palms, Betty's love for Lenore wouldn't have sold too many Hallmark cards. I'd been puzzled all along by her allegiance to Saunders over her daughter—if Saunders had believed that Lenore had suffered from postpartum psychosis when she'd killed Max, why couldn't Betty?

"From everything you've told me about Lenore, we could be talking about a psychopath," Irene Gurstner said.

Irene is five years older than I am. She's a congregant in my shul and the psychologist who helped me after Aggie died. She has become a friend. I was impatient to talk to her as soon as I returned from Santa Barbara, but traffic had been heavy, and I didn't get home until after five, not a great time to bother a mother of two small children. I was also eager to read the trial transcripts Bergen had loaned me, but there were four volumes, and between my trips to Twentynine Palms and Santa Barbara, I was behind in entering *Crime Sheet* data. So I worked at my computer until seven, at which point I couldn't wait any longer and phoned Irene.

"*Psychopath's* such a scary word," I said now.

"You can use *sociopath* if you prefer. Whatever you call it, planning to kill your own child *is* scary."

"If it's true. I don't know that she did."

"I don't either. I'm just going by what you've told me, Molly. The father skipped. The mother was in and out of her life in her formative years, and when she *was* around, she was cold and verbally abusive. Lenore was in a series of foster homes when she was young. Makes it hard to form the normal attachments crucial to a child's early development. Add the fact that she was molested, and you have a history that would fit with that of a psychopath. Was there other physical abuse?"

"I don't know. The mother was very strict and, according to Lenore's best friend, she was rough on her. They didn't have much money. That's why she pushed Lenore to marry rich."

"Talk about learned behavior." Irene sighed. "Lenore's mother hooks up with some rich guy and gets pregnant. He marries her and skips when the baby's an infant. The mother pushes the daughter to marry rich. She finally does, and gets the guy the same way, by getting pregnant."

Like mother, like daughter, I thought.

"But the daughter wants to do it better, not like mom, who went from guy to guy and ended up with nothing," Irene said. "Lenore wants Daddy to stay. In her head, she's remembering all those times the mother told her Daddy wouldn't have skipped if she'd been a good girl, if she hadn't cried, if she hadn't kept them up nights."

"Basically, if she hadn't existed," I said. "So you think Lenore intended from the start to kill her baby?"

Donna Bergen's theory. I thought about the hospital birth card for Baby Boy Saunders that I'd found among the playbills in the lavender hatbox, souvenirs from Lenore's starring roles. A sad memento, or another playbill from her most challenging performance?

"This is just a hypothesis, Molly," Irene warned. "I never met this woman. I could be way off base."

"She's not going to sue you, Irene. She's dead."

"God, you're terrible!" She laughed uneasily. "She may have started out intending to succeed where her mother failed. We all think we're going to do better than our parents. She wants security, doesn't want to be abandoned again. So when she suspects her husband of fooling around, she can see the end of the story: She'll have the baby, he'll leave her. The baby will be left without a father, and she'll be without a husband. And without money."

*Lenore had waited a long time for Robbie. She would've done anything to hold on to him.* "So she kills the baby."

"Because she thinks she'll get to keep Daddy. But, surprise: Daddy leaves anyway."

"So she tries again," I said. "She gets pregnant, thinking Robbie will dump the fiancée like he did last time, and marry her. But this time the charm doesn't work. What if it had?" I wondered aloud.

"I don't know," Irene said. "Psychopaths don't just turn into normal people overnight."

The prosecutor had phrased it in starker terms: "Lucky for the fetus Lenore died, or eventually she would've killed it, too."

"If it's true, is she sick or is she evil, Irene?"

"Now you're getting into murky waters. When people do bad things, is it because they're evil or because they're disturbed as a result of their upbringing or genetics or something else? Most psychologists will agree that a psychopath is evil, but even psychopathy generally comes from abuse."

"And if a person's born a psychopath?"

"Then it's genetic, isn't it?"

I was frustrated and told her so.

"I told you, there's no clear answer. Maybe the Torah has a clearer perspective. Ask a rabbi."

Twenty-four hours ago I would have asked Zack, but I wasn't really interested in talking to him about this, or anything. Still, I wondered who Lisa was, and where he was taking her tonight. I never learn. . . .

"Would she feel remorse?" I asked. "Would she try to kill herself?"

"A psychopath doesn't feel guilt or depression, Molly, so why would she kill herself? Psychopaths have no conscience.

They're manipulative and use people to serve their own needs and goals. They usually have above-average intelligence, too, so that would fit Lenore. And they're incredibly charming. You could live next door to one and have no clue."

"Or be her best friend."

"As long as she needs you."

I thought about Cathy Johnson, Lenore's best friend until Lenore dropped out of her life. I wondered what purpose Nina had served. Someone to adore her? Someone to believe her lies? If it's true, I kept reminding myself. If it's true . . .

"The prosecution psychiatrist thinks Lenore's two suicide attempts were gesture suicides," I said. "Is it plausible that she'd fake another suicide to manipulate Robbie and make him feel guilty so that he'd marry her?"

"It's plausible. Whether she did it, I don't know."

"Dr. Korwin, Lenore's shrink, thought the suicide attempts were genuine. But that was before she testified. The prosecutor thinks Korwin realized she'd fooled him, but how is it that Korwin didn't see through her right away?"

"We're not infallible, Molly. We don't have X-ray vision. No psychological Geiger counter. Sorry."

"So why *did* she call me, Irene? Why did she tell me she was afraid?"

"If she's a psychopath, she's manipulative, remember? Maybe she wanted to authenticate the suicide attempt with you because you're a reporter. Maybe she wanted you to call her mother or alert the nurses. It's also quite possible she really *was* afraid she was in danger, and she figured no one else would believe her. Enter you."

I didn't like thinking Lenore had fooled me. But I'd seen her in her hospital bed, a victim of a hit-and-run driver. Injured, weak, trembling with vulnerability and anguish. Naturally, she'd aroused my sympathy. Had she been acting then, too?

"If she's a psychopath," I asked, "do you think anything she said to me was real?"

"Other than her name, I wouldn't count on it."

I finally had some answers about Lenore, but they weren't the answers I'd wanted. I still didn't know whether she'd faked a suicide attempt too well, or whether she'd been murdered. And I still wasn't any closer to figuring out who had killed Betty Rowan.

# CHAPTER THIRTY-FIVE

ISAAC HAD SAT ON THE PORCH IN WAIT FOR ERNIE THE postal carrier, so my mail was intact—bills and a reminder that I was due for my annual eye exam.

I had listened to my phone messages earlier, when I'd returned from Santa Barbara. Mindy, wanting to know if her client had been helpful and reminding me to be careful. Saunders, sounding pleasant this time, and wanting to discuss something. Maybe he wanted to pay me to keep quiet or find out how much I knew.

I'd been hoping to hear from Darren Porter. It was after eight, so either he wasn't home yet or he hadn't checked his mailbox. Or he didn't want to talk to me.

I tried finishing the *Crime Sheet*, but kept thinking about

Lenore, reviewing what she'd said to me. *Nobody believes me. I thought I'd have a second chance.* What if Donna Bergen was wrong? She'd based her conjecture on a smile and an embrace and a look on a mother's face, and I'd been quick to agree. Twelve jurors and a judge had believed Lenore. Maybe Bergen was smarting from losing.

And then I wondered if I was hoping to disprove her because if what she said was true, then I wasn't such a good judge of character after all.

Zena Lopost looked nervous when she opened the door, probably worrying that my visit meant she'd be finding another dead body. She was wearing the same housecoat as the other night, the same sandals, but her hair was in a top bun and she had on lipstick.

"I'm sorry to bother you," I told her. "I just had a few questions."

She welcomed me into her green-and-white kitchen, which smelled of apple pie and cinnamon. She offered me a slice, which I declined, but I did accept a glass of iced tea.

"They're saying on the news that Betty was murdered," Zena said. "So I guess the police are sure. She's had a rough few years, and to die like this . . ." She shook her head.

"I imagine she was devastated when her grandson died."

"She looked like a ghost. She went up to Santa Barbara for the first day of the trial, but it was too much for her." Zena slid a piece of pie onto a plate and set it in front of her. "You're sure?" she asked me.

I told her I was. "Did she blame Lenore?"

"She didn't say, and of course I didn't ask. Well, except for when it first happened. I'd heard about it on the news, and I didn't see her that next day. I was kind of worried, so I went over there to see if she was okay. Of course, she wasn't. I told her I didn't come to pry, just to make sure she was all right, but I guess she had to talk to someone. She told me Lenore had killed her baby, and how could she, Betty, not have seen Lenore was in trouble, and everybody was going to think she'd raised a baby killer."

It was amazing but not surprising, I thought, how even in those first hours Betty Rowan's concern had been focused on herself.

"I tried to give her comfort," Zena said. "I told her that everything is God's plan, that she'd done the best she could for Lenore. Betty had told me what she'd been through with Lenore. It isn't easy, being a single mom, having no help from anyone."

I bit my tongue and drank my tea.

"And I *do* think Lenore wanted to be a good mother," Zena said. "I saw her just before she and her husband moved to Santa Barbara, about a month before she had the baby. I think I mentioned that the other night."

She probably had. I didn't remember. "Lenore was visiting her mother?"

"Actually, I saw her at the Beverly Hills Library, over on Rexford? I took my grandson there—he needed a book for a school project on dinosaurs." Zena smiled. "Anyway, I saw Lenore sitting at one of the tables, reading, with a stack of books next to her. I don't think she recognized me at first when I said hello. She seemed kind of embarrassed about it when I told her who I was. Her face was red."

I had that prickling feeling, like the one I get when I'm watching a movie and the bad guy's about to jump the good guy. "What was she reading?"

"Oh, some of those books on motherhood. The top one

had something to do with the baby blues, but they used that medical term."

My mouth was suddenly dry. "Postpartum depression?"

"That's the one," Zena said, nodding. "All the gals read so much now before they have their babies. My daughter-in-law practically owned a library on the subject by the time her first was born. I didn't read one book when I was pregnant, but I think I did all right with my three." She smiled again and ate a spoonful of the pie.

"Did you tell Betty that you'd seen Lenore?"

"Well, I told Betty I *saw* Lenore, but I didn't mention the books, not at the time. I didn't want to worry her. Lenore looked happy, so I didn't think . . ." Zena sighed and put down the spoon. "I did tell Betty later, after it happened. I thought it would be a comfort to her to know Lenore wanted to be a good mother, that she really tried. Looking back, I don't know if I did the right thing, telling Betty. But I never, ever thought Lenore was ill."

She was defensive now, the color in her face high, and she was clearly sorry she'd told me.

"I mean, it's wonderful to be prepared, but sometimes you can scare yourself silly, don't you think? There are so many things that can go wrong, but it doesn't mean it's going to happen to you."

# CHAPTER THIRTY-SIX

THERE'S A YIDDISH PROVERB THAT SAYS THERE'S NO SUCH thing as a bad mother or a good death. Now I wasn't sure it was true. I told myself it was ridiculous to feel betrayed by a woman who had, after all, not asked me to write about her or spend an entire week trying to figure out whether she'd killed herself or had been murdered.

And this wasn't about my feelings. This was about a dead child. I had driven home on autopilot and was sitting in my parked car, overwhelmed with sadness for poor little Max Saunders, shaken to death not by a mother too ill to know what she was doing, but by someone who had planned that death before he'd taken his first breath. He'd have been dead either way, but it made a huge difference.

I've seen my sisters and sister-in-law pregnant. I've placed my hand on a swollen belly, felt the fetus's quickening, the later months' rumbling movements. A knee, an elbow, an arm.

A miracle. And that's before the baby was born.

What had Lenore felt when the baby had moved inside her? What had she felt the first time she'd held him, seen his first gassy smile? Was there an instant in which she'd reconsidered? At what point had she decided to do it? How had she chosen the day?

I couldn't bear thinking about Lenore another minute. I stepped out of the car into the dark night, locked it, and was on the porch, my house key in my hand, when I heard footsteps behind me.

I whirled around, my heart in my throat, keys poised to strike. It was Zack.

"You scared me half to death!" I said, breathing hard and pressing my hand against my chest.

"I'm sorry. I wanted to talk to you, Molly."

"There are phones."

"In person. I came straight from shul. I don't like the way last night ended."

I didn't like it either. I was about to say, "Is that why you called Lisa?" but I wasn't in the mood for verbal jousting. "I drove to your office last night with cheesecake from Maison Gourmet, to apologize for being late and ruining the evening. I heard you on the phone, making a date." God, this was so high school.

"If you'd stayed, I would have told you the woman I was arranging to meet is my married cousin."

I was glad it was dark. "I didn't know you had a cousin."

"I'm thirty years old, Molly. I stopped playing games a long time ago."

I sighed. "I'm sorry. I obviously jumped to conclusions. I seem to be doing that."

"You still don't trust me, do you?"

"I said I'm sorry."

"And the next time?"

He was right, of course. "I've had a rough day, Zack. I'm exhausted. Can we talk about this another time?"

"I'd really like to talk now, Molly."

The night was still warm, so we sat on the glider on the porch, the jasmine Isaac had let me plant in the earthenware pot scenting the air. I thought Zack would start, but he was waiting for me.

"It's not just you," I told him, my eyes on the sliver of moon, because even now talking about this was hard. "Ron cheated on me. That's why we divorced. It's not something I talk about, and I'm only telling you so you'll understand."

"That must have been terribly painful," he said quietly. "I'm so sorry."

"It's definitely not something I want to go through again."

"I'm not Ron, Molly."

"I know that."

"I'm not the guy who dumped you twelve years ago. But I can't keep trying to prove myself to you."

"I know that, too." I pushed my toe against the brick floor and set the glider in motion.

"I thought we really had something going when I was here Sunday."

"We did," I agreed.

"Then why would you think I'd throw it away?"

"I don't know. I was late. You were upset."

"Couples argue," he said. "They get irritated with each other. That doesn't mean they're over."

"History," I said. "I'm not interested in getting hurt again."

He didn't say anything for a while. "I can't promise that you won't be hurt, Molly, just like you can't promise that I won't be."

"I know."

"I'm a rabbi of a shul. I'll be meeting with women who are seventy-five and women in their twenties, and sometimes I won't be able to tell you who I'm meeting, or why. I need to know that you trust me."

"It's like a learned response," I told him. "It's hard to un-learn. But I'm willing to try."

From the way he was looking at me, I knew that if he weren't a rabbi, he would have leaned over right then and kissed me, and I would have let him. It's just as well. Sometimes a kiss will let you believe that it's a promise sealed, instead of hope. Sometimes it can confuse or, like Ron's kisses, lie.

We rocked on the glider for a few minutes, the silence easier between us.

"You mentioned that you had a rough night," Zack said.

Bubbie G says a heavy heart talks a lot. I don't know how long I talked, but I told him every detail about Lenore and her mother that I'd learned during the past few days, told him how devastated I was. He listened without interrupting, and I felt a little better after unburdening myself, though not at peace.

"I'd like nothing better than to find out I'm wrong," I said. "And it's not as though I have hard evidence."

"But you believe she killed her child intentionally."

"I don't want to. I can't understand how someone could in-tentionally kill *any* child, Zack, especially her own. But then, I can't understand a person who has no conscience, who'll do anything to get what he wants."

"The Torah talks about people like that," Zack said. "Pha-raoh, for one. He ordered his people to drown all male babies born to Israelite women. And there's the woman who came to King Solomon with another woman. Her baby had died, and she'd switched it with the woman's live child, but claimed that the other woman had done the switching. Solomon announces he's going to cut the baby in half, and the real mother cries, 'Let the other woman keep the baby,' because, of course, she can't bear to have him harmed. So the true mother is revealed."

I nodded. Everybody knew the story. I'd studied it several times in high school.

"The commentaries discuss the syntax each woman uses," Zack continued. "One woman says, 'Her son is dead, mine is alive.' The other says, 'My son is alive, hers is dead.' The order reveals that the first woman was lying, that what was most important to her wasn't the fact that her son was alive, but that the *other* woman's baby was dead."

"But the *other* woman focused on the fact that *her* baby was alive. I get it." I wondered whether something in Lenore's testimony would reveal what she'd been thinking.

"I was always puzzled by the woman who lied," Zack said. "Why didn't she do what the real mother did—pretend to care by telling Solomon she was willing to give up her baby? The commentaries ask the same question."

"And?"

"According to some, the two women were mother-in-law and daughter-in-law living in one house, both newly widowed, and it was the daughter-in-law's baby that had died. Some say she switched babies because she wanted the inheritance that would come to her through the live child. Others say because her husband died childless, she was obligated to perpetuate his name through her dead husband's brother—the mother-in-law's newborn son. And she would have to wait years until the brother reached his majority and could release her, through a ritual, so that she would be free to marry."

"So she was stuck," I said.

"Right."

I frowned. "But that isn't fair."

"Only according to our understanding, which is limited. We

can't presume to understand God's laws, Molly, or understand His plan. The point is, this woman didn't want the baby because she *loved* it. She wasn't grief-stricken about her own child's death. She switched her dead child with her mother-in-law's *live* baby because he would set her free. And that's why she didn't care if Solomon killed the child. She had no *interest* in suckling and raising a child that wasn't hers. The child was an impediment to her happiness. He wasn't a human being. He was a thing."

"Just like little Max Saunders," I said. "But there's a big difference. That baby lived, Zack. Max died. An innocent two-month-old died. I don't understand that either." Or Aggie Lasher, I thought, but didn't say.

"I met with a couple once who had just lost a newborn," Zack said after a moment. "They were heartbroken. I was, too. I didn't know what to tell them. So I phoned Rabbi Frank in Israel. He told me a beautiful story about a special heavenly hall for the souls of infants, souls so pure they need only the shortest amount of time on earth to complete their missions. A few minutes, a few hours, a few days, a few months. And then they go home."

"And that helped them?"

"It didn't take away the pain, or the numbing loss. Nothing will do that. But I do think it helped a little. I think it was a comfort."

We sat a while longer, until the air turned chilly and my yawns came one after another although it was only after ten.

"I'll call you tomorrow," Zack said. "By the way, did you get the invitation?"

Honesty, I decided. "I tossed it."

He smiled. "I'll have them send you another one."

"That's okay. I know where and when. I haven't decided yet if I'm coming."

"No pressure. So how was the cheesecake?"

"Divine, both slices. Lucky for me, sulking doesn't affect my appetite."

He waited until I was inside, my door locked and bolted, and I watched through the living room window as he walked down the block to his car.

I'd eaten hours ago, and the mention of cheesecake had made me hungry. I did serious damage to a carton of Häagen-Dazs, and, my exhaustion replaced by a second wind that was nine-tenths curiosity, I went to my office, where I'd placed the trial transcripts.

The phone rang. I looked at the Caller ID and picked up the receiver.

"I asked Robbie about the nightgown," Jillian said. "He said he'd gone to the kitchen to get her coffee, to calm her down. When he came back into the living room, she was wearing my nightgown. He didn't tell me because he didn't want to upset me. I just wanted you to know."

I pictured Lenore opening Jillian's drawers, taking the nightgown and slipping it on, staking her claim.

"They were together one time. *One time!*" She spat the words. "He felt so ashamed, so *stupid*. She'd come crying to him one night when she knew I wasn't home, begging for help. She was lonely, she was depressed, she was afraid she might hurt herself. The usual bullshit. And he fell for it." There was contempt mixed in with the anger. "He tried comforting her, and next thing he knew, they were in bed. He thinks she drugged him with one of her pills."

A day ago I would have thought Robbie was fabricating. Now I wasn't sure. "I suppose Robbie wanted to prepare you, now that the police are investigating Lenore's suicide and all this will come out."

"He told me the day after it happened. I didn't tell you because he'd be upset, but I don't want you to think he was hiding anything from me. We tell each other *everything*. You can't build a marriage on deceit." She spoke doggedly, almost by rote, like a prisoner reciting her name and serial number.

"Robbie made a mistake, Molly. Of course, I was hurt. But Lenore tricked him, and we both knew that. He told her he wasn't about to let her trap him again. That's why she killed herself."

I'd wondered why she'd called to tell me.

No secrets, no motive.

# CHAPTER THIRTY-SEVEN

I SKIMMED THROUGH THE FIRST VOLUME OF THE TRAN-
scripts, which included the voir dire and opening statements
from Bergen and then Chapman. Nothing I hadn't already
known.

The second volume and the first half of the third presented
the prosecution's witnesses.

One of the paramedics who responded to Saunders's 10:22 P.M.
911 call was first. He testified that the baby was dead when he
arrived. Reading the testimony, I could imagine the horror the
jurors had felt listening to the grim details. Donna Bergen had
begun her case well.

Robbie was next. His description of finding the baby dead

in Lenore's arms was almost verbatim what he'd told me, but the details were still chilling—more so now that I suspected Lenore may have acted not out of delusion but malice. He testified that she'd told him several days before that the baby's cry hadn't sounded normal, that he'd reassured her.

MS. BERGEN: That first time did your wife tell you she thought there was a demon inside your son?

A: No, she didn't. I think she was afraid to tell me.

MS. BERGEN: Move to strike, Your Honor. The witness can't know what the defendant was thinking.

THE COURT: The jury will disregard the last statement. Proceed, Ms. Bergen.

FROM MS. BERGEN: Did it occur to you, when you discovered your baby dead and your wife told you what she'd done, that she was lying?

A: No.

Q: That she was afraid to tell you she'd lost her temper and shaken the baby too hard?

A: Lenore wouldn't do anything to harm the baby. I believed her.

Q: The thought didn't cross your mind?

FROM MR. CHAPMAN: Asked and answered, Your Honor.

THE COURT: Move on, Ms. Bergen.

FROM MS. BERGEN: How was your wife that morning, Mr. Saunders?

A: She was tired, as usual. She hadn't been sleeping well since the baby was born. But in the last few days she'd seemed different. Not like herself.

Q: Can you explain what you mean?

A: It's nothing I can put my finger on. She just wasn't Lenore.

Q: You stated that the housekeeper was out sick that day. Did your wife ask you to stay home and help her with the baby?

A: No.

Q: She didn't seem like herself, but you weren't worried about leaving her alone with the baby?

A: No. I realize now that I should have been.

MS. BERGEN: Move to strike, Your Honor. Not responsive.

THE COURT: You opened the door, Ms. Bergen. Continue.

FROM MS. BERGEN: You were in your Santa Barbara office that day. How far is that from your home?

A: About ten minutes.

Q: Did your wife phone to tell you she needed help with the baby?

A: No.

Q: Did you phone her during the day?

A: Yes, around three in the afternoon, to see how she was doing. I had to drive to L.A. and wanted to make sure she was okay.

Q: What did she tell you?

A: That she was tired but okay. She sounded tense.

Q: More tense than usual?

A: It's hard to say. She was constantly anxious.

Q: Well, if you were worried, you would have gone home, especially since she was all alone with the baby. Isn't that correct?

A: I guess so, yes.

Q: So there was nothing to indicate that she was about to have a psychotic episode?

MR. CHAPMAN: Objection. Mr. Saunders isn't qualified to make that kind of assessment.

THE COURT: Sustained.

FROM MS. BERGEN: Did you phone her later that day?

A: Yes, at a little after six. I wanted to make sure she was okay.

Q: Was she?

A: She didn't answer the phone. I thought she was resting.

Q: Did your wife phone you?

A: No, she did not.

A few pages later in the transcript . . .

MS. BERGEN: Do you feel responsible for your son's death, Mr. Saunders?

A: Yes. I should have been home more. I should have seen the signs and made sure Lenore got help.

Q: You don't think she should be punished for killing your son?

A: She needs help, not prison.

Q: Is that why you're lying here today, Mr. Saunders? Because you feel guilty?

A: Lenore would never have wanted to hurt our son. I believe my wife.

In his cross-examination, Chapman focused on the fact that Lenore had seemed different during the past few days, and he had only a few questions for Robbie: Did he believe that Lenore had heard frightening voices from the baby? Did he believe that was why she'd shaken the baby?

"I believe my wife," Robbie had said. "She would never have done anything to hurt Max."

One of the two uniformed police who initially talked to Lenore took the stand, followed by Detective James Jordan, who testified that, following her husband's advice, Lenore had refused to answer any questions without an attorney present. She'd been distant, detached, calm. She showed no remorse. Donna Bergen had made that sound damning, but Chapman had turned it around.

> MR. CHAPMAN: Detective, in your work, have you questioned individuals who have been in shock?
> A: Yes, I have.
> Q: Would it be fair to say, from your experience, that people in shock can appear to be detached and distant?
> A: I guess so.
> Q: So is it possible that Lenore Saunders was in shock?
> A: It's possible.
> Q: Detective, were you familiar with postpartum psychosis when you arrived at the Saunderses' home?
> A: No, I wasn't.
> Q: So at that time, were you aware that a mother experiencing a psychotic episode can be convinced that her baby is the devil?
> A: At the time, no, I wasn't.
> Q: Or that the mother might believe the only way to save her child is to rid the child of this evil?
> A: At the time, no.
> Q: Detective, if you believed you had saved your child from demonic forces, would you be calm?
> A: I guess I might.

Was it the calm of a woman in a postpsychotic state, I wondered, or of a psychopath who feels no remorse for the life she's taken?

Lenore's obstetrician testified that the birth had been normal, and that Lenore had never complained about depression, prenatal or postnatal, although he admitted under cross-examination that he had no way of knowing whether patients were depressed unless they told him so, and because she'd moved to Santa Barbara in her ninth month, he'd seen Lenore a total of four times, including the day of delivery and a postnatal exam six weeks later.

"Not much time to develop a relationship," Chapman had noted.

The baby's pediatrician testified that Lenore hadn't mentioned hearing voices, though she had seemed anxious about the baby's well-being, asking if he appeared normal, and she'd worried because he was crying incessantly throughout the day and even more so in the evenings, a condition the doctor attributed to the colic typical of many newborns.

> MS. BERGEN: Mrs. Saunders brought the baby in twelve times in a period of two months. Is that normal?
>
> A: It's somewhat excessive. She was anxious about his weight, and then about the crying. She was nursing, and didn't know whether he was getting enough milk, or whether her milk was agreeing with him. She needed reassurance, but that's typical of new mothers.
>
> Q: But still, Dr. List. Twelve visits in two months?
>
> A: I've had mothers who bring their newborns in every other day. It doesn't mean they're depressed, or that something's wrong with the mother or the baby.

On his cross, Chapman elicited what he had before: Just because Lenore hadn't said she was depressed, didn't mean she wasn't.

> MR. CHAPMAN: In fact, Dr. List, didn't Mrs. Saunders tell you that she felt overwhelmed, that she wasn't sleeping? That she found herself crying for no reason?
>
> A: She mentioned the crying a few days after giving birth. I attributed it to the baby blues. Since she didn't mention it again, I thought she was doing better. As for feeling

overwhelmed and being unable to sleep, that's typical of new mothers.

Q:  Aren't those some of the symptoms of postpartum depression, Doctor?

A:  They could be. I've found that many new mothers feel like that. Once the baby sleeps through the night, things work themselves out.

Q:  Not always, Doctor. Did Lenore Saunders ever give you the impression that she was frustrated by the crying or angry with her child?

A:  No, she didn't.

Q:  Did you think she was a loving, devoted mother?

A:  Yes, I did.

I was reading words on paper—there was no nuance, no body language—but I have to say Chapman had succeeded in making Lenore sound depressed. Maybe she really *had* been. I had to keep an open mind.

Or had she been setting the groundwork for her defense? If so, she'd been clever. Reporting symptoms that could be indications of depression, but not saying she *was* depressed, because if she'd done so, then someone—the obstetrician, the pediatrician— would have recommended therapy and medication, and of course, she hadn't wanted that. Not if she'd planned to kill her baby and claim she'd been suffering from postpartum psychosis at the time. Which would explain why she hadn't asked Robbie to come home, even though she'd been tense and alone, the house-keeper coincidentally absent that fateful day.

The coroner was the state's last witness. He testified that Max Saunders had been dead several hours by the time the paramedics arrived. The cause of death was a broken neck resulting from vigorous shaking and a "coup-contrecoup injury" to the brain.

A baby is fragile, and the coroner described Max Saunders's other injuries, internal and external. I wish I hadn't read them.

"Your witness," Donna Bergen said when she finished her questioning.

Chapman didn't cross-examine, and I understood why. No one was denying that Lenore had shaken little Max to his death, and I assumed the defense attorney had no desire to reinforce the particulars on the jury.

# Chapter Thirty-eight

THE DEFENSE HAD ONLY TWO WITNESSES, KORWIN AND Lenore. The psychiatrist's testimony corroborated a diagnosis of postpartum psychosis, and Donna Bergen was unable to gain any ground.

MS. BERGEN: Dr. Korwin, have you ever had a patient who fabricated?

A: Patients lie all the time. It's my job to separate fiction from truth.

Q: And you've never been fooled?

A: Not to my knowledge.

Q: So it's possible that you *may* have been fooled.

A: Anything's possible, Ms. Bergen. But Lenore Saunders

didn't fool me. She shook her child when she was experiencing a psychotic episode.

Q: You'd stake your reputation on that?

A: I thought we were in a courtroom, Ms. Bergen, not Vegas. But yes, I would. She loved her child deeply and would never have done anything to hurt him.

Korwin couldn't have been more emphatic. I was impatient to hear Lenore's story in her own words, to read the lies that, according to Donna Bergen, had worried him.

"I wanted stability," Lenore told Chapman and the jury after he'd led her through the trauma of her childhood. "I wanted a family like everybody else, but I didn't have it. Looking back, I think I was depressed. I guess that's why I loved acting so much. It gave me a chance to forget my problems, to be somebody else."

She talked about meeting Robbie, falling in love.

"How did you feel when you found out you were pregnant, Lenore?" Chapman asked.

"Nervous," she admitted. "I didn't know how Robbie would react, and I was afraid of raising a child on my own. I didn't want to repeat my mother's mistake. I wanted my child to have two parents. But Robbie was wonderful. He insisted that we get married right away."

"Were you looking forward to having the baby?"

"Very much. I wanted to be a good mother. I wanted to provide our baby with love and security, with a stable home."

"The very things you didn't have growing up," Chapman said. "So what happened, Lenore?"

"After the baby was born, I felt miserable. It wasn't what I'd expected." She talked about the crying, the sleeplessness, the listlessness, the anxiety. "I thought it was the baby blues, that they were just lasting longer."

"Your husband testified that he wanted to hire a full-time nurse, but you objected," Chapman said.

"I thought I'd feel better, and I wanted to take care of the baby myself, I guess because my mom wasn't around much for me when I was young. I didn't want strangers taking care of my baby."

"Did you tell your pediatrician your concerns?"

"I tried to. He said I'd feel better as soon as the baby slept through the night. He said that a lot of new mothers felt like this."

"Did you tell him about hearing frightening voices?"

"No. The voice said not to tell anyone."

"You didn't tell anyone?"

"No."

"Not even your husband?"

"The voice said not to tell anyone, not to trust anyone, even the doctors. Not even Robbie."

"There are books and articles on postpartum depression and psychosis, Lenore. There have been television shows on the subject, and it's been on the news. Why didn't you get help?"

"I didn't read those books," she said. "I didn't watch those shows. They're too frightening. I heard about postpartum depression, but I never connected it with what I was going through. I thought the voices I heard were real."

*She lied.* My mind flashed to the books Lenore had been seen reading in the library, and my face burned as though she'd slapped me.

"When Max was born," Chapman said, "the hospital gave you a pamphlet about postpartum illness with a number to call for help."

"I didn't read the pamphlet. I didn't keep it. I didn't know I was ill. I thought the voices were real."

"What happened on that Thursday, Lenore?" Chapman asked.

She'd had a rough night, and the baby hadn't stopped crying all day. She'd wanted to get some sleep, but the housekeeper hadn't showed. So she'd rocked the baby all day, and then toward evening, she'd heard voices saying strange things. Horrible things.

"It was a deep voice, a male voice, coming from inside the baby. I'd heard the voice a few days before, but not this strong."

"What things did the voice say?" Chapman asked.

"He said there was an evil spirit trying to kill the baby and me. He said the evil was growing and would kill us soon. I knew then that's why the baby was crying so much, because this thing was inside him. I knew I had to shake it out of him or we would all die."

"Lenore, there are people who think you shook your baby so hard that he died because you were frustrated and lost control. They say you pretended to hear voices because you were afraid you'd be punished."

"I had to shake Max to save him. I didn't shake him because I was frustrated."

"That made sense to you?"

"At the time it made perfect sense. I loved my baby. I would never do anything to hurt him. I wanted him to be safe."

She said it over and over, every chance she had, during the remainder of Chapman's questioning and during Bergen's long, relentless cross-examination. "I love my baby. I would never do anything to harm my baby."

MS. BERGEN: Mrs. Saunders, when did you first hear these voices?

A: I think it was on Tuesday.

Q: Tuesday, March 5?

A: Yes.

Q: And what did you do?

A: I didn't know what to do. I asked Robbie if he thought

the baby sounded normal. Robbie didn't hear anything, so I thought I was just overtired.

Q: But you didn't tell him you'd heard strange voices.

A: No.

Q: On Thursday, March 7, two days later, what time did you start hearing these voices?

A: Sometime in the early evening.

Q: Can you be more specific?

A: I'm sorry. I don't remember.

Q: They worried you?

A: Yes. I was terribly frightened.

Q: Why didn't you phone your husband and ask him to come home?

A: The voice said not to.

Q: Did you talk to your husband earlier in the day?

A: Yes, he phoned me in the afternoon.

Q: What time was that?

A: I don't remember.

Q: Your husband testified that it was around three o'clock. Does that sound right?

A: I guess so. He would know.

Q: And you didn't mention the voices to him at that time?

A: I didn't hear them at that time. I started hearing them later.

Q: Actually, Mrs. Saunders, during the preliminary hearing you stated that you'd phoned your husband and told him you were nervous.

A: I may have.

Q: Did you phone him, or did he phone you?

A: I don't remember everything that happened during the day clearly. I was very tired. I'd been up all night with the baby.

Q: But you remember talking to your husband?

A: Yes.

Q: And you told him you were worried.

A: I may have.

Q: But you didn't mention the voices.

A: No.

Q: Did you phone your husband later that day?

A: No.

Q: Because the voices told you not to call him?

A: Yes.

Q: And you did everything the voices told you to do?

A: Yes.

Q: So you didn't phone anyone?

A: No, I don't remember calling anyone.

The prosecutor introduced into evidence Robert Saunders's cell phone records for that Thursday, then gave a copy to Lenore.

MS. BERGEN: Looking at page seven, the eighth line. The phone number highlighted in yellow is the number from which a call was placed to your husband's cellular phone at five twenty-six in the evening and a message was left. Do you recognize that number?

A: Yes. It's our home number.

Q: You testified that you were home alone in the house, that the housekeeper wasn't there. Is that correct?

A: Yes.

Q: So Mrs. Saunders, can you tell us who made that call to your husband's cellular phone?

A: I don't know.

Q: Did the voices make the call?

FROM MR. CHAPMAN: Objection!

MS. BERGEN: I'll withdraw that. Can you explain the phone call, Mrs. Saunders?

A: It's what I said before. I guess I must have called him. I don't remember doing it.

Q: You don't remember doing it.

A: No.

I could imagine Donna Bergen's sarcasm and assumed the jury had heard it, too. Yet, judging by the manslaughter verdict, they'd believed Lenore. So, obviously, had the judge. In spite of the sarcasm, or because of it?

MS. BERGEN: Your husband testified that he phoned you a little before six o'clock that evening, but you didn't answer.

A: I was probably sleeping.

Q: You testified earlier that you were exhausted that day because you hadn't been able to sleep for even five minutes.

A: I tried lying down. I may have fallen asleep for a few minutes. I don't really remember.

Q: Maybe you didn't answer the phone because you were shaking the baby.

A: I don't remember hearing the phone.

Q: Mrs. Saunders, what were you doing when you first heard the voices?

A: I don't remember exactly. I think I was lying down.

Q: What did the voices sound like?

A: They were male voices. They were loud and angry.

Q: Can you demonstrate for the court what they sounded like?

A: I—I can't.

Q: Why can't you?

A: I have no sense of it now.

Q: Maybe that's because you never heard them.

A: I heard them, but I have no sense of it now.

It was an odd phrase, I thought, yet strangely familiar. I wondered why.

MS. BERGEN: Where was the baby when you heard the voices?

A: He was in his crib.

Q: During the preliminary hearing, you said you were holding him.

A: I took him out of the crib, and held him. That's what I meant.

Q: But it's not what you said. If he was saying terrible things, and you thought something inside him was going to kill you, why would you take him out of the crib?

A: I don't remember everything exactly. I remember hearing the voices. I probably picked him up because he was crying, and then heard the voices.

Q: What did they tell you?

A: To kill the baby. They said the baby was evil.

Q: What did you do?

A: I loved my baby. I wanted to shake the evil out of him, to make the voices stop. I wanted to save the baby.

Q: You wanted to save the baby, so you shook him so hard you broke his neck?

A: I loved my baby. I had to save the baby.

Q: How long did you shake the baby?

A: I don't know.

Q: Two minutes? Ten minutes? Twenty minutes?

A: I don't remember. It didn't seem like a long time.

Q: Long enough and hard enough to kill him. And then what happened?

A: And then the voices stopped.

Q: What did you do?

A: I think I put the baby in the crib, so he could rest.

Q: Your husband testified that he found you in the rocking chair, holding the baby.

A: I guess I must have picked him up again later. I don't remember the details.

Q: It's interesting that you remember exactly what the voices told you, but you don't remember other things at all, like phoning your husband's cell phone.

A: I heard the voices. They said I should kill my baby, so I had to save him.

Bubbie G says a liar must have a good memory. I could see why Donna Bergen hadn't believed Lenore—I didn't believe her—and why Korwin, hearing her testimony, might have been troubled.

I had wondered why the prosecution's psychiatrist hadn't testified, but I found Leonard Vogel's testimony in the state's rebuttal, after the defense rested its case.

Vogel insisted that Lenore had been fabricating; that there had been no prior history of bipolar disorder or manic depression typical of patients suffering from postpartum psychosis; that she had said nothing to her pediatrician about hearing anything strange in her baby's cry. Chapman had brought up Lenore's difficult childhood and suggested that depression hadn't been diagnosed because she'd never sought help.

MR. CHAPMAN: Do you think that's possible, Dr. Vogel?

A: Sure, it's possible. But it's a far cry, if you'll excuse the

pun, from general depression to postpartum psychosis.
It's a major leap.

MR. CHAPMAN: So you think Mrs. Saunders invented
all this?

A: I do. It's a great defense.

Q: And you're basing your assumption on the fact that she
didn't mention hearing voices to her pediatrician?

A: That's one of my reasons. It's not the only one.

Q: Since Dr. List isn't a mental health expert, is it possible
that Mrs. Saunders was reluctant to reveal something she
feared might make her sound crazy?

A: Sure, it's possible. It's equally possible that she didn't say
anything because she invented all that later after she realized she'd killed her baby.

Q: But it's possible, Dr. Vogel?

A: Yes, it's possible.

Q: And if the voices told a psychotic person not to tell anyone, including her doctor, would that person obey the
voices?

A: If the person were truly psychotic, yes.

Even Vogel hadn't suggested Donna Bergen's theory: that
Lenore had planned on killing Max. Bergen never brought it up
either, not in her opening, and not in her closing statements, because it hadn't occurred to her until after the trial was over.

She *did* raise all of the inconsistencies in Lenore's testimony.
She also raised the fact that Betty Rowan, the defendant's
mother, hadn't testified for her daughter:

"Who better could have told us about Lenore Saunders's de-
votion to her newborn son? Who better could have given us in-
sight into the depression that supposedly afflicted the defendant
throughout her adolescence and adulthood? Who better could

have persuaded us that her daughter was telling the truth about the death of Max Saunders? I find it interesting that the defendant's mother chose not to testify, don't you? I can't understand why, unless she didn't believe her own daughter and knew that you and I would realize that if she took the stand."

It was a powerful statement, and a compelling condemnation, but it hadn't been compelling enough to persuade the jury to convict Lenore of second-degree murder. I was reading the rest of Donna Bergen's closing statement and was annoyed when the phone rang, but my annoyance disappeared when I looked at my Caller ID.

"You said to call till twelve," Darren Porter said. "So I guess it's not too late. What's this about?"

# CHAPTER THIRTY-NINE

*Thursday, July 24. 9:05 A.M. 11300 block of Stevens Avenue. A woman reported that her mail had been stolen from the front-door mail slot of her house. The victim had left the outgoing mail in the slot. The victim knew the mailman had already come by that day. Outside, the victim found an empty envelope that had contained a $35 DVD. The other piece of mail had been a bill with a check for $73. (Culver City)*

I WAS BECOMING ADDICTED TO "THE LADY FROM 29 PALMS." I have an unhealthy attachment to the Internet as it is (ask my family), and I'd listened to the song on the town's Web site last night after talking with Darren Porter, who, it turned out, used to do property management for Saunders Enterprises. He'd agreed to meet me during his lunch break at a coffee shop on Pico and Beverwil, just a few blocks from his current workplace.

I listened to the song again this morning, thinking about Lenore, wondering who she was. I'd just finished rereading her testimony, and like Donna Bergen, I was convinced she'd been playing a role.

During his closing statement Chapman had explained Lenore's inconsistencies as the natural confusion of a woman coming out of a postpsychotic episode. Maybe if I'd heard her on the stand, if I'd seen the grief on her face, maybe if Zena hadn't told me she'd seen Lenore reading books about postpartum depression when she was pregnant. Maybe then I would have believed Lenore, too.

I checked my e-mail, replied to several posts including one from my agent, who wanted to know if I had an idea for the new book. Then I looked at my Amazon numbers for *Out of the Ashes*. 84,101. *Rock-a-Bye Baby* was on the same Amazon page, in the column to the left, because I'd checked out Korwin's bestseller on Monday. I clicked on the link.

His star had risen—the book's ranking was number four. The news reports associating him with Lenore probably hadn't hurt. Which didn't mean it wasn't a great book. Even Bergen, cynic that she was, had acknowledged that Korwin was tops in his field.

If Korwin had been troubled by Lenore's testimony and suspected that she'd shaken the baby to death in a fit of frustration, he wouldn't be thrilled to learn that the woman he'd helped beat a second-degree murder charge had killed her child in cold blood. I wondered what would happen to his Amazon numbers if the truth came out. Probably nothing. Notoriety is like a bad review—it's better than *no* review, as long as they spell your name right.

But what about his credibility? Maybe psychiatrists *can't* always detect when patients are faking symptoms, but Korwin had staked his reputation on his certainty. Any good interviewer would find that out and bring it up, embarrassing Korwin in front of the audiences watching all those national talk shows he'd been booked on. And his peers. And his patients, and all the prospective patients banging on the clinic's doors. Not great timing.

Of course, he could reject what was, after all, conjecture. The smile, the embrace, the look on Betty Rowan's face. Even the fact that Lenore had been reading up on postpartum depression when she was nine months pregnant. He could argue that Lenore had been a conscientious mother-to-be, that we don't always recognize in ourselves the things we see in others, that we deny. Which is all true.

And the fact that Lenore had lied about it under oath?

Maybe she'd been frightened to admit that she'd read books about PPD. Maybe she'd worried that the jury would damn her with the knowledge, just as I was willing to.

Half a truth . . .

The point was, Korwin *hadn't* known the truth. At most, he suspected that Lenore had panicked and fabricated the postpartum psychosis. Unless . . .

Betty Rowan had known. She'd known the truth on that first day of the trial, and when she'd looked under the rock and had seen something nasty, maybe she'd seen part of herself. She had known, and that explained the rift between her and Lenore.

I wondered if Lenore had written the truth in her journal. That's what journals are for, right? Your secret thoughts. Had Betty blackmailed Korwin with the truth? Had she teased Robbie with it?

*Don't you want to know what really happened to Max?*

Maybe she'd given Robbie a copy *before* Lenore died.

And if Korwin had discovered the truth and worried that

Lenore would tell? She had nothing to lose. They couldn't try her again, because of double jeopardy. Had he weighed the worth of a psychopathic killer against the needs of all the women trapped in postpartum depression, women he'd no longer be able to help if his reputation were ruined? And what about his clinic, his dream come true?

Suicide or murder. I still didn't know, and it was making me jumpy. As Bubbie G says, you can't sit on two horses with one behind.


On the way to my meeting with Darren Porter, I stopped at the Hollywood station. I had to wait a few minutes before I could see Connors, who told me he'd received the preliminary autopsy report on Betty Rowan that morning.

She'd been strangled with a scarf—silk, judging from the fibers. Bruising on her arms, along with tissue under her finger-nails, indicated that she'd struggled with her assailant.

"She was killed sometime between ten P.M. Sunday and two A.M. Monday," Connors said. "She was dead when she was put in the tub and her wrists were slashed. Very little bleeding from the wrists, and the M.E. found no water in her lungs."

Connors also had a list of the phone calls Lenore had made the night she died.

"Lenore phoned Saunders repeatedly between one and three in the morning. The last call she made was at two fifty-five, just before the nurse did her rounds. She also phoned Nina Weldon, at two-twelve, and left a message on her machine, asking her to phone Saunders."

I wondered again why Nina hadn't told me about the call when we'd first talked.

"At eleven thirty-five, Lenore phoned Korwin's exchange.

She phoned him again at two thirty-five. The service said they tried contacting Korwin both times but couldn't reach him. He says he never received the pages."

"Interesting." So was the fact that Lenore hadn't tried phoning her mother—it was a sad commentary on their relationship. "She didn't try to call a nurse?"

"The call light box was on the floor, near her bed. Lenore either dropped it or someone did it for her."

"Did you ask Saunders about the calls?"

Connors gave me a look. "Duh. He and his fiancée were out until around two. Then they went to sleep and didn't hear the other calls."

I sniffed. "All those phone calls, and Robbie and Jillian didn't hear anything?"

"Maybe they were otherwise occupied and didn't want to be interrupted."

"More likely they thought she was crying wolf. I can't blame them."

"Do I hear sympathy?" He raised a brow. "I thought you were on Lenore's team."

"I thought so, too." I repeated what Bergen had told me and what I'd read in the transcript, and my conversations with Irene and Zena Lopost. "Apparently, Lenore and her mom were both manipulative and scheming."

"Just when you thought it was safe to go into the water," Connors said, but he sounded sad.

That's one of the reasons I like Connors. He has heart. "What did Lenore say when she called Saunders?"

"That she needed to see him, that she was going to kill herself if he didn't come to the hospital. That's what he claims, anyway. He erased the tape."

"Do you know for certain that he was home?"

"The neighbors were all asleep. I couldn't find anyone who can say whether or not Saunders left the house around the time Lenore died."

"And Sunday night?"

"He and the fiancée went to dinner and a late movie."

"They could be lying to alibi each other."

Connors widened his eyes. "Hey, let me write that down!"

I'd opened myself up for that. "Did you talk to Brad Messer, Andy?"

"Yesterday afternoon. He's committed to the environment and he was outraged—*outraged!*—when I suggested he was more committed to another kind of green." Connors grunted. "As for Betty Rowan's murder, he claims he was home with his wife the entire night. No other witnesses. Ditto for the Hortons and Maureen Saunders. Home alone. Mrs. Saunders's maid is off Sundays."

"So no one really has an alibi."

"Why I love my job, by Andrew Connors."

I debated, then figured, what the hell. "Can I run something by you, Andy?"

"Like it would matter if I said no?"

"Remember I told you Betty Rowan kept calling me, saying she wanted to get together? I think I know why."

"I'm listening."

And he did, intently, his eyes narrowed into slits as he swiveled back and forth in his chair with his cranelike arms laced behind his head until I'd finished my spiel.

"So you're thinking Betty mailed teasers to prospective buyers and hedged her bets by dangling you in front of them," he said. "Saunders. Messer. Maybe Horton. Who else?"

"Nina Weldon." I voiced my suspicion about the phone call. "It's odd that she didn't mention it right away. Maybe she made it up, after you started investigating Lenore's death as a homicide."

"Why?"

"She and Lenore were close. Nina told her *everything*. Nina's words. She probably discussed intimate details of her life. What if Betty threatened to expose all that?"

Connors looked skeptical. "Details about what?"

"Her depression. She may have some deep, dark secret. She definitely has a thing for Korwin. She almost snapped my head off when I suggested that patients become attached to their shrinks. Maybe she's sleeping with him."

"Maybe you need a vacation."

"And there's Korwin." I told him what Donna Bergen had said, that he'd realized Lenore had fooled him. "He staked his reputation on his diagnosis. What if Lenore wrote the truth about Max's death and Betty sent him a copy of the pages, telling him she'd make the knowledge public unless?"

Connors didn't answer.

"It's not just about humiliation, Andy. Korwin told me he's hoping to get another book deal. That won't happen if his credibility's damaged. And he can forget about being an expert witness, about attracting more patients. Six months ago his clinic was in trouble, by the way, and now it's going gangbusters." I had liked Korwin, I really had. But I'd liked Lenore, too.

"I don't know, Molly. He sounds genuine to me."

"That's the point, Andy. He's doing a scientific study. He wants to help all these women, but he can't, not if Betty Rowan discredits him. And the fact that he didn't get Lenore's messages from his service is awfully coincidental, don't you think?"

"I'll check it out," Connors said.

At least he wasn't laughing.

# CHAPTER FORTY

"I DON'T THINK SAUNDERS WILL BE HAPPY IF HE FINDS out I talked to you about Lenore," Darren Porter said, and laughed uneasily. "But at least he can't fire me. I left Saunders Enterprises around a year ago."

I'd noticed Darren at the funeral. He was in his late twenties, I guessed, tall with dark brown hair, a football player's build, and small blue eyes set a little too close together.

"I saw the beautiful sunflowers you brought Lenore when she was in the hospital," I said. "I wish my boyfriend brought me flowers like that once in a while."

"They were nice, weren't they?" He ate a bite of the tuna sandwich he'd ordered and wiped the mayonnaise that dripped down his chin. "I didn't get a chance to talk to Lenore, though, 'cause she was sleeping. The nurse wouldn't even let me go in. I can't get over the fact that she's dead. I mean, how could that happen in a hospital?"

"The two of you knew each other long?"

"About four years. We started working for Saunders around the same time, right after I got my degree from Santa Monica City College. She'd been working somewhere else before."

"What was she like?"

"Smart. *Real* smart. She worked her way up fast, too, faster than I did. Well, I couldn't marry the boss, could I?" He laughed and took another bite of the sandwich. "That was a joke. I wouldn't want you to get the wrong impression. Lenore worked hard, and Saunders appreciated that."

"Did you ever go out socially?"

He laughed again. "I wish. You've seen her, right? She's not hard on the eyes. I asked her out, and she said yes, but told me right off she just wanted to be friends. I figured out why pretty soon—she was saving herself for Saunders."

"She made a play for him?"

"Saunders didn't seem to mind."

"He was engaged at the time, wasn't he?"

"He was, but Lenore didn't know. She was upset when I told her."

Or pretended to be. "That didn't stop her from going out with him."

"Well, that was up to him, wasn't it? It's not like they were married. He was in the driver's seat. And she would've gone to the moon and back for him."

Several drivers' seats, apparently. "So you and Lenore kept up after she and Saunders married?"

"Some. We weren't best buds or anything. She'd call and say, did I want to go to a karaoke bar or grab a bite. She could stay out all night. And she'd send me a birthday card every year, never forgot. Well, except that one year right after the baby died. The thing is, I think she felt kind of lonely with his crowd, and she couldn't let her hair down. Then they moved to Santa Barbara, and, well, you know what happened."

"Did you see her after that?"

"Every once in a while. I felt bad for her, especially when I heard Saunders was divorcing her. She didn't talk about it, but I could see she was hurting."

"How did you know she was in the hospital?"

"We went to a movie and pizza the Thursday before she got run over. She was pretty upset that night, so I called her Saturday to see if she was okay, but she wasn't in. When she still didn't answer the next day or the next, I called her mother. She told me. I heard the mother was murdered, huh?" Darren shook his head. "Isn't that something."

"Why was Lenore upset?"

He twirled the straw in his soda glass. "I don't know if I should be telling you Lenore's private stuff."

I waited.

He let out a deep breath. "It was my fault. I told her I heard Saunders had set a wedding date. I only told her 'cause I knew she'd never get over him if I didn't. But she took it bad. She was cussing him out. She said she was going to bring him down. I heard on the news that she was pregnant, so I guess that's why. I guess it was his kid."

Had Lenore gone to Robbie on Saturday night to threaten him or seduce him? Probably the latter, since she'd put on Jillian's nightgown. And then he'd thrown her out.

"Listen, I'm not a fan of Saunders," Darren said. "He can be a mean son of a bitch, and he's out for number one. Plus I don't think he's always on the up and up. That's why I quit. If he went down, I didn't want to go down with him."

"Did you hear rumors?"

Darren shrugged. "There's always rumors. He lost a bundle in the market, and he was having problems with some projects. His father-in-law bailed him out. *Future* father-in-law. But I can't blame Saunders for not wanting to have another kid with Lenore. He went through hell the last time and stood by her. I was with him the day it happened, you know."

I looked at him with interest. "Were you?"

He nodded. "I was helping him set up the Santa Barbara office. Everything was going wrong. The secretary he hired never showed, the computers were down. And this deal he'd been working on for six months fell apart. On top of all that, the housekeeper called in sick, and Lenore kept phoning, telling him the baby was crying and she didn't know what to do."

Not what either one of them had testified, and you didn't have to be Johnny Cochran to figure out why. Donna Bergen hadn't known that, because Saunders's office and home were only ten minutes away and probably had the same area code, so the calls wouldn't have shown up on the phone company's records.

"What did Saunders tell her?" I asked.

"Well, you have to remember he was in a foul mood, okay?" Darren sounded uncomfortable. "He told her he was sick and tired of her bitching, that if she hadn't gotten herself knocked up she could be out shopping instead of taking care of a crying baby, that he'd offered to hire a nurse, but she didn't want one, so what the hell did she want him to do?"

"Nice," I said. Robbie definitely had a way with words.

"Well, he was just blowing off steam. He probably wasn't getting much sleep either. He called her back and asked should he come home instead of going to L.A., and she said no, go ahead. I'm sure he felt bad about what he said, especially later, when he found out . . ." Darren sighed. "I'm sure he blamed himself. If he hadn't yelled at her, maybe she wouldn't have flipped like that. 'Cause the doctors, they still don't know what makes a woman think she's hearing voices like that, right?"

"Right," I said, although from what I'd recently learned I knew that postpartum psychosis wasn't triggered by an argument, and Robbie had known it, too.

"I saw him a few days later," Darren said. "He asked me not to say anything about the phone calls. He said the police might get the wrong idea about Lenore. They might think she got fed up and took it out on the baby, and that's not what happened, but they might think so anyway. So I said okay. I never said a word to anybody, but now she's dead, so it doesn't matter, does it?"

It might matter to Korwin, I thought. It might matter a great deal. "So Saunders drove to L.A.?"

Darren nodded. "I stayed in the office a couple of hours longer, and Lenore called again, saying she'd tried the L.A. office but everyone had gone for the day, and she'd tried Saunders's cell, too, but he wasn't answering and did I know where he was?"

"Did you?"

Darren was blushing. "Well, I had a guess, but I didn't tell Lenore."

"Jillian?"

He nodded. "She figured it out, though, and she asked me. I said no, why would you think that? He's probably in a meeting and shut off his phone. But after I hung up, I reached him on his cell and told him Lenore was looking for him, and I heard Jillian's voice in the background."

That explained the phone call Lenore had made, and explained why Saunders had phoned her back. And did it explain why Lenore had picked that night? Had it been part anger, part desperation?

"Did you ever tell Lenore?"

"Two Thursdays ago, the night we had pizza. I thought she should know, so she could get him out of her system. I don't know if I did right, telling her. She flipped. She said he'd been lying to her all these years, and she was sick of it, and she hoped he spent the rest of his life locked up where he belonged, and she knew how to do it. She had it all written down."

# CHAPTER FORTY-ONE

YOU PROBABLY THINK I WAS THRILLED TO LEARN ROBBIE had lied to protect Lenore because he'd felt guilty. Not only had he yelled at her, but he'd been two-timing her while she was home alone with a crying infant.

But I wasn't. I was troubled. When you write crime fiction, you can go back before the book's in print and change things you don't like, things that don't work. You made a character too old, too nasty, or too nice? Change it. You don't like the dialogue you gave someone on page 127, or the facts of a case or a clue you planted, or the way characters behave or interact or dress? Change it. You can change it all. It's just words on a computer screen or paper.

But I wasn't writing crime fiction. I was writing about real events and real people whose actions and words were inconsistent. And I couldn't go back and change anything. Not words I'd heard from those who had no reason to lie, not words in the court transcripts. I was writing true crime and was stuck with characters who didn't ring true. My editor wouldn't buy them. I didn't buy them either.

For instance, why was Korwin so nervous and defensive? I didn't believe that he'd never received Lenore's late-night messages. If he was a caring, committed psychiatrist, why hadn't he returned her call?

Why would Robbie, a nasty, self-serving, unethical man who had cheated not only on his wife but on his former fiancée, twice, and probably didn't know how to spell "guilt" let alone feel it—why would he lie under oath for Lenore?

"Lenore would never have wanted to hurt our son," he'd kept saying. "I believe my wife."

Had she threatened Robbie even then to expose his shady business dealings unless he backed her up?

And what about Lenore? "I loved my baby," she'd sworn. "I would never do anything to hurt my baby."

*My baby is alive, hers is dead. Her baby is dead, mine is alive.*

Was Lenore a psychopath who had planned her child's death to hold on to her man? Had she done it out of vengeance? Or was she a loving mother, frightened because she'd done the unthinkable after a tongue-lashing from her two-timing husband?

But if that were so, why had she seduced another woman's fiancé and put on her nightgown?


Marie O'Day was shopping for groceries, something I should be doing, but her husband, Tom, was home.

"I guess you can take another look," he said. "I'm wondering when we can clean the place up and who's going to take her things, now that her mother's dead."

He walked with me to Lenore's apartment and inserted a key into the new lock. "Let me know when you're done, and I'll come lock up," he said, and left me alone.

The air-conditioning hadn't been on in a week. The place was hot and smelled mustier, but it looked the same. Books and photos on the floor, goo on the linoleum, broken dishes, a pink pregnancy tester.

A lavender hatbox filled with broken dreams.

I wasn't sure why I'd come—maybe to take a look at Lenore's things, now that I was seeing her differently. Maybe I hoped I'd find something she'd hidden, something the vandal had missed.

Well, I didn't. I searched for about half an hour and gave up. I looked in her closet and under her sink. I checked her refrigerator and freezer. I held her books upside down, one by one, and fanned the pages in case she'd hidden some evidence inside one of them. That's when I noticed that one of the books was missing. *Rock-a-bye Baby,* by Lawrence Korwin.

"Done, are you?" Tom said when I knocked on his door and told him I was leaving. "Find what you were looking for?"

"No."

"Neither did that other gal, Lenore's friend."

I can't describe what I was feeling. A frisson, I think they call it. "Nina?"

Tom nodded. "Jittery thing, isn't she? Came by Monday. Thought she'd left something when she picked up some things for Lenore. Didn't find it. Hard to find anything in that mess. I asked her what it was, maybe Marie or me would find it when we clean the place up, but she said never mind, it wasn't important."

———————

Sometimes when my mind is too crowded with thoughts, I need to do something physical. At home I changed into shorts, a tank top, and running shoes, and climbed onto the treadmill.

It's boring, isn't it? Tedious. Kind of pointless, too—walking or running, sweating and getting nowhere, tenths of miles and minutes creeping by with painful slowness and no frequent-runner coupons to show for them. I usually put on the TV or my CD headset, but today I stayed with my thoughts.

Lenore and Robbie, Jillian and Betty. All swirling around, talking to me. Korwin, who had been unnaturally nervous when I'd asked him whether he was close with Lenore—I didn't care what Connors said.

And Nina. What had she been looking for in Lenore's apartment, and why had she taken Korwin's book? She'd probably noticed it last Wednesday, when Lenore had asked her to go to her apartment. Maybe she'd been jealous that Lenore had an advance copy, although as far as I knew, Nina had a copy, too.

I hadn't checked the book's inscription, but I assumed it was standard fare. "All best wishes." "Enjoy the book." Maybe something more personal: "I'm proud of what we've accomplished together." Unless the good doctor had written something intimate? "Let's get it on—Larry"?

To tell you the truth, my suspicions had been leaning to Korwin. Because he had so much to lose. Because he'd been so nervous, because he had an ego and a temper. But there *was* something jittery about Nina: I'd noticed it during our phone calls and on our visit. And she hadn't mentioned the call Lenore had made to her, until later. She'd told me Lenore had written in her journal information that could harm Robbie—names and dates and monies involved. But I only had Nina's word for that.

She was passionate about Korwin and his work. *He gave me*

*hope. He did that for so many other women. . . .* And if she thought he might not be able to help other women because of something Lenore had written and Betty had been about to expose?

Maybe Korwin inspired passion in all his patients. Maybe I was reading something complicated into nothing. I tend to do that. With Lenore dead, Nina may have taken the book to rescue it from the trash bin or from Betty Rowan's shelves, where it would have moldered. And what was wrong with that?


I showered and changed, and after some hesitation, called Nina to sound her out. She wasn't home. I checked on Mindy—the obstetrician had said nothing would happen for at least another ten days. As if he knew.

On a whim, I phoned my mom and talked her into joining me for a manicure and pedicure—my treat, I told her. It was five-thirty. On the way to my parents' I drove to the post office before the lobby was locked for the night. I won't lie and tell you I receive thousands of fan letters a week, but I do receive some, and I hadn't visited my P.O. box in a while.

The pampering was a good idea, the time with my mom even better. We sat on adjoining chairs, our feet soaked in deliciously warm water, and she told me she was worried that Liora was rushing, for which I had no answer, and that my dad was working too hard, which all of us knew would never change.

She asked me about Lenore, and I told her what I knew. Too much, too little. "I think she was acting. She slipped up a few times, but they bought her story anyway. And when the D.A. asked her to demonstrate for the court what the voices sounded like, she couldn't."

"I have no sense of it now," my mother said.

I frowned. "That's exactly what Lenore said when she testified."

"Mary Warren in *The Crucible*. That's what Mary says on the stand when the judges want her to demonstrate how she faked hearing spirits along with Abigail and the others."

Lenore's favorite play, I remembered.

My mother asked about Zack. "I'm not pushing," she said.

"I know." I told her that I'd jumped to conclusions, that it was hard to trust. "But I'm trying. How did you know Dad was the right one?"

"I just knew."

"I thought I knew with Ron. I thought I loved him." Too much flash, I'd known even then. Too slick. But so full of life, so much fun.

We talked about other things. What did I think Mindy was having? How was my mom's new book coming? Was she looking forward to classes in September?

When I dropped her off an hour later, our toenails and fingernails were buffed and polished and so were my spirits. Not bad for twenty dollars apiece plus a tip.

I stopped for a slice of pizza on Fairfax, then at a nearby supermarket where I filled a cart with enough groceries to last two weeks. At home I put away the perishables and stacked the cereals and cans neatly in my small pantry. I knew they wouldn't stay that way.

I had forgotten my mail in the trunk of my car. I slit open the small envelopes first and scanned the notes. One from a man who loved *Out of the Ashes*. Another from someone who hated it and me and everyone who wasn't pure white and hoped I burned along with every copy of my horrible book. One letter was from a young reader who hoped to be a writer someday and did I have any advice? Read, I would tell him. Read, read, read.

I'd been right about one of the larger envelopes. It contained a 467-page true-crime manuscript entitled *Love Me, Kill Me*, written by a woman I remembered meeting at a book signing over seven months ago.

The other envelope had no return address, but the letter inside was from Betty Rowan.

# CHAPTER FORTY-TWO

THERE WERE PAGES ACCOMPANYING THE HANDWRITTEN letter, which was dated Saturday, two days after Lenore died.

Dear Miss Blume,

Your probably wondering why am I writing to you, with my daughter just dead. I have been sitting here, thinking about my poor baby.

She was only twenty-six. She had a hard life, and she made mistakes. Which we all do, I think you'll agree. But I think her story should be told, and I think you could be the person to tell it.

She liked you, Miss Blume. That day you visited

with her, she enjoyed talking to you. I know because she told me.

Lenore wrote a journal, that she gave me just before she died. It tells her story—the good parts, and the ugly parts. She told me to ask would you be interested in writing about her life. Its one of the last things she said before I left her hospital room that night.

Your probably wondering, how can I be thinking about this write now with my daughter not even buried? Well, its hard, but it was important to my daughter, and I promised I'd ask. So here I am.

I don't know if you will think this would make a good book, or maybe a movie, too. There's parts in it that don't make me sound so good, but its Lenore's story, and she has the right to tell it the way she saw it.

I am sending you a few sample pages which I copied from the journal. There is lots more, where she talks about the trial. If your interested, let me know, and we can meet.

PLEASE DO NOT TALK ABOUT THIS WITH ANYONE!!

Betty Rowan

She'd sent me selected photocopied pages, the first dated a month after the trial. The bottom entry on the page, and several entries on the other pages, had been blacked out with marker. I suppose she hadn't wanted to give away the barn.

*Thursday, July 18*
*Dr. K says all his patients write journals, and I should, too. He says no one will ever see it but me, but how do I know he isn't lying?*
*He lies, too.*

*Everybody lies.*
*Write that down.*
*He asked me if I think about the baby.*
*I told him I do, every day.*
*Write down what you think, he said.*
*Mirror, mirror on the wall.*
*Who's the greatest liar of them all, you or me?*

*Monday, July 22*
*Dr. K assured me again that anything I tell him is*
*confidential. Do you want to talk about why you lied on*
*the stand?*
*I asked him if he was angry.*
*This isn't about me, he said. You seem troubled, and*
*I want to help you.*
*The truth will set you free.*

*Thursday, July 25*
*Dr. K won't be happy until I tell him something,*
*so I said I shook Max because I was exhausted*
*and frustrated, and I panicked when I saw he*
*was dead.*
*Tell me how you feel about that, he said.*

*Friday, November 15*
*Robbie brought me flowers and kissed me and told*
*me he can't spend Thanksgiving with me. He said*
*he has to be with Maureen. I know Jillian will be*
*there.*
*Did you kiss her, too? I asked. Did you sleep*
*with her?*
*I'll not have your suspicion anymore.*

*Then let you not earn it.*
*Everybody leaves me, nobody stays.*
*I don't know if I can stand one more month.*
*I don't belong here.*
*I don't.*
*Belong.*
*But I can't tell.*

*Monday, December 9*
    *I'm free at last—without the truth, Dr. K.*
    *Where is Robbie? Why doesn't he call?*

The next entries were dated this year:

*Wednesday, February 12*
    *Robbie said filing for divorce is just for show. He needs*
*Jillian's father to invest in the company, and her daddy*
*won't do it unless his baby girl is happy.*
    *You are my valentine.*
    *It's just for now.*
    *My only valentine.*
    *Promise.*
    *Don't tell.*

*Wednesday, March 7*
    *The anniversary of our lie.*

*Wednesday, March 14*
    *Nina's baby sister drowned when Nina left her*
*unattended in the tub for a minute. She blamed the*
*Hispanic housekeeper, who fled the country.*
    *Nina told me her secret, but I can't tell her mine.*

*Yours and mine, entwined.*
*Promise, she said, don't tell.*

Wednesday, April 2
    *Dr. K says I have to let go of my fantasies of getting*
*back together with Robbie if I want to get on with*
*my life.*
    *I told him it's not a fantasy. Robbie loves me, too.*
    *Get some sleep, he said. We'll talk more tomorrow.*
    *And I have many miles to go and many promises*
*to keep.*

Saturday, May 3
    *I told Robbie I'm tired of playing games. I'm tired of the*
*lies, his and mine. He says he's trying to work things out.*
*These things take time, Lenore.*
    *Suspicion kissed him when I did.*
    *Nina heard me on the phone. I told her I know names to*
*use if Robbie doesn't stop the games and wrote them down.*
*Robbie warned me that games can be dangerous.*
    *I said, so am I.*
    *I didn't tell Nina the truth.*
    *Promise.*

Monday, June 9
    *Betty told me Jillian moved into our house. I think she*
*enjoyed telling me, but I didn't let on how upset I was. Betty*
*knows. She guessed right away.*
    *Sometimes I want to tell Maureen.*
    *Shall I tell you what happened to your grandson?*
    *You don't want to know.*
    *Only I know what I know.*

*And you, my love.*
*And I will tell,*
*I promise.*

*Thursday, June 12*
*Jillian will be away, the rats will play.*

*Sunday, July 6*
*I phoned Jillian and told her, and she called me*
*a liar.*
*I wore your nightgown and lay with him on your bed.*
*I wear it every time. Ask him why.*

*Friday, July 11*
*They set a date! I told Dr. K Robbie has been lying to me*
*all this time, and he said, did you really expect him to take*
*you back, and I said YES! and that's why I did what I did.*
*YES! and he said it would be all right, we'd be together. Yes!*
*Yes! Yes!*
*Dr. K figured it out. He asked me and I didn't say no.*
*I'm not worried because he can't reveal what I tell him, but*
*I could tell he was upset. What are you going to do, he*
*asked.*
*Promise, don't tell.*
*I think he's going to terminate therapy.*
*He is leaving me, too.*

*Saturday, July 12*
*Robbie says he set the wedding date because the Hortons*
*are suspicious. After the election he'll tell Jillian.*
*Dr. K is worried. Do what you have to do, he said again,*
*but I see the lie in his eyes.*
*I played him for a fool.*

And Nina. She knows.
There is nothing like the sting of betrayal.
Rock-a-bye Baby no more.
The truth doesn't set you free.

# CHAPTER FORTY-THREE

I SHOULD HAVE GONE STRAIGHT TO CONNORS. I KNOW that now. Instead I drove to Zena's house. She had a pinched look around her mouth and was unhappy to see me. She probably regretted our last conversation and didn't want to become involved, but she opened the door and invited me in. She was wearing an apron, which explained the wonderful aroma wafting in from the kitchen. Not apple this time. Peach, I think.

"I'm wondering if I could take a look in Mrs. Rowan's house," I said, standing in her tidy living room.

She wiped her floured hands on the apron. "Why?"

I explained that I was looking for Lenore's journal. My guess was that Betty had made a copy, and had hidden it when she became frightened. She may have given the original to Saunders when he'd first asked her to get it. Or she'd handed it over to her killer, hoping to save herself.

"Shouldn't you leave that to the police?" Zena asked, eyes narrowed.

"I intend to give it to Detective Connors if I find it. I'm anxious to see if it's in Betty's house."

"A friend of Lenore's came by here just yesterday and asked me to let her into Betty's."

"Nina?" I asked. My chest tightened.

Zena nodded. "We met one time before. She was in the car when Lenore came to see Betty. I happened to be there. She said she'd loaned Lenore a book, and Lenore may have given it to her mother, so she wanted to look for it. But I can't let people in just like that. It's not my place."

"You can call Detective Connors," I told her. "He'll vouch for me."

Zena thought that over, and I guess she decided it was okay. She left me in the living room and returned a minute later.

"My husband and I are leaving in five minutes to see a movie. Drop the key in my mailbox when you're done."

I promised I would.

It's creepy entering a place when you know the owner's been murdered. The house was hot and filled with dead air. I switched on a living room lamp and the chandelier in the dining room to dispel the gloom. Whoever had killed Betty Rowan had no doubt searched before me, but I checked behind crockery and glassware in the china cabinet and underneath the living room sofa and cushions.

Betty's bedroom hadn't been disturbed. The white eyelet coverlet, surrounded by blue and white pillows of different sizes and shapes, lay smooth on the bed. I unzipped the cases but found nothing. The dresser drawers were filled with packets of floral sachet whose cloying fragrance rose like ghosts when I touched them.

I had an uncomfortable moment as I entered the small, paneled den where Betty had been killed—an image of her struggling with her killer flashed in front of my eyes. I blinked it away. She had few photos. Most of them were in a cardboard box in a closet. Betty with Lenore's father. Betty and Lenore. Betty and a series of other men, some more handsome than others. One photo was on a lamp table: Betty with Lenore and Robbie, her future secured.

She did have a dozen albums filled with pictures and articles she'd cut out from magazines of movie stars, old and new, and of Hollywood. Her true love. Some of the pictures and articles had yellowed beneath their plastic sheets.

I searched the rest of the house and returned to the albums. I opened one and flipped through the pages, and that's where I found a photocopied page of the journal, inserted between a glossy, full-page headshot of Susan Sarandon and the narrowly corrugated backing that kept her from slipping. My heart thumped. I searched through each album, and when I was done, I had found fifty-four pages. I went through the albums again and searched behind every photo, but I didn't find the list of names Nina had told me about, individuals Robbie had bribed and the amounts he'd paid them, and when. Lenore's insurance.

I'd wondered earlier whether Nina had lied to send me down the wrong trail, but according to Lenore's journal, it was *Lenore* who had lied to Nina. *I didn't tell her the truth.*

What truth? And if Lenore wasn't holding that list over Robbie's head, what had she meant when she'd warned him that she was dangerous? What information did she have that, according to Darren Porter, would send Robbie to jail for the rest of his life?

In the next-to-last entry, Lenore wrote that Korwin had figured "it" out and so had Nina. But what had Korwin meant when he'd told her "do what you have to do"?

And why would Lenore tell Nina she'd planned to kill her child?

I sat down in the middle of the room on the carpeted floor and spread out the pages, which were out of order.

I found the first entry, the one I'd seen, dated Thursday, July 18.

*Dr. K says all his patients write journals, and I should, too. He said no one will ever see it but me, but how do I know he isn't lying?*

*He lies, too.*

*Everybody lies.*

*Write that down.*

*He asked me if I think about the baby.*

*I told him I do, every day.*

*Write down what you think, he said.*

*Mirror, mirror on the wall.*

*Who's the greatest liar of them all, you or me?*

I thought I knew.

I'd been looking at Lenore through Donna Bergen's eyes. People had told me Lenore was obsessed with Robbie, that she'd do anything to hold on to him, and I'd taken a giant leap and assumed that she'd killed her child.

But maybe she'd *lied* for him.

I read the rest of that first page, the part Betty had blacked out on my copy.

*Monday, July 22*

*Robbie loves me so much. When they took me, he came*

*every day to see me, to tell me everything was going to be okay.*

> *Remember Elizabeth Proctor, and this isn't prison. I'll be out in nine months at the most, maybe six, and then we'll be together. The pills they watch me swallow make me drowsy, and sometimes I wonder what is real and what isn't.*

*Tuesday, August 6*
> *I was so angry when I phoned him at the office, and*

A door opened.

I froze and stopped breathing for a few seconds. Maybe I was wrong. I strained, trying to detect something in the silence, but I couldn't hear because my heart was pounding in my ears.

Another sound. The click of a door being shut.

"Molly?"

Saunders's voice.

I'd locked the front door behind me and wondered how he'd gotten in, but then I remembered: This was his house, not Betty's. He had a key.

There was a cordless phone on the small brown sofa. I stood, careful not to make noise, and walked to the sofa. My hand shook as I lifted the receiver to my ear.

No dial tone. The battery was dead. My purse with my cell phone was on the dining room table.

"Miss Blume? Where are you?"

I knelt on the carpet and gathered the pages, cringing at the explosion of rustling. There was an air-conditioning floor vent next to the sofa, against the wall. The door to the den was open, and I could hear his footsteps on the wood floor. Holding the pages in one hand, I removed the grate as quietly as I could and shoved the pages inside. I replaced the grate and was moving away from the vent when he stood in the open doorway.

"There you are." He expelled a breath of what sounded like genuine relief, but I knew better. "For a minute there I was really nervous. Why didn't you answer me?"

"Thank God it's you," I said, dancing the dance because I didn't know what else to do. I placed my hand on my chest and felt my heart racing. "I didn't recognize your voice. I was frightened."

"I don't blame you." He took a step into the room. "Mrs. Lopost's keeping an eye on the house for me. She phoned to tell me you were here looking for Lenore's journal and wanted to make sure that was okay. She said Nina Weldon had been by to look for something, too, and I started worrying. This may sound crazy, but I'm wondering if she killed Betty and thought she'd left some evidence."

"You may be right." Terror was pinching my throat, and I found it hard to talk. "Nina seems extremely nervous and tense. I think she was jealous of Lenore's relationship with Dr. Korwin. I think Lenore knew, and wrote about it in her journal. Maybe Betty blackmailed Nina with it. That's why I was looking for the journal, but I couldn't find it. I think we should phone Detective Connors right away, don't you?" I made a move toward the door, but he just stood there, his large frame blocking the opening.

"Good idea." His eyes were on the albums on the carpet, many of them still open. Vivien Leigh smiled at me.

My heart thudded. "Those are amazing, have you seen them? Betty has wonderful pictures of all these movie stars, she must have been a real fan." I was babbling, and I hoped he didn't hear the edge of panic in my voice.

"I have to hand it to Betty." He shook his head in admiration. "I never thought to look there. You did. But I guess as a writer you have to have imagination. Where'd you put the pages?"

There was a door to my left, but I had no idea where it led. I took a baby step toward it. "I told you, I couldn't find the journal."

"Good try." He smiled, apparently amused. "Betty gave me the original, then phoned me the next day and said she'd made a copy. She wanted money, as if I haven't been giving her enough all these years. Greedy bitch."

"Why?" I was nauseated with fear, talking to a man who had killed at least one person and wouldn't hesitate to kill me, but I had to know.

"Don't play games, Molly. You obviously read the journal. Lenore told Betty I was the one who shook the baby. It's ridiculous, of course—Lenore was on drugs half the time, and the other half, she was delusional. But I wanted to keep Betty happy. She helped me convince Lenore to sign the divorce papers." He took another step toward me. "Give me the journal pages, Molly."

"I don't have them. Maybe Nina found them after all." I shrugged and used the opportunity to look around for a weapon. I didn't see one. I took another step to my left.

"The journal's crap, Molly. But it could be embarrassing to me, especially now. I'm willing to pay you for it. Not that I have to. But I'm willing to do it."

Was this what he'd told Betty? "I wish I could help you."

He sighed. "Molly."

I've never heard the promise of so much menace attached to a name. "I put the pages back in the albums," I told him and pointed to the carpet.

His eyes followed my finger. In two steps I was at the door. I yanked it open and ran through a laundry room into a long, narrow, dark kitchen. I found the nearest drawer, opened it, and felt around with desperate fingers. Towels and papers.

A pair of scissors.

He was right behind me. I grabbed the scissors. His hand clamped down on mine and squeezed my fingers until I screamed in pain, but I wouldn't let go of the scissors.

He clamped his free hand on my mouth. I bit at the palm and tasted blood.

"Bitch."

I shoved my elbow behind me into muscle and heard him grunt. I shoved again and met air. He slipped something soft and smooth around my throat and jerked it tight. A scarf. I let go of the scissors, heard them clatter to the tile floor as I tugged at the silky length of fabric that was squeezing my windpipe. Oh God, was this how Aggie felt before she died?

I couldn't breathe, I was dizzy and faint. Bracing myself against the counter, I lunged backward as hard as I could, surprising him. We fell together, the scarf around my throat looser, and I heard a thunk as his head hit first the wall, then the floor.

I used both hands to wrest the scarf away from him, but he pulled it tighter. Keeping one hand between my neck and the scarf, I reached behind me and pinched hard at the skin on the inside of his thigh, my freshly manicured nails digging deep. He yelled and grabbed my arm.

I pulled away, the scarf no longer a noose, and crawled on the floor, stretching out my hand in a wide sweep as I felt for the scissors. His hand gripped my ankle like a vise. I kicked free and scrambled to my feet, wheezing, my throat raw and aching, every breath a fiery pain, and still I couldn't get enough air. He grunted again, and I knew he was getting up, too.

My eyes had adjusted to the dark, and I made out the shape of an appliance on the counter. A blender. I raced for it, grabbed it, and turned around, holding the thick, heavy glass container high as Robbie came at me with the scissors aimed at my throat.

I slammed the container into his nose. He screamed. Blood

spurted out of his nose, but he was still coming toward me. Raising the container higher, I slammed it into his forehead until he fell to the floor. I think it was only two times. It could have been three.

He'd dropped the scissors. I picked them up and approached him gingerly. The rise and fall of his chest told me he was alive, and though he looked unconscious, I took three dish towels and knotted them together, then rolled him over and tied his hands behind his back.

I found my cell phone in my purse and phoned Connors.

# CHAPTER FORTY-FOUR

LATER, I READ SOME OF THE OTHER JOURNAL ENTRIES.

*Tuesday, August 6*

*I was so angry when I phoned him at the office, and later on his cell phone.*

*Was I sleeping when he came home? He says I was, even though the baby was crying, but I was so tired. He tried holding him, tried giving him a bottle with formula, but nothing would quiet him.*

*I know he didn't mean to hurt the baby. I know how tired he was because Max hadn't slept all night, how frustrated from the long day. And I didn't help. Calling* him so often, bothering him at work, accusing him of being with Jillian. That really made him angry, and I don't blame him. And I was the one who refused to have a nurse.

So it's my fault, too, isn't it?

He says he didn't realize how hard he was shaking the baby until Max suddenly stopped crying and he saw that something was wrong. He was terrified, and I believe him. I would have been terrified, too. It could have been me, couldn't it? He loved Max, so why would he want to hurt him?

He was sobbing when he woke me and told me the baby was dead. He wanted to call the police right away. If I were a mother they'd understand, he said, but now they'll lock me away for years, and we'll never be together.

*Thursday, August 8*

Sometimes I don't remember who came up with the idea first. I think it was me. Elizabeth Proctor lied for John, even though he cheated on her. She went to prison for the man she loved, and I didn't want to lose my lover and my son on the same day.

He came to see me every day. You're so brave, he said. I can't believe you're doing this for me, and I told him it was for us.

*Tuesday, September 10*

I think about Max every day, and even when I press my hands against my ears I hear his cry. Robbie says we can have another baby right away, but the emptiness will always be there.

Three more months.

*Maternity.*
*Eternity.*

*Friday, February 14*
    *Sometimes I think he's lying to me, and we'll never be together. He says he can't upset Donald Horton now, and I understand. But what if that's just an excuse?*
    *I threatened to tell the police the truth, but who will believe me?*

*Friday, May 5*
    *Betty says if I don't sign the divorce papers Robbie won't let her stay in the house. Why should I care?*
    *You owe me, she says. I could have had an abortion.*
    *Sometimes I wish she had.*

*Friday, June 13*
    *Robbie set the table with candles and wine. After dinner we went into the bedroom and he had me put on one of Jillian's nightgowns. It's exquisite, cream silk with lace.*
    *It looks much more beautiful on you, he said.*
    *Be patient.*
    *You know I love you.*

*Friday, July 11*
    *Dr. K says I should tell the police the truth, but I have to be prepared that they might not believe me. Don't worry about me, he said. Do what you need to do. But I think he is worried.*
    *What I need is Robbie.*
    *I shouldn't have told Nina the truth. She is angry that I fooled Dr. K, and hurt that I lied to her.*

*Saturday, July 12*

   Robbie told me Jillian's away. He begged me to come, he wants to explain. I'm so angry, but he has a right to know about the baby.

   A second chance, his last.

# CHAPTER FORTY-FIVE

*Tuesday, August 12. 6:02 P.M. Corner of Crescent Heights and Olympic Boulevards. A suspect approached the victim at a school and said, "You are not going to have that baby." (Wilshire)*

A FEW DAYS AGO I ASKED CONNORS WHY ROBBIE DIDN'T use his key the night he killed Betty Rowan. Why mess with the lock? That bothered me, but Connors thinks Robbie wanted to deflect suspicion in case the police didn't believe Betty killed herself.

Robbie's a smart guy, and a great storyteller.

He told Connors he drove to Betty's after Zena phoned him, to see if he could help me search for the journal. He heard screaming and thought I was inside, with Betty's killer. So he ran into the kitchen and was knocked down by someone he couldn't identify, and the next thing he knew, I hit him in the face with a blender and broke his nose. He'd suffered a concussion, too, but he told Connors he wasn't going to press charges against me because he knew I'd been too frightened to know what was going on.

Talk about chutzpah.

As for the journal, he insists Lenore was delusional and what she wrote was fantasy.

Chapman is his lawyer, but I don't think Robbie will wiggle out of this one. The lab found traces of Betty's blood on the scarf (Jillian's), and his fingerprints were all over Lenore's Four Runner, which he parked in her spot (labeled L. SAUNDERS). Connors said it's definitely the car that hit Lenore (the O'Days hadn't seen Lenore leave, and had assumed that her car had been there all night). But the D.A. will have to prove that Robbie had intent.

I think he did, but then, I'm biased.

I think she drove up there in a fury and he did what he always did, calmed her down, promised her the moon and marriage as soon as the election was over and Horton's money was in the bag. Had her put on Jillian's nightgown.

Then Lenore told him she was pregnant, and they'd have to get married, now. And he said, baby or not, we have to wait. And that's when it all fell apart.

I think she threatened to go to the police and meant it this time. I think he knew it. I think he grabbed her car keys and said, let's talk about this. So she ran out of the house and left her car.

Maybe he did follow her down Willow Glen to catch up with her and sweet-talk her one more time. More likely, he thought she'd always be a noose around his neck, and though most people would believe she was lying, jealous because her ex was getting married, he couldn't risk the publicity. Not with the election coming. Not with Horton breathing down his neck.

So was there intent?

You tell me.

I try not to think about her final moments, but the images come unbidden. I see her running down Willow Glen in Jillian's nightgown, crying as she stumbles along in the moonless night in those backless sandals. Maybe she trips once or twice. Maybe she keeps looking over her shoulder, wondering when he's coming. Because she knows he will. As she nears Laurel Canyon she hears the car. She keeps going, because he's hurt her, hasn't he? He should feel sorry, he should worry. And then she turns around and sees him behind the wheel of her Four Runner, and she's smiling, because she believes in happy endings and she knows he's come to tell her he'll marry her after all. But the car doesn't stop, it's coming too close, and she wants to run, but she's paralyzed with fear and horror, she can't believe he'd hurt her.

I think he visited her in the hospital that one time to find out how much she remembered and was relieved to find out, not much. I think he worried when Betty told him she was starting to say things and a reporter had been by.

You'll be pleased to know Jillian admitted she lied when she alibied him for the morning Lenore died. They both heard all the phone calls, and Jillian said, why don't you make her stop bothering us once and for all?

I think he did. I can see him walking into Lenore's room after the nurse has gone and he's created that diversion by pushing another patient out of his bed, clever guy.

"Hey, sweetheart. I just heard your messages and got here as fast as I could."

She's been agitated all night, so they've been giving her Haldol. She tells him she's starting to remember things, but they don't make sense. Something with her car? And her journal is missing.

"We'll find the journal," he tells her. "We'll get married right away and we'll have the baby, but you have to get well first. Why don't you take this, it'll help you sleep."

She believes he loves her because to do otherwise is unthinkable, and she's sedated. He has her purse, remember, and Nina told me Lenore always carried Haldol tablets with her. He gives her enough to knock her out, which I found out can take just minutes, and then he slashes her wrists.

Nevermore, Lenore.

Jillian says she was asleep when he came back, and he told her he never saw Lenore, he changed his mind. People believe what they want. I learned that a long time ago, with Ron.

I'm sure Robbie trashed the apartment after Betty put on the squeeze, in case Lenore had left anything that would incriminate him, but he was careful not to leave fingerprints. And I think Betty went there Thursday to look for more evidence to strengthen her hand.

Nina told me that Betty had mailed her journal pages that referred to her private hell and the fact that Lenore had duped Korwin, something Nina already knew. Lenore had been in a rage after Darren told her the wedding date had been set and, by the way, Robbie was with Jillian that fateful March day. So Lenore told Nina the truth about Max's death.

*"Ask Nina. Tell her I said."*

Nina thought Robbie may have killed Betty. She wasn't sure and she had no proof, and she was terrified, and furious that her best friend had kept a secret that could ruin Korwin. So she'd gone to Lenore's to make sure there was nothing else to damage his reputation. And she'd taken the book. *(To new beginnings, Yours, Doctor K.)* She didn't admit to jealousy, but I think there was some.

And there was outrage, too, that Lenore's charade would cast its shadow on all those poor women trapped in the grip of post-partum depression and psychosis.

I'm sure Korwin shared that outrage. He insists he never received Lenore's messages, but my guess is he ignored them because he wasn't in the mood to hold her hand. I'm sure he felt guilty, and maybe that's why he was so defensive. Plus he knew the truth about Robbie, but couldn't reveal what Lenore had told him in confidence, and maybe part of him didn't want to, because what would that do to his credibility? He says that when Betty Rowan was killed and he'd read some of the journal pages, he'd worried that Nina might have been involved because she'd been unusually nervous and distraught but hadn't been willing to say why.

It's amazing how much we think we know, how little we actually do, how ready we are to jump to conclusions. I had done it, too. Donna Bergen had opened the door, but I had willingly walked through it.

Korwin's book is still on all the bestseller lists, and for the two weeks after Saunders was arrested, his Amazon rank kept bouncing between one and ten. I watched him on *Good Morning America*, and I have to say he handled himself with grace and dignity and good humor, and even a little humility. I hope he reaches a lot of women.

I'll never know why Lenore phoned me. Maybe she had a lucid moment when everything clicked. Her journal was missing, and she was remembering things about the accident, but she didn't want to believe what she knew deep inside: that Robbie had run her down.

For a little love, Bubbie G says, you pay all your life. And sometimes, *with* your life.

————

Mindy gave birth to a boy two weeks ago. She was in labor during Monday night mah jongg, doing her Lamaze panting in between picking and discarding tiles until her contractions were five minutes apart and we made her leave.

She and Norman named the baby Yitzchak for Bubbie G's late husband, Zeidie Irving. Zack came to the bris on Tuesday morning, and I introduced him to everyone, including Bubbie. Even with macular degeneration, she can see through people better than anyone I know.

"*Gitte schoyreh,*" she told me when she took me aside. Good merchandise.

But I already knew that.

As I told Zack, it's hard to unlearn a learned response, but I'm highly motivated. We've been talking late into the night and seeing each other four or five times a week.

Tonight is the eve of the fifteenth day of Av, a special holiday. During the era of the Holy Temple young maidens would dress in white garments and go out into the fields. They would dance in the vineyards and say, "Young man, lift up your eyes and see—what do you choose for yourself?" The beautiful maidens would say, "Look to beauty." Those from good families would say, "Look to family." And those who were plain would say, "Look for the sake of Heaven and adorn us with gold."

Tonight is the meet-the-rabbi reception at the shul. "Will you come with me, Molly?" Zack had asked three nights ago while we sat on my landlord's porch.

I know that Reggie will be there, and other young women looking to dance in a vineyard, each one hoping to find her young man. But it won't be the rabbi. Zack has lifted up his eyes and chosen, and so have I.

Yes I said, yes I will, yes.

Last Wednesday night, on the eve of Tisha b'Av, the Ninth of Av, I ate a hard-boiled egg dipped in ashes and began my fast.

At shul I sat in my tennis shoes on a pillow on the carpeted floor in the women's section as several men, including Zack, took turns reading aloud from Jeremiah's *Lamentations*. It is a grim elegy, chanted softly in a haunting, solemn melody that tugs at your heart, of the destruction of the Temple, of the accompanying famine that led to unspeakable acts, of desolation and despair.

I spent the day fasting with Bubbie G, reading stories to her from different Judaic texts, and in the afternoon, the first two chapters of my manuscript, *The Lady from Twentynine Palms*. Bubbie is curious about the nightgown, and I said, wait, you'll see.

In the evening we broke our fast at my parents' house, and I ate too much, as usual. Then we all went to visit Mindy. Bubbie sat in Mindy's rocker, and I placed the baby in her arms.

The Three Weeks were over, and what better way to rejoice than by celebrating a new life.

## ABOUT THE AUTHOR

ROCHELLE KRICH is the author of ten acclaimed novels of suspense, including *Shadows of Sin, Dead Air, Blood Money,* and *Fertile Ground.* An Anthony Award winner for her debut novel, *Where's Mommy Now?* (which was adapted as the TV movie *Perfect Alibi*), Ms. Krich lives in Los Angeles with her husband and their children.

Visit Rochelle Krich's Web site at www.rochellekrich.com.